KU-728-284

angel stations

Gary Gibson works as a graphic designer, and was previously a magazine editor, in his home town of Glasgow. He has been writing since the age of fourteen, and this is his first published novel.

GARY GIBSON

angel stations

TOR

First published 2004 by Tor

This edition published 2005 by Tor
an imprint of Pan Macmillan Ltd
Pan Macmillan, 20 New Wharf Road, London N1 9RR
Basingstoke and Oxford
Associated companies throughout the world
www.panmacmillan.com
www.toruk.com

ISBN 0 330 42017 8

Copyright © Gary Gibson 2004

The right of Gary Gibson to be identified as the
author of this work has been asserted by him in accordance
with the Copyright, Designs and Patents Act 1988.

All rights reserved. No part of this publication may be
reproduced, stored in or introduced into a retrieval system, or
transmitted, in any form, or by any means (electronic, mechanical,
photocopying, recording or otherwise) without the prior written
permission of the publisher. Any person who does any unauthorized
act in relation to this publication may be liable to criminal
prosecution and civil claims for damages.

3 5 7 9 8 6 4 2

A CIP catalogue record for this book is available from
the British Library.

Typeset by SetSystems Ltd, SaffronWalden, Essex
Printed and bound in Great Britain by
Mackays of Chatham plc, Chatham, Kent

This book is sold subject to the condition that it shall not,
by way of trade or otherwise, be lent, re-sold, hired out,
or otherwise circulated without the publisher's prior consent
in any form of binding or cover other than that in which
it is published and without a similar condition including this
condition being imposed on the subsequent purchaser.

Thanks to all from the Glasgow SF Writer's Circle past and present for their advice and suggestions, to my parents for their support, and of course to MJ, for suggestions, tea and reading out bits from *Fortean*.

Prologue

Sagittarius Arm, Approx. 15,000 light years from Galactic Core.

Space twisted briefly around the probe as it emerged only a few thousand light years from the Galactic Core, the very weave and warp of the universe briefly exposed in a burst of exotic particles that destroyed themselves in minuscule flashes of energy. The probe was tiny, small enough to balance on the fingertip of one of the scientists who had designed it, a compact and powerful bundle of molecular circuitry that stored information on the deep quantum level, recording and collating everything it saw or detected.

It unfolded like a silver flower, a gossamer-leafed bauble catching the cosmic wind, at its heart a microscopic bud of molecular circuitry: the hub of a dizzying assortment of sensors directing their mindless yet infinite attention towards the stars of the Core.

Its aim had been off by a mere .23 light years – as good as dead-on; fourteen thousand light years closer to the heart of the Milky Way than the nearest of the Angel

Stations, and over twenty thousand light years from Earth. The device that had been used to fire the probe across half a galaxy, in less time than it took for a human eyelid to begin to twitch downwards in a blink, had only consumed the energy equivalent of a thousand Hiroshimas.

Like a flower turning its head towards the midday sun, the tiny probe used its photovoltaic leaves to aim itself now in the direction of the Core.

It watched, and it waited.

There. Algorithmic formulae began spinning through the heart of the machine: analysing the background radio noise, the red and blue shift of the nearest stars, comparing what it saw with the stellar maps stored in its powerful memory. Other, similar probes had spun throughout the galaxy, appearing and then disappearing again, all looking for the clue, the sign. For one star dimmer by far than the stellar records showed.

The probe updated its stellar map, and then ran new routines that seemed to point, again, in one direction, concentrating on an object enormous in physical size, but so lacking in effect on the local star systems as to suggest it had no gravitational attraction. It also radiated no human-visible light, but the probe was no simple machine: it analysed and cross-correlated data from across the entire spectrum, picking up the blast of X-rays emanating from that one particular area of the sky.

It floated there, so far from home, like a bird of prey nervously circling some enormous, snuffling beast.

One

Sam Roy

The boy was there again, watching from a distance. Sam ignored him. He placed his hands against the smooth polished surface of the stone, and pushed. It rolled forward a few inches, then stopped. Sam grunted under the strain. He could still see the boy standing near the top of the cliff. He looked a lot like his father. Sam noted the frightened expression on the boy's face.

Sam's mind ran over the conversation they were going to have – the boy terrified his father would find out, wary of the powers his father possessed. Soon, despite these fears, he and his father would clash. In the meantime, he desired knowledge: why his father hated Sam so. Why he forced him to endure this eternity of punishment.

But first they would talk, Sam and the boy, about beginnings, but most especially about futures.

A recent wound had reopened across Sam's thigh, where he had been slashed the night before with a long knife. It bled for a few seconds then began to heal again, rapidly. Sam's flesh was a fine network of stab wounds, gouges from the million flicks of a lash. The chains that secured him to the rock pulled at his arms, tearing the skin. He had known nothing else for seemingly an eternity.

The boy glanced backwards, then down at Sam. He was young, perhaps thirteen. A cold breeze blew across the frozen landscape, dropping to the unsuspecting valleys far, far below. The boy began to walk down the steep path that led upwards to water and food at the top. Sam did not wait for the boy to arrive. He had not tasted water or food in days and, although he was more powerful than almost any other human being who had ever lived, there were limits to what even his body could take. When he next looked up from his labours, he saw the boy was just a few feet away, his lips set in a thin line of determination.

'We need to talk,' said Matthew.

Elias

Once Elias was safely under the city roof, some of the cold winter chill lifted from his bones. It was dark down here amongst the ruined causeways, and as he moved he could discern figures in that grey twilight world, lost amid the shadows of what had once been a busy shopping centre. Occasionally, as they cut through the shafts of evening light that found their way through the broken ceiling far, far above, the figures resolved themselves briefly into human beings with fear and resignation cut deep into the lines on their faces – the look of the terminally downcast.

There were rules here, in the Arcologies, as in all places. If not reflecting human civilization as it was more commonly understood, then they at least constituted an etiquette of living, albeit an occasionally deadly one. This was a place long abandoned by the city authority's security forces, and in their place an understanding existed between the various gangs that plied their business here, far from the constantly scrutinized streets of London itself.

It would get dark within the hour, the worst time. Everyone was finding a place to sleep for the night or, better yet, to hide.

When night fell in these Arcologies, there were no electric lights to illuminate either the giant causeways or the once brightly coloured streets, and the only people who prowled the spiderweb-thin bridges criss-crossing beneath the cracked roof were the Mala Pata and their turf rivals, the Reavers. Elias had no business with the Reavers, his business was solely with Mik. Mik had been with the Mala Pata since birth, given over to the gang before he could even walk, for the Mala Pata had never been above kidnapping or trading in children and newborns.

The Mala Pata weren't hard to spot: they all carried facial wounds, gained through ritual contests. Mik's was a jagged wound running across his cheek, from just below his left nostril, then up past his ear. Ugly, certainly, and the kind of thing that could still be fixed with cheap medical cosmetics, but if Mik'd done that, it would have demonstrated a serious lack of cojones, tantamount to resigning from the Mala Pata. And the only way out of the Mala Pata was death.

'Hey.' A whisper out of the shadow. Elias looked up, saw a murky silhouette on one of the bridges, twenty metres or so above his head. 'Up here, Elias. It's me.'

Elias could see a bank of twenty or so escalators, which hadn't functioned in decades, stretching upwards to the next level. He walked over, put one foot experimentally on a metal step and listened as it creaked and shifted ominously. He stepped back, glanced up again. Mik gestured down, waving his hand towards a staircase at the far end of the row of ruined escalators. Elias walked over to it, and climbed upwards.

'Murray, 's you, right?' Mik squinted at him as Elias traversed the thin bridge. Elias disliked these bridges because they looked so flimsy, but they had been well designed, made by using nanocarbon tube technology that meant you could drop a house on this bridge if you liked, and the bridge would win. Still, Elias kept one hand on the wire-thin rail and avoided looking down.

'Yes, it's me,' he said. 'Where is she?'

'We'll get there, we'll get there,' said Mik. 'No hurry, right? I mean, not like she getting any better. They're expecting you. Don't want to be first to get to the party. Meantime, we can take a stroll through the neighbourhood.' Mik glanced at Elias's face. 'You nervous?'

Elias looked at Mik, standing there on that thin strip of material forty metres long, which seemed to be supported by nothing but air at any point except where it began and ended. Mik was probably no older than thirteen, but he already had a reputation: he liked to kill.

'I'm not nervous,' said Elias coolly. 'It's just cold.' The winter chill was reaching to him on a stiff northern wind that blew in from above. Elias looked up to where the roof had once been. It looked like it might even be snowing.

'That's good,' said Mik. 'I wouldn't want to think you were frightened. I mean, in your position I would be, you know, frightened. Are you sure you're not frightened?' Elias felt his lips compress in a thin line. Mik was goading him. The boy was wearing an expensive-looking leather coat, under which a barely concealed weapon was strapped across his chest, its blunt muzzle shifting languidly as Mik moved from foot to foot. A sonic slammer, thought Elias; something that could make a not unimpressive mess out of whoever it happened to be fired at. But usually only good for one shot. After that it was about as effective a weapon as an attractively shaped tin can.

If Mik was interested in carrying a weapon that looked less impressive but might actually be of some use, he'd have carried, say, a small flechette gun – a tiny, palm-sized one that could be concealed in the smallest of hiding places. Something like the gun Elias now carried, as a matter of fact.

'I'm *very* sure, Mik. Maybe we should get going,' Elias replied. He was constantly aware of the drop below him. How had people been able to use these damn bridges back when they first built them? Then he remembered: each bridge used to be surrounded by a transparent tube, completely enclosed. The cheap plastic tubing was gone, but the bridges remained.

'I don't know,' said Mik, as if reading his thoughts. 'I like these bridges. You can have some real fun with them.' Mik started to jump up and down in the middle, and to Elias's horror it started to vibrate under the impact of his boots. He tightly gripped the narrow railing, trying to make the gesture look casual and unhurried. Heights were not his strong point. He reminded himself that these bridges were far tougher than steel, near as damn unbreakable, but Elias could have sworn he heard an ominous creaking, although it might just be the wind sighing through the cracked ceiling far above.

'One time, Elias,' continued Mik, while seeming to use the bridge like a trampoline, 'I saw this guy who'd been messing with the Mala Pata. He got dropped from a bridge and his head went boom! When he hit, it went everywhere like a big red rotten egg, ha ha!' Mik cackled with childish delight.

Elias just stood there and waited, his face an impassive mask, unable to head further in the direction they were going until Mik let him pass. For a moment, in his childish pleasure, Mik actually looked like a real child, rather than a murderous monster. Somehow, this only made the horror of it all that much greater.

But Mik had stopped now, suddenly bored. 'Anyway, we can go now.' He turned, looked over his shoulder. 'You're something, scared of heights like that.'

Up they went, higher still, until Elias could feel the sting of the occasional snowflake on his cheek. It didn't take a genius to recognize Mik was deliberately leading him on a long and convoluted trail. The higher they got, the more inclined the boy seemed to lead him across yet more of those spiderweb bridges, high enough to make Elias's head spin if he risked looking down. At first he thought it was a ploy to confuse him and thus make it hard for him to find the safe house again if he wanted to. But after a while he realized his companion was only playing with him, wanting to see Elias lose his cool, to buckle at the knees, or balk at crossing one of the uppermost bridges running just below the Arcology ceiling.

Finally, finally they left the damned bridges behind and went deeper into the Arcology's internal structure, farther from the soaring central atrium. The Mala Pata graffiti was now everywhere, while faces emerged from the shadows, both men and women, all cruelly scarred.

The only light now came from a string of coloured bulbs crudely tacked up along one side of the long corridor, above walls dented and scratched. Music blared out of open doors from sound systems ramped up to ear-splitting levels.

Elias thought he could hear someone screaming behind the intense noise, a woman, perhaps. He kept walking. Interfering would just get him killed.

They came eventually into a long, low-ceilinged room that looked like it might have been a corporate meeting area in another era. A heavily scarred table stretched almost the entire length of one wall, and the original wallpaper was hidden under years of graffiti and water stains. Boxes of contraband were stacked up in one corner, and two tall, bulky men stood by the table itself. They were dispensing white powder out of a crate, using a set of scales to measure it before pouring the powder carefully into small plastic bags, which they tied at the neck with practised ease. Both men wore small, surgical-style masks, and a couple of rifles lay further along the table, within easy reach.

Then, Elias saw it: a small, plain-looking attaché case sitting by the far end of the table, leaning against a leg. He felt his hands grow damp and clammy. Objective achieved. He wasn't even supposed to get it out of there, that was for the genuine professionals. Elias was just supposed to confirm it was there, then get out.

Unfortunately, there were certain niceties still to be dealt with.

Mik had stepped ahead of him in the few seconds it had taken Elias to appraise the large room, and now he stood by a darkened doorway at the far end. He nodded into the gloom beyond, and Elias followed.

Her face had been so badly cut up it took Elias a few moments to be sure it was really her, Mia. Her brother Josh was high up in the Mala Pata, a loyal soldier. A distant memory came to Elias, still surprisingly sharp: a smile, soft breath against his earlobe, softer hands caressing his back. She'd have been, what, seventeen, back then? Late twenties now. Although it might have been due to the relative gloom within the cramped space Mik had led him to, it had been difficult initially for Elias to tell whether the body he observed had even been a woman. She lay naked on a sheet spread across a bare mattress, and as Elias's eyes adjusted to the low lighting, he realized that not only had her breasts been cut off, but also her heart had been pulled halfway out of the ribcage. Elias turned away, then, automatically, almost grateful that her face had been so badly mutilated it was impossible to discern what the final expression on the once beautiful features might have been.

'That is Reavers making a joke,' explained a voice from the far side of the room. He'd been so preoccupied with the state of Mia's body, he'd failed to register her brother Josh sitting in a far corner.

'Joke?' said Elias, stepping away from the mattress. The stench of death in the room was almost unbearable.

'Think they funny.' Josh stood and stepped towards Elias. He wasn't the hardest man to spot in a crowd, because he'd had his nose sliced off in a particularly nasty fight a few years before and, like the rest of the Mala Pata, he refused cosmetic surgery and wore the mutilation like a badge of honour.

Of all the Mala Pata, it was probably Josh – brutal, psychotic Josh who used white-hot pokers to torture and then murder his victims – who most struck fear into Elias.

'Take my sister, kill her Mala way. Big joke to Reavers. Get me?' he growled.

'I get you,' said Elias. Almost to his disappointment, things were going exactly as Hollis had predicted they would. 'What do you need me for?' Elias asked, already knowing the answer.

'You do stuff for Mala. Now you do stuff for me. Tell me who do my sister. Then I cut their balls and eyes out and make their mother eat 'em for lunch. You say who, I give you reward. You be grateful.'

Elias glanced at Mik, who was still hovering in the room. Mik had a cocky smirk on his face, though he gazed with open admiration at Josh. Clearly, for Mik at least, there was some very definite mentor–protégé stuff going on here.

'It true you do what they all say, Elias?' Mik asked him then. 'You do stuff like magic, all kind shit?'

'Not magic,' said Elias carefully. 'Something else. It's hard to explain.'

'Bullshit. Not magic, what then?' said Mik. 'I hear about you. Stuff you do, no people dare lie to me. They tell truth. I hear you only half-person: fucked-up mongrel made in lab.' Mik's voice had taken on a jeering quality.

'Shut up, Mik,' said Josh and, to Elias's relief, the boy shut up. 'I don't give shit what you do, just you find out who kill Mia. Then I give you reward. Okay?'

'Sure,' said Elias. 'Give me a couple of minutes.' His mind was racing. Maybe Mik was just guessing about the lab, but he'd stumbled on the truth. Somehow Elias didn't think so. And with stories about him like that flying around, it would get harder and harder to avoid official government attention. And if it came to that, maybe Elias would be better off dead.

Josh and Mik fell back into the shadows, leaving Elias to do what he had to do. He forced himself to sit by Mia's broken, ruined corpse, breathing through his mouth to alleviate the stench. He touched her hair, soft and dark, knowing as he did so that in future any time the memories came back of those few days when he had known Mia so long ago, they would be mixed with the memories of now kneeling on a bloodied mattress, studying her ritually mutilated corpse.

Elias let the light take him. He thought of it as a tiny star, bright and fierce, something that had always been with him, part of him. Like a star, it seemed to flicker in his subconscious with a thin, pale light, which neither he nor Trencher had ever been able to find appropriate words to describe. It was as if they could each open a mental valve and let it spill out into the world beyond. With that thought in mind, he felt it flow out of him, discharging through his fingertips, seeking out the flickering trace of life still trapped somewhere inside Mia's body. Josh and Mik meanwhile stood near the wall, staring, but unable to see the light.

So he reached out, touched the flickering residual life within Mia, already deep into the terrible abyss it sought and craved. In his mind's eye he pictured his hand probing to grasp that last tumbling fragment of Mia's life-force, feeling it writhe, holding it back.

Mia's eyes twitched rapidly, then widened. Someone nearby gave out a low moan of horror, but Elias didn't look up to see if it had come from Mik or Josh. A keening sound, almost like whistling, now came from Mia's throat. Elias didn't want to know what it felt like to be trapped again, no matter for how short a time, in that shattered body.

'Tell me who did this, Mia. Tell me, and you can go.' He glanced up, saw Josh standing right above them, clenching and unclenching his fists. Elias ignored him, looking back at Mia's face. Muscles writhed like snakes under her cheeks. He wondered if she could feel anything.

'Let me go,' Mia whispered weakly, partly in Elias's

mind, partly out loud; it sounded as if she were gagging on the words.

'Tell me first,' said Elias. 'Tell me who did this to you, Mia. Tell me now or I won't let you go, do you understand?'

'Macey,' she said, her voice so small and frail Elias could barely hear it. The flickering life within her seemed to grow a little weaker. Elias tweaked here and there, and Mia's back arched, a high keening sound escaping her lips. 'Oh fuck,' she whispered, entirely in the real now. 'I can't, I can't—'

Her back arched again, and blood sprayed out of her open mouth.

'Stop it,' said Josh. 'Stop it now. You're hurting her.'

'I can't help that, Josh. She says Macey did it. What else do you need to know?'

'I – nothing. Tell her I love her, Murray. Just tell her I love her.'

Elias stared at him for a moment, unable to imagine Josh capable of ever expressing any emotion remotely like love. But maybe he was wrong. Maybe people really were that unpredictable. He turned back to Mia, grateful now to let the life within her slip away, her body slumping down as that brief spark of light left her eyes for the last time.

'Did you tell her?' asked Josh, his mouth twisted in distaste.

'Sure, Josh, I told her. I can't guarantee she heard me, though.'

'You tell me how to do that,' spoke Mik from the corner in a low, awed whisper, 'I make you a fucking king.' Elias ignored him, kept his attention focused on Josh. 'Macey? The name means something to you?'

'Does, yeah,' said Josh. 'You done good, Elias. You deserve reward. Mik, take him next door. Make sure he gets his reward. Okay?'

'Sure,' said Mik with a wide smile like a shark's. Mik beckoned to Elias, heading back through the door they'd come through, and back into the large room where the two men had been bagging drugs on a long table. Elias stood studying Josh's features for a few moments, before turning and walking slowly after Mik. Something felt badly, badly wrong here. It wasn't so much what Josh had said . . . it was the way he had said it.

Back in the larger room, the two men were still there. Elias cleared his throat, and watched as Mik walked over to the table and picked up a tiny diskette. He swaggered back over to Elias, a wide grin on his face.

'Here,' said Mik. 'That what you wanted?'

Elias took the diskette, and looked down at it cradled in the palm of his hand. So tiny, but it held the secret to a man's life.

Elias nodded, and pocketed it.

The attaché case Hollis had told him to watch out for still sat unattended to one side of the table. Like it signified nothing, nothing at all. It seemed strange they would leave it just sitting in open view like that—

Unless they knew?

Elias looked casually towards Mik, but the kid, damn him, just grinned like he was playing some game. Then Mik walked over, picked up the case, and hugged it to his chest.

He stood in front of Elias. 'So. You lookin' for this, maybe, Elias?'

Elias heard the gentlest movement behind him, then the unmistakable chill of a steel gun barrel being laid against the nape of his neck.

'Elias,' – he didn't need to turn around to know it was Josh speaking, Josh holding the gun to the back of his head – 'you did me a great service tonight, a very great service. Macey will not live out the night. His death will be protracted, painful. Thank you.'

Elias cleared his throat, preparing to speak. Then he stopped in his tracks, the boy Mik still standing in front of him, grinning and clasping the attaché case to his chest. Elias didn't turn, didn't want to stare straight into the barrel of a gun. 'You're welcome. But you've – got an odd way of thanking me, if you don't mind me saying so.'

'You been lyin' to Mala, Murray, set us up good. That bad. Mala good to its people, but very bad, though, when you fuck 'em. Don't want fuck with Mala, no,' said Josh, and it seemed to Elias that the other man's voice was filled with genuine sorrow. Like the pity a man might feel for some injured animal found by the roadside, right before he breaks its neck.

'I haven't been lying to you, Josh. I'm your friend. The Mala Pata have been very good to me.'

The blow came suddenly, unexpectedly. Elias found himself slumping to the ground, lying directly between Mik and Josh. Pain filled his head, and at first he thought Josh might have shot him. Then he realized Josh had merely slammed him across the back of the head, presumably with the gun butt.

He was distantly aware of the two other men, still measuring a crate of powder into those little bags. One of them glanced briefly in Elias's direction with an expression of amused contempt.

'Heard everything, Murray: you meetin' with police, passin' information. So bad, bad. You tell police, London, everything want know about Mala Pata, about Arcologies. What you get for that, Murray? What price they give you, even when you know anyone fucks with Mala Pata, always end up dead? So don't lie to me, Murray. I know everything.'

His head still throbbed, but at least he could think again. He rolled slightly over to one side, trying to keep alert. He could see the case still clasped in Mik's small sweaty hands; enough Blight contained in it to waste half of Europe.

'When did the Mala Pata start dealing in biological warfare, Josh?' Elias asked from where he lay. 'You must know what's in that case. They call it the Blight.'

18

'And it better in your hands?' Josh scoffed. 'I told you I'd give you the information you wanted. And you got it, though it's not much use to you now. You think stuff in that case be better in hands of London Authority? Or in hands of people it came from? You think they make any better use, huh? Least if we all gonna die, Mala Pata get a little reward on way. This *your* reward, Elias. You told me who kill Mia, and I grateful, really.' The gun had been hanging by Josh's side, but now he levelled it at Elias's head.

'Killing me is no way to thank me,' Elias protested. 'Killing me isn't going to fix anything.'

'Other part of reward is, Murray, you die quick, not long and drawn out like you would do otherwise. Gettin' tired talkin'. What say we finish this?'

And then, it came to Elias. If he only had the strength . . .

'Mia,' Elias said, and Josh frowned.

'What you say?' said Josh, staring angrily at him. 'You want die slow?'

'It's Mia,' Elias said, most of his attention seemingly focused elsewhere. He didn't know if he could do it, didn't know if he had the power. Always, before, he'd touched them, like Trencher had done, laying the hands on and feeling the light spill out. But Mia was in another room, and that made things very different. But having a gun pointed at your head, he was finding, tended to encourage remarkable levels of motivation.

Something shifted and banged in the room they had

left only seconds before, and everyone around Elias froze on hearing it. The only thing in the room the noise had come from was Mia – and Mia was very, very dead.

What was it like, reaching in again, into that terrible place for a second time, finding the thin, delicate cord that led from this world into the abyss beyond life, somehow still connecting Mia's spirit to her body? Like burying your face in wet, greasy compost and breathing in, he thought. It was the taste and the scent of death, the sensation of a dead soul being pulled back from the brink one more time, back into the light.

It's lucky I don't believe in God, thought Elias, *or I'd burn in hell for this.*

Mik and Josh now had their attention firmly fixed on the room with Mia's corpse in it. The two men at the table had also moved towards the room door, picking up the two rifles that lay on the table. Nobody, for a few seconds at least, was now paying any attention to Elias. Mik was still standing transfixed directly in front of him, only a few feet away. Elias propelled himself forward, finding it easy to push the kid over onto his back, pinning him down with his knees pressing the metal case into Mik's chest. Mik's eyes grew wide with surprise and fright, and could not even look behind him and see what Josh and the other two men were up to.

What happened next lasted only seconds. In his struggle to escape, Mik let go of the case. Elias snatched it up and flung it, hard. Words started to form on Josh's lips just as the case slammed off his forehead. Meanwhile, the two nameless men with the rifles swung around and raised their weapons, aiming them straight at Elias's head.

Then they noticed the case, which had burst open across the floor, a fine dust settling amongst shards of broken glass. For the briefest moment, it was as if the whole world had come to a halt.

Elias, still half-kneeling on the floor, realized it could only be the Blight he saw swirling through the air: that same gene-altered alien phage that had already devastated so much of Asia. He turned to see Mik come at him, snarling.

Elias caught Mik's leg with one hand as the boy kicked out at him, reaching up with his other hand to grasp the handle of the sonic slammer where it was strapped against Mik's chest. Finding the trigger, he pulled it.

The boy disintegrated. Or rather, the portion of his torso between his upper shoulders and his hips seemed to turn into a fine red mist that expanded rapidly outwards to fill one half of the room, mixing together with the fine, deadly powder of the Blight.

Elias only realized he himself had been shot at when he felt the bullet rip through the side of his arm. The sonic slammer had deafened him, the world around him reduced to death and silence. He groped for his small flechette gun and turned, firing rapidly behind him, while half-scuttling, half-crawling towards the shelter of the long table. He'd been lucky, the bullet hadn't hit his gun arm, but it turned out that it wasn't necessary.

Josh stood still in the centre of his room, one hand stroking almost absent-mindedly at the base of his throat. The tiny flechettes had found their targets all over his shoulders and chest, but it was soon clear they weren't all that was killing him. Elias could feel the Blight working on himself too, as the gun slipped from Josh's hand, his mouth working silently, his eyes becoming unfocused.

Behind Josh, the two other armed men were sagging to the floor, the rifles slipping from their hands. It had all been so quick, surely no more than a few seconds. Yet Elias was still alive. For the moment. Josh staggered forward, a thin line of drool slipping from his mouth, through air still filled with a mist of blood and Blight. Elias coughed, and coughed again, feeling the strength sapping from his own bones.

He forced himself to crawl towards the door that led back outside, all too aware that he would find more of the Mala Pata beyond it. He reached inside himself once again, trying to summon both the strength to reach the door and the healing light inside him, coaxing it out, willing it to propel his muscles towards the door – and any chance of safety, however slim.

The door opened, and a heavily tattooed face appeared, staring over Elias's head to take in the attaché case, Josh still standing empty-eyed in the centre of the room, the shattered fragments of Mik's body . . . everything.

'Jesus fuck,' the newcomer gasped, and ran off again.

Elias kept crawling – reaching the door, passing through the door. His hearing was coming back gradually. He could hear people screaming, could understand why. The Blight was still working at him, tearing at his nervous system, and all the time he willed the inner light – the healing light that flowed from his fingers, the same light that had brought Mia back – to resist, to get him out of there, out of the Arcology, away from the Mala Pata.

After a while, the ghost came to him again.

He had silvery grey hair, and walked slowly along beside Elias as he crawled through the now deserted Mala Pata safe house. Not even the Mala Pata, it seemed, were brave enough to stick around for the Blight.

'Fuck off,' Elias gasped, once he realized the ghost was there.

'Now, now, Elias.' The ghost had lines on his face, but distinguished lines, like an elder statesman or a movie star who's put his best work behind him. His eyes even seemed to twinkle. 'No need to be rude. What you did back there wasn't very nice, was it?' The words were spoken with the hint of a smile, as if only mock-stern.

'They were going to kill me,' Elias gasped. He was

getting near to the wide atrium, the great open space filling the centre of the Arcology.

'I meant Mia, who was once your friend. Bringing her back like that, not once but *twice*. I imagine her pain must have been beyond words.' Elias knew it wasn't really a ghost, that its name was Vaughn. But it was hard to think of this wraithlike thing that appeared and disappeared as anything remotely human, regardless of what Trencher had taught him. Vaughn stepped up to the railing, inspecting what he saw below like the king of some abandoned castle surveying his erstwhile domain.

Elias said nothing to that, because the ghost – Vaughn, whatever – was probably right. So he changed the subject.

'Why don't you leave me alone,' he wheezed, pulling himself towards the railing and hauling himself up into a roughly sitting position. 'I didn't ask for you – but you keep on coming.'

'That Blight powder must have been extraordinarily concentrated to do what it did to those men,' the ghost said, as if ignoring him. 'Usually it takes days, or at least hours, to strike people down. But look at you: still alive, still moving. Truly, Elias, you are remarkable.' He said this without the least hint of irony. The City Authorities would be here soon, Elias thought, and he didn't want to be here when they arrived. His bones seemed to be on fire, the Blight was spreading through his system, but despite his resentment he knew the ghost was right:

24

he was still alive, still moving. He pushed himself from his sitting position and somehow, miraculously, pulled himself upright, holding on to the railing. The world swayed around him, and for a moment he looked down into dizzying depths, the roof of the Arcology only a few metres above his head. He retched, coughed, started to walk. There were shouts in the distance, and he saw people moving, all moving downwards, away from the Mala Pata safe house.

He decided this seemed a good idea, and found his way to one of the bridges, hauled himself across it.

He didn't look back to see if the ghost was still there, but it was following silently. Voices echoed from far below, too distant to be made out. 'They're going to hurt you for this, you know,' Vaughn said. 'You let the Blight escape. Imagine the fuss that's going to cause.'

'I don't need your fucking comments,' Elias croaked, making himself turn around at last. But the ghost – Vaughn – was gone, vanished. As always.

Two

Ursu

It was on the fifth day of the Ceremony of Commencement that Shecumpeh 'called' to Ursu, and he found himself awoken in the depths of the night by Master Uftheyan. He had been dreaming of the orchards beyond the mountains, although he had never seen them. But his mother had, before he was even born, and he wondered how he came to dream of something he knew well he had never seen. He wondered what those orchards really looked like.

Not that he was ever likely to find out, the way things had been going recently.

Master Uftheyan was bent with age, his brow grey and mottled, but his eyes remained bright and piercing. When he shoved Ursu awake, he woke to see the old priest's eyes gazing down at him. The old one was hard enough to read at the best of times but, for once, as Ursu sat up on his rough stone pallet, it seemed to him there was some hint of emotion in Uftheyan's eyes which he could not readily identify.

26

The cell had a single window, covered over with wooden shutters inscribed and embellished with the teachings of the Speakers. From what dim light filtered through from the sky beyond, Ursu could tell that it was just after dawn.

His first reaction, on being woken at such a strange hour, was fear – fear that the invaders had launched their final attack, and were now scaling the walls of the city. But as he listened hard, his short, triangular ears twitching at either side of his elongated skull, he could make out hardly a sound. So perhaps it was something else.

'Get up, Ursu. We all heard it,' Uftheyan urged with a trace of excitement. Normally the old priest was careful to reveal no hint of emotion. He had been a soldier in his youth, apparently, but never spoke of his military life. There were rumours that he had grown tired of the killing, so had become a Master to remove himself as far from his previous lifestyle as possible.

'Heard what?' Ursu asked sleepily.

Uftheyan glared at him, revealing a mouth full of long, sharp teeth. 'The voice of Shecumpeh,' he said, in a tone of barely restrained anger. The name he uttered was a compound of words from the old language – the one spoken by the first race of city-builders, before they died amid snow and darkness. It translated, more or less, as *the-one-who-speaks*. Ursu stared stupidly at the old priest, not sure what he was saying.

Then he remembered.

In his dream, he had been walking through the orchard his mother had once spoken of. The smell of ripe fruit had filled his wide nostrils, and his long narrow tongue had flicked out and across his muzzle. It was a familiar dream, but this time he had not been alone; there had been another beside him. But in the dream it had never occurred to him to turn and see the face of that companion. Its voice had been moderate and pleasant, almost musical in tone. But for the life of him, Ursu could not remember the actual words it had spoken.

But, now he took the time to think about it, in those first blurry moments after waking there had been something about that voice – something that frightened him.

He looked up at Uftheyan. 'I don't know. I'm not sure that—'

'You thought the words of a god would be clearer than that,' the old man said, 'like thunder from the skies?'

Ursu nodded. 'Yes, exactly like that.' Perhaps he had heard the voice of Shecumpeh after all. To hear the voice of the god, speaking directly to you? Raw excitement filled him, and he began to tremble.

Shecumpeh had spoken to him. And they had all heard it.

This early in the day the city was relatively quiet. Shecumpeh's House was situated directly in the centre of the city of Nubala, so that the god was at the heart of all things that mattered most in the lives of its citizens.

This had always been so, even in the depths of the Great Cold.

Ursu went over to the narrow window and peered through at the empty marketplace below. It occurred to him that almost a year had passed since the last great market held there, but that had been before Xan's great army had come. As anniversaries went, it was unlikely to inspire much celebration.

Ursu felt his stomach rumble, and he thought again of those orchards from his dreams. Likely the same soldiers encamped outside the city walls had long ago trampled their trees and gardens under their boots and wheels. Out there you were more likely to find the frozen bodies of the elderly, ready for the embedding rituals.

Uftheyan made a sound of irritation and Ursu turned away from the window. 'I'm sorry,' he said. 'I was just thinking.'

Then down the clammy stone steps they went, shivering at the chill wind that blew through the window slits. Ursu's cell was high up in the god's house, and from there he could just about see over the city walls to the encampments beyond, faint and almost hidden in the misty morning light. After a year, now, war had almost come to seem a normal part of their life. Along with starvation, and endless fear.

The god lived underneath the main edifice, in a cellar created for that express purpose (according to the Order's holy book) more than forty-five generations before, during which time the city had not fallen once. Throughout the course of a normal year, acolytes such as Ursu were permitted to see the god on only three occasions: the Festival of Frost, the Festival of the Sun, and the Festival of the Waning.

Only a few from outside the Order – the city's current rulers and various dignitaries and people who held hereditary honoured positions – were allowed to take part in just one of these: the Festival of the Sun.

Into the main hall next to the entrance, a chill morning wind came gusting through the open wooden doors, accompanied by a fragile chink of sunlight. Other acolytes and a few Masters were moving about, hurrying from the kitchens to the stables where the icebeasts were housed, and back again. A few of his fellow acolytes stopped and looked startled when they saw Ursu descend the rough stone steps accompanied by his Master.

Ursu himself had been handed over to the Masters at the very young age typical of most acolytes. Nubala had strict laws on this: if you had produced three children who survived into adulthood, then any further offspring had to be offered up for consideration by the Masters. Ursu had been the fourth in his family. Though an elder brother had died of the recurrent blackface plague some years into his adulthood, by then Ursu had been too far advanced into his training for the priesthood.

Being selected for service by the city's god was not

a rare occurrence, but neither was it an everyday event. It usually meant celebrations for the other denizens of the House, even a day or two of holiday. It had been four, maybe five years since the last acolyte – a female named Ewenden, Ursu recalled – had been called to serve Nubala's god. Ursu himself had been a lot younger then, barely sentient a year, so Ewenden was only the vaguest memory. Her name was remembered, though, as being the one who had died so tragically, drowning in the well immediately beyond the House. Being called meant you were destined for better things than most, to join the elite of the Masters who guided all religious life in the city and, perhaps, if you played your cards right, destined to become part of the ruling Council itself.

And so it was that as Ursu picked his way through the great entrance hall of the House, yawning and scratching at the tangled fur beneath his robes, he noticed that the normal indifference with which he was treated had been replaced with respectful gazes. Some pre-sentients – canthres – dashed past him on all fours, having somehow found their way inside the temple, their eyes glinting happily and devoid of adult intelligence.

He exchanged some casual greetings with other acolytes, their tongues touching and tasting each other's fur. Uftheyan, behind him, allowed his claws to briefly unsheathe, and the other acolytes scattered out of their way.

Being an acolyte required no special calling: you were there to fulfil the menial or degrading tasks the Masters regarded as below them.

But now things were different; he had been called. He would be permitted into the awesome presence of Shecumpeh. And if you were called, you became a Master-in-Waiting. You were housed in better quarters; you were even assigned an acolyte to run around for you. Uftheyan's hand occasionally touched his shoulder as if to guide him, but Ursu could have found his way down these steep stone steps leading deep into the ground with his eyes blindfolded.

Ursu stepped on down into a familiar darkness, where the scent of sticks of burning sweetgrass filled the air like perfume. This was supposed to be a solemn occasion, but Ursu could hear the sound of muffled yawns and low muttering from the dozen or so Masters who waited in the chamber below, somewhat spoiling the ritual atmosphere. It seemed likely they hadn't been up for long themselves. Ursu's long-toed feet sought out the edge of each step carefully, not wanting to witness the reaction of the Masters if he managed to trip and make a fool of himself.

The morning chill seemed to fade as Ursu heard the great wooden door that separated the Lower Chambers from the Main Hall above squeak shut. There was little light, but as his eyes adjusted to the dim candlelight flickering over walls laden with mosaics so ancient that many of them had almost merged into the surrounding stone, he saw the Masters he had served almost all his young life waiting there – for him.

It occurred to Ursu that his bladder was uncomfortably full.

Uftheyan was gone, merged with the shadows, and Ursu stood alone in the centre of a circle of watchers. He felt a nervousness tinged with excitement, and the delight of a new life now awaiting him.

And there, straight ahead of Ursu, sat Shecumpeh itself, the beating heart of Nubala, on its throne of brass and gold.

The god of the City was represented by a clay figure moulded loosely in the form of Ursu's own people, with spiralling incisions to indicate fur, a long tongue sliding downwards over the torso and a broadly grinning tooth-filled snout that might be interpreted by some as menacing. Shecumpeh was as old as the city itself – was in fact indistinguishable from the city. By an ancient Plains tradition, each of the Great Cities maintained its own god, and when it chose to, the god spoke to its citizens. Ursu had been taught how, at times, these gods would speak of things beyond nature, beyond understanding.

And suddenly the spirit of Shecumpeh was within Ursu. The attentive Masters could feel it too: an accompanying sensation, not quite taste nor smell, like the way the air feels the morning after a thunderstorm. Something clean, and sharp and bright.

He heard nothing that might be described as sound,

nothing like words spoken. It was as if suddenly revealed memories, images, sensations flooded into him.

Ursu knew the god was asking him for his *true* name.

'I—' he said out loud, then remembered himself. He was alone now in the centre of the room. *I am Ursu*, he spoke in his thoughts, and he wondered if the god could hear him.

And that was when the god spoke his *true* name, his private name, the name of his soul.

When Ursu had been five summers old, his adult mind so recently implanted in his canthre body that it still seemed a strange thing to be walking on two legs, he had undergone the same ritual that every other child of the city experienced, receiving his true name in the shape of just one of many hundreds of intricately carved pieces of wood picked at random from a great urn. This was to be his inner name, and he had been solemnly warned how demons would try to steal into his dreams to root it out. The horror was that once they had it, they owned your soul.

The only entities who should know your name – your *true* name – were the gods. And so it was that Shecumpeh spoke to Ursu.

More sensations, sounds and smells overwhelmed him. And this time, Ursu saw the image of a small, weak-looking individual in a robe too big for him, slipping through the streets of Nubala at night. And strapped to his back was . . . was . . .

Ursu stared at the idol of Shecumpeh that sat before him. Surely there could be no doubt about the message the god of the City was giving him? He realized now that he was the one in the god's vision, struggling through the city, this very same effigy crudely strapped into a bag slung across his back.

Then there he was again, slipping as if invisible between the ranks of the enemy marshalled outside the gates. On to the orchards beyond, and – on again. At first clear and sharp, the images flooding into Ursu's mind began contradicting themselves, as if several separate visions were being presented to him at once, each slightly different in outcome.

And then on, further into confusion and madness, as Ursu envisaged fire raining down from the heavens, the great city of Nubala burning in invisible light, all its territory being reduced to death and ruins.

As vision after vision assailed him, he became lost to the basement temple around him, his mind stretching out to explore something he could only dimly, distantly comprehend. Yet it seemed to be his own life, evolving along in a seemingly endless multiplicity of paths.

But there was one strand that still shone as brightly as a path of stars through an endless sea of night. That enduring image of Ursu the acolyte, now a Master-in-Waiting, stealing away with the figure of the god, and carrying it – somehow – through the walls of the city, and beyond.

Sam Roy

'Where's your father?'

'In the Citadel. I don't think he has any idea what's happening here while he's been in there. You know how it is.'

Sam did. Time and space ceased to operate as they should, once you were deep inside the Citadel. There were ways to navigate it, to find your way into its hidden depths and uncover the treasures that lay there, but it wasn't without risk. Matthew was older now, side-parted blond hair flopping across his forehead in an unruly wave. The sun was high overhead.

Sam gently rubbed his arms where they had chafed under the chains that secured him to the great round boulder. He already knew how much time they'd have. *All the time in the world*, he thought. Matthew's father was discovering what Sam already knew, that the Citadel was a patient mistress, a place where something was always waiting to be discovered.

'How old are you now, Matthew?'

'Fifteen.'

'Remind me why you hate your father so much.'

Matthew stared at him. 'Why I—? You hate him too. Look what he's done to you. You couldn't help but hate him!'

'He's your father. He's done nothing to *you*.'

Matthew stared out across the wide mountain plain. Sam followed his gaze, taking in distant peaks wreathed in cloud and, nearer at hand, a village almost like a resort in its picturesqueness, like someplace you might find far up in the Rocky Mountains, with a hotel and a bed for the night. But of course, they were a very long way from the Rockies.

'My father is insane,' Matthew explained at last. 'A girl in my class went crazy, started shouting that my father was evil, that we shouldn't be here.' Matthew licked his lips, then turned hollow eyes to Sam. 'They took her away, and a couple of days later he had her body left in the square so we could all see.' The boy was trembling now. 'He wants me to be like him. I could never . . .' He shook his head, the words trailing off.

'When we talk, Matthew, I don't necessarily get any sense of what you want to do, if and when you find a way to defeat him. Remember, *I* tried,' Sam raised shackled hands, 'and look what happened to me.'

'I don't understand.'

'Say you're left in charge of all this,' Sam said, nodding at the village, 'what are you going to do?'

Matthew looked defiant. 'Go home. Leave this place.'

'This is your home. It's where you were born.'

Conflicting emotions crossed the boy's face. 'There – there's so much else out there. We shouldn't even be here!' The boy actually stamped his foot. Sam raised one eyebrow and waited. 'We belong out there with the rest of the human race. You knew that, didn't you? That's why you did what you did!'

'I did what I did because your father wants to destroy a world, and I couldn't permit him to do that. No one sane could allow that.'

'That's what I want, too. And the others.'

Sam nodded. It was strange that Matthew's father had made the decision to have a family and raise a son after so long. He suspected Matthew's father intended to begin a dynasty.

'Very well, then. We should make plans. As long as you understand you might die.'

Matthew swallowed. 'I know that.' Sam studied the boy carefully until his eyes widened and the blood drained from his face. 'I will die, won't I?' said Matthew, taking a step back.

Sam said nothing, his expression remaining calm.

'Tell me,' said Matthew. 'I have to know. He'll find us out, won't he? We should stop.'

'No, you won't die.' *But some will*, he thought. He knew who they were, their faces and their names. They came in his visions, such strong, rich visions. He wasn't going to tell the boy this, though. 'You're right to do what you're doing, Matthew, so maybe you'll succeed where I didn't. But there are risks: this is life and death stuff.'

'He didn't kill you,' observed Matthew.

'He can't kill me, remember? And I can't kill him.' Sam's smile was more like a grimace. 'That's our gift, our sentence – that and the future.' Sam laid a hand on the boulder he had been chained to for so long. The path upwards waited again and, at the top of the path, food and water. 'Besides, in case you hadn't noticed, he gets much more of a kick out of torturing me than killing me.'

Kim

It was Fitz again. Fitz, with the bright red shock of hair that seemed to defy gravity in the way it floated in jagged wisps around his head. An emergency light flickered just behind him, and in the intermittent glow it provided, she could only briefly see his features outlined from second to second.

Fitz was saying something. 'We have to get out of here. Come on—' And then he said a name, and it was someone else's name, not hers. 'We have to get out of here now,' he repeated, and she could hear despair in his voice.

'No, wait,' said a voice sounding suspiciously, unpleasantly like her own. She struggled away from that voice, from the name Fitz had mentioned. Someone else.

'Fitz, fetch Odell and the others. We can still get this stuff out.' Great stone slabs surrounded her, their rough surfaces carved with arcane symbols and alien scripts that her practised eye recognized as Middle Period Shipbuilder. She was stepping into a corridor that curved abruptly just ahead. A faint trickle of memory came into her mind about what lay beyond, and then she realized . . .

She was dreaming, and she knew her worst nightmare lay around that curve. The worst thing she could possibly imagine, ever, lay a few feet away, in a building abandoned by the race who had constructed it untold millennia before.

She was dreaming, and with an awful certainty she knew Fitz was dead. She discovered then that no matter how much she wanted to, she could not cry, could not shed tears, because this, after all, was a dream.

Somewhere, on the periphery of her awareness, something significant was happening. She knew it was imperative that she now wake up.

Must wake up.

And suddenly she was back in the Goblin – shockingly so. *Oh dear God*, she thought, *that was bad*. She'd actually forgotten just how bad it could be. She had to find Bill, and fast.

The Goblin was her ship; after the botched expedition to the Citadel, she'd acquired it after finding herself still in the Kasper system with enough money left to purchase a long-range, deep-system hauler and a retrieval contract to go with it. That had been over two years ago, and since then Kim had developed into a rock hermit. Every now and then she'd bring the Goblin back into the Kaspian system's Angel Station, way far out where the Kaspian sun was just one particularly bright pinprick of stellar light in the deep black of night.

Now she was coming back in after a particularly fruitless haul and knew they'd be reviewing her contract. That knowledge just made her usual state of mind all the worse.

When she'd seen the inside of a Goblin for the first time, she'd thought she could maybe make sufficient cash by going out in it for a few days at a time, as the idea of living in it for weeks or months seemed hardly appealing. But she knew people did so – had been doing so, one way or another, for decades. Yet, after the first month or so on her own, travelling through the Kaspian system as captain and sole passenger on board her refitted Goblin, she had discovered the will to keep living.

To some degree, she had Bill to thank. In a sense, Bill had given her something she could have found without ever leaving the Angel Station, if only she had known. It was one of life's ironies that she'd had to spend a while going quietly crazy in a flying hermit's cave before she could discover that.

Kim had, so to speak, fallen asleep at the wheel – if only the Goblin had a wheel to guide it. She had passed out, entering one of those frequent waking dreams she'd long been suffering, a kind of relapse into the memories that the Books brought to her.

The Angel Station showed itself on two subsidiary screens as well as on the main viewscreen. One of these screens – nestled in a nook just above her left knee, glowing brightly from its niche between the co-pilot's seat and hers – revealed the Station as a computer-generated torus with an empty centre. The other, smaller screen, situated at head height, displayed a star map. One of the thousands of dots represented there glowed a different colour than the rest. That was the Kasper Angel Station she was about to dock with. Another brightly glowing dot represented Earth and the home system, several thousand light years away. An arrow pointed in the opposite direction, towards the Galactic Centre – which might well have been the next stop from this system, if anyone had ever found an Angel Station that led that far in.

She glanced up. Only a few seconds having passed, she still felt groggy and confused. She'd already had an inkling this was going to be a really, really bad day.

First, Bill had stopped answering her calls. Kim had tried contacting him previously during her long weeks of approach, but nothing. She had checked in with some other people in the human-habitable portion of the Station, and they'd confirmed having seen him around. So she knew Bill hadn't checked out and caught a shuttle back through the Station's singularity to some other system – which begged the question, why was he ignoring her?

And the whole time, her air and rations were running lower and lower, and now if she got back and Bill wasn't there . . . she wasn't sure what she would do.

And then she noticed a red light was blinking at her. She'd never seen it blink red before, but then she'd never functionally passed out on an approach vector before, either. Kim reached out with an unsteady hand and hit a button. A stream of dialogue had been trickling along so quietly as to be almost subliminal. Hitting the button knocked the volume up and, with a cold rush of fear and horror, she wondered just how long she had been floating along effectively dead in space, with only the autopilot to keep her alive.

'. . . Damn it, Goblin 4PX, do you read? I . . .' The voice grew briefly fainter as another voice interjected. Kim couldn't quite make out what they were saying, but she recognized the tone: angry, worried, someone in charge. 'No, I'm not in the habit of blowing anyone out of the sky. She's on auto, okay? We'll just bring her in. No, there's no danger, I—'

'This is Goblin 4PX,' Kim said rapidly, the blood draining out of her face. Stupid girl. Stupid, stupid girl! 'I'm sorry, my comms system has been having problems. I don't know what happened.' She swallowed, her throat suddenly dry. 'I, uh – sorry about that.'

'We hear you, but you know the rules. I'm afraid we may have to insist your ship undergoes a thorough overhaul before you can go out again.' The voice was reproving, but not too harsh. Kim had met the man behind the voice, once, not long after she'd arrived there. A gentle bear of a man who confessed to her one drunken night that he'd had enough of civilization and living in crowded hives, while alien diseases killed off entire continents. He'd put on his official voice this time

43

presumably for the benefit of whoever was standing next to him. One of the military guys, almost inevitably.

They called it the debriefing room, but it looked a lot like a cell.

'Thing is, Miss Amoto, there are rules and procedures here.' The Sergeant held out a clipboard in front of him. Every now and then, as he spoke, he'd let it drop down to his side and tap it against his thigh, so Kim could see a couple of shiny plastic sheets with a really bad photo of her attached. 'You *must* be aware of this.'

'I am, Sergeant.'

'Hm.' He nodded and looked over at Pierce, her lawyer – everybody's lawyer here on the Kasper Angel Station. He was also Earth's ambassador to Kasper, except of course the Kaspians didn't know that fact. He was further, by virtue of a strange public relations sleight of hand, the Station's Mayor. Apparently it had been decided that in order to foster a real sense of community amongst the Station's non-military personnel, they should have their own Mayor. It was, by Pierce's own admission, one of the stupidest ideas around. She knew he was also a pretty mean cook when it came to Mexican food, which came in handy because he really didn't get much else to do out here. Kim had been to a couple of his barbecues.

'Well, at the risk of telling you something you

already know, this Station – this entire system, as a matter of fact – is under military jurisdiction until any possible further threat is checked or identified. Now, the man in the docking control room at the time you were coming in would have had every right to fire upon you after you failed to identify yourself.'

'My ship was on autopilot, Sergeant. I've had a look at the ship myself, and there were some problems with the atmosphere control. My oxygen levels were too low, so I passed out. It happens, especially when you're out solo for long periods of time.'

'But you then carried out those repairs before an official inspection team could take a look at your craft.'

'Yes, because they were necessary.'

The Sergeant pursed his lips until he almost looked like he was pouting. Kim had a feeling *he* didn't have much to do with his days either. 'Miss Amoto, there are specific clauses in your contract to do with our rules and procedures. There are ways of dealing with situations such as this, and you didn't follow them.'

Pierce looked away from the blank wall he'd been gazing at for several minutes. 'The contract is thirty pages in length, Sergeant, and in very small type. People don't have time to read thirty pages of small type when they're dealing with potentially life-threatening situations.'

Kim willed her cheeks not to burn; she had never considered herself a good liar. Before she had finally docked, she had deliberately damaged a small valve to the rear of the craft, and then fixed it with the repair kit. She had come up with a story and started telling it to Pierce as soon as she'd found him. Pierce had just looked at her with a weary expression; he wasn't going to buy it.

'Whatever you say, Kim,' he'd sighed. 'Just make sure you get your story straight before we go in, all right?'

The Sergeant glanced at Pierce. 'She was right next to the Station then. How long would it have taken before we could pick her up from one of the navy ships?'

'I don't know, Sergeant. How long does it take someone to suffocate in a ship without a functioning oxygen supply?' Pierce asked dryly. He leaned back in his seat. 'There's really no need for this, Sergeant. The only reason we have these procedures in the first place is because of what happened – whatever happened – to the original occupants of this Station. But you well know there's no immediate threat to anybody here, and hasn't been for a very long time. If there *was* ever anything here, the danger is gone. One lone prospector falling asleep doesn't constitute a crisis.'

'Mr Pierce, I follow the set procedures laid down by my superiors, otherwise I have to answer to them.'

'Yeah, and this is a farce,' said Pierce. 'You don't have the legislative power to make any decisions here. I move we adjourn this meeting until the Station Commander can actually be present.'

The Sergeant stared at Pierce like he wanted to rip

his head off. Then he looked at Kim. 'Miss Amoto, I'm not convinced you're fit to pilot anything right now.' Kim's head was pounding, like needles were being worked into the backs of her eyeballs. 'I'm impounding your ship pending the payment of a fine for endangering the lives of the people on board this Station.' The Sergeant stared at her for a moment, then spun on his heel and left, an awkward expression on his face.

'Here, knock these back, do you a world of good.' Kim took the pills and swallowed them dry. Pierce tried to give her a glass of water but she waved it away.

'Really, I'm fine. You shouldn't concern yourself.'

'I thought you were going to pass out all over again back there. You should have seen the look on that Sergeant's face. He thinks everybody here is crazy, you know.'

'We *are* all crazy. Why the hell else would anybody be out here?'

'What?' he said, his cheeks dimpling. 'And turn down the chance to investigate the only extant civilization apart from humanity in the known universe?' Kim rolled her eyes at him.

Pierce had been good enough to get this accommodation sorted out for her while the Goblin was moved to another dock, where it would be impounded until she could either appeal the fine or pay up. The room was a tiny cube whose facing walls were maybe only a couple of metres apart, but for all that it felt like luxurious roominess after the time she'd spent in the Goblin. She sat on the edge of the room's tiny fold-down bunk, rubbing at her temples with the tips of her fingers. The Station's Mayor sat cross-legged on the floor in front of her.

'Listen, Pierce – I need to do some things. I need to get some things sorted out.'

'Sure, I know. Try not to worry too much just yet about the review of your licence. To put it bluntly, a lot of these people aren't too worried if any prospectors get themselves killed out in the middle of nowhere. Apart from the fact you screwed up in front of their noses, the only reason they're kicking up a fuss is that nothing ever really happens out here – aside from the usual observations of life down on Kasper.'

Kasper, thought Kim: the planet and the system had been named by a Polish member of the first exploratory team to come through this particular Angel Station. He'd named it after one of the Three Wise Men, and the name apparently meant treasurer. She supposed he'd meant to suggest this planet was full of valuable things. It was the kind of hint that made you wonder if he'd come up with the name before or after they got around to investigating the Citadel.

'Yeah, well, that asshole Sergeant seemed to think something was waiting to pounce,' Kim said, glancing down at Pierce. Her headache seemed to be abating. 'But listen, if they tell me I can't do prospecting here any more, I'll just – I don't know – go somewhere else, you know? It's a big universe.' Bill? Bill would be around somewhere; the Station wasn't that big. Once she found him, she could . . . get things sorted.

'Kim. Cards on the table, you have Observer bioware, don't you?'

She looked at him warily. 'Sure, yeah,' she said after a moment. 'Yes, I do. You already know that. What about it?'

Pierce shook his head. 'Take it easy. I'm not asking in any official capacity. The bioware – official or off-record?'

Kim surprised herself with her honesty, or perhaps she had been too long out amongst the asteroids of the Kaspian System with no one to talk to. 'Off-record,' she said.

'No problems?'

She squinted at him. 'No, no problems. Why?'

'I know a little about how you came to the Kasper Angel Station – and I know Bill. I don't know if you're aware of it or not, but your behaviour can sometimes be a little—'

'It's not like that,' she said, cutting him off. 'It works fine. It's a fairly straightforward surgical procedure. The thing does most of the work itself once it's inside your skull. After that, no problems.'

Kim could see the faintest hint of a grimace playing on his lips. Some people didn't like to think of that, something alien and slimy living in their skull next to their brain, reaching into their flesh and entangling itself inextricably with their neurons, ultimately conjoining with their mind. 'I had it done by someone reputable but, yes, off the record.'

'Do you remember why you had it done?'

'*Why?*' She hesitated for a moment. 'It . . . I had my reasons.' She looked at him angrily. 'I don't like you prying, Pierce. There's nothing I want to say to you about it. What happened out there was an accident, and nothing to do with it.'

'Okay, okay,' he said, raising his hands in placation. 'I'll keep you posted about what happens with the Goblin, all right? And maybe we can get some kind of an appeal sorted out.'

'All right,' she agreed.

Elias

When he got back to London, Elias dumped the taxi in a back street, sliding a knife under the cheap aluminium panel which hid the vehicle's brain, thus damaging it beyond repair; if he could make it look like the vehicle had been vandalized, there was maybe a little less chance that anyone would analyse the onboard computer's log and trace his journey from the Arcologies to this part of London.

He couldn't have imagined the pain might get worse, but it had. He pressed the heel of his hand into his face, then forced himself to walk away, looking for the first subsurface entrance he could find. The city extended as far below the ground as it did above, and he needed to get himself out of sight. It was a part of town he knew, but he couldn't go back to his cramped quarters in the Camden Maze; too dangerous until he figured out what was happening.

Which meant the only way to go was downwards.

He found a service entrance he'd used a couple of times over the years when he'd needed to get lost quickly, and soon lost himself in the warren of sewers and service tunnels that honeycombed the city's infrastructure. There were people down there, shadow-people like the ones that populated the Arcologies outside the city, surviving by whatever means they could.

He went looking for Danny, and found him in the deserted Tube station which had become a kind of home to some of London's abandoned folk. He was standing with a small cluster of people who were struggling to pick up one of their own from where he lay on the cracked concrete. Danny turned at Elias's footsteps, then frowned and started forward when he noticed the blood.

'Elias, what happened to you?'

'Don't ask, all right? What happened to your friend there?'

Danny frowned again, then glanced back at the men carrying away the body of their dead companion. As they disappeared into the gloom of the station, Danny shrugged and shook his head. 'Died of despair, probably. Don't tell me if you like, Elias, but you need fixing up.'

Danny led Elias back to his hospital: a long, low, luxury-sized mobile home rescued from a scrapyard that now doubled as a clinic. Elias let the priest inject him with something that seemed to distance the pain. Somewhere between the horror of what had happened to him out there in the Asteroid Belt and his present existence, Danny had found religion. As Elias told him about the Blight, Danny stared at him in horror.

'You should be dead,' Danny observed eventually. 'You shouldn't even be alive.'

'It doesn't always kill,' Elias insisted.

'You need to tell me more about exactly what happened.'

'I can't.'

Danny stared at him with fierce anger and disappointment.

'Just trust me, please,' continued Elias. The room around him swayed for a moment, till he felt Danny's firm grip on his upper shoulder. 'I was just trying to do the right thing.'

'The right thing?' said Danny, his lips set in a thin line. 'I wonder where I've heard that before. Tell me you weren't responsible for bringing it here, into this country?'

'I wasn't responsible.' Elias's voice was now a thin wheeze. 'I was trying to help stop it, all right? But something went wrong.'

Danny smiled humourlessly. 'That's the wonderful thing about people. They're always so surprised when things don't work out exactly the way they expect them to. I myself always expect the worst, which is why I'm still alive – you should remember that.' He seemed lost in thought for a few moments. 'Patching up your wound I can do, but the Blight is another matter. I can't help you with that. No one can. But if it's any consolation, you really should be dead.'

'Thanks.' Elias coughed. 'That really makes me feel so much better.'

'Listen to me, Elias. What they did to you and the others, they did to me too, remember that. It didn't work with me, or almost any of the rest of us, but what you possess is priceless. What you can do is . . .' He stopped, looked down at his hands, which were trembling. He stared at them until they became still. 'If I didn't know better, I'd have said it was miraculous. You could have helped so many people.'

'Not if I was dead. Trencher tried, and now he's gone. City Authority catches me, I'll be dead too.'

Something trilled in the background. Danny stepped away, and tapped a paper keyboard spread across a fold-down table. 'That's the analysis just done on your nervous system.' Danny eyed Elias with a carefully neutral expression. 'It's not looking good, I'm afraid. Your body seems to be resisting the Blight, but it's still pervading your system. Enough, I think, to constitute Slow Blight.'

Elias felt his flesh go numb.

'You know what that is, right? It's still in there – can't get it out. It's part of you now.'

Elias looked at him blankly.

'Elias, the Blight is some kind of biological *machine*. It's much more than just some random bug. It locks itself into your nervous system and tries to change the way your body works. Nobody knows just what it intends, but nobody ever lived long enough to find out.'

'I've heard of Slow Blight. Takes about a year to kill you, right?'

'The good news is, it's a non-infectious form of Blight. But it eats you from the inside out, starting with the nervous system. First thing you get is the shakes. I'm sorry to be so blunt about it, Elias, but you should know.' Elias noticed Danny seemed to be having trouble meeting his eyes. 'Don't believe what they tell you when they say it isn't going to spread beyond India,' Danny continued. 'I've been hearing otherwise.'

Slow Blight? Somehow he couldn't quite take it in. What Danny hadn't said, but Elias already knew, was that there was no cure for it. *Now there's a time limit on everything I do*, he thought.

He would die slowly, his nervous system rotting away, dying from the inside out.

Three

Autonomous Mining Collective 'Essex Town'
(Mars/Jupiter orbit; Asteroid Cat: No. 2152 NZ20)
Ten Years Before

Something had happened to Pachenko. Elias moved ahead, scouting out the further curve of the corridor, his combat rifle gripped ready in the hands of his armoured pressure suit. These corridors were carved from bare rock, the flickering emergency lights that illuminated them bathing the walls in a blood-red glow.

'Pachenko,' barked Elias over the intercom. 'What's wrong with you?' Elias looked around. Pachenko had been at the rear.

A howl of pain and despair came over the radio. Elias turned back, pushing past Farell and Eduardez, heading back in the direction of the military transport that had brought them to this pressurized asteroid. He found Pachenko huddled against a wall.

'They're going to die,' Pachenko babbled, as Elias knelt beside him. 'I can see it,' he said. 'I can see it.'

'What can you see?'

'Blood, and pain and bodies,' howled Pachenko. 'I can see them, Elias. Can't you see them?'

'No, but I believe you.'

Another voice came over the intercom. It was Farell. 'Sir? Everything's gone to shit, sir. A firefight has broken out between Company A and the miners. I can't contact Command. What should we do?'

Be anywhere but here, thought Elias. The miners had siphoned the atmosphere out of half the asteroid seconds after Elias and the other troop companies had boarded. Things were clearly not going the way Command wanted. Elias knew what Pachenko meant, what Pachenko was experiencing.

The mining community had carved itself into one of the scattered boulders of the Asteroid Belt. It was a kilometre-long slab of nickel and iron, positioned somewhere on the route between Earth and the Oort Angel Station, which only merited a serial number in a catalogue. The miners made their living by supplying raw materials to huge-bellied cargo ships that plied their way between the Oort Station and Earth. The nature of the Belt, its disparate communities scattered in lengthy orbits around the Sun, made any attempt at control or policing impossible. Corruption and lawlessness were the way of life here. Political expediency meant the attempt at control was made, nonetheless.

'Pachenko, Liam, listen to me. I'm going to have to leave you here. Make your way back if you can – do you understand me?' Pachenko nodded, his eyes still staring in horror at something Elias couldn't see, didn't want to see.

Pachenko was the one who'd made the scientists proud. *We're going to make special soldiers of you boys*, they'd said, before beginning the gene-tweaking process. *You'll heal faster, live longer.* They hadn't mentioned any of the other stuff: being able to catch glimpses of the future, the nightmarish visions experienced. So many of the other men had gone insane within days. Scientists had then been replaced by smooth-talking men in civilian suits, reminding them of their duty, of the terms of the permissions they had signed.

Elias had more than a good idea what Pachenko was going through, and would go through, slipping slowly into insanity. Elias could only pray he himself wouldn't end up going the same way.

Command had described the situation here to them during their briefing: a self-contained economic unit, a semi-socialistic enclave of God's Pioneers who, it seemed, had been extorting neighbouring miner communities while themselves being in the pay of a corporation seeking a monopoly on mineral extraction rights.

Later, Elias would find out that Command had been wrong – disastrously, terribly wrong. There was no extortion. Their sources had been wrong, misinformed.

They came to a kind of crossroads, Farell and Eduardez both flanking Elias. Something drifted down from above, from out of the darkness. Elias looked up to see a young girl, perhaps seventeen or so, her young round face barely visible inside a several-times-patched pressure suit. She held a weapon. She raised it. She fired. Elias heard Eduardez yell, even as the three of them brought their weapons up simultaneously.

A girl, thought Elias. *A little girl?* He took aim, but someone else fired first. The girl exploded.

Heat and flames filled the cavern. They fell back, taking refuge in the same corridor from which they had just emerged. 'Oh Jesus, what was that?' yelled Farell.

'Explosives,' Elias heard himself say numbly. 'They must have packed her with explosives.' He was now finding out what Pachenko had meant. He knew now it was going to get worse.

More miners in pressure suits came crawling out of the dark, firing as they moved. Elias and his men returned fire, their armoured suits protecting them, but there were just three of them, and scores of miners. It was only a matter of time before they were over-whelmed. Elias signalled for the other two to retreat further back.

New orders came through from Command. A 3D map came up on the inside of Elias's helmet, showing him the route to take. He signalled to Eduardez and Farell, and they moved off again, re-entering the cavern they had just retreated from, and meeting with

Company B coming from the opposite direction. A Korean named Lee Huang led them. The miners had vanished into the darkness.

'We got 'em,' said Lee. 'They're retreating now, pulling back. They weren't prepared for this kind of onslaught.'

Elias thought of saying something, like, *How do we even know they've done anything illegal*? But he kept his mouth shut. They moved off together, coming to what the Command map indicated was a central dormitory complex.

It was open to the vacuum.

'*We* didn't do this,' said Eduardez. 'Who did this?'

Messages flew between Command and the three companies who had boarded the asteroid. Something had gone very wrong. Company C was on its way. The miners had simply pulled back, ceased resisting.

So where were they?

As they moved into the dormitory complex, they found miners everywhere, faces slack, their twisted bodies floating in the airless vacuum. *Blood, and pain and bodies*, thought Elias. They were all dead, so Pachenko had been right, not that Elias had ever doubted him. *Blood, and pain and bodies*.

They had suicided, down to the last man, woman and child. He turned to see Lee vomiting inside his helmet.

Things became very strange after that; his memory of subsequent events grew patchy. One memory remained strong: they had attempted to rescue some of the miners. Like trying to fix something that can't be fixed, he'd thought crazily. But one thing he remembered well, above all else. Something he would never forget.

There had been a child, her face blue with hypoxia. He had watched as the girl was cut from her pressure suit and placed on a gurney. There she had lain in the stillness of death. He stared at her, and touched her face gently, a hollow feeling deep within him, in a place where a part of him had once lived but now seemed lost forever. He wanted so badly to bring her back, to rectify all the things that had caused her to be here, in this time, this place.

Then the miracle had happened.

The miracle that had sealed the fate of anyone who had emerged, transformed, from the gene treatments.

Especially Elias.

Getting back home had been far from easy. Once the mission was over, Elias had a gut feeling they'd try and find a way to hold on to all of them forever. They were, he realized, too valuable or too dangerous to be let go. So Elias had bribed a sergeant to stow him in a deep-sleep coffin on board a cargo shuttle that took a year to wind its automated way back to Earth after a long, slow solar orbit. After that, well, losing yourself in London was easy, if you knew how, and Elias had become an expert.

The experiments had left him changed, different – and not just because of the nightmares that he knew would haunt him forever. And one day, sitting in the secluded corner of a bar, the darkness obscuring his features, he was listening to an old man telling a story he hadn't heard in a long time, and felt a chill run down his back as the details of it flooded back to him. He distantly recalled the childhood stories, something whispered in those steel and concrete playgrounds that were the streets he'd always known from infancy. It was a story of someone blessed with a kind of second sight, the power to heal. Sometimes the Primalists came into the story – and someone who was the Messiah the Primalists had been waiting for. But always, in these stories, he'd eventually deserted the Primalists, instead of leading them into the Promised Land, wherever that was.

Studying any one particular variation of this legend, it was easy to find yourself realizing, only when it was much too late, that you'd been following the wrong path, and the truth lay elsewhere. Some variations on the story maintained he'd been a soldier serving on the re-contact missions to the colonies which were originally lost for two centuries, thanks to the Hiatus. He had, the legends further claimed, the power to bring people back to life, a power he'd gained when he met an Angel, the last of its kind. Nonetheless, there was a resonance to all these stories that Elias couldn't have been conscious of before the events he experienced out there amongst the Rocks.

Listening to the old man's story, Elias remembered the twisted, ruined bodies of the God's Pioneers, and became suddenly obsessed with uncovering the truth behind the legend.

And if there might be someone else like himself.

He began to scour the streets of London, hustling contacts and information, until he found himself standing before the entrance to a service tunnel running under one of the big maglev stations servicing London's lower levels. The kid who'd shown him the way there led him through a broken vent tucked behind an abandoned access corridor, which only a few people knew about. Down there, the kid had whispered, you could hear people walking about, people from all over the world.

That was when he'd found the name behind all the stories.

Trencher.

Trencher told Elias he remembered what it was like before they excavated the great tunnels that carried the maglev trains between continents, but Elias doubted that. The tunnels had been in place for over a century and Trencher was an old man, but Elias knew he couldn't be that old. Elias returned to the service tunnel many times, and once Trencher trusted Elias enough, Elias got to see the miracle worker at work. He watched the old man cure a woman of cancer simply by touching her, and again he remembered the miracle out amongst the Rocks.

Whenever Elias asked him about his past, Trencher had been guarded, but it was clear to both of them that they shared a gift, though a gift that was more like a curse. In turn, Elias told Trencher about his life in the military, the terrible things that had happened there. Elias came across Dan Farell who had been in the Rocks with him, and found that Danny had escaped not long after Elias himself, and had since become a priest. Elias became part of *his* world too, and for a while, his life found a meaning and a depth that he had never realized was missing from it. It was from Trencher he first learned about Vaughn and about the Primalists.

'You mean this guy Vaughn is like a ghost?'

'Not a ghost.' Trencher had coughed. They were somewhere high up, near the curve of the Dome, the bleached grey wall of some vertical slum visible through an open window. Rain streamed through a crack in the city's facade, falling a quarter of a mile or more to the streets far below. 'He's human. As human as you or me, at any rate. It's as if he can be in two places at once, like a kind of astral projection.'

Elias cocked his head to one side. 'Is it something we can do?'

'There are only two I know of, Vaughn and one

other, who have that ability.' They drank mint tea out of stainless steel mugs that belonged to an elderly woman Trencher knew, who to all intents and purposes ruled the building Trencher was now sheltered in. 'Vaughn comes to me sometimes, *like* a ghost, but that's because really he's far away. He wants me to go back to the Primalists.' The old man laughed. 'Imagine? Did I ever tell you about the Primalists, Elias?'

'No,' said Elias, wondering if he should say anything else or wait and see what the old man said next. He'd been trying for months to get some idea of Trencher's origins, but the other had remained taciturn.

Until now.

'I'll tell you, then,' said Trencher.

The Primalists had started out in Japan a long time ago, before the Stations were found, and centuries before Elias was born. They'd used a different name back then and their philosophy combined elements of eastern mysticism and western millennialism – a real fire-and-brimstone, the-end-is-coming kind of ideology. When the Angel Stations were first discovered, the Primalists decided they were there for the sole purpose of taking a chosen few out to safety amongst the stars, where God would get things right this time.

By this point, they'd grown powerful and influential, spreading outwards from Japan into America and Europe, using the pooled funds and knowledge of their richer members to make investments in high-yield research industries, particularly those reaping rich rewards from inventions linked to the newly discovered alien technologies recovered from other star systems.

It seemed that the Angels – or whatever they'd actually called themselves – had carried out genetic manipulation on an unimaginable scale. This much had been public knowledge for centuries, and had led to the development of Angel-derived technologies such as read/write bioware for recording memories and experiences by biochemical means.

Any of the worlds the Angels had visited, where life existed, they'd altered in some way, travelling between those worlds via great waystations that could carry them across vast interstellar gulfs in the blink of an eye: the Angel Stations. Identical strings of apparently 'junk' DNA had been found in species on worlds light years distant from each other.

And somewhere during the time that came to be known as the Hiatus, when the Oort Angel Station had nearly been destroyed by the scientists studying it, and contact between the scattered fragile colonies around other stars had subsequently been lost for almost two centuries, research into the Angel-altered gene sequences had continued unabated. Paradigm-altering discoveries about human DNA were then made, and it didn't take long for some of the new theories to be tested out on human beings. *If I'd known more about these things*, thought Elias, *maybe things would have been different*.

It didn't take long for Elias to realize what the old

man was telling him. The Primalists had actually created Trencher, in a breeding programme designed to bring about a new Messiah – but a Messiah that would serve only the needs of the Primalist religion.

Elias had listened appalled to Trencher; appalled at what they had done to him, appalled that they had succeeded in so many ways.

'I didn't want any part of it,' Trencher assured him. 'And I told them so. They didn't want to let me go either, but they had made us too powerful. The Primalists were going to kill all of us but one, but we rebelled. *I* rebelled. This was all a long time ago, Elias. A long time ago.'

More than three centuries ago, Elias realized. It was indeed a long time. He wondered if the old man would ever die, or if he'd just keep going. 'You said "us"?'

'Sure, Elias, *us*. Three of us. Three supermen, and the Primalists couldn't control any of us.' The old man sipped again at his mint tea with merry eyes, enjoying the consternation, the confusion in the other man's face.

'But they didn't breed *me*. We were all adults, all soldiers, when we underwent the treatments that made us the way we are.'

'Dangerous,' said Trencher. 'How many of you now left with the power? Just you, you said? Pity. The rest weren't strong enough to handle it, I suppose, not in the body or the head. Now they're after you too.'

'But the Primalists are still looking for you, right?'

'Sure. They can't necessarily account for me, and I could screw things up for them.'

'What are they planning?'

'Things.' Trencher looked out to the rain as a bird flew by, navigating the cavernous spaces between the buildings. 'Look at that, Elias. I swear, must have been years since I saw a bird flying down in here. Not so many of them left outside either. Things're getting bad.'

'What are the Primalists planning?' Elias persisted.

'You'll know, Elias. Best you don't torture yourself till the time comes. We've all got a burden to carry, and yours is greater than most.'

Unsettled, Elias put down his mug. 'You're talking about the future?' Trencher's ability for precognition was extraordinary, while Elias's own visions were like faded family photographs, bleached images so vague in detail they could represent almost anything. But Trencher saw so much more. The old man had known precisely when to glance out of the window, Elias realized: just at the right moment to see a sparrow fly past, its tiny wings beating furiously in the still dead air.

Trencher had sighed heavily then. 'I told you there were three of us. Vaughn was one of the others. He's going to come to you, soon. Don't listen to him, Elias, whatever he says. He's powerful, dangerous. He believes in everything the Primalists taught him, and more.'

The old man was silent for a few moments. 'Something bad's going to happen, Elias,' he said at length.

'I'm going somewhere soon, and I need you to do something for me, okay?'

'Something bad? How bad?'

'Let's just say I'll be gone for a while. I want you – I want you to do the right thing.'

'What?'

'The right thing – when the time comes.'

'You've lost me.'

'When the time comes,' Trencher had repeated patiently, 'you'll know what to do.'

That had been one of the last times Elias ever saw Trencher. Elias came by one day, found half the block burning, its ruined apartments gaping open as masonry tumbled downwards.

Elias thought about these events, and after he'd thought about them some more, he went looking for Hollis.

Ursu

It had not been a good morning.

Ursu had woken to the thunderous sound of the army encamped outside the walls, yelling and hooting enough to drive fear into the hearts of all the citizens. Ursu was now a Master-in-Waiting, and in the three days since the god had spoken to him, he'd tried to find some kind of precedent in the Book of Shecumpeh.

He pored through thick, heavy pages rich with ink and platitudes, but discovered nothing that described anything like the situation he now found himself in.

The Book of Shecumpeh was kept in a vault below the stables, attended by an elderly amanuensis named Turthe. Ursu was aware that Turthe was seeking someone to learn the arts necessary for making new copies of the Book and, perhaps, eventually take his place. For in many civil matters decisions made were based on sayings found in the Book of Shecumpeh.

Ursu knew that there were other communities, beyond the valley and still further away, which also revered their own city gods, each as jealously guarded as Shecumpeh was in Nubala, and that many of those cities also kept their own great books. But there was only one Book of Shecumpeh, much as there was only one city of Nubala. All the Masters-in-Waiting were required to learn the words of the book by rote, but it was Turthe's task to repair and maintain the current copy.

The pages were heavy, the covers made from fine beaten leather. The paper had been handmade, sheet by sheet, by Turthe himself. Mostly, its text consisted of stories of all the leaders of Nubala since the city had been founded at the beginning of the Great Cold, when the ice came. But also within it were stories of the great heroes of Nubala, and the battles they had fought. Fables, legends and prophecies filled these pages.

Ursu's mind drifted constantly back to the deeply certain knowledge he'd been given by the god; in those strange half-images that seemed to suggest words, there had been absolutely no confusion, no doubt of what was being asked of him.

Which left the question of when he should do it. It wasn't like he could just tumble down those stone steps, snatch the thing up, and vault to freedom over the city walls. Lack of opportunity combined with his own fear, and Ursu could not help but dither on a heroic scale, waiting always for some sign he could not be sure would ever come.

So he waited, and the longer he waited, the harder the waiting became. But despite all this, he could still reason, use his rationality. Shecumpeh had shown him the world fallen to fire and death, if he failed. Therefore failure simply was not, could not be, an option. Ursu planned his move, although he greatly doubted his own ability to carry out such an impossible task.

Over the yells and hoots of the enemy, the sound of screaming closer to home became apparent. Ursu felt the fur across his back prickle, and across the tip of his snout. He raced down the cold stone steps, only to find turmoil in the Great Hall. Its doors were wide open, and he witnessed Masters and acolytes alike shouting and running about outside. The well just beyond the entrance seemed to be the centre of activity, as they drew buckets of water up and ran off with them some-where, as if attempting to put out flames. Ursu began to step forward hesitantly, to help. He still remembered that story the older acolytes once told, about the ghost of the girl, Ewenden, who still haunted the well, and dragged the unwary down after her.

'Just put that fire out!' screamed one of the Masters, and Ursu stared around as gibbering acolytes ran past him. It was then he spotted the buildings across the way with their wooden roofs ablaze.

No matter how fast the acolytes hauled their buckets from the well, it was clear they would never have enough to douse the flames before the stricken buildings burned to the ground.

Nubala had been built in the time of the Ice Giants, and had been well prepared for siege. But since then, the ice had retreated, and in its place a great river flowed down the valley, deep enough for conquering armies to float their supplies dangerously close.

When Xan's army had first approached, the city council had had some forewarning, and therefore time to build up stocks of vital supplies. But these great catapults that hurled flaming missiles over the city walls were an innovation that Nubala's original architects could never have predicted.

'Sometimes I think we should just give them what they want, and fuck tradition,' muttered a voice near Ursu. He glanced to one side, and recognized the long, sad face of Nepuneh, until recently a fellow acolyte. Ursu stared at him, and Nepuneh looked guilty.

'I – sorry. I didn't mean that,' he said hastily, his fear

evident from the way his ears flattened themselves
against his skull. He ran off quickly, and Ursu watched
him go.

Give them what they want, he reflected. Why had it
taken so long for him to understand Shecumpeh's true
purpose?

Xan wanted one thing, and one thing only: the living, beating heart of Nubala. And the essence of the
city, the one thing whose removal would mean the end
of the city, was Shecumpeh itself.

'Hmm.' Turthe smacked his long lips and lifted, one
after the other, several huge pages of the Book, looking
for the most recently inscribed passages. 'Here we are.
Xan's armies arrived peacefully enough – well, as peacefully as any potential invasion force can.' Turthe looked
up at Ursu and slid his black, unsheathed claws through
the fur that coated his lengthy skull.

Every bone in Ursu's body ached from the endless
carrying of water that had lasted until almost sunset. It
had, of course, not been enough to prevent all the
buildings standing opposite the House of Shecumpeh
from burning to the ground. There were now injured to
be attended to by Shecumpeh, and the dying also.
There were also many corpses whose families would
wish embedded by nightfall.

'You know all this already, Ursu,' said Turthe. 'Why
refresh your memory now?'

'It has to do with what Shecumpeh communicated to me when I became a Master-in-Waiting,' he replied, knowing he could hide behind the truth as long as he phrased things the right way. Turthe's lips made a sucking sound and he left it at that. It would have been very impolite, if not a little sacrilegious, for him to inquire as to the nature of that privileged conversation between god and acolyte.

'Well, as recorded here, Xan's generals sent us a delegation seemingly to remind us that Xan is the reincarnation of the Fhide, and therefore Nubala was now part of Xan's empire – lucky us.' Turthe mumbled rapidly as he ran his fingers along the lines of symbols. 'Naturally, being the race of canthre-licking piss-snow-eating troglodytes that they are, they saw fit to make demands. Well, that's a bunch of inbred southerners for you. Anyway, as we all know,' with this, he glanced up, 'they also demanded we hand over Shecumpeh, in accordance with the Prophecies of the Fhide.'

The Prophecies of the Fhide? The Fhide had been a great ruler before the snows came, one of the First People, who had sought – briefly succeeding – to unite all the city-nations, including Nubala. Shortly before his death – in this, most of the Great Books of the various cities were agreed – corruption and betrayal destroyed his loose-knit empire from within. Most histories also agreed that the Fhide had predicted on his deathbed that he would come again to rebuild his empire. Inspired by this prophecy, Xan had led a so far successful campaign to consolidate the fractured lands on the opposite shore of the world, and had recently even proclaimed himself the reincarnation of the legendary Fhide. If anyone in Nubala actually believed that, few would publicly admit to it.

'Remarkable.' Turthe shook his head. 'Nonetheless, before we became trapped in here by the siege, it was coming to light that Xan's armies had already succeeded in stealing the gods of different cities all across the known world. Even now, perhaps, the lunatic is planning to encroach on great Baul itself.'

'But we won't hand over Shecumpeh to Xan, will we?' said Ursu.

'Of course not. And bring the ice storming back in again, once it sees there is nothing to protect us from it? My own grandfather used to tell me what life was like in Nubala when he himself was a boy, and he described his piss freezing so fast, when he went to take a leak, that he could see the ice reaching for his delicates before he'd barely started.'

Ursu smiled; Turthe was always a lot more approachable than some of the other senior Masters.

'But if they do succeed in entering the city, and taking Shecumpeh from—'

'Careful what you say, young Master-in-Waiting,' said Turthe. 'Shecumpeh will triumph as always. Does it not say so, in the Great Book itself?'

Ursu nodded.

'One hopes you do not have doubts, Ursu,' the old

one continued. 'In times of war and desperation this may be forgivable, but perhaps not admirable.' Ursu tried to look appropriately reproachful. Turthe emerged from behind the low table on which the Great Book rested and placed a hand on his shoulder.

'The whole matter of the siege is fairly straight-forward. They want Shecumpeh, but we don't want to give it to them.'

Ursu gazed into his wide black eyes. 'Nonetheless, if they . . .'

'Enter the city?'

'Yes.'

'Then they . . .'

'Will take it anyway?'

Ursu glanced through the pale light cast by burning tallow towards the entrance to Turthe's workroom. Nobody was in there, but he still felt as if every word he said was somehow being conveyed throughout the whole of the House of Shecumpeh.

'Perhaps,' said Turthe sadly. 'Perhaps even inevit-ably.' He looked at Ursu for the longest time. 'And whatever shall we all do then?' he asked.

'I – don't know,' Ursu said carefully.

'No?' Turthe's ears twitched alongside his skull. 'Pity. I was rather hoping you had been imparted some ideas.'

Kim

Kim fell into old routines with what felt to her like depressing ease. Unless there were some really exciting new nightspots down on Kasper, the Angel Station was about as good as it got for several thousand light years.

In design, the Angel Station consisted of a fat torus, with the singularity at the centre of its ring-shaped structure. When Kim first acquired the Goblin, she'd had to pay someone to teach her how to pilot it and then issue her with a pilot's certificate. The tutor – a middle-aged woman who moonlighted occasionally from her work in one of the main research departments on board the Station – had tried to explain to her how the Angel gate worked. The only phrase that had really stuck with Kim was *phase transition* – like when water suddenly became ice, once the conditions were ideal.

She'd told Kim that, as far as anyone could tell, the singularity worked on a similar principle. Not a black hole – black holes being neither shaped like flat discs nor lacking gravity – but sharing some of the same properties. Somewhere inside the torus, space and time were forced into a controlled phase transition, where the laws of physics operated differently, and this made it possible to jump from one end of the galaxy to the other.

After that, it seemed to Kim, all you really needed to know here was where to find the best bars, because drinking, doping and screwing were pretty much the only forms of entertainment you were likely to find.

The human part of the Angel Station was built around the circumference of the original alien-built torus, bolted on to its exterior surface. As a result, a large part of the original Angel Station was now hidden behind ready-assembled living quarters, medical bays, converted fuel tanks that housed everything from exo-biologists to lapdancers, as well as docking bays, military barracks, and pressurized tubes winding through it all like spaghetti. And beyond that were the ever-present military escorts, sleek, buffed-up, long-range cargo haulers with heavy shielding built around the hull, and pressurized living quarters where once there had been only vacuum.

Kim headed for the Hub immediately after speaking with Pierce. A long time ago, this part of the Hub had itself been a heavy cargo lifter, but it was now permanently welded to the Station torus. Some budding entrepreneur had recognized the need for providing entertainment for upwards of several thousand people scattered at various points throughout the Kaspian system. He had gutted the whole thing after the post-Hiatus investigations into the disappearance of the original crew turned up nothing but blanks, then filled it with bars, music and a variety of exotic entertainments. The Hub, Kim knew, was where she stood the best chance of finding Bill Lyndon. Her supply of Books was already lower than she felt comfortable with. Not just any Books, of course – special Books. Ones that were hard to get hold of.

She caught sight of herself in a mirrored wall and saw her mouth was set in a thin line of anger, with maybe something uncomfortably like desperation in her eyes.

She noticed one or two other asteroid hermits like herself, almost certainly passing time on the Station between their contracts. They nodded, or exchanged a few words with her, at most.

Kim was more used to communicating with them from inside her Goblin than in the flesh, and it felt strange to see some of them now wandering around the Station's fleshpots. She imagined they must feel the same way about her.

And then, at last, she found Bill Lyndon.

He was over six feet tall with a long beard brushing his barrel chest and thick black hair on his head. He sat alone in a small alcove near one of the bars, tapping through pages on a smartsheet. Video clips and pictures of naked actresses scrolled blurrily in front of him. She slid into the booth beside him and waited.

He gazed at her for a few short moments before it clicked with him. 'Oh, hi, Kim,' he said. 'I didn't know you were on your way back here.'

Kim smiled, more tightly than she'd meant to. He must have received at least a dozen voice, screen and text messages from her over the past few weeks. 'Mind if I join you?' she asked.

'Sure, sure, sit down,' he said, although she was already seated. 'Want a beer?'

'Not right now, thanks,' she said. 'I've been trying for some time to get hold of you.'

Bill sighed, and flashed a wide grin. He shook his head slowly, in a theatrical way. 'If you knew what my life's been like.'

'Bill, I'd like to get some more of those Books I ordered from you last time.'

'Well, things are kind of difficult right now – after the big find, and everything. You know they've raised the security rating for the whole Station?'

'Big find? What big find?'

He peered at her. 'You have been out of the loop, haven't you? One of your rock hermit friends found something way out by Doran – stuff that looks like real old Angel technology.' He leaned in close to her. 'Something that might turn out to be Angel Books too, maybe. How about that?'

She stared at him. 'Angel Books? Are you sure?' Probably, it was something else altogether. Real Angel Books were still a fantasy. It didn't take much imagination to picture how lucrative a find like that would be.

Doran was an irregularly shaped lump of rock barely worthy of being called a planet, really a captured asteroid with an orbit that kept it far from the heat of Kasper's star. It had little in the way of mineral deposits worthy of exploitation, and so had been largely ignored both by the Station authorities and the rock hermits.

Even so, it struck her as strange that something so significant could have been missed by the initial exploratory missions into the system.

'I never heard anything on the Grid,' she said. During those long, slow weeks of approach, her mind had been too preoccupied to pay much attention to whatever random information was bouncing around out there. Maybe she should have listened more closely.

'That's because they're keeping it all hush-hush up there in Command,' said Bill, referring to the nexus of pods and living quarters that housed the bureaucrats and military types who administrated life on board the Station. 'So whatever it is, it's back *here* now. So up goes the security rating until they know what they have. End result is,' he raised his eyebrows, 'it's a little harder now to get people some of the things they ask for. They're paying a lot of attention to anyone going in or out through the Gate.'

'I just saw some people come in off a ship who looked like scientists, not tourists. They let *them* in.'

'Yes, but that's coming in, not going out,' he said. 'What this means is, for the next few weeks, very little of anything is going back out – of anything.'

Kim shook her head. 'So what? It's only Books I'm after, and you know the only Book distillery is in Command. They're just Memory Books. It's not like an addictive drug.'

At that, Bill gave her a long, cool stare, and she found herself flinching from his gaze. 'Everything's addictive, sweetheart. Just depends how badly you want it – or need it.'

There was silence, then, for several long seconds, as music drifted through the air, emanating from hidden speakers. The way Bill looked at her, and spoke to her; it always made her feel as if she'd done something wrong. Books were just something she needed. Because her own bioware had come through the black market, she required Bill as a point of contact, because official channels for the distillation of Books weren't accessible to her. But maybe he didn't realize that.

After the silence had dragged on long enough to get uncomfortable, she opened her mouth to speak – but Bill beat her to it.

'You know, Kim, I make a lot of money just sitting here getting old and fat. I don't intend to do it forever, though, and believe it or not I do sometimes give a damn about some of the people who come to me. But do you know what?'

He looked at her like he was waiting for an answer. She shook her head.

'You I don't get. I heard of people like you, and what you're doing isn't even against anybody's laws. But what you're doing to yourself is suicide, plain and simple – the worst kind. Losing your own memories for somebody else's.'

'Bill,' she said, 'I don't need lectures.' And with that, an image sprang into her mind: a grinning face with a bright red shock of hair. Then the same face shouting at her to get out, and she pushed it down, hard, hard.

'I still have some distillate of the memories I need,' she said, picturing the vials of precious liquid in her mind, tucked away in her quarters.

The distillate technology allowed raw memories to be siphoned in liquid form from a person's bioware and turned into Books – small, easily digested pills. Anyone else with the same bioware could then consume these pills, and thereby relive the memories and experiences of whoever the distillate had originally been taken from.

Having the bioware, Kim had found, was the easy part. Getting the raw distillate turned into something she could actually use was an entirely different matter. The distilleries were astonishingly expensive – and very hard to get access to if you didn't have fully authorized documentation. There was one on board the Station, in a highly secure area to which she, as a regular civilian, did not have access.

There were ways, of course. Bill was one of those ways. She had enough distillate to last her a long time, but the levels of bribery involved in getting the Books processed into a usable form meant she could only afford to have relatively few manufactured at a time.

'As long as they're keeping those artefacts up there in Command, they'll be watching everybody going in and out of there like a hawk. But I might be able to do something for you – if you can do something for me. A favour?'

Kim regarded Bill with a wary expression. 'What kind of favour?'

He reached into his pocket and brought out a tiny plastic case. 'I knew you'd been looking for me, and heard you'd just got back. It's like this.' His voice dropped to a semi-conspiratorial whisper, and she leaned towards him a little. 'I'm not telling you who made the find because if it gets out, it might end up being traced back to me. Seems someone working inside Command suggested a little unofficial deal. If they could be provided with a tiny quantity of the memory distillate, the person who made the discovery got a little cash above and beyond what the joint Government committees might provide.'

Kim nodded. She could well imagine what untried – even alien – memory distillate could fetch on the black market, especially when the official channels wouldn't be able to match the price.

'Well, that person talked to the rock hermit in question, and then that same person talked to me, and then we had a couple of drops of that distillate made into Books. Unfortunately, you're the only person around here who's got the necessary read/write bioware to tell us what's in them without crying wolf. So how about a couple of those to tide you over?'

Kim felt like crying. 'Bill, this isn't something you snort or stick in your arm. For God's sake, it's *chemical* Books. It's memories and experiences. It's not a drug, it doesn't work the same way.'

'Baby,' he said, 'it's all about escape, one way or another, isn't it?' he said, smiling. Kim said nothing, knowing he was perfectly right, dead on target. It was always about escape – only the means varied. But knowing that made no difference to her own very real need.

'Look,' he said, keeping his voice soft and low, 'you know how it works out there, bouncing from rock to rock with nothing to do but talk to a bunch of other deranged Goblin jockeys. There are no secrets. And these guys,' he said, nodding discreetly towards a bunch of military-looking types sitting at the far end of the bar, 'are no better. Information gets bought and sold out here, same as anywhere else. So, I get to hear things: like they think the raw distillate they discovered might be the real thing, real Angel memories. Not animals, or dinosaurs or whatever, but actual Angel memories. Think about it, Kim. I heard they found this stuff frozen in a block, like amber, still viable after God knows how many millions of years. Maybe including memories of the things that built this place – maybe. That's the kind of Books I'm talking about. There are always people from the . . .' Bill scratched his cheek, apparently looking for the right words. '. . . the *private* sector who want to know what's in them.'

'You mean criminals,' Kim said carefully.

Bill leaned back, studied her. 'That I can get my hands on right now. The other kind, you're going to have to wait for.' He smiled, shrugged. 'Sorry.'

Four

Roke

There was a tower Roke liked to visit on mornings like this. It stood at the eastern limit of the high-walled valley in which the city of Tibe stood. The walls of the valley fell away to the north, spreading wider and lower to provide space for a network of wide-bodied rivers that led to the Great Northern Sea. As you approached by ship from the north, you saw the city of Tibe spread before you, between wide, rounded hills that rose gradually behind the city to the mountainous terrain of Southern Tisane. But first you saw the mass of the Emperor's Rock, rising from near the centre of the city: a great lump of basalt on which the palace stood, home to kings and despots and lunatics since the beginning of time. It was impossible to walk through the streets of the city below, and not crane your neck up to see the Emperor's home, balanced there as if by magic.

Where Roke now stood, in a tall whitestone tower on one of the high hills that embraced the metropolis like great encircling arms, the Emperor's Rock rose slightly to the right of his vantage point. This far up the valley wall, you were almost – but not quite – level with the palace itself. To Roke's left were ships coming into port or sailing out to sea. Most of them were warships; even the merchant ships mostly carried military supplies these days. This was a sight that had stunned Roke the first time he had seen it, when he had been brought here as a captive more than half a lifetime ago. He had believed he would die, horribly, for resisting the armies of Xan. And now, here he was, one of the Emperor's most trusted advisors.

However.

Bright sunlight fell through the clouds that tumbled down from the high mountains to the south, bathing Roke in sudden warmth. It was not enough to lift his mood, though. The meeting was scheduled for that evening, after most of the city's inhabitants had retired for the night. Always, after nightfall, the Shai came, and Xan consorted with devils out of a child's fairytale or some story taken from the great Book of some flea-bitten city's history. Even so, the Shai frightened Roke, frightened him to the core, for although it was like nothing else in the world, strange and alien, it seemed to Roke that behind its words hid other intents.

Roke had attempted to speak to the Emperor about his concerns, but Xan had only seemed to half-listen. The Emperor Xan, after all, was the conqueror of the known world, the reincarnation of the Fidhe. Roke, for all his respected status within the court, was still at heart a refugee from a captured city. There were many in Tibe who would be reluctant to let him forget this.

– Master Roke.

Roke stiffened, but did not turn. He did not wish to see the figure that had appeared behind him. He did not know the creature's name, but it seemed apt to think of it simply as the Monster. He felt, rather than saw, its ravaged face staring out at him from the shadows by the stairwell.

– I can see why you like it up here, it said. – It reminds me a little of a place I once knew.

Roke looked down to where the hills descended below the tower, all the way down to the distant streets. He could hardly imagine what world such a phantom might call home. 'I find it peaceful here,' said Roke.

– Ah. Peace. All intelligent beings seek peace. Even I.

Roke forced himself to turn around and look. 'The Emperor's men have sought out the god from the city at the edge of the world, and are preparing an assault. There is no sign as yet that the god has been removed from the city without our knowledge.' Roke cleared his throat. 'But then, you have foreseen that this will happen, haven't you?'

– I have, yes. It's why I'm here, Master Roke.

The Shai's voice was not unlike the voice of a god, that same spill of images or suggestions of faded memories half-remembered that somehow translated into comprehensible words. His lips moved, speaking the language, Roke presumed, of the Shai, though he could hear no actual sound pass from the Shai's lips.

But *not* a god. Roke had to remember that. Something else, altogether, that had come here to Tibe, travelling over some unimaginable distance that Roke suspected he could not possibly comprehend. Roke and the Shai had spoken several times now – here, in this tower, where he knew they would not be disturbed.

It had taken some time for Roke to reach the point where he could believe the monstrous Shai when it claimed it stood against the other Shai he had witnessed appearing before the Emperor Xan and his court. The monster could genuinely see into the future, and nothing it had predicted had failed to take place.

'Then tell me,' said Roke.

– Your Emperor is going to send you northwest of the Teive mountains, said the Shai.

'North of Nubala.' Roke's throat was suddenly dry.

– He wants you to look for something. You will find it, but it will be too late for Xan.

Roke nodded, staring out across the roofs of Tibe for long seconds.

'Remind me why I should trust you more than the other Shai.'

– Because that one does not have your best interests at heart, soothed the creature.

'The other Shai has brought technology and science to our Empire. It . . . it says it wants to help us.'

The creature bared its teeth. They were black

and broken, a nightmare vision which Roke found unnerving. – Come, Master Roke. You've already described to me your misgivings about the company the Emperor has been keeping.

'But you don't tell me *why* you wish to destroy this Shai, or any of the others you have told me about. Why would you war against your own kind?'

– Perhaps because they did this to me, Master Roke. Because I discern the lie in what they say. And I tell you that if you do not do as I describe, your people are quite genuinely doomed. The Shai have anything but your best interests at heart. You already know this, even if Xan is not prepared to accept it.

'So.' Roke paused, trying to collect his thoughts. He would walk into the council meeting tonight filled with lies. He only hoped Xan and Feren, the Emperor's spymaster, would not be able to read them through his skin. 'I am to go north, you say?'

– Yes. And when you get there, there is something you must do.

'Which is?'

And then the Shai told him more than he ever wanted to know. It was a dispiriting and terrible thing to find out the true nature of your world. That truth wasn't an easy burden to carry, but Roke was made of stern stuff. He'd fought in battle side by side with Xan, first as an opponent and then later as an ally, once Xan had won him over and they had become friends. He, Roke, would prevail. As Xan would prevail. As perhaps the Empire would prevail, despite its recent losses. And he came to understand that the Shai was, indeed, correct when it said Roke would know what had to be done.

And when this meeting was over, when the twisted form of the Shai, with its bent and broken teeth, faded gradually once more into the shadows of the stairwell, like a phantom from a nightmare fading into nothing, and Roke was again alone, then he knew it was time to prepare for that evening.

Xan had summoned him – and, it was reasonable to assume, Utma and all the others – to a meeting with the Shai. Roke picked his way down the long, spiralling stone stairs, thinking about what the Monster had just said.

Elias

Elias watched as Hollis came out of the building and walked over to a private car. An expensive one, Elias could see; it even had manual drive, judging by the steering wheel visible through the windscreen. As Hollis started to climb in, Elias stepped forward out of the shadows, sliding the flechette gun from his sleeve, guiding it between his fingers until it was firmly in his hand. He reached out as Hollis bent to get into the car and pressed the muzzle against the side of the man's neck.

When Hollis jerked back, Elias gripped his arm and whispered at him to continue getting in.

'Elias.'

'Get in, Hollis. Then we can talk.'

Elias then pulled the rear door open and slid in behind him, keeping the gun pointed at Hollis's ear. The man moaned with fear, turning white as the cold metal of its muzzle touched his ear.

'You were behind that, Hollis? You're really up to your neck in something this time, aren't you?'

'It wasn't what you think. Put the gun away, I'll explain.'

'I'll keep it right here, thanks. So start explaining or say goodbye to your head.'

Hollis' breath was loud, ragged. 'I'm not the only one whose neck is on the block, Elias. I'm not your enemy. Without me, you'll never get out of London alive.'

Out of London alive – that was what it came down to, now? The city was a world in itself, sprawling across the entire southeast of England; huge, implacable. But he'd seen what was on the diskette Josh had given him.

'If I hadn't been lucky, Hollis, I'd be dead right now, thanks to you, so I really wouldn't go making any threats. The Mala Pata knew I was snitching on them, and you handed me over to them on a plate. So here's my idea: you tell me why the fuck somebody wants to take Trencher offworld, and I'll let you live. And don't think you can get away from me, because I've got plenty of friends who owe me really big favours, friends who make the Mala Pata look like play time at the fucking nursery.'

Hollis swallowed; he was a policeman, after all, and knew all too well that Elias wasn't lying.

What rankled with Elias was how Hollis had managed to blackmail him for so long. *Do what I tell you*, Hollis had told him, *or I hand you over to the City Authority*. Except now Elias knew exactly how corrupt Hollis really was, and how careless. That threat was almost certainly empty. If Hollis had ever blown the whistle, he himself would never have seen daylight again, the instant Elias opened his mouth.

'We're going to circle round for a while,' said Elias.

'And then what?'

'We'll get to that. For now, take it off manual.' He thought for a moment. 'Take it to the Camden Maze.'

The car pulled out.

'You're in trouble, aren't you?' said Elias.

'Yes, I am,' – and the policeman's candour surprised him – 'a lot of trouble. But you'd better understand something, Elias. We're both in this together, whether you like it or not. They'll get rid of you even quicker than they do anything about me. And I can pull strings, which you can't.'

'Josh clearly knew everything, *everything*. And now the Mala Pata and half of London believe I can't be trusted. The only place they could have found anything out from was you.' It was a statement rather than a question. But Hollis nodded, and Elias felt a grim sense of satisfaction.

'Here's what I think happened, Hollis. You've been bleeding blackmail money out of me for years now, just so I can keep the City Authority from finding out where I am. The way I see it, I think you then got scared you'd be caught so you set me up. Bad idea, Hollis, very bad. Because now I have nothing to lose.'

'They don't know about you,' Hollis babbled, 'but if I'm not around to help you, they'll find out who you are and hand you back to the military. I won't be able to protect you any more. So you need to disappear.'

'Which reminds me,' said Elias. 'Stop just here.'

As the car slowed Elias leaned over Hollis's shoulder, and punched a series of commands into the car's console. It moved off slowly, turning a corner into a quiet alley near the edge of the Camden Maze.

'Take a look at this.' Elias pulled out a crumpled smartsheet and dropped it onto Hollis's lap, still keeping his gun pressed against the back of the policeman's neck.

'What is it?' asked Hollis shakily.

'Just look at it.' Elias reached over Hollis's shoulder, touching the smartsheet here and there. As information began to scroll down, a long sigh escaped Hollis's lips.

'See that?' said Elias. 'It's a ship's manifest. I got it from Josh – just before I killed him. Not an official manifest. It's got details of where they kept him, where they're moving him to.' There were other things on the sheet. A pixellated image of a man being lowered into a deepsleep coffin, his body sprouting wires. Trencher.

'I didn't know about this, Elias. Really, I didn't. You have to believe me.'

'I thought Trencher was dead,' snarled Elias, his voice rising. 'All these years, I thought he was dead. And now I find he's still alive – if you can call that living.' He pushed the gun harder into the other man's neck, forcing Hollis to lean forward under the pressure. 'If you even intimate for one second you didn't know about this, it'll be the last thing you ever say. Does he know where he is – or what's happening to him?' Elias pressed his free hand over one side of his head; it felt like he had a headache. No . . . worse than that. *Not now*, he thought. *Not here*. The pain was growing.

'I don't know. We don't have him anymore. He was given over to a private research group for storage and research. They said he died during procedures. That's all I know, Elias, believe me.'

'I don't know, Hollis. You've always been a slippery little bugger, haven't you? Maybe you're still lying. Maybe I should just kill you.'

'No.' Hollis was weeping. Elias scowled, feeling sickened. His finger touched the trigger, and he pushed forward again until Hollis's head was forced down even further. Pain filled one side of his skull. There were images, thoughts flickering in the back of his mind, unwelcome ghosts of people and places he'd never seen or been to, all crammed together in a meaningless jumble.

Do it, thought Elias. He's worthless, scum. The world would be a better place. Remember all the threats, all the living in fear.

Elias shook his head, while staring in wonder at the corrupt policeman. 'You people truly never fail to amaze me.' He pulled the pistol back and hit Hollis twice, hard, in the back of the head. Hollis slumped, unconscious, face pressed against the console.

Then it hit: a wave of nausea and pain, and then the visions. Not the tiniest fraction of the power of precognition Trencher had been blessed or cursed with, but an overwhelming experience nonetheless. A tiny scrap of the future tumbled out of the sky, and fell between Elias's eyes.

Nothing. Darkness. The negation of being. He howled with pain and terror, as his altered cells showed him the end of everything.

Vincent

'Hey, Vincent.'

Eddie Gabarra. Vincent Lani hadn't seen Eddie in years. He grinned despite himself. They'd worked together, briefly, at Arecibo, before Gabarra had been moved upstairs, literally.

'Eddie.' Vincent leaned his bicycle against the door

to his office and shook the other man's hand. 'Long time, no see. I thought you were—' Vincent made an upwards-pointing motion with his hand.

'Still ILA? Yeah, I still am. This is my first time back in, oh, two years.' Somehow, in the surprise of finding Eddie waiting for him outside his office at the University, Vincent had neglected to notice the pair of crutches Eddie was leaning on.

'Oh, you're . . .' Injured? 'I'm sorry, I had my mind on other things . . .'

'Thank you, Vincent. Yes, I'll be just fine,' Eddie said, deadpan.

Vincent thought for a moment. One of the problems with working in low-gee had always been the deleterious effect on the human anatomy. The longer you had to live in low or zero gravity, the harder it got to deal with normal gravitational levels. But these days there were medical techniques that could deal with that kind of thing: tailored viruses and medical processes that could more or less rebuild your skeleton from the inside, with relatively little pain or fuss.

Expensive, though. As far as Vincent knew, the treatment cost about the same as getting someone up to the ILA and keeping them there for a couple of years. The ILA was the International Lunar Array, a complex on the dark side of the moon, which itself formed part of the Deep Space Observation Array. Eddie was Head of Operations for the Array, one of the sweetest jobs an astrophysicist could have.

The refectory was bright and busy, stark polar light slanting in through tall angled windows. If you stood at the room's east side, you could see the rows of wind turbines stretching off into the distance, like an army of giants encamped on their way to torture a Spanish knight. The rest of the view was blocked off by an extension to one side of an Arcology, one of the seven Arcologies that housed the three million population of Antarctica City.

Inside the refectory, palm trees brushed the thick, protective glass, bathing in sunlight. Vincent deposited Eddie at a table there and fetched a couple of coffees for them both.

'How long you been back?' Vincent asked, sitting across from Eddie. 'If you don't mind my saying so, it seems a little mysterious, you turning up out of the blue like that.'

'I pree-fer to be . . . mysterious,' Eddie replied, in mock-sinister tones. 'Well, I guess I didn't want to draw too much attention to myself. Besides, I wanted to talk to you.'

'Uh-huh.' Vincent sipped at his coffee, and thought about that reply for a couple of moments. 'So let's see. You came all the way – from the moon – because you wanted to talk to me?'

Eddie shrugged. 'Sure, why not?'

'There are easier ways. Phone? The Grid?'

Eddie just looked at him calmly and waited.

'Okay, then, why are you down here?'

'Well, put it this way, you know I run the ILA. It's a pretty demanding job, and more about politics and not enough science for my taste, but the money and the prestige that come with it are just ridiculous,' he said with a smile. 'Every now and then, though, something comes up which really blows your mind. I mean the big stuff, Vincent. Up there with finding the Angel Stations big.'

Vincent nodded and leaned back. He glanced around the cafeteria, where students milled about, and he could see a couple of other lecturers in the distance, getting fuelled up for their morning classes. Vincent liked real science, but he liked teaching as well. Sometimes, while explaining things, he could work something out in his head, often connected to what he was actually teaching at the time by only the most tenuous link.

Eddie, on the other hand, was the kind of guy you'd have at a party because you knew he was someone people could connect to, who could make things happen socially, but he was also a brilliant scientist, renowned for his abilities, on Earth and other places too. Vincent knew Eddie well enough to know that when he said something like this, he really didn't mean it lightly.

'Are you sure this is where we want to talk?' Vincent asked him. 'It's kind of public.'

'If anybody really wanted to listen in to our conversation, they'd have bugged your office. If they've bugged you personally, we're screwed anyway. But here we can just sit and talk and nobody will pay much attention.'

Vincent nodded, not really thinking about how he had gone all the way from greeting an old friend to worrying about surveillance in the time it took to drink a cup of coffee. 'Okay,' he said carefully.

'Okay, first your research.' *My research?* thought Vincent. 'How's it going?'

Vincent blinked. 'Are we talking about the import-ant thing now?'

Eddie wore a very patient look. 'Yes.'

'Fine, I guess,' Vincent said with a shrug. 'Most of it's just librarianship, keeping up with the data coming in from the other deep-space arrays, collating and cross-referencing it all, comparing it with other information gathered by other people over the centuries since they found the first couple of Angel Stations.'

'Discovered anything interesting?'

'Lots,' Vincent said immediately. 'The most import-ant finding would involve fluctuations in levels of gamma radiation on a galaxy-wide basis. The Angel Stations aren't spread evenly enough to provide a truly accurate picture of how the galaxy's evolved over the past couple of hundred million years, but, using the Array here, and at the moon, along with the Arrays they've re-established out at the other Stations now, what you get is pretty remarkable. Sudden surges of gamma radiation, separated by huge periods of time.

More than might be accounted for by typical burster activity.'

'Big surges, right?'

'Yes,' Vincent said carefully, wondering where all this was leading. Eddie maintained an intense expression, while Vincent kept talking. 'Big surges – more like explosive.' Explosive? That was the word he'd been looking for. 'That's what you basically have. Maybe some kind of a super-burster. Evidence seems to suggest there are regular explosions of lethal gamma radiation, emanating from the core region of the galaxy, and spreading outwards from there over periods of thousands of years.'

'Lethal?'

'Sure, almost certainly. But it's hard to be accurate. We found the first Angel Station out in the Oort Cloud at the end of the twenty-first century. Now, that let us jump to other Angel Stations at different points throughout the galaxy. Some are closer to the galactic core, others are further away. The one in the Kasper system is the closest to the core. So that gives us several vantage points from which we can measure these fluctuations.' Vincent beamed at him.

'Go on.'

'Okay,' said Vincent. He could feel himself slipping comfortably into lecturer mode. 'When the Oort Angel Station failed three centuries ago, we lost contact with all the other Stations and their associated human colonies for two hundred years.'

'The Hiatus.'

Vincent nodded. 'Observations from those other Angel Stations resumed a century ago, when the Oort Station's singularity was successfully reactivated. Now, the Hiatus made for some big gaps in our knowledge. I've been correlating data gathered before the Hiatus along with data obtained since we re-established contact. It's long been thought that similar surges or explosions might have been responsible for mass extinctions here on Earth. The geological evidence is there, in the rock. That's also part of my research.'

'And how certain of that are you?'

'Pretty certain. Can't test it out, obviously, but I'd say all the evidence is strongly in favour.'

'I'd agree.' Eddie nodded. 'I've got something you should take a look at. No, make that *have to* look at.' He reached inside his jacket and brought out a smartsheet with bright red edging. He rolled it up and put it in Vincent's hand. 'I want you to take a good look at that. But, before you do, I want to ask you not to show it to anyone else, or talk about it to anyone. When I say the stuff on that is confidential, I really mean it. And once you've finished reading it, I want you to dispose of it, carefully.'

Vincent laughed nervously, but Eddie's face remained grim. 'Oh, come on, Eddie, what do you expect me to do – eat it? I mean, grilled or boiled?'

Vincent caught the glimmer of a grin at that remark, but immediately it was gone. Still, Eddie had relaxed a little. This was not like the man he knew, and Vincent had an inkling of the kind of pressure the other's job must put him under. 'So can you give me any idea of what's on this thing?'

'Only a little. It's information that corroborates and supports your theories, too much so for my liking. But it's really important you don't spread this around, okay? I can't say that often enough.' Vincent raised his hands, palms displayed towards Eddie, in a placating gesture: point taken. Eddie rolled his eyes and swirled the coffee around in the bottom of his paper cup, then put it down again.

'Listen,' he said, 'I'm only down here for a few days. I'm not even officially here, kind of, so I'll have to come back. I'm going to shake some hands and do some politics, and I'll be back here in two days' time. Then you can tell me what you think of what's on that smart-sheet.'

Ursu

More days passed, and Ursu waited for some further sign that he suspected, in his more candid reflections, would never come to pass.

He spent more time with Turthe, fulfilling his new duties as a Master-in-Waiting, but with less fervour or pleasure than he might have otherwise done.

'Did I ever tell you how I came to be the Guardian

of the Book of Shecumpeh?' Turthe began one time, while Ursu studied some of the ancillary texts Turthe kept stored on shelves in his workroom. Most of those other works recorded events in other cities, other lands, information gained through trading or war.

'No, I don't think you ever did,' said Ursu. He had earlier been helping Turthe grind down a particular form of stiff, puttylike fungi – called icewort – which grew mostly under the eaves of buildings, particularly after it had been raining. It was slimy to the touch and possessed a foul smell, but was a vital ingredient for producing ink.

Rumours continued that the army outside the walls was preparing for a grand assault any day now. There had been an exchange of messages during the last two days, and Ursu had been there when Nubala's own message-bearer had re-entered the gates of the city. Ursu noticed how the messenger's face had looked drawn, his ears spread flat and stiff across the back of his skull.

The icebeasts in their stables had finally been sacrificed to the needs of the people, and were even now being roasted, their meat cut into long strips and salted to preserve it. The hardships of siege had long since made Turthe painfully thin, and Ursu worried lest the old Master was too frail to survive much more of it.

'It happened when I was young,' Turthe continued, watching his pupil work.

'Shecumpeh showed you the Great Book and told

you that you were to be its Guardian?' Ursu spoke more sharply than he had intended. 'You told me so.'

'So I did,' he said. 'But I lied, you know.'

Ursu looked up. 'You did?'

He nodded. 'Shecumpeh in fact showed me something quite different. But you never told me what Shecumpeh revealed to you. Did he ask you, too, to guard the Great Book?'

Ursu blinked and almost dropped the bowl of half-mashed weed in his hands. 'Turthe!' he erupted, briefly forgetting the elderly scholar was by far his superior within the House of Shecumpeh. 'You know I can't speak of that! It's—'

'One of the sacred bonds between a priest and the god he worships? Piss and excrement, my lad.' Ursu simply stared at him, dumbfounded. 'The enemy is at the gates, and we may all be dead within days. We've kept them waiting too long, so say rumours from the Council. They may exact revenge on us, as a lesson to others.'

Ursu made to leave. 'I can't stay and hear any more of this,' he said, with an irrational fear that someone might be listening.

'You really don't have to tell me if you don't want to,' said Turthe. 'If Shecumpeh has directed you to be my replacement, fine. But otherwise, I think you are being less than honest with me.'

Ursu stared at him. 'I'm sorry, Master Turthe. I have had so much on my mind. The siege and everything.'

'Will you be leaving the city?'

He knew! He had to. Otherwise, why would he ask such a question?

'I – am a loyal citizen, Master Turthe.'

'But not a soldier, eh? Where's the use in sticking around for a bloodbath? You're young, so it's not right for you to burn with the rest when the time of retribution comes. Besides, I suspect Shecumpeh has something special in store for you.'

Ursu kept silent, waiting to see what would emerge next. He felt how his ears had flattened themselves to his head, the unmistakeable indication of being trapped and cornered.

Turthe came towards him. 'I think I can trust you,' he said. 'For there's something you should see. But first let me tell you this. You have been the first one called by Shecumpeh in some time. And it is now almost a given that the siege will come to a head within the next few days – if not sooner. If decisions are to be made, there is not much time for them to do it. You've been sneaking around with your ears all flat ever since he spoke to you, so it doesn't take a genius to realize that whatever Shecumpeh said to you, it wasn't easy listening.'

Turthe drew back and went over to where a slightly tattered curtain screened off part of his workshop. He pulled it to one side and secured it to a hook set in the wall. As Turthe beckoned to him, Ursu stepped forward, slipping between the wall and the broad platform supporting the current Great Book of Shecumpeh. He stepped into a deep, low-ceilinged alcove which he had noticed Turthe use for storing materials.

Ursu lit a candle while Turthe kneeled down by the lowest shelf. For the first time, Ursu noticed a small door in the wall below the shelves. He wondered why he'd never noticed it before, then realized that there had always been a pile of rolled-up manuscripts stacked in front of it.

'It's small,' Turthe muttered, bending low to duck under the lintel of the tiny door, 'but even I can squeeze through it without too much trouble.'

He watched Turthe scrabble through and, after a few moments' hesitation, he followed.

The walls beyond were cold, slimy, rough-hewn. The flickering candlelight made the space beyond feel primitive and old, as if it hadn't been visited for a thousand years. Ursu shivered, the fur on the top of his head brushing against the ceiling. By the dim light of Turthe's candle, he could see that beyond the door was a long, low tunnel.

'This one runs near to the lower Temple,' explained Turthe. 'Look – see there?' He stopped and raised his candle, so that Ursu could see steps, falling away into darkness just ahead. Ursu turned to look behind him: a faint, distant glow was the only hint that the tiny door leading into Turthe's workshop still lay open.

'Turthe, I don't understand, where exactly are we?'

The Master Turthe raised a long digit to his wide, broad lips. 'Voices carry farther than you'd think down here. And, in answer to your question, we are on the threshold of the deep catacombs below this part of the city. There are other caves far below here. Come further.'

Ursu gradually became aware of a distant roaring sound that only barely distinguished itself from a vibration. He had always known caves existed below the city – as did all the citizens – but this was the first time he had ever had cause to venture into one.

Ursu noticed he could see better, in part because of his eyes adjusting to the stygian blackness of the tunnels. But a certain faint luminescence was becoming evident the farther they progressed. Aware of a familiar odour, he stopped. As he reached out to touch the wall, he realized the rock was damp.

The walls were speckled with icewort, that same foul-smelling fungus he had been mashing up only minutes before for Turthe's benefit. Here, in these godless depths below the city, it had transformed itself into something infinitely more beautiful than the grey rot manifested by daylight.

'You see that, yes?' said Turthe. 'That's how they can make armour sparkle in the night. Now, look ahead of you.'

Turthe waved him forward, where there was just enough light for him to see he was standing on a surface of natural, uncarved rock. The passageway had given way to something like a shore; his feet were now resting on rough slimy pebbles.

Ursu looked up, and saw bare rock curving into a dome above him, also speckled with the same dimly shining icewort. Water gushed in a torrent through a great crack in the far corner of the cavern they were now in, before pouring through another great rent in the floor, and into some unknowable abyss. The darkness gave itself easily to his imagination.

'What is this?' Ursu asked.

'One of the tributaries of the river Teive,' explained Turthe. 'It runs down from the Teive peaks, which rise beyond the valley of Nubala.' Ursu was familiar with the Teive peaks – great rocky giants, blue with haze, at the furthest edge of the horizon; they could be seen from the top of the city walls.

Ursu stared around at the cave, feeling a certain kind of awe that this magical city he had grown up in could still, even after all these years, surprise him. The darkness was misleading; the cave was not, on closer study, so very large. No larger than some of the rooms in the House of Shecumpeh above it. Still, Ursu couldn't help but wonder how many years, how many lifetimes, it had taken the torrent to carve the deep groove of its passing in the floor of the cave.

'The river flows fast, and hard, before it re-emerges far from the walls of the city,' said Turthe from somewhere behind him. 'It would be a dangerous journey even for someone as young as you.'

'This is why you brought me down here?' Ursu turned and stared at the old priest, his features hidden in the thin light. But he was already contemplating the journey ahead, regardless of the obvious dangers. But what chance was there of survival? Slim, certainly – more likely non-existent.

'I am not suggesting it,' said Turthe. 'I am merely saying that there are . . . *alternatives* to be considered, should circumstances here grow much worse.'

'I don't understand why Shecumpeh cannot protect us,' said Ursu. 'Why he doesn't repel the invaders.'

'Some might suggest,' said Turthe, his voice mild, 'it's because we haven't shown ourselves worthy of Shecumpeh.'

'No!' Ursu said. 'I mean . . . there is no difference between us and any other generation of Nubalans since the beginning of time. We are a good people. We don't deserve this.'

'Then consider Xan's claim to represent the fulfillment of the Prophecy of the Fidhe.' Turthe's voice was still calm and reasoning, and Ursu had to strain to hear him over the sound of the rushing water. The thin mist that filled the air all around had left them drenched, their robes heavy with moisture. 'He does reveal some of the major qualifications,' Turthe continued. 'He has, after all, conquered much of the known world. Under such circumstances, it might seem a given that we should yield the god Shecumpeh to him.'

'You don't believe that,' Ursu said, turning to face him. So far beneath the earth, he was sure no one else could hear him, except perhaps Shecumpeh himself.

And what Shecumpeh had asked him to do was a heresy against the god itself. It was almost funny, and he felt his ears begin to twitch at the humour of it, but suppressed that reaction quickly when he saw the annoyance on Turthe's face. 'There are still questions that have to be asked,' said Turthe. 'Outside the rooms occupied by the City Council, this is one of the few places I'd say is safe to discuss them without the risk of anyone overhearing and accusing us of treason.'

'Would they really? Give Shecumpeh to Xan?'

Turthe's ears twitched in thought. 'Perhaps – if it meant the survival of the city. However, I suspect many members of the Council fear what would happen to them if they did so. Some of our more devout citizens'd happily see them torn apart for giving away the beating life and soul of our city to any crass invaders. And if they survived Xan's army, what would happen if what few crops we manage to grow then failed, or our hunting expeditions brought back no game? Who would be to blame then but the Council, for letting our enemies take our god away from us?'

And what of my own torment? thought Ursu. Knowing that he might be the one to remove Shecumpeh from Nubala, wouldn't that mean abandoning his own people to death at the hands of the invader – unprotected now by the god he'd stolen from them?

But it was Shecumpeh himself who had commanded Ursu to carry the god's effigy beyond the confines of the city, and whatever Shecumpeh directed, any acolyte or Master-in-Waiting hurried to undertake. Or so Ursu had always been brought up to believe. Now, he wasn't quite so sure.

And Turthe – what drove him to bring Ursu here now, to this place? Ursu's mind was filled with a horror that somehow the old man knew what Shecumpeh had asked of him. Yet . . . Turthe was showing him a safe way out.

'But what of Shecumpeh?' Ursu said carefully. 'Shecumpeh must have spoken of this, must have seen this coming?'

Turthe had been staring deep into the churning water; now he turned back to Ursu, looking suddenly weary. 'Yes, I think he must have realized in some way. I think he might have spoken to someone.'

Ursu found himself trembling, only partly from the cold and damp. 'Do you think so?'

Turthe studied him carefully. 'Whenever there has been a crisis in our history, the god has spoken to someone – whereupon Shecumpeh's word is carried out.'

'Because that is the way things always have been, Master Turthe?'

'Yes, Ursu, always.'

Five

Kim

Kim studied the tiny vial of Books in her hand. She knew she'd taken up Bill's offer without really thinking it through, and only because he'd hinted how he might be able to help her if she did. The Books were an unknown quantity, possibly even dangerous. Maybe I'm in over my head, she thought. Maybe I should take them back.

The guilt was starting to return – and with the guilt came the reason for her guilt. And with that reason for her overwhelming, almost unbearable guilt came everything else – a tidal wave of dark memories and sorrow that might well suck her under. She stopped her progress, found her way into a convenient toilet which was thankfully deserted, and leaned her head against a wall.

'My name is Kim Amoto,' she whispered. She pressed her hands against the cool surface of the bulkhead and studied her wrists, turning them so as to study the healed-over slash marks that had created narrow white strips of insensate flesh. There had been a reason for her not having surgery to hide these marks, but that reason had been lost in some other life. That other life – that other person – was gone now, dead and buried forever, along with all the things she had achieved, as well as all the guilt and pain and terror that same person had been forced to carry and that, even as she struggled against them, were threatening to overwhelm Kim all over again, for the first time in so many months.

No. She brought her arms down, pulling at the long sleeves of her jerkin until the scars were well hidden again. Most of her fellow rock hermits had their own, far worse, secrets to hide.

She headed back into the Hub, but now the noise and movement all around her acted like an intolerable pressure on her, like too much information was being thrust towards her and she was drowning in sensations. She felt a constriction in her chest, like some invisible giant had wrapped one enormous hand around her chest and was beginning, ever so gently, to squeeze her. As panic rose in her, she thought perhaps she'd been out here in the middle of nowhere for too long, forgetting what it could be like with other people around. And here she was surrounded by hundreds of them, pushing and jostling, drinking and dancing and hanging out all at once. She thought about stumbling back out of the Hub, but where was there to go, where the oppressive thoughts and memories wouldn't follow her?

So she found her way to a bar and ordered a tequila. And then another one. She tried to think. Bill couldn't be the only one in this place who could give her what she wanted. But she'd left it almost too late. She ordered another tequila, a double this time. After that, the room began comfortably swaying. Better, she thought: the anxiety had dropped, she was feeling calmer. But still the pressure of all the bodies and noise around her was hard to take.

She pushed away from the bar, thinking there had to be somewhere better to go. A brief image came to her of somehow opening one of the triple-security airlocks scattered around the Station and throwing herself into the naked vacuum, but she pushed it away.

There were better ways than that – less painful ways.

Elias

Two days later, Elias was on his way out of London forever.

He'd taken Hollis's car deeper into the Camden Maze, a horizontal and vertical mishmash of building units and crumbling megatowers, filled with low-rent residences and makeshift shops, built on top of the Old Camden. There were so many access points between the Maze and the relatively unpopulated lower levels, it was one of the easiest places to disappear in at very short notice. Elias had been telling the truth when he'd told Hollis he had friends. Not only through favours owed – of which there were many – but through payments that had been made to Elias, all saved up towards that inevitable day when he knew he would have had to make a break for it.

He took some of the money accumulated and paid to have Hollis iced for at least a week, allowing enough time for him to get away. There were those who knew how to track the streams of data passing through the complex computer networks of the City Authority, and they confirmed what Elias had found on the diskette Josh had given him: Trencher was still alive, iced down, and already offworld.

Trencher was on his way, in fact, to the Kaspian system. It was as far from Earth as it was possible to get. But if that was where Trencher was going, Elias would go after him. He couldn't even begin to guess why anyone wanted to take Trencher there, or to what purpose. He owed it to the old man to find him, and bring him back.

And so Elias found himself, here and now, on a landing pad on top of one of the mighty towers of the city, surrounded by helicopters and VTOL craft. A cold February wind whipped across his face like a frozen blade. Smelling smoke, he peered out across the great, semi-translucent panels that partially roofed over the streets of London, separated by dully gleaming metal interstices.

Dozens of other buildings rose above him, their windows now reflecting the early morning sun. The smoke, he realized, was drifting up from campfires below, and he could see a huddle of makeshift dwellings erected between two great exhaust towers. Although Elias knew about these rooftop shanties, this was the first time he'd ever seen one. It made the city seem that much more forbidding, even more like a medieval walled fortress surrounded by starving supplicants being refused shelter.

A sign pointed to an office where someone in the uniform of the city's militia came out and studied the smartsheet with Elias's passport details. Elias waited, not sure if his fake ID would pass muster, but all that happened was that he was escorted to one of the larger VTOLs, a great black aircar with curving mirrored windshield obscuring the cockpit.

Stubby black wings protruded towards the rear of the craft, and the fuselage flared outwards at four points, partially shielding from view enormous jet nozzles, now folded neatly away but still visible. The vehicle rested on four fat wheels.

As Elias got in, he found Vaughn inside, waiting for him. Elias stared at him for a long, long moment then took a seat across from the ghost, but ignored him. Vaughn seemed happy to say nothing for the moment. The pilot was separated from them by a blank wall.

The aircar banked as it lifted, so Elias could see London shrinking away below him. He had now accepted that his chances of ever seeing the city again were slim, but he didn't feel as depressed about that as he'd imagined. It was a place he had lived in for much of his life, and when he'd been younger, the city had seemed a complete universe in itself. Now, as it fell away, it seemed to fade in his memory as well, becoming merely a part of the past.

The curved glass of the exterior looked almost transparent from the inside, and every time the aircar tilted in its flight Elias found himself gripping the material of the couch, as if he might fall out.

Vaughn observed this reaction with a bemused expression. 'Don't worry, Elias, I'm only here to give you some advice.'

'Oh, lucky me.'

'Always so hostile.'

Elias looked out of the window rather than reply.

'You owe those people nothing,' Vaughn continued, adopting the same light conversational tone as before. 'The unaltereds, I mean. To them you're nothing but an Illegal, a criminal simply for existing – the product of dangerous alien biotechnology.'

Elias felt his face grow hot. 'I'm not a criminal. And I didn't ask to be this way.'

'Really? I thought you'd volunteered. But as far as the people back there are concerned' – he pointed over Elias's shoulder, as if back at the city of London – 'you may turn out to be a vector for something they can't predict. Nobody expected the Blight either, and that came about as a result of meddling with Angel biotechnology. *You*, Mr Murray, are the result of Angel biotechnology, and that makes you dangerous – to them.'

'Fuck them. I'm gone now. You might as well go away too, Vaughn. I can make my own path through life.'

Then, to Elias's confusion, Vaughn started to laugh. 'What happened to you back there in that Arcology wasn't an accident. There *are* no accidents. Everything that happens, occurs because it's part of a plan and, unlike most, you're privileged to see glimpses of that plan, some little brief snatches of the future. And you still persist in thinking you can change things? Why is that?'

Elias pursed his lips, studied the smartsheets he had brought with him. Kasper – Trencher's destination – was the seventh solar system to be discovered by humans exploring through the Angel Stations' network. It was the only system in which intelligent life had been found. The Kaspians themselves had been declared off-limits in order – so went the official line – to allow their culture to evolve uninterrupted. They had been studied ever since nonetheless, either by long-range satellite or by microscopic spycams that could eavesdrop on their daily lives.

It was also publicly known that researchers landed in unpopulated areas there, to collect flora and fauna or retrieve artefacts from abandoned buildings and ruins. Yet the Kaspians had no idea they were no longer alone in the universe. However, Elias continued reading, those studies had been interrupted by the Hiatus until someone managed to figure out the arcane alien technology of the Oort Station, thereby re-establishing its singularity.

Elias glanced out of the window. All he could now see below was endless grey sea, cut through with long pink streaks which glittered and undulated through the water.

'You won't find any details of that in those smartsheets,' Vaughn said. Elias glanced up to find the ghost was still there.

'Details of what?' Elias asked, not sure if Vaughn was referring to the pink streaks he had noticed below.

'Details of the Blight. It's everywhere, Elias. It's gone too far. Pollution, environmental disaster after disaster, and now the Blight spreading across the globe, and either transforming or killing everything it touches. There's no turning back – not now. The Primalists have known this for a long time.'

Elias stared down at the Atlantic far below, not wanting to believe what Vaughn was telling him. 'What does that have to do with Trencher?' he asked uncertainly.

'You care about him? I suppose he was the nearest thing you had to a real father.'

'He saved my life,' said Elias, 'more than once.'

'But you let him go, let him get captured. Not a good way of demonstrating your gratitude.'

Elias struggled not to let Vaughn see how deeply he

was affected by these words. The worst thing Elias could think was that, somewhere down in that drug-induced state, Trencher himself believed Elias had betrayed him.

'Since you know so much, then I'm sure you know exactly what happened.'

'Trencher was a failure: he betrayed the Primalists, and he betrayed himself. Mentally unbalanced, all he could tell you was the vilest nonsense.' Vaughn leaned forward then, as if peering into Elias's soul. 'You still see glimpses of things to come, Elias? Tell me what you see.'

Nothing, bleak, dark nothing, an absolute negation.

'Nothing,' Elias said carefully. It was probably the truest thing he could say.

'I see things, too,' said Vaughn. 'Sometimes it's one thing, sometimes it's something else, only *slightly* different. That's the problem with being one of the chosen, one of God's true children. All you see are glimpses of the truth, of the grand masterplan. He allows us that much. Sometimes what you see seems to confound more than inform. We are still only mortals, tiny things in the eyes of God.'

'I'm not a Primalist,' Elias replied. 'I don't think Kasper is the new Eden. I don't think it's anything other than what it is.' Elias looked at the Ghost with tortured eyes. 'Why me, Vaughn? Do you think any of this stops me wanting to look for Trencher? Or is this the only way a sick fuck like you can enjoy any kind of entertainment?'

Vaughn leaned back and gazed at him coolly for a few seconds before replying. 'Because it's been seen, Elias. It's been seen. God has chosen us. Godless you may be, but nonetheless you do God's purpose, as do we all. Remember that when the time comes.'

And then Vaughn was gone, and Elias found himself staring at an empty seat.

Sam Roy

Sam tasted blood on his lips. He could see his own essence, red against stark white, where blood had touched snow and ice.

'Go to hell,' he said weakly. He lay half stretched out across the boulder that was his world, his universe. Blood ran down his back and his body from the fresh wounds. He was past the threshold of being able to feel anything now, and Vaughn knew it. He'd wait for a while, until he was sure Sam would be able to feel again.

'You think I didn't know?' rasped Vaughn. 'You thought I wouldn't find out?'

'Of course I knew,' he said weakly. 'More than you ever could understand.'

Vaughn coughed in the chill mountain air. He'd pushed Sam and the boulder back down the steep path that led to the top of the plateau; he lay crumpled like a rag doll.

Vaughn coughed, was silent for several minutes. Sam waited, something he'd become very good at. 'You were behind it,' Vaughn said, more quietly now. 'You pushed them to it, turned them away from the path they should have been on.'

'I didn't,' said Sam when he felt he had the strength. His bones had begun to knit back together, with extraordinary speed. It was quiet, the night as still as death, and Sam imagined he could hear his own bones creaking like oak trees swaying in a heavy wind as shattered fragments found each other, re-knitted.

Vaughn cocked his head towards Sam, in a motion that was extraordinarily bird-like.

'I had nothing to do with it,' Sam said, forcing the words through his throat. 'I only advised them. As I knew I would. As I always have known. The impetus, the desire was theirs. They would have done it anyway.' He tried to clear his throat, spat blood onto pristine white snow. 'Or couldn't you see it coming?' Sam said, unable to keep the taunt out of his own voice.

Several of the conspirators were dead. Sam had heard a scream, far into the night, abruptly cut off; had immediately known it was Marjorie, Vaughn's young wife. She'd fallen in with them, of course. After all, one of the conspirators was her own son, Matthew. Now . . . she was in that place neither Vaughn nor Sam seemed able to reach. He thought of the people who had created them, Vaughn and Trencher and himself, and wondered at the blindness of their fanaticism. Marjorie's death at the hands of her own husband was just one more reason to hate them all the more.

He glanced at Vaughn, saw the briefest flash of real fear deep in his eyes. Vaughn turned, climbing the path back up to the plateau, back to the light and warmth of an everyday life Sam hadn't experienced in an eternity.

Roke

'Master Roke,' said Utma, walking towards him as he entered a courtyard within the Emperor's Palace and passed into the inner ring of buildings, a storm of kitchen staff and servants hurrying around them. 'Are you well?'

'As well as I can be,' wheezed Roke. 'Are you attending this meeting of Xan's?'

Utma blinked, taking on a more furtive expression. 'Master Roke, please. Who knows who may be listening?' Utma took Roke's arm and spoke into his ear as they walked rapidly towards Xan's Sanctum at the heart of the Palace.

'Nobody's listening, Utma,' Roke said wearily. 'And even if they were, I haven't said anything about the meeting. Xan does have a lot of meetings, I might remind you.' But Utma didn't look comforted, just apprehensive.

More guards swept the Sanctum's great doors open and they entered, seeing other Masters favoured within the court standing some distance away, sunlight streaming down from the windows near the ceiling, far above. Roke could see Feren, the Emperor's Spymaster, who gazed in their direction for a few moments, before looking away.

'Backstabbing widow-makers, the lot of them,' muttered Utma. 'If I thought I'd end up consorting with people like that when my mother gave me away to the priesthood, I'd have run away and joined the tribes.' Roke nodded in agreement. He counted few true friends within the court, but Utma was one of them. They approached the other Masters, also waiting for their audience with Xan. Mostly they made cordial small talk, and Roke heard some news about the siege against the northern city, Nubala.

'A shitstained hovel, been there once, never again,' muttered Riteyan, who maintained Tibe's great book. 'And cold, too. Very cold.' He shivered, as if in illustration.

'I hear they have as yet failed to retrieve the city's god,' Roke interjected mildly.

'But nothing insurmountable,' argued Feren, stepping up to stand by Riteyan, a cool expression on his face. 'I'm sure the Emperor will have no trouble completing his great Plan. What do you think, Roke?'

Roke noted the way in which distant walls and ceilings suddenly became the objects of great fascination for his fellow Masters. 'I would say that none have greater faith than I in the Emperor's Plan,' said Roke, 'but I would not wish to insult other members of the Court with such an arrogant conceit.' He smiled, taking pleasure at the flash of anger in Feren's one good eye. Oh, but I must be losing my love of life to take chances with Feren, thought Roke. Or perhaps I have simply ceased caring.

'Riteyan,' said Utma, 'I might remind you that Master Roke comes from one of those shitstained Northern hovels. Your own Great Book tells us it used to be just as cold here as there, and colder, only a few generations ago.'

'Enough, gentlemen,' said Roke wearily, as the doors to the inner court were opened by the Palace Guard. 'Let's get this over with.'

It was dark enough within the court that the otherwordly light that surrounded the form of the Pale Ghost – the Shai – was very apparent. Pink and hairless, with tufts of fur where its flesh was visible outside of its garments, the creature's head was disturbingly lacking in ears until you noticed the tiny, shell-like shapes on either side of its skull. They looked strange, malformed. It stood close to an enormous map of the world, which rested on a wide table half as long as the chamber itself.

This map was composed of carefully carved representations of mountains and valleys and seas that Emperor Xan himself had ordered to be created some years before. The Great Northern Sea, of which Tibe was a southern port, filled up much of the map, as did the bulk of Tisane even further south, and the Tieve mountains to the north.

The Emperor Xan himself stood at the far end of the table. The Shai, which called itself Vaughn, stood near him. Roke noticed immediately how frail Xan looked.

'Roke!' Xan hurried around the table.

Not as young as he used to be, thought Roke, but he felt genuine fondness for the Emperor, both the one he knew now and the one he had first known, many years before. Roke smiled, and went to meet his Emperor.

'My lord,' said Roke, 'I hope you are feeling better.'

'Much better, thank you. I have received a new treatment from Vaughn. His men of learning believe they may have found a cure for my illness.'

Roke nodded slowly, trying to hide his feelings. But Xan had not become ruler of an empire through a lack of perception.

'Oh come, Roke, forget your misgivings. I believe Vaughn here may be able to help us in locating the final part of the Plan.' As Roke followed Xan around the great round table, he looked over and found Vaughn gazing at him intently. Roke had the uncanny sensation the creature had heard every word that had just passed between him and the Emperor.

A bundle lay nearby: the sheen of metal gathered in rough cloth. Roke stared at it, and the Emperor also looked to the bundle.

'What do you think, Roke?' The Emperor strode over and pulled the cloth aside. 'This is a gift of Vaughn's great knowledge.'

'It's the least we can do,' said Vaughn – or, to be more precise, the Shai held up a small box and the voice came from there. At first Roke and Utma had speculated that the creature was mute, totally incapable of speech. Then he realized that could not be so; he had heard it gabbling into the device using its own, bizarre tongue. Rather, as the Emperor had explained, those boxes enabled the Shai to communicate by transforming its words into those of true folk. The result was a ghastly, flat, though comprehensible din that carried none of the pleasant qualities of Tisane's dominant dialect.

Roke stared at Vaughn, not sure how to react. The creature was looking back at him, and Roke knew the Emperor expected him to respond. How could one tell what it was thinking, when it possessed such inexpressive ears?

Xan picked up a long, steel tube from the cloth-covered bundle and called the Masters to approach. They gathered near him, an attentive audience with the great map spread out to one side. Roke studied the tube, and saw it was more than that: a carefully manufactured artefact that grew wider at one end where a shaped piece of wood had been fitted. Other protrusions had been attached with painstaking intent, although to what end Roke could not imagine.

'What is it?' asked one of the other Masters. Though Feren, Roke noticed, looked like he was enjoying their puzzlement, which suggested he had already witnessed a demonstration.

'It's called a firearm,' said the Emperor, glancing towards the Shai beside him, whose head bobbed in agreement for a few moments. 'It's the solution to our Great Plan. I'm afraid I've not been very forthcoming with you, this past year, although I'm sure you've heard rumours nevertheless.'

Roke had indeed, and he caught Utma's eye. An unknown weapon, being used on the Northern shores, far from Tibe? The cities of the Empire had, indeed, been buzzing with rumours about this new technology.

'You should demonstrate it for us, my Lord.' Feren sounded positively gleeful.

'As I will do!' said the Emperor. Raising the tube to his shoulder, he pulled at a small metal hook set underneath. Sudden light flashed before Roke's eyes, then he heard someone give a high-pitched yelp of dismay. He hoped it hadn't been himself. The explosion the device had made was impossibly loud, and Roke looked up to see all the Masters with their ears flattened against their skulls, looking around bewildered.

The Emperor's own ears were flicking with sheer joy. He strode forward, all the way to the far wall, and waved a beckoning arm for his court to follow him. Among them, Roke observed Seyferen, the Captain of Guards, hovering with a grim expression on his face.

'There, see that?' The Emperor was pointing to a statue of some honoured officer of guards at least two centuries old, who had suddenly and dramatically lost one arm. Roke was, indeed, impressed.

'Gentlemen, equipped with these devices, our specially trained squadrons have thrown our enemies into disarray. But remember, you have the Shai here to thank for our victory.'

'I'm sure the Emperor himself had hardly a small part in such triumphs,' said Roke.

'Perhaps I did, Master Roke, and I'm not inclined to false modesty, but great changes are afoot in our world.' Xan casually lowered the firing end of the weapon towards them, and one or two of the gathered Masters stepped back.

'My dear fellows, don't worry. I'm not sufficiently displeased with any of you to use you for target practice.' The Shai had stepped forward. 'And I may be getting old, but I am, believe me, in full possession of my faculties.' Xan looked around at them. 'But I felt it was time for a proper demonstration of what benefits the Shai can provide. Many of you here, as Masters, are entrusted as caretakers of the gods of other communities who now reside in this city. This Shai called Vaughn,' the Emperor pointed the weapon at the Shai, 'walks with our gods. I am your Emperor; my victories in reuniting the ancient empire should be all the proof you need that I am the Fidhe reborn. Yet I suspect some of you do not quite believe the truth of this.' He lifted the weapon and fired it directly at the Shai.

The Shai remained unharmed, mute, impassive, but there was an eruption of powder from the plastered wall behind it. Yet clearly the weapon should have wreaked terrible damage . . .

Roke felt a chill deep in his belly. *Demons, ghosts*, he thought immediately. But of course he knew from the monstrous Shai he had met in the tower that they were something entirely different. He looked around at the rest of the Emperor's audience, and saw nothing but awe and horror struggling for dominance in their expressions.

'I need your allegiance, good Masters, not your doubts,' continued the Emperor, his expression suddenly serious. 'Remember that, the next time you whisper sedition behind my back. You may all leave now.' The Masters gathered around Roke stood still for a few moments more, then gradually began to break into small knots heading for the great doors. Roke noted their appalled expressions; only Feren looked untroubled.

As he himself turned to leave, he caught Seyferen's eye, and walked beside the Captain of the Guard as he too stepped towards the door.

'You knew about this?' said Roke, and Seyferen nodded stiffly. 'But you don't approve?'

'Master Roke, I am the Emperor's loyal servant.' He glanced around, wary of twitching ears. 'But I'm less than comfortable with these new weapons. They are . . . ignoble.'

'Times change, Captain.'

'In their own good time, Master. Only in their own good time.'

A servant came up to Master Roke and handed him a rolled-up note, which he opened. The Emperor was inviting him to a private meeting in his antechamber. Roke hoped the Shai would not be in attendance.

Xan, he was relieved to see, sat there alone on a stone bench.

'Roke, my old friend, come join me. I hope my little demonstration of strength hasn't alarmed you.'

'Perhaps a little. But may I speak freely?'

Xan looked at him in surprise. 'Why, of course. But don't expect me to pay attention to a word you say,' he said, his tongue flicking good-humouredly around his nose. 'I've never been averse to straight talking.'

'Your assessment that some of the Masters entertain doubts concerning the Shai would be more than accurate. I can't myself see what the Shai possibly have to gain from this alliance. Until you can assure the other Masters of that, they can hardly be blamed for harbouring some doubts. Though I must stress I have no reason to believe any suffer from a lack of loyalty.'

'Feren might disagree with you,' Xan replied wryly.

'Feren is a foul little snake.'

'Yes he is, but he's very good at his job. As to the Shai, well, I'm not so sure it or the other creatures it claims to represent are genuine Shai – not in the fairy-tale sense. Ghosts and goblins don't normally show you new ways of smelting metals or constructing machines, or concocting new medicines, do they? As to what they gain from us in return, well, I have to confide in you, old friend, I can't be sure.'

Roke felt as if his heart might stop. 'Yet they *claim* to be Shai, the ancient messengers of the gods.'

'Who were usurped when the gods favoured us instead, and the Shai were left to wander the ice for eternity. Yes, I know the stories of the Pale Ghosts as well as you. But this is an enlightened age and we know these accounts to be just stories. Or so I believed myself until the creature appeared less than a year ago. And you know how much things have changed since then.'

'My lord, it pains me to hear you talk so.'

'My campaign was failing, Roke, and you know that. Seyferen knows that, too. Even Feren knows that. I overreached myself by invading the Northern continent. My generals were then complaining of their men deserting in droves, returning to their families rather than starve and freeze amid the ice. My health is . . . not what it used to be, and such setbacks lent encouragement to those claiming them as the proof that I am not the Fidhe. But then the Shai came.'

'The weapons it has given you are certainly potent, but how do they work?'

Xan sighed. 'Simply a mixture of powders ignited by a flint, which hurls a steel ball down the barrel fast

133

enough to cause terrible damage to anything unlucky enough to be standing in the way. Imagine, Roke, having one for every soldier in my army – small and manageable enough to carry over the shoulder. Could you yourself turn down such an opportunity?'

'Everything has a price, my lord, but some prices—'

'Are too great? I am an Emperor, Roke. They acclaim me the Fidhe reborn, the uniter of nations. I have brought civilization and order not only to this land of Tisane but also to so many territories beyond. Victory is worth any price, Roke, but I will tell you one thing. And I tell you this because you are a valued friend, and because I feel sad at hiding these new weapons from you for so long. I begin with a question: how many stories does one hear, even in Tibe, of the Shai? Or of the mountains they haunt?'

Roke shrugged. 'They traditionally haunt the glaciers and high places. You hear most accounts of them, I believe, in the north, because it is so cold there.'

'Let us be more precise, then. Within the past few generations, the Teive mountains are where most claim to have encountered the spirits of the Shai. You must have heard there are areas of those mountains where the superstitious never stray? And where travellers have been known to disappear?'

'There is little to substantiate such tales,' Roke replied.

'And that's where you're wrong,' said Xan vehemently. 'And that is one reason why Feren makes such a good spymaster. I have sent my cartographers to the Teive mountains in the wake of our armies, to study the geography. But the areas they cannot reach are the same parts that have been associated with the Shai for centuries. Which is why,' added the Emperor with relish, 'I have come to believe that is where these strange creatures are hiding.'

'You haven't explained why you're telling me this.'

Xan stared at him. 'Perhaps so. You know me better than most others here in my court. And I only ever hear the truth from you, and value what you say. The Shai came to me originally out of a professed sense of altruism, supposedly because I was the Fidhe. But I don't profess to understand the real reasons for its wanting to help me.'

'My lord, it must have said something else to explain.'

'Only that it believed that helping me in my task would bring about a universal state of paradise. Which is flattering, of course, but peace in itself would be nice enough.' Xan's ears flicked in amusement. 'I don't trust it, however, and so believe it would be to our advantage to learn precisely whereabouts in the world it and its brethren are located.'

As Roke realized what the Emperor was telling him, he felt a chill as he remembered the Monster's words. 'You need me to go there?'

'I need you to lead an expedition to evaluate our newly conquered territories. That's the official purpose,' said Xan. 'The real purpose of your trip remains between you and me, and just a few others.'

Roke nodded. 'And if I do find them, what then?'

'My dear Roke, I wish to know if they are truly as immaterial as this one appears to be.'

Six

Vincent

'Christ, Vincent, you look like shit.'

'Ah,' said Vincent, 'that would be the famous Gabarra wit. How I miss it. Really, I do.'

Eddie peered past the door, looking over Vincent's shoulder. 'You alone?'

Vincent tried to think of something funny to say, but all that really came to mind was: *It's three in the morning. Couldn't it have waited?* But of course Eddie couldn't have waited any more than Vincent could have – or wanted to. He was tired, but as much as he had wanted to sleep over the past few days, he'd been unable to do more than grab random catnaps. Sleep had come to seem ephemeral, a barrier to the greater understanding. His life had come to revolve, it seemed, around the flimsy smartsheet Eddie had left for him.

'Sorry?'

Eddie stared at him. 'I'll take a guess, you're alone. Let me in and I'll make you something to keep you awake. Then we can talk.'

137

'It's the middle of the night,' Vincent insisted, as Eddie brushed by him and headed for his kitchen.

'I have to be back on the moon within seventy-two hours,' said Eddie. 'That means I can only stick around here for maybe two hours, maximum. We can do some serious talking in that time. Then you can get ready.'

'Ready for what?' Vincent half-stumbled to the kitchen, where Eddie shoved a mug into his hand, filled with something hot and black. He sipped at it, scowling as the coffee burnt his tongue.

'For the moon,' said Eddie. 'You're coming with me, then you're going on to Kasper.'

'Kasper?' Vincent registered the information, nodded his head. Somehow it seemed the logical conclusion. It was, after all, the closest star system to the Event.

The Event – he mulled the word over as he went back into his living room and found Eddie already tapping away at the coloured buttons on the smart-sheets. That was how he had come to think of it: it was the Event. Such a mild word, really, to describe something so enormous and yet far away. 'What do I do when I get there?'

'Liaise,' explained Eddie. 'Talk to people there who'll be expecting you. You're going to be my representative, since you know as much as I do – more, as a matter of fact – about what's going to happen. You do realize the implications of this business, don't you?'

Vincent drank down more of his coffee. 'Sure, of

course: a galaxy-wide event that threatens life everywhere. Like a big gun firing off gamma bullets from the heart of the galaxy, ripping through space at the speed of light, regular as clockwork every few hundred million years. We have to prepare for it, find a way to block the radiation – maybe some kind of shield that can save the Earth. But it could be a lot worse, of course.'

'A lot worse.' Eddie nodded. 'A lot worse how?'

When he thought about it, it wasn't so much the fact that Eddie had proven a theory that, until mere days ago, had constituted little more than theoretical abstraction which bothered him. It was that Eddie had known things Vincent might never have found out himself, or at least not until everyone else had found out too. The only way, after all, to really find out about what was going on in the heart of the galaxy was to actually go there. That wasn't possible, of course, or so Vincent had thought.

The Angel Stations acted as bridges between widely separated corners of the galaxy, yet as far as Vincent had known, until only a few days ago, they were the only way that mankind could access distant star systems within something less than a lifetime. In just a few days, everything regarding that had changed.

You could never really know exactly what was happening in another part of the galaxy while you were looking at it, because what you were seeing through an optical or radio telescope was something already long dead, a snapshot of the galaxy as it had been ten, twenty, thirty thousand years before. Knowing what was happening *now* was a whole different ball game. That was possible, thanks to the Angel Stations, but only to a limited extent. The Arrays stationed near several of the Angel Stations, spaced out over a volume of space approximately twenty thousand light years in diameter, were sufficient in themselves to lend historical truth to Vincent's theories.

Regular surges of life-destroying radiation would be created as stars scattered across the galaxy violently exploded almost at once, although what might bring about such a cataclysm Vincent couldn't even begin to imagine. Nothing in nature could possibly account for such a phenomenon: it was like switching on a Christmas tree big enough to light up the universe.

The radiation produced by this cataclysmic event would then sweep through the galaxy, implacably destroying higher-order species, leaving other organisms to rise to the top of the food chain in their place.

But sometimes, Vincent had realized, you could be too abstract in your theorizing, so that when the cold hard implications of what you had discovered came knocking at the door, your gut instinct was to run and hide. But even that realization paled next to what Vincent now knew, and he wasn't sure whether to be awestruck or appalled that this had been going on so long without his – or almost anyone else's – knowledge.

'It could be a lot worse, Eddie, because we're thousands of light years from the nearest of the gamma-ray bursters – tens of thousands, in fact. That means we have a lot more time than civilization has even existed on Earth to get ready for it, to prepare for it and . . . I don't know, prevent it or something.'

'Okay. But what about the Kaspians?'

Vincent had thought about that, of course, but only in an abstract sense, one more factor to be accounted for in an overwhelming mass of new data he needed to absorb. Perhaps, *too* abstractly.

'The Kaspians?' Vincent shrugged. 'I don't know, Eddie. I'm open to ideas. I know they're a lot closer to the wavefront.'

'Vincent, they have barely a year before the gamma wavefront hits them, and then the only civilization – the only extant intelligent life outside of the human race, for all we know – will simply cease to exist. Have you thought about that?'

'There's *too much* to think about. What about these probes, for God's sake?' Tiny things, marvels of molecular design constructed in the utmost secrecy before being flung across the galaxy. It was all there in Eddie's smartsheet, along with digital images of vistas unimaginable, of the great blaze of stars towards the galactic core. 'I had no idea, Eddie. All this time, and not a hint, no clue of any kind we'd discovered how to build an ftl drive from the Angels.'

'Yeah, well, it's still a secret – for now, anyway. And remember it's just a few tiny probes we've sent in towards the galactic core, and I really mean *tiny*. You have no idea the' – Eddie spun his hands around, in small circles in front of his chest – 'the magnitude of the cost, in money as well as energy. Really.'

Eddie stared at Vincent, saw his friend's hurt expression. 'It's a secret, for God's sake, Vincent. And it's still a secret, right? You read the security clause on the first sheet, I hope.'

'Yeah, yeah. I read it.' Legalese, but Vincent had paid no less attention to it nonetheless, when he'd realized just what kind of information was contained on the smartsheets. Just by having accepted them from Eddie, he'd become part of a Big Secret. And if he told anyone about that Big Secret, it warned with unswerving explicitness, he'd be in Big Trouble. 'I understand, Eddie, I really do. This is – huge. It's just a lot to take in.'

'That's fine, Vincent. But you've got a lot of work to do. We both do.'

'So what are we going to do now? Save the Kaspians?' Vincent thought of the popular image of the Kaspians; wolf-like, sharp-toothed things almost like talking animals out of a child's fairy-tale book. But in fact they were real, living creatures that fought and dreamed and died on a world far, far away. He tried to picture them assembling in great queues extending over far horizons, quietly stepping up onto long platforms to board great cavernous spaceships with welcoming humans standing by the entrances, but that was an absurd thought. There were big starships available –

almost always military craft – but how many Kaspians could be rescued before the radiation arrived in less than a year's time? A pitifully small number, he suspected.

'Maybe. Yes, if we can. What do you think?' Eddie's eyes, bright and round, were watching Vincent carefully. *He really wants to know if I've got any ideas,* thought Vincent. But Vincent couldn't think of anything. All he could register in his mind's eye was tragedy.

'We've known about this for a while, haven't we?' said Vincent, finishing his coffee. He slumped down on a couch, stretching out and letting one leg slide to the floor while the other pushed into the cushions. The fatigue was coming back again, as it had many times over the past two nights – before some sudden new thought occurred to him and he began poring over the smartsheets, making notes and muttering quietly to himself.

'Not that long: less than a year since we've had enough data. Not all of the probes make it back. The ftl technology is still in its early days, so sometimes there was guesswork involved.' Eddie stepped through to the kitchen again for a moment; his voice became briefly muffled before he returned, carrying an empty wastebasket. 'Then, because this is a secret, the funds for the probes can't come through the normal civilian channels, since too many questions would then be asked. So, mostly it's military money. Top Secret all the way. Very expensive.'

'How expensive?'

'Don't ask – really. You'd be shocked. Expensive enough to make very sure smartsheets like these can't fall into the wrong hands.'

'Oh.' Vincent reached again for the smartsheet, now lying on the table next to the couch, but Eddie picked it up and dropped it into the wastebasket. 'So, what about the Kaspians? Are you really going to try and rescue them?'

'No.'

Vincent felt a shock run through him. 'But you said—?'

'I didn't say anything, I just asked you for ideas. The people in the know have been talking for a long time about what to do with the Kaspians, but that's all they've been doing – talking. There were even some idiots who said we shouldn't even try, that it would be interfering with the course of nature, the natural evolution of the planet. Can you imagine that?'

Vincent watched Eddie carefully. A bright gleam had come to his eyes, and something else that – when he thought about it later – brought the word *haunted* to mind. 'Look, when I say no,' Eddie said, 'I don't mean me personally. I mean the issue of what to do has been bouncing around so long that it's already, effectively, too late. The Kaspians – all the higher order, more intelligent species – are doomed, that much is clear. But there must be a way to rescue some of them at least, maybe enough to keep the species from becoming extinct. That mustn't be allowed to happen, Vincent, do you understand me?'

Eddie was almost standing right over Vincent now, and Vincent shifted uncomfortably on the couch, feeling nervous and unsure. He'd never seen Eddie like this before, ever: the wild gleam replaced by something much more like anger, a righteous kind of anger.

'You want me to help you, then? Help you save some of the Kaspians.'

'Yes. That's exactly what I want you to do. Most of the people on the Kasper Angel Station don't know what's happening yet, but in a few months' time every human being alive there is going to want to know what's going on, and they'll soon find out – but too late for the Kaspians. There are already teams of scientists and scientific observers on their way out there to study the gamma radiation when it hits, and to watch the effects of it. Other people, too. I can't go myself, so *you* need to. Talk to the people out there, Vincent. You'll be working directly for me. Be my voice. Talk to whoever you need to, but find some way to save at least some of them.'

Vincent realized Eddie had been clutching a lighter for several seconds. Eddie seemed to suddenly remember where he was, and flicked the lighter until it burned with a steady blue flame, then he dropped it into the wastebasket. A few moments later, the acrid smell of burning plastic filled the flat as the smartsheet smouldered and dissolved.

Ursu

Ursu woke to the sound of distant screams. He stumbled upright, finding his robes and pulling them on. *We are being invaded*, he thought. The thought had been with him even before he had become fully conscious. He found the jug of water he kept on the floor in the corner, and drank from it to chase away the dryness in his throat, all too aware how badly his hands were shaking.

He then picked his way down the winding steps, scared of what he might find below. Then he was running down, the sound of his feet slapping against bare stone loud in his ears. But eventually he started to distinguish other noises, and the distant yelling of voices, panicked and angry.

Down into the great Hall, which was empty. The massive doors lay wide open, and he saw figures running about beyond. He started to move towards them, then heard someone call his name, just behind him. He turned to see Turthe emerging up the steps that led to his workshop. The Master beckoned to him and Ursu halted.

'Ursu, not out there! Over here!' Turthe disappeared again, retreating downwards. Ursu had absolutely no idea what his plan of action should be now. There had always been a vague notion of escaping with Shecumpeh, but the actual *how* of it was another matter. He realized to his shame that he had not actually made any concrete plan. But it was too late for that now. He could hear shouts and screams from outside, as he ran towards where Turthe had appeared, then down into his cellar workshop.

'I was right, wasn't I?' said Turthe when Ursu stepped into the cramped workshop. The Master's voice was strained and high-pitched. Ursu thought of saying nothing, still afraid of the consequences, but it was clearly too late for that. 'Yes,' he said, listening to his own voice cracking. 'Yes.'

'The god, Shecumpeh . . .' Turthe's tongue lolled inactive for a moment as he unconsciously matted down the fur on his cheeks, 'you're taking him, yes?'

'Yes I am,' admitted Ursu, feeling strangely stronger for having said it. But now he had said it, out loud, he knew it was true. He was removing the god. Escaping. Leaving Nubala behind.

'Shecumpeh himself commanded it.'

'I knew that, I knew that.' Turthe nodded. 'You weren't the first, Ursu. No, not the first to be asked.'

Ursu was thunderstruck. 'Who—?' But then he saw how the heavy worktable Turthe used had been shoved to one side, and as he stepped forward he saw that the tiny door leading into the secret caves Turthe had shown him earlier now lay gaping open. In his fear and worry it did not occur to Ursu to wonder precisely how an oldster like Turthe could have pushed such a heavy table aside without any help.

'Come with me,' beckoned Turthe, 'back into the

caves. There's a way out.' And with that Turthe got on his hands and knees and scrabbled through the door. Ursu had no choice but to follow.

Strong hands grabbed him as he emerged through the tiny entrance, and Ursu yelped and struggled. But those same hands hit him hard on the side of his snout, and he felt his head go numb, a sick feeling spreading through his guts. He felt himself being carried briefly, until at last he was dropped to the ground. As he opened his eyes he realized from the faint luminescence and the sound of running water that he was back in the cave Turthe had shown him barely more than a day before. Others, however, were assembled here with them. Looking up from where he lay, Ursu recognized all of them.

'Get up,' said Uftheyan harshly, and Ursu pushed himself upright. There were four of them, all Masters, including Turthe and Uftheyan. They glared at him with hatred and contempt. 'To think,' began Uftheyan, 'that we welcomed you into our holiest place, we fed you and educated you, so that you could then steal the very soul of our city away from us, you contemptible—'

'He wasn't to know.' Turthe turned to Uftheyan and yelled at him. 'False visions,' he said, turning to Ursu, 'brought about by the armies outside. What you experienced was not true.'

Ursu stared at him. 'Shecumpeh *spoke* to me. He

told me what would happen. Our city will be taken. I have to remove Shecumpeh to safety.'

'Safety where?' screamed one of the other Masters, a heavyset figure called Meleter. 'There is no *where*, you idiot child, only Nubala.'

The fourth Master, Irubus, whose role was to instruct the House acolytes in history and doctrine, nodded vigorously. 'Quite so,' he said. 'You should have known better, Ursu. Nubala has stood secure for countless generations, protected by Shecumpeh itself. What do you think will happen to us when it is removed, eh? Didn't it occur to you that Xan might try and incur false visions in our priests and acolytes, so that they would give him exactly what he wanted, Shecumpeh itself?'

'Do it now,' added Meleter. 'Do it now, while Shecumpeh still has faith in us, in our ability to serve him.'

Do what? Ursu wondered, a sudden chill in his bones. Hands gripped him again, hauling him upright, hands that were stronger than he would have suspected. Fear made him feel weak, as if his legs would give out from beneath him.

'Perhaps,' Turthe quavered, 'perhaps we should consider what the boy said. We were all there when Shecumpeh spoke to him, weren't we? And even if he were misled—'

'Turthe, you dolt!' raged Uftheyan. 'It's too late for that now. The enemy has broken through the walls.'

'He's right,' moaned Meleter, his voice heavy with

fear. 'Kill him now – do it. Show Shecumpeh we still have faith in him.'

'No, listen to me,' someone spoke, the voice low and mumbled. Then Ursu realized it was his own. 'He spoke to me, really he did. I'd have known if it were someone else. I—'

Another blow and Ursu sagged, strong hands still holding him at the shoulders, immobilizing him. Ursu stared into the eyes of Uftheyan, which were seething with hatred. Despite himself, Ursu felt ashamed, terribly ashamed, for disappointing him.

But the god had spoken to him. He *had*. Someone grabbed him by the fur on the back of his neck and pulled his head right back, sharply. Ursu felt too numb even to yell in pain.

'Swim, when you have to,' said a voice, barely above a whisper. There was a sudden commotion, as Ursu saw Turthe being pushed to the ground.

'What were you whispering there, you old fool?' yelled Uftheyan. 'Maybe we should throw you in as well!'

'Why, Turthe, have you changed your mind now?' cried Irubus. 'I thought we were all agreed. You seemed willing enough the last time!'

The last time? Ursu stood rigid, still held fast by the shoulders. The last time.

Ewenden?

'You said there had been another,' Ursu mumbled.

'I wasn't the first to hear Shecumpeh tell me to leave the city?'

His ears flattening, Turthe stood, staring at Ursu. As he looked away, shame filling his face, Ursu knew he was right, that he had not been the first. Shecumpeh had asked the girl to carry it out of the city. But when? It must have been not long after the besieging armies had first arrived outside the city gates. It could only have been her; no one else had disappeared so suddenly, so completely. Contempt and anger filled Ursu, and he snarled at them. For the merest moment, he felt the grip on his shoulders loosen the tiniest fraction.

'It's only for the good of our city, boy,' said Uftheyan. 'Our enemies want Shecumpeh gone from the city, because with Shecumpeh gone, the city is theirs.'

'The city is already theirs,' rasped Ursu, his throat sore from his beating. Uftheyan stared at him, and then the elder's fists started hammering at him.

'Into the water – now!' a voice cried, and Ursu felt himself lifted. And then a shock beyond pain, a freezing rush, as if all the warmth in the universe had fled, leaving him in a place of unending, cold darkness. Water filled his nose and ears and mouth and he reached up, feeling his hands break through the surface of the water, feeling himself being dragged along by the current.

He thrashed out instinctively, clawing for air, his mind filled with primordial terror, reaching out for life at any cost. He saw them there on the tiny shore, surrounded by the sparkling dim light of the glowing fungus for the tiniest of moments, a frozen tableau of murderers almost certain to be the last thing he would ever see.

And then he was gone, sucked down into rushing blackness. He thrashed, and screamed, but water rushed into his lungs and a heavy darkness spread out from the centre of him, grabbing for his very soul, and in panic and terror he reached out blindly once more, desperate for the slimmest, tiniest chance of a miracle, of a way back to life – not ready to give up, not yet. His hands touched smooth wet rock, the walls of the underground tunnel slipping by him, then miraculously his face felt the air. He gripped onto a roughened protrusion, the water still battering at him, and vomited water. Air, he realized gratefully. Air. His head was still singing with the beatings he had taken, his muscles as if on fire. Then he spotted light: the familiar thin glow of icewort.

He had emerged in a tiny cavity of rock, several feet in height, a natural deformity in the tunnel that narrowed upwards to a paper-thin crack reaching through the stone. He listened to himself whooping, hyperventilating, sucking in as much air as he could manage, gripping on desperately, his feet braced against a rocky outcrop by the side of the tunnel to prevent the icy water from sucking him away. Slowly, gradually, he regained some composure, but the terror still lingered, and it took every ounce of effort to keep himself from slipping into blind panic.

Even if he didn't drown here, the cold would take him soon enough. And the air would last him only so long; minutes, maybe. Perhaps this was fate's cruel joke on him, to give him one last taste of life before dragging him away to the merciless underworld where all such enemies of Nubala were doomed to languish.

But perhaps there were other air pockets; and perhaps the tunnel was not so lengthy, after all. But the water spilled out of the hills miles away, and if there were no further air pockets between here and there . . .

No, he mustn't think of that. Shecumpeh would not have entrusted himself to Ursu if the god had thought him incapable of his task. To think otherwise was to remain here until the air became stale, until he froze to death, until he became weak enough for the current to snatch him away once more.

He remembered those childhood tales, those horrible stories passed around amongst the youngest acolytes, that some had heard a voice calling up from the well outside the House of Shecumpeh, only days after Ewenden had disappeared – had been murdered, in fact, by Turthe and the others, for experiencing the same vision as Ursu had.

How could they have made her disappear so completely? Surely not by bundling her body out of the House . . . and then where would they have disposed of the body? There was nowhere obvious inside the city, and beyond the walls an enemy army was waiting. Then it must have been done the same way: dragging a frightened young girl, guilty only of trying to serve her god, into that underground cave and throwing her into the water to drown her. Perhaps she had also found herself trapped here in this same diminishing bubble of air, only to be swept away eventually.

She must have survived for a brief time. Under the well, of course. Clearly the river ran under the well shaft and replenished it.

The thought of it was even more terrible than that childish ghost story. Perhaps she had indeed been trapped alive at the bottom of the well, too weak after the beating to call out for any length of time. Perhaps some young acolyte had indeed heard her calling out in the night, in the days immediately after her disappearance. Perhaps he would have run to Turthe, or Meleter, or Uftheyan, and told them. As Ursu pictured the scene unfolding, anger began to burn within him, anger strong enough to almost make him forget the terrible cold seeping through into his every bone.

He could feel his strength sapping away with every passing second, but he held on grimly, not willing to return to the rushing blackness until the force of the icy current finally pried his feet and hands loose. But eventually the Teive would claim him, regardless.

He sucked in air several times, filling his lungs, feeling the air grow denser and warmer each time he did so. Then he let go, feeling strangely calm now, yielding himself to the river spirits that gurgled and roared around him, as they snatched him away from the tiny bubble of life that had so briefly given him sanctuary.

Then, suddenly, the river seemed to twist downwards, plummeting. By some miracle Ursu kept his mouth closed and resisted the urge to scream.

And then, just as suddenly, he encountered air again. Though it felt like an eternity since he'd first been submerged, by a miracle he was still alive. His feet touched a mound of pebbles and loose shale, covering what he realized was the base of the well. Some of the surrounding brickwork had given way, allowing him enough of a handhold to scrabble part of the way up out of the water, before he could be swept away again.

Aware of light coming from above, he looked up and saw a tiny disc of sunlight. Apart from where the walls had occasionally crumbled, the sides of the well were composed of smooth brick offering little to hold onto. But he could see a water bucket hanging down, just out of reach, and maybe . . .?

He yelled out several times, hoping someone could hear him, but no answering call came, no sudden welcome silhouette peering down from far above. He paused and listened intently for a few moments more, hearing sounds that might be screams, and other less recognizable noises. But deep in the well, with the water still surging around his chest, it was impossible to guess what was happening above. He now refused to even think of the girl, Ewenden, trapped down here unheeded until she had died. Instead he negated her from his memory, thinking only of surviving.

The bucket, he realized, was not so far above him. Normally it was reeled up to the top after use, but for some reason it had been left hanging a short distance above his head. Not near enough that he could easily reach it, so he scrabbled frantically for handholds, some way to brace himself against the curved brickwork and then raise himself up. He had to reach that bucket, and then . . .

And then what? He didn't know. But he was now freezing cold after his immersion, and it was getting steadily harder to move, or even to think. The water swirling around his chest tugged at him constantly like the souls of the dead trying to carry him away to the underworld. He knew his time was limited as his fingers sought out spaces between the bricks where some mortar might have been loosened. One of the bricks came loose all of a sudden. He jerked back in surprise, then put his hand in the gap it had left, finding it made an excellent handhold.

Again his fingers sought among the bricks, looking for a way to loosen more of them.

One seemed to give way the tiniest amount, so he began working at it with his hard, stubby claws, wrenching it from side to side until finally it gave way enough for him to pry around its sides with desperate fingers and slowly tug it loose.

Now he had created two handholds, which would

raise him much closer to the bucket. Just close enough so that he might be able to reach upwards. His long clawed feet sliding and slipping desperately against the smooth bricks below, he scrabbled up, and thrust a hand into one of the inviting gaps, then lunged for the other one a short distance above. Now that he had his clawed fingers firmly inserted in these two handholds, he found the bucket was just above his head. Even so, he was not at all sure he had enough strength left to reach it. Then he thought of the water waiting below him, ready to suck him away again, and knew somehow he must find the strength. And it had to be now.

He reached up with one long leg, finding a foothold next to one of his hands in the loosened brickwork, and for a moment hung sideways across the diameter of the well shaft, just above the foaming water. Then he swung the same leg out in a frantic arc, so that it caught the side of the bucket, batting it against the far wall of the well, and watching as it bounced back towards him.

He reached out quickly from his second handhold, and caught the edge of the bucket with one hand, pulling it down just enough so that he could get a firm grip on its rim. His mind sang with joy, but he wasn't safely there yet.

With fingers still clamped grimly onto the rim of the bucket, he let go of the wall and for a moment hung there precariously by just one hand, before reaching up and grabbing the bucket's edge with his other. He pulled himself up slowly, the painful effort forcing tears from his eyes.

The bucket suddenly tipped under his weight, and in desperation he scrambled upwards, with what remained of his strength, till he had both hands and both feet securely around the rope. Fortunately the bucket had remained above the treacherous water. By some miracle, by the merciful hand of Shecumpeh, Ursu was still alive.

But for how long now? He couldn't shimmy up the rope; couldn't perform the impossible. He would still have to rely on a rescuer. As he rested for a while, his robes felt soggy and damp and uncomfortable around him, drying only slowly. He realized he had every chance of dying first from exposure. As he shivered miserably, he wondered what was happening far above him, as the city his people called Nubala succumbed to the armies of the Emperor Xan.

Time passed.

He had taken the rope he used to tie his robe around himself and knotted one end tightly around the curved iron handle of the bucket, and had tied the remaining length around himself. He then kept his arms wrapped around the handle, his flesh becoming sore where it pressed against the bucket's wooden rim.

But now he could feel very little of anything; even his fingers had lost all sensation. He had forgotten what it must be like to be warm, and his fur had dried out in thick, uncomfortable tufts, which he longed to drag his claws through. The cold was gradually seeping into his brain.

Sometimes, he heard sound from far above, but the fact that nobody had come to draw water from the well was not a good omen.

As more time passed, the night drew in. Ursu clung onto the bucket, staring longingly upwards. After a while, he found himself playing childhood games with Ewenden. First they played stone rounds, a favourite game of Ursu's, on the pebble-strewn ground near the well. From time to time, Ursu would look over at the well. Then he would turn back to Ewenden, her skin pallid and rotting, ears and fur tangled with weed, and ask if she wanted to play some more. She would reach over to groom his fur, licking and stroking it into place with her tongue and sharp, canthre-like claws.

Sometimes he would be back inside the well, and he could see the flesh of his hands swelling where they gripped the bucket's rim. Sometimes he would see smoke drifting overhead, obscuring the well mouth. And sometimes, he dreamed.

He dreamed he had been rescued. This was a comforting dream; he had felt a tug at the rope and the bucket swaying. Slowly, slowly he ascended, and it seemed so perfect, just the happy ending he longed for but knew would never happen. He then dreamed of strong hands lifting him over the lip of the well, and when he called out to Ewenden, called out to

Shecumpeh, he heard them shushing him. As if anyone might hear him down at the bottom of that deep dank well.

He listened to the voices around him, waiting for the dream to finish so he might continue clinging to the bucket, deep down in the well.

'But what was he doing down there, Master Turthe?'

'Never you mind. Just carry him. He obviously fell in while he was trying to raise water to douse the fire. Now carry him inside.'

Another voice: 'But how did you know he was there?'

'I don't have time now for these questions,' came the exasperated response. 'And in the name of Nubala, keep your voice down. Do you want the soldiers to hear us?'

Ursu woke, his nostrils filled with the smell of something burning – so thick and heavy it made him double over choking. As he vomited noisily someone took his head and guided his mouth towards a bucket. As his head fell back the pain returned twice as severely as before. Faces were all around him now, blurred visages that failed to resolve themselves. He saw his own hands, looking thick and misshapen. It took a moment to realize that they had been bandaged.

The next time he woke, he could make out his

surroundings more clearly. The pattern of bricks in the walls around him and the carvings on the wooden door looked unfamiliar, unlike anything in the House of Shecumpeh. There was little light, and he could only discern his surroundings by the starlight coming through the window. He moved his head, and saw a figure watching him from a corner of the room. Turthe.

'You're awake.'

Ursu felt his hackles rise. He was lying on a heap of rags and the air around him smelled of animal shit. He realized they were in the stables where the icebeasts had been kept, only a short distance from the House of Shecumpeh. As Ursu tried to raise himself a blackness welled up inside him and he let himself flop down again.

'No thanks to you.'

'I rescued you from the well.'

'You put me down there in the first place,' rasped Ursu, feeling tired even from the effort of speaking. 'You tried to drown me.'

Turthe leaned forward, out of the shadows, and raised his hand. When Ursu saw his face it was as if years had passed since they had last spoken, not just a day and a night. Blood stained the old Master's lips, and he seemed greyer, as if something vital had been leached from his soul.

'Yes, I did,' said Turthe. 'And, for my sins, we are all being punished.'

'The invaders—?'

'Are everywhere,' Turthe interrupted. 'Shecumpeh

has failed to protect us.' Turthe shifted forward. Ursu could see more clearly the lines of pain in his face, saw the way Turthe reached down to clutch his chest, as if something had been damaged beyond repair. *This is death*, he thought. Turthe was dying.

'The others – where are they?'

'Uftheyan is dead,' said Turthe, 'killed by Xan's soldiers.'

'Shecumpeh – they don't have the god?'

'No.'

'Do you know where the god is?'

Turthe smiled, a wan, thin smile. 'Yes I do. It was true, wasn't it?' Turthe's sad grey eyes stared into Ursu's own. 'Shecumpeh commanded you to carry him to safety outside the city.'

'Just as Ewenden was instructed, and you repaid her obedience by murdering her.'

'Help me up,' Turthe said, by way of an answer. 'I need to get up.'

Ursu's head felt a little clearer. He pushed himself up from the rags he'd been laid on and looked down at his hands, at the ruined flesh of his palms. Then he grudgingly helped the old priest to stand, and glanced briefly out of a window. Snowflakes drifted through it onto Ursu's fur.

The window directly faced the side wall of an adjacent stable, and to the right of it a wide lane leading, in the distance, towards the wall surrounding the city. Closer, he could see figures dressed in armour looming in the dim twilight, their black ears encrusted with heavy jewelled rings, as favoured by mercenaries. They seemed to be just standing and talking. Probably standing guard, Ursu guessed, but over what?

There were no other signs of life on the streets, which was very unusual, and no lights burning. Only the constellations shone down on the ravaged city, casting thin shadows under the encroaching night. He looked up at the stars spread across the sky in the thick glistening band of Hesper's Crown.

'Is there some kind of curfew?' whispered Ursu, glancing at Turthe. It was strange to think how, a few days ago, Turthe had been a symbol of authority, but that had all gone now.

'I don't know,' Turthe replied. 'I've been hidden here since before night approached.'

Ursu made a disgusted noise. He had every right to take his revenge on Turthe. Instead, he supported him out into the night.

'Be careful. There's been a lot of death, Ursu. Too much death,' the old one whispered, wary of the soldiers nearby.

'I'm taking the god,' said Ursu. 'Do you understand me?' He grabbed Turthe's arm and led him through the darkened streets, moving quietly and slowly. There were indeed many bodies; some, men from the city militia, left slaughtered on the cold ground. As they came across a dead child, Ursu's heart grew colder than an

163

icy grave. Who would do such a thing? Who would encourage an army to do such things?

As Turthe hobbled along he had to stop frequently to rest, and Ursu anticipated the old Master dying at his feet. But Turthe kept grimly on, and finally they reached the shadow of the House of Shecumpeh – or what was left of it.

It was a burned-out ruin, and snow hissed on smoking embers mixed amongst collapsed masonry. There were footprints across the thin covering of snow on the open square facing the main facade. Someone had been here within the last hour.

'What happened to you, Turthe?' Ursu whispered, pausing for breath on the edge of the freezing square. He could hear no sound, only absolute silence, as if everyone in the world had died but them. Smoke rose in great black drifts across the skyline, even obscuring the stars. It was the end of their history, he thought; the end of Nubala, the end of everything.

'When the soldiers came, I hid the god. Myself and the other Masters were attacked by Xan's soldiers as we tried to reach a hiding place, and I pretended I was dead even though I was only badly hurt. But the other Masters . . .' He pointed to the shadows obscuring a far corner of the square, and Ursu realized that one darker patch of soil was in fact a great pool of frozen blood and mutilated flesh.

They slipped over to the wreckage of the main

entrance. 'We can't get in that way,' Ursu protested. 'It'll collapse on us.'

'Nevertheless, you have to try, for the god's sake,' said Turthe. 'I will tell you where to look, so listen carefully.'

Of course, there was more than one means of access to the labyrinth of tunnels that riddled the rock below the streets of Nubala. The soldiers of Xan had come all this way to seize their god, but despite so much time and effort, they had not yet found it. Ursu didn't want to think what retribution they might exact if they remained unsuccessful. He didn't want to think what would happen to the surviving population of Nubala.

'Maybe we should just give them the god after all,' said Ursu. 'Maybe they'll spare us all if we do that. Wouldn't that be the best thing?'

'When Shecumpeh spoke to you, he must have shown you what would happen if you followed the wrong path. What did you see, when the god revealed what would happen if you failed?'

'A blackness,' said Ursu, remembering all too vividly. 'Like the whole world had come to an end.' He stared into the gaping maw of the ruined doorway.

'Stay out of sight,' he muttered to Turthe. Then Ursu stepped into the shadows of what had once been the House of Shecumpeh.

It was more difficult than he had expected: the mighty stone walls of the House had once supported huge wooden beams meeting far above the heads of acolytes and Masters alike. But these had crashed to the ground as they burned, leaving little level space for him to squeeze through. Here and there a thin layer of frost had formed on the stonework.

The great House of Shecumpeh, he thought, was now like a corpse after the spirit has left it; vacant but still containing memories of its prior vitality. Yet, the god was still in here somewhere. As he hunkered down and crawled through a narrow gap between the broken stone slabs of the floor and a tumbled beam, fearful of its huge weight and dimension pressing against his back, something moved and he froze.

Realizing it was only a nearby beam settling its weight, he kept going, squeezing further into the shadowy ruin of the House's great hall. Occasionally, vague shapes resolved themselves into corpses, burned partly to the bone.

Ah, here: a little beyond the winding stone stairs that had led down to Turthe's workshop. Here, where double doors had opened onto a passageway leading down to the room where the god had spoken to him. The doors themselves had been smashed to fragments, presumably by Xan's soldiers. Why had they burned the House down, when they had still not found the god? He wondered if the fire had been started by someone other than the soldiers. Maybe it was an attempt to hamper them.

He stepped through into greater darkness, his eyes still adjusting, and he paused there, at the top of the stairs. The darkness reminded him of the river – like a black liquid waiting to swallow him. He felt his throat tighten and stepped back. He picked up a still-burning wooden stake, cursing as hot ashes fragmented onto his long narrow fingers, and carried it down into the blackness.

The ember barely illuminated the wide chamber with its flickering light. It seemed so much less now, just an ordinary room, but one of great significance to the citizens of Nubala for dozens of generations. The stone slabs beneath his feet had been polished smooth as glass by the endless legions of acolytes and Masters, coming here to beseech the god. Now he was here all alone, and it seemed just a room.

Now, where had Turthe said . . .? Ah yes.

Shecumpeh had rested on that wide stone plinth near the far wall, but the god was no longer evident. Ursu touched one hand to the wall, and felt the faintest vibration of distant water coursing through the rock beyond.

Carefully placing the burning ember on the ground beside him, he studied the wall hangings and carvings adorning the walls: the intricate work of thousands of craftsmen devoted to Shecumpeh, extending across some unfathomable period of time.

Enough of this dwelling on the past, he reproached himself and, even as this crossed his mind, another part of him stood detached and wondered that he could now be so emotionless, even ruthless, about the heritage of his home.

There. A wide square slab set into the wall, the deep grooves around its four sides the only thing distinguishing it from the surrounding brickwork. Ursu would never have noticed it himself if Turthe hadn't told him exactly where to look. He pushed hard on it, until he felt the rock slab start to slide and shift from side to side as if on some hidden pivot. It rotated slowly to reveal a tiny space on its right side . . . a tiny space, yet just big enough to hold the effigy of the god Shecumpeh.

He slid long fingers around the smooth, varnished skin of the god inside, slowly dragging it out of the tiny space. The effigy was heavier than Ursu had thought. For all its interior power, its carved eyes stared sightlessly outward. It seemed more fragile, somehow, than Ursu had remembered.

Cradling the god in both arms, he picked his way back across the chamber to the door that led into the stairwell, the discarded embers casting flickering shadows on the chamber walls around him. When he reached the darkness of the passageway, he sought out the steps with his prehensile toes, climbing back up through fragmented stone and burned timbers.

Voices.

He froze, only the light of Hesper's Crown illuminating the night beyond the city walls. Perhaps the soldiers had returned.

After a few minutes, he crawled and wormed his way

back through any navigable gaps in the collapsed masonry, to the spot where he had left Turthe. The bulky statue in his arms made progress a lot more difficult and, despite himself, he wished Shecumpeh could be . . . well, a bit lighter, maybe.

Back to the shattered entrance, where he realized to his horror that there was a small group of soldiers gathered in the square. Ursu watched them from the safety of the deeper shadows, wondering if he could make a run for it if they came near the House. He hefted the god in his arms and waited.

He could sit tight, or he could do something – they weren't particularly looking his way – and clouds were beginning to obscure what little light there had been. The ruined House cast a long shadow across the square, as Ursu half-crawled, half-hobbled out of the door, towards the near corner of a neighbouring building.

There was no sign of Turthe.

As he scuttled around the corner and out of sight of the square, he looked up to find three soldiers walking towards him from the far end of the street. One of them had clearly spotted him, his mouth opening wide when he saw the effigy clutched in Ursu's arms.

Go to the well, spoke the voice of Shecumpeh, in words like thick-flowing liquid. Ursu's limbs seemed to swivel without his volition, and he fled back into the square.

Time seemed to slow to the point of stopping. A thought raced through Ursu's mind, for the smallest fraction of a second. It hadn't been a voice he had heard, really; more like the wind shivering through the trees, or rain tapping against cobblestones. Shecumpeh was speaking to him again. And with that same deep-seated knowledge he had felt that previous time, a lifetime ago in a warm and smoky cellar, Ursu knew the god was urging him to jump into the well.

No, a part of him screamed.

Despite this, his feet carried him towards the well – the worst place imaginable. He was going to die.

At a shout from behind him, the soldiers standing in the square turned, bleary-eyed, and stared as he ran past them with the effigy clutched tightly in his arms.

Even as the soldiers nearby started moving towards him, his feet left the ground and he hurled himself over the lip of the well, his arms still clutching the god of Nubala. He felt their fingers snatch at his leg, even as he fell into darkness.

He plummeted headlong into blackness, felt bones shatter as he hit the bottom, then the torrent tugging at his broken body, freezing water filling his lungs. There were no pockets of air now to give him a brief respite. The intense blackness swallowed him whole, like a great dark serpent coiling around him, squeezing the life out of him.

His grasp on the god loosened, as his lifeless body was swept towards the distant sea.

Seven

Kim

One afternoon, not long after she'd spoken to Bill, Kim noticed a ghost staring at her from a distance.

More of a glance really, enough for a sudden frown to form before she ducked out of sight and down a busy corridor, past people pushing and pulling in every direction. She still carried the Books in a little plastic capsule in her pocket.

She half walked, half flew back to her tiny quarters, almost floating in the Station's minuscule gravity, not looking back to see if he was still there, following her. Back inside her home, she hooked one foot in a wall-strap to stop herself floating away, and took out the capsule filled with the Books given her by Bill. Perhaps a dozen: enough memories to drown in, after a fashion.

A ghost, she thought. His name floated to the surface of her memory, but she pushed it down. She still had some of the other Books left: the Books with Susan in them. She had been rationing them out, like someone lost in the desert taking measured sips from the last of their water supply. Until she could get someone to replicate the Susan Books with the distillery in Central Command, that was all she had.

Her bioware had not come cheap. Despite the terrible things that had happened in the Citadel, the expedition had reaped lucrative rewards, and she had subsequently become moderately wealthy. Most of the fees for installing the bioware had gone on locating the specialists prepared to put it in her skull while sidetracking the usual legal and medical permissions.

There were a lot of different theories about the purpose of the Angels' bioware. The standard texts claimed the bioware had been intended to record the memories and experiences of the widest possible variety of different species. An entire branch of human experiential art and even diplomacy had grown around the bioware, including practitioners who referred to themselves as 'Observers': those who went to places and recorded what they saw, what they felt. Which had the advantage that it couldn't be altered, couldn't be misinterpreted, so long as you took into account that the emotional responses of any one Observer would inevitably be tied to their own long-ingrained tendencies and belief system.

She met . . . then the thoughts stalled. She blinked. She was an Observer, trained on Earth. The memories were now there: a life spent growing up under clear blue skies in Canada (growing up in a cramped corridor deep under the surface of an ice moon), her graduation (first trip to Earth). She . . .

(confusion)

Kim gripped her skull, filled with Susan's conflicting memories and thoughts. She thought of the alien Books she was carrying, of what might be in them. Another way to lose yourself. She had told Bill she was interested in no other memories but Susan's.

She remembered Bill's admonition. With enough will and determination you could *lose* yourself in other people's memories. She'd even heard that it was a recognized psychological condition, designated by a long string of Latin vowels and consonants.

She sighed.

She could look for Bill now and return the new Books to him, tell him the deal was off.

Instead, she sat down on the edge of her narrow bunk, opened the capsule and shook out one of the new supply of Books. She ate it, thinking, it'd probably be nothing, that probably whoever supplied the original distillate to Bill had lied or been misled. The Book broke into dry flakes on her tongue, dissolving rapidly as she chewed it. Within seconds it was into her bloodstream, swarming up towards her brain and towards the bioware that interpreted it, translated it into something her mind could understand and interact with. Made it real.

She let herself drift over to a small fold-down table and tapped into a smartsheet lying there, looking for something to distract her until the Book had fully taken hold.

It only took her a minute to realize something was wrong.

She wondered if the light was burning brighter. She looked up, saw it was. *This shouldn't be happening*, she thought with dismay. *Ride it through, then find Bill.*

She dropped off for a moment, fatigue and tiredness taking their toll. That was twice within a few days, so she'd have to be careful. Pull that trick next time she took the Goblin out, even Pierce wouldn't be able to save her skin.

To Kim's surprise, the whole universe appeared to rip open.

It was as if her room, the Station, simply peeled away. She found herself falling into an abyss, and a deep certainty filled her that she was going to fall forever and ever and ever. A billion years passed then, at a crawl, and still she fell. She pictured the universe tumbling away somewhere far behind her, forever out of reach.

After several more eternities, her own life, her memories, were stripped away. There was someone else underneath.

She was still distantly aware that none of this was real, and it was this knowledge that allowed her to maintain her sanity. Now in another world, her fingers sought out, and found, felt the edge of the table. Breaking the spell of the Books was not easy, but it could be done. It was so much easier to completely subsume yourself in the thoughts and actions the Book recorded, an activity Kim normally pursued with a single-minded devotion bordering on the fanatical. Pain, though – pain could break the spell.

Then they came.

They fell towards her like stars glowing in the eternal stygian night, and in her mind she could hear them calling to her. They tasted her thoughts, her feelings, memories and emotions, and she found herself like a passenger in her own life. She remembered her mother's womb, then being born, lying screaming and puking in her cot as a tiny baby. It all unravelled in real time – the great darkness was now long gone. She lived again through those years spent growing up in the confined, leafy corridors of the Hellas C Ice Station. She stared up in wonder at the striped outline of the gas giant her home orbited, then looked across to the ancient alien ruins towering on the horizon. She had been Sol-standard thirteen when she had first stood on that same hill, the heavy environment suit feeling light as a feather in the low gravity.

She lived through her studies again, that moment of learning that she was to travel via the Hellas Angel Station to study xenoarchaeology on Earth. She relived her late twenties for the first time, seeing a *blue* sky with her own eyes, staring up now at the moon, her freshly re-engineered bones flexing under the unaccustomed weight of Terran gravity.

Then her first trip to the Kasper Angel Station,

working amid the abandoned Angel ruins in the isolated, unpopulated northern wastes of the planet Kasper. Kim tried to scream, to break the grip the Book exerted on her, but it was like nothing she had ever previously experienced. She was going to live through it all over again, in intricate, painstaking detail.

She was now back in the tunnel, deep within the Citadel. She sobbed, feeling for the edge of the table in her quarters with a ghost-hand, then slid her fingers under, seeking out the hard steel edge of the bracket on which the tabletop pivoted. She smashed her fist against it, trying to use pain to snap herself out of it.

She could feel the pain, but it was only a distant thing. She managed to hit the bracket again, harder, and something wet and warm trickled down her wrist and arm. It wasn't working.

Susan – whose hair smelled like mint. *A better person than I ever could be*, thought Kim, thinking how strange it was that they seemed to share some of the same memories, as if they were almost the same person . . .

Susan.

It all came back then in a rush, memory after memory. She would relive every moment with the added torture of foreknowledge – of what would happen to them all, and how horribly some of them would die.

*

Kim woke, suddenly, a feeling of deep anxiety lurking inside her, as if she were about to be attacked. She looked up at the thick plastic walls of the sleeping bubble she shared with Susan. Kim was expedition leader, in charge of three others: Susan, Fitz and Odell. Kim had meant to rise early today, to get the imaging equipment set up for their morning's work.

She pulled herself out of her sleeping bag with the minimum of grace. That was one of the first differences Kim had ever noticed between them: Susan was a morning person, Kim most definitely was not. For Kim, mornings were something to be endured, rarely enjoyed. She wondered what had woken her so suddenly, what had made her feel so frightened. She was still fuzzy with sleep, but when it repeated a few minutes later, she knew what it had been.

A tremor – definitely a tremor. Not a good sign. It could mean their expedition being pulled out.

Still, she was head of the expedition, a considerable honour. Susan, however, had been her equal at university, and although it was in Kim's nature to look for some tiny sign in Susan that might betray resentment that Kim was expedition leader here, she found none. In fact, Susan showed every sign of being glad of Kim's career success, an unconditional pleasure for her lover that Kim sometimes found hard to accept.

'Of course I mean it,' Susan had said, once Kim brought herself to ask.

'You're the better at the job,' Kim had argued,

staring at the blonde woman through her fringe of dark hair. 'Everyone knows it. They knew it, back on Earth.'

'I did well, but that's not what I am first and foremost.'

'Yeah, right.' An Observer. Kim hadn't really met many other Observers, but apart from Susan, she'd come away with an impression that they tended to be portentous and not especially well endowed in the humour department. Susan had gone through all the psych tests, the evaluations and the training, and finally the surgery.

Kim didn't like the thought of that: something alien and slimy stuck inside your head like some kind of passenger in your brain. *Nasty*. Still, Susan also had training in anthropology, and knew more about the Kaspians and their culture than anyone else Kim had ever met.

Kim had made the inevitable joke about the sex lives of Observers when they first met, a crude attempt at breaking the ice. Susan had just sailed over this faux pas.

'I've made Books of it, sure,' Susan said, her voice matter-of-fact. Despite herself, Kim felt shocked. Susan was attractive, no doubt about it, with that strangely compact shape as against the tall and gangly Kim, a loose-limbed product of a lower-gravity environment.

Life on her native Hellas was more conservative, with old-fashioned ideas of propriety and public behaviour that had come with the first, primarily Quaker settlers arriving in that system. And, although she hadn't brought herself to admit it at the time, Kim had found this other woman both unsettling and exciting from the moment they first met. That didn't take long to turn into strong mutual attraction, the discovery that Susan, in turn, found Kim exotic, alien, different too. It was on that first get to know you meeting – it was only later Kim had come to think of it as their first date – that Susan had explained her Books.

'It's not just being inside someone's head. It's *getting* them.'

Kim shook her head. 'You've lost me.'

'Everyone has a different way of looking at the world, different ways of interpreting it. If you eat enough Books that carry the thoughts and memories of one particular person, to a certain extent you sort of become that person.' Susan had a faraway look as she spoke, and Kim could see she was searching carefully for the right words. 'You come to understand them, appreciate their reasons for being the way they are, because you also experience their emotional reactions to the world around them, and you can learn to at least understand how someone else might come to hold different views from you – even quite radically different views.'

Kim frowned. 'Sounds horrible. I can think of some people whose viewpoint I don't want to understand. Murderers, people like that. I'd feel' – she waved her hand in the air – 'tainted. Marked.'

'Not just anyone can do it, you know,' Susan said. 'Takes training, a lot of psychology before they let you acquire the bioware. You have to be pretty strongly committed.'

Maybe I should have listened harder to her, thought the part of Kim still aware that this was all a kind of dream.

She felt sure she could ride it out, get through it. Her arm had stopped hurting a while back, had become even less than a ghost pain. She was still very much caught in the moment, in the illusion. It was like being buried alive – but in your own memories.

The curious thing was that Susan had been right. Kim *was* getting it, enough so she understood for the first time what her dead lover had been trying to tell her all those years ago. She was inside her own head, experiencing her own half-dissolved memories, learning what it was really like to be Kim. She was actually able to stand outside herself, outside her own life, like watching a tragedy being played out to its inevitable and sorry climax, able to become her own critic with a surprising degree of objective analysis.

The Citadel lay beyond a ring of mountains situated at Kasper's north pole. The current consensus was that it hadn't been built by the Kaspians themselves at some point in the distant past – that it was created by the Angels, a great, aeons-old network of rooms and tunnels that led deep below the planet's surface. Everything about it, from the arrangement of the molecules in the stone from which it had been constructed to the apparent violations of the laws of space-time that could be found in its maze of corridors, surely pointed to the Angels. Outside of the Stations themselves, it was the most remarkable work of engineering left behind by those long-departed aliens.

The rules were, you couldn't interfere with the culture on Kasper, and that meant no flyovers, and almost no clandestine visits unless they'd been carefully approved by half a dozen committees who each had the power of absolute veto over all the other committees if they felt so inclined. The Citadel, however, presented an exception; the geography of the surrounding area, plus the frozen climate, made it utterly inaccessible to the natives. That was because a long chain of mountains, stretching east to west, made for an entirely adequate barrier to interference or observation. Subsequently, a small research station had been set up near one of the entrances to the Citadel, half a dozen prefab units manned by a rotating skeleton crew of half a dozen.

And now she was there, deep within the Citadel, on her first ever trip to the Kaspian surface. Its warrens and corridors stretched for hundreds of kilometres beneath the frozen soil. There was something about the atomic structure of the rock from which the Citadel had been created that made it extraordinarily resistant to collapse or decay – but a million years was a long time. There were caved-in corridors to be found near the expedition's base camp, but sonar and imaging equipment showed the outlines of shapes beyond the rubble. Fitz had been excited by this, but for Fitz excitability was a core character trait.

'Angel tech,' he had pronounced, a gleam in his eye. Kim had just radioed in their findings, along a cable that connected to a comms room in the research station.

'Don't jump to any conclusions,' Susan had said. They'd celebrated First Landing the night before, following an old Hellas tradition, drinking 'ponics wine Kim had brought all the way from home for a special occasion, until their breath stank. Kim had wondered if this centuries-old tradition might seem provincial, but Susan and the others had seemed to enjoy it. Susan seemed to enjoy everything, however, even if it meant being stuck for weeks in cold, empty caves and corridors with the freezing dark lurking only feet away, beyond the lights and the portable heaters.

The way the electric lights flickered, swinging gently in the breeze coming from the heating units, brought to mind old childhood stories: of the Old Man lurking in the corridors of Hellas C, ready to snatch the unwary off to their doom.

And now there was every indication they'd found a major new branch leading off the tangled maze of tunnels and rooms located on one of the lowest levels of the Citadel – almost a mile below the Kaspian surface, a long way down.

Sometime in the past million years or so, part of the tunnel complex had obviously collapsed. This region wasn't particularly prone to seismic shifts, but it was clear something drastic had happened. Seismometers stationed in and out of the Citadel had picked up disturbances, and an initial investigation with remotes showed that a new collapse in the building's lower levels had uncovered previously inaccessible areas. That had been the impetus for their expedition, and Kim had fought hard to get in on it, and then fought just as hard again to get the right people in there with her.

There was something big on the other side of a vast mound of rubble and, according to the readings they were getting, something was happening there; still active machinery, perhaps, but certainly something unprecedented. Their findings – via video and audio, plus deep scans – were fired in encrypted packet bursts out to the Angel Station. Now they had to wait for permission to clear the rubble. That delay took time, and involved a lot of bureaucracy, and a lot more radioing back and forth with the Station authorities.

There had been a sour note to the First Landing celebration, as she'd been arguing with Susan, a lot. It hadn't taken much more before they'd started arguing in front of the others, once they had both become too drunk to stop themselves. That hadn't been good at all.

Even the work wasn't enough to distract them from their personal problems; it only took a word, even a look, to set them off again.

Why couldn't life be simpler? Kim had wondered a dozen times, knowing deep down it was her own jealousy of Susan that was the problem. Susan was everything Kim wanted to be herself: comfortable with people in a way that Kim had never been able to comprehend nor imitate. She'd lie there at night, and wonder why Susan was still with her. And how long it would be before Susan would leave her, if Kim didn't drive her away first.

Fitz, yawning and full of morning tiredness, squatted wordlessly next to Kim, where she'd fired up a heating unit. The others were starting to rise too. The camp was constructed of heat-reflecting multi-layered plastic sheets coating its floors and ceilings, with airlocks at either end to keep the internal temperature bearable. The bright lights of the camp shone through its translucent plastic walls, illuminating the broken alien corridors beyond.

She went over to the monitors, where monotone images flickered on the screens, revealing vague shapes not unlike banks of machinery, but seeming to regularly fade and then brighten.

'Do we have an active camera through yet?' Kim said, sinking down beside Fitz.

Fitz shook his head. 'I put another one through last night, during my watch, but it broke down again. Didn't see a thing, beyond what we've already spotted on the infra-red. And no evidence of dangerous radiation either.'

'Anything weird otherwise?'

'You mean glitches in time, wandering space, stuff like that? No, nothing that hasn't been mapped out already by previous expeditions.' Time would skip forwards or backwards by a few moments; you could move a few feet and find yourself at the far end of the same corridor with no idea of what had happened in between. To anybody watching, it appeared you just vanished, for the tiniest moment. And then, of course, there were those who had vanished completely. Some parts of the Citadel were still restricted to access by anything but automated robots, and most of the time those didn't return either. 'We'll just have to let the remote mapping experts take over and see what they can find with robots.'

Kim glanced at Fitz. 'We could do it ourselves,' she said.

'You're joking, right?' Fitz grinned. 'We performed all the requisite scans. If there's any more tremors, we'll be pulled straight out of here, file our reports and let the local Artefacts Committee figure out what to do next.' He shrugged. 'Besides . . .'

'What?'

He peered at her. 'Kim, we have absolutely no idea what's through there. It could be anything. Could be dangerous. Can't be too careful.'

'Fitz, where's your rugged Hellas spirit?' Kim said with a mocking grin. Fitz was also a native of Hellas, and had grown up in a corridor not so far from her. 'Don't tell me you came down here just to take pictures, then duck out. Whatever would the Founding Families say if they could see you?'

'The Founding Families were hardcore individualist nutcases so far gone in their political and religious beliefs that living on an ice moon light years from home seemed like a good idea to them.' Kim stared at him. 'Look,' he continued, taking a more reasonable tone, 'I just think we should be careful.'

'Fitz, whatever caused the recent cave-ins, it's not going to happen again anytime soon. It's the kind of event that takes place here maybe once every hundred thousand years. There's nothing to worry about.'

Fitz said nothing. If they did now send in remote diggers, they would probably be operated under the direction of the Kasper Angel Station's Artefacts Committee, which would itself be responsible to the Station's Central Command, the nearest thing around to a government. Kim and the rest of them would be taken out of the process by then. She'd still be project leader, of course, but it wouldn't be the same. She'd be back there in the Station's busy corridors, far from the real action here.

Events seemed to fast-forward again. Her arguments with Susan got worse. In the meantime, there were other things to worry about, like the seismic readings coming in from the outpost. The tremors seemed to be centred on their camp.

Odell broke the bad news. She was a dark-haired girl from Oslo, the expedition's planetary geologist. 'We're looking at rumblings, mainly. You know that one of the things we did down here was install new seismometers, to try and figure out how innately stable the structure of the whole Citadel is. If these readings are anything to go by, Kim, it looks like the Citadel's not nearly as stable as everyone assumed.'

Kim frowned. 'It's been here a very long time. I don't think it's likely to collapse right now.'

'I didn't say it was going to.'

Kim was acutely aware of Susan sitting nearby.

In the end, they voted to sleep on it. The expedition was not in any apparent immediate danger; there was no real reason, seismic readings or otherwise, to suspect that the Citadel had become suddenly unstable over-night.

Nonetheless, there followed yet more inexplicable tremors, getting worse this time. Kim woke again in the middle of the night, instantly alarmed. There was a sound like . . . like nails being dragged across some hard surface? Like two mountains being ground together? She waited, tense, and the sound passed after a few seconds.

She heard Odell and Fitz talking. Kim got herself dressed, went over to them.

Odell looked pale. 'I don't know what's causing the tremors.' She rubbed her hands together. 'I mean, there's no apparent cause that makes any rational sense, anyway.'

Kim's eyes slid over to the rubble-packed corridor, somewhere beyond which alien machinery quietly worked away. The most recent tremors had shifted some of this rubble, now revealing a possible way through – if they were very careful. And if the Citadel didn't collapse around their ears in the meantime. Maybe.

Maybe not.

'Too dangerous.' Fitz shook his head. 'We shouldn't be taking any chances. We're not here to grandstand.'

'Kim's the expedition leader,' said Susan unexpectedly, not even looking at Kim as she said it. Her tone was matter-of-fact, detached. 'So it's up to her.'

Kim merely stared at her.

Fitz shrugged. 'It's your call, and I never said otherwise. God knows, I'd like to know what's through there.' She could see Odell nodding absent-mindedly. They all wanted to know what was through there. 'But I have a . . . a gut feeling, if you like. There were tremors during last night, more than once. We're talking about something completely unprecedented. Even if we miss out on something, we can still watch it develop from outside, or from the Angel Station in complete safety.'

'We stay,' said Kim. 'Because if I give up now and let someone else take the credit, I'll regret it for the rest of my life – and frankly, so will all of you. Look me in the eye and tell me I'm wrong.' She scanned their faces. Fitz's eyes flicked away from hers; Odell looked uncertain. 'We're lucky to be here at this time,' said Kim. 'Apart from the chance to discover something untouched for millennia, we stand to make a lot of money if it turned out there's anything usable. That won't happen if we walk away and take the chance of some bureaucrat being assigned to run everything by remote. You all know how the laws on technology salvage claims work.'

They took a vote, deciding to stay on, though Susan abstained. When Kim glanced at her it was as if she were looking into the eyes of a stranger. Kim felt her face flush, and turned away.

Events moved on towards their ultimate finale. *Let it end*, thought Kim, part of her still in the here-and-now, her body wedged into a corner of her tiny quarters.

'Not sure,' Fitz was staring into a monitor, 'but it looks like something. Can you work it through a little more?'

Kim watched as Odell fed the camera further through a long metal pipe drilled through the rubble. The tremors overnight had been extremely minor, which gave hope that the worst might be over. The tiniest notion of doubt had meanwhile slid into Kim's mind, but she dismissed it as irrational. They were more likely to get killed by a passing asteroid than to have the Citadel suddenly decide to fall on top of them. What could possibly be causing it?

They had their own remote digging equipment that they could use to excavate these tunnels at a safe distance before entering them themselves. They now retreated far outside the camp, running operating cables for half a mile away from the blocked corridor, before sending the diggers in. Kim realized ruefully that, in this age of technology, this was as hands-on as it really got.

She wondered what Howard Carter, who had almost burrowed his way into the boy-king Tutankhamun's tomb with his bare hands, would have thought of it all. The cameras hadn't told them much, so far. Something was clearly scrambling their signal, and she trusted it wouldn't do the same for the diggers. However, it didn't appear to be dangerous – she hoped. Just something new that they couldn't understand. Like all Angel technology, in fact.

Then followed the memory she most dreaded. They had sent the diggers in, to clear a path through the rubble. For the first time, they saw the blue glow of what lay beyond, and knew that something was still functioning around the curve of the corridor, even after untold aeons. They stayed well back, watching images flicker across screens, the long tangles of cable twisting along the corridor floor like shiny metal snakes.

'We've got no radiation levels evident around there,' said Fitz, watching the screens with the rest of them.

'That light . . .' said Susan, 'what is it?'

'Nothing natural, that's for sure,' said Fitz. 'Do you see those markings on the walls? That's Angel stuff. They look pretty much the same as any other language samples discovered in the past.'

The tell-tale symbol was there on a wall, like the shape made by a child lying on his back in pristine snow and scissoring his arms and legs. A snow angel – the reason they'd become known as the Angels in the first place.

Kim listened hard, imagining what would be said about their discoveries when this went public. There'd be controversy, of course, since they'd broken some rules. But in the long run, that didn't matter: their names would live forever. Whatever lay around the curve of the corridor would ensure that.

'So what's the current danger to us?' she asked.

'The remote sensors indicate a sharp drop in air pressure over a distance of two feet a short distance inside the corridor,' said Fitz.

Kim nodded, feeling light-headed. The Citadel included areas where invisible, undetectable barriers kept some sections in vacuum. With any luck, all they'd have to worry about now was whether they'd be able to breathe. There were other things that might be of concern, of course . . . after all, the Citadel seemed to defy all the known laws of nature.

Past expeditions had run into similar problems, so now pressure suits had become standard issue. She looked at the other two, Odell and Susan. Neither looked like they would object to entering the corridor. Susan's expression was carefully noncommittal, lacking in any emotion. *Perhaps we could still come out of this as friends*, Kim thought, knowing even as she thought this that it would never be enough. She needed Susan a lot more than Susan needed her. That would be a problem, but she'd deal with it. She promised herself she would.

The first of the fresh tremors came as she stepped, in her pressure suit, towards the now partly cleared corridor. The blue light was strange, because it seemed to come from all places at once. There were no shadows at all, as if the molecules of the air itself were glowing slightly. Amorphous brighter patches billowed gently, almost like smoke, and continued to do so even once they passed through the pressure barrier and entered near-vacuum.

Susan was beside her now, her face only half-visible inside the helmet of her suit. Fitz and Odell had stayed behind to monitor their progress from around the corridor's far bend. She knew Susan wanted to 'Observe' everything, to get it all down for posterity. Kim blanched at the thought of how future Observers would see herself, in this moment, through Susan's eyes. The thought made her feel awkward, clumsy. She chose her words carefully.

'We'll go on past this rubble, keep following the curve. Take some pictures, recordings, stuff like that. See if we can figure out what we've got here.' Susan turned her helmeted head, and Kim caught the hint of a small smile, like Susan had found something ironic in what Kim said. Even to herself, Kim sounded a little stilted, too much playing a role.

'Fine by me,' said Susan. Kim was still looking

towards her when Susan frowned. 'Hey, did you feel—?'

Kim did. She had felt it even as Susan spoke, at first mistaking it for some aberration of her own body, then realizing there was something external: a vibration, no, a roar.

I was wrong, Kim had thought, about what the tremors sounded like before. This is what two mountains sounded like when being ground together.

For one heart-rending moment Kim was sure the whole corridor was about to collapse on top of them. It didn't, but its walls – the super-strong walls created by an alien race to last an eternity – sagged inwards. *What's causing this?* wondered Kim. She glanced at Susan who, like her, had frozen, waiting to see what would happen next.

Kim listened. Nothing more. 'Fitz? Odell? Can you hear me?'

'Odell here,' crackled her helmet comm. 'That was bad. We lost some of our equipment. There's been some kind of major shift. We're getting messages down the wire from the guys at the research station. They picked up the shaking too, and want to know if we've experienced anything significant.'

Have we experienced anything? thought Kim. Some joke.

'Listen,' said Odell. 'I'm taking readings here. This whole section of the Citadel, it's . . . I don't know, it's like it's sagged or something. You need to get out of there.'

'Maybe it's settled now,' said Kim. It had been tens of thousands of years since the last corridor collapse. Why now, just as they were approaching that particular curve in the corridor? More than ever, Kim ached to see what lay around there. Going back and sending in cameras wouldn't be enough. She wanted to *see*.

'Maybe it has, maybe it hasn't,' said another voice over the radio, Fitz this time. 'Just get out of there.'

'I'm still in charge of this expedition, Fitz.'

'Kim, I'm sorry, I've already spoken to the Station Command via the outpost relay. They want you to pull back, abort.'

Anger flared through her. He'd gone behind her back. 'Fitz, you can't do that. What's through this corridor will change our lives forever. It's Angel tech.'

'Not much use to us if we're dead,' came back the reply. 'Look, I'm sorry. But we've already broken too many rules, and the rules are there for a reason.'

There weren't any words to describe the emotions she felt: an awful kind of betrayal. She turned to Susan.

'I guess you had something to do with this,' said Kim. 'Feel better for it?'

Susan looked back at her with clear, calm eyes. 'Kim, this is as much news to me as it is to you, believe me.'

But I don't want to believe, thought Kim. Her reputation would be destroyed by this, she was sure, and she'd barely even started out. 'We're going ahead,' said Kim.

Susan looked as if she was about to say something, but Kim turned away and started ahead.

'Fitz, if there's a real chance of tremors causing some kind of collapse, it's all the more important we rescue what we can before it gets lost forever. Do you understand?' *Say yes, you little bastard*, she thought.

But the radio merely crackled; then silence. Whatever had affected the cameras was affecting that too.

They moved forward in silence, now unable to communicate except by gesture. Kim turned the corner first, blinking at the haze beyond her helmet. The air seemed to glow more intensely. There were objects visible ahead, machines of some kind. She felt her scalp tingle. Then something moved. Something alive? She tried to peer through the haze. It was like someone had taken the very air and twisted it in a fist, like a piece of cloth bunched between fingers.

The air twisted again, and the ground shuddered. Kim stumbled, slapping one gloved hand against a wall for support. She felt a sudden rush of vertigo, as if *down* was suddenly becoming *up*. There were objects lying nearby, glowing with that same unearthly light. She reached out for one, grabbed it. She looked to Susan, nodded towards them. Take some, she gestured. Kim looked about, grabbing whatever she could of the random junk that seemed to be scattered around them.

195

GARY GIBSON

Not much time, she thought. Susan was doing the same, picking up whatever she could. They carried it back around the curve of the corridor where they had approached. Ominous tremors rolled through the dust beneath their feet. Kim thought again of the miles of layered rock above them, then tried not to think about that.

When they had got far away enough, Fitz came back online.

'. . . hell have you been?'

'It's the corridor that's blocking transmission,' said Kim quickly. She was sweating inside her suit, but only partly because of physical effort.

'Odell's on her way,' said Fitz. 'She's fetching one of the tractors.'

'Thanks, Fitz.'

'This is under protest, Kim. We've already taken too big a chance.'

Kim didn't reply. Odell appeared a few moments later, the tiny electric tractor whirring down the gentle incline leading to the corridor. 'Load it all in,' Kim heard her say over the intercom. 'Is there more?'

'Lots more,' said Kim. Odell was close enough for her to see the uncertainty in the geologist's face. Kim was scared, but they had to get it all out. 'Fitz is right,' said Odell. 'It's too dangerous. I'd rather be alive and poor than rich and dead.'

'Just take this stuff up to Fitz. We're going back for more.' Susan said nothing, just watching, 'Observing'.

They tramped back into the corridor and out of communications range again. This time they found something that looked roughly like a lathe. It also looked big, heavy, but when they tried to move it, it turned out to be as light as a feather. They took either end of it, and by the time they shifted it out of the corridor, Odell was back; her mouth now set in a hard thin line. Two strong tremors rolled consecutively through the ground beneath them.

Susan kept twisting her head around, trying to record everything she saw. Her memories alone could be worth a fortune by the time they got out of there. They loaded the lathe-thing onto the tractor. 'Come on, let's get out of here,' insisted Odell, her voice shaky as the ground shifted again beneath their feet.

'Just one more trip,' said Kim.

'She's right,' said Susan. 'It's time to go.'

'Only one more trip, I swear. It'll take just a minute or two. I'm not being crazy here, I'm being realistic. We could find something that jumps science forward a century or more. These corridors aren't going to collapse a second time just because *we* turned up.'

'Kim, look around you,' Susan almost shouted over the intercom. 'The place is falling down around our ears. We have got to get out of here.'

Kim turned away, moving as fast as she could in her heavy suit.

'Kim,' Susan called after her. 'Kim.' Then her voice crackled out of range as Kim entered the glowing corridor. *One more trip. Bring back just one thing more.* Maybe the secret of living forever. Maybe something like the Observer bioware, yet even more amazing. One more thing.

She found something, started to carry it back out. And saw to her surprise, as she turned, that Susan had followed her in. She caught a glimpse of Susan's face: the mask of passivity had slipped, and Kim felt curiously relieved to see the anger there. She realized it was something she'd been trying to achieve, to break through that mask of calmness. They both carried out whatever they could in silence.

'Okay, that's it,' said Kim. 'Let's get out of here. I—'

The world caved in. Kim watched in horror as the end of the corridor nearest to the scattered artefacts first sagged, then collapsed, the ceiling rushing down to meet the ground.

'Go now!' said Kim, and they jumped on board the tractor, Odell already pulling away up the long ramp towards where Fitz was stationed. A rumbling surged up through the wheels, through their pressure suits, almost rattling the brains in their skulls.

Fitz had the other tractor's engine already running when they found him. 'Forget the stuff, forget everything,' he said. 'Just come on.' Behind him, a screen strobed through the empty darkness: an icon flashing emergency red.

Kim glanced at the first load of artefacts Odell had

fetched up from the corridor. She moved towards them, picked one up.

'Kim, we have to get out of here *now*,' said Fitz, his voice sounding high and cracked.

'No, wait. We can't leave all of this behind.' She looked warily at the great stone slabs that surrounded her, their surfaces rough with carved symbols and alien scriptures. 'We can load up both tractors.'

She turned, looking at Susan, and remembered . . . remembered she wasn't really here. And then the foreknowledge came to her, of what was about to happen. Kim glanced up, saw the high ceiling fragmenting, then falling towards them, and time seemed to slow down to a crawl, so that she witnessed it all, as the great slabs of stone crashed down upon Odell and Susan. Research equipment spat sparks and died under that crushing weight . . . and they fell into darkness. She felt a hand grab her and yank her away.

'Kim! Give me a hand!' It was Fitz. The collapsing stonework had crushed both Odell and Susan and one of the tractors beneath it. The lights had shorted out, leaving them in total darkness.

Kim remembered she had a flashlight strapped to her thigh, and she pulled it out, switched it on. What she saw wasn't pleasant. Odell had been horribly crushed under a great boulder. Blood pooled around what little she could see of her. Susan lay under some smaller rocks, but the faceplate of her helmet was shattered, her open eyes staring out. Kim stepped forward, too numb to feel real horror yet. Fitz began shoving a rock from on top of Susan.

Kim moved forward to help him. *It's too late*, she thought, looking at the shattered faceplate. Susan's dead eyes stared back at her, accusing. She busily helped, nevertheless. Medical technology could do wonders – you never knew. She kept that thought in her mind as she helped Fitz pull Susan free.

Fitz ran back to the surviving tractor, and pulled out a survival cocoon. This was a long tube of flexible plastic, which could also monitor vital signs. *But will it keep her warm?* Kim wondered. She didn't know. She helped strip the pressure suit from Susan, doing whatever she could.

We're putting a corpse in this thing, she thought, manoeuvring Susan's body into the bag. It was like handling a sack of loose rocks. The ground trembled again. They then loaded Susan and whatever else they could strap onto the tractor, and shot back up the long ramp to the next highest level, aiming for the exit.

We did this, thought Kim suddenly, as the corridor walls slid by them. There were still miles to go, but a roar sounded from far behind them, and she could swear it was getting closer. She glanced to one side, at Fitz mounted in the open driver's seat, his expression grim. He glanced back at her briefly, then away again.

She thought again of Howard Carter, and all the other explorers who had gone before her. Of the dead kings who had left traps to catch thieves and the curious. *We did this*, she thought, *just by being here. Maybe someone doesn't want us here.* She wasn't so sure later, but that idea still stuck.

All my fault, she thought, and realized there was blood running down her arm, partly drying now. She hadn't even realized she'd been injured. A dull ache filled the arm and she felt dizzy. Looking around her, she saw the fold-down table and the contours of the tiny room she lived in, so claustrophobic and so narrow.

The effects of the Book were still clinging to her, so that it seemed in some way she was still racing through the lost corridors of the Citadel, her dead lover beside her. *Who am I?* she wondered, and was not sure what the answer was.

Elias

Three days after he reached the Angel Station, Elias located Eduardez.

The micro-gravity environment brought back unpleasant memories.

He carefully watched the people who lived there, who didn't seem to walk so much as hop from wall to ceiling to wall in their movements around the pressurized zones of the torus. Then he followed their lead, and soon got the hang of it. Just like old times.

Eduardez was scraping a living carrying out odd jobs in and around the Station. He'd spent several years outside as a rock hermit, then moved into the local black market, supplying unregulated gene treatments and drugs to soldiers as they were rotated through. The Station seemed to provide excellent opportunities for black marketeers: every six months or so a whole new clientele turned up with nowhere to spend their money but the Angel Station.

Like Elias, Eduardez had lived under a dozen false names, finding his own niche somewhere along the way. For Elias it was a lucky break that Eduardez happened to be in the same system he'd arrived at.

'Never heard of the guy,' said Eduardez, flipping the picture back at him. 'What you doing out here, anyway?' he asked. 'Get in trouble with the law?'

'Something like that, yeah.'

Eduardez studied him for a long moment. 'Gene treatment did nothing for me, man, not that the military authorities seem to think that makes a difference. You're the one with superpowers – you and Pachenko. If you've cut some kind of a deal with anyone to hand me over, I got a lot of friends who'll cut you down 'fore you even know you're mincemeat, you hear me, Elias?'

'I hear you. It isn't like that – that's the truth.'

Eduardez glared at him. 'Yeah, well maybe it is and maybe it isn't. You just remember what I'm saying, okay?'

'I'll remember.'

'Yeah, well. Anyway, you hear about Pachenko?'

Elias hadn't heard anything more about Pachenko

since they'd found him curled up in a ball in the same spot Elias had left him. 'No. No I didn't.'

'Went crazy after we all got back from the Rocks – you know that much, right? They locked him in a cell, then went looking for him one day. He wasn't there. No window, no way out, just gone. Weird as shit.'

'You sure about this?'

'As sure as I'm sure they didn't give us one single straight answer when they fucked around with our DNA. I've got contacts, heard stories how people used to see Pachenko, crazy and still screaming about bodies and blood and stuff, him wandering around, even when they knew he was still in the cell.'

'I don't understand. You mean he *did* get out?'

'No, Elias, I mean he was in two places at once. You ever hear of anything like that before?'

Elias thought of Vaughn. 'Maybe. I'm not sure. Listen, I'm looking for that man in the picture. He's here somewhere.' He showed Eduardez a smartsheet, then tapped at it until figures and names scrolled up. 'This is a ship's manifest.'

'The *Jager*? Yeah, I know that one. One of the big cargo ships. He on the crew?'

'Not exactly. He's on ice, somewhere aboard. I need your help.'

A look came over Eduardez's face. Not sly exactly, but calculating. 'Anything for an old friend, Elias, but times are hard, you know?'

'I can pay you.' Elias had discovered, to his surprise,

that he was rich: payments from people, from deals over the years, all accumulated in anticipation of just such a day.

'Hey man, I'm not being greedy. I'm just saying—'

'I can pay you, okay? Now I need to know, can you – or anyone else – get me on board that ship?'

'Sure,' said Eduardez. 'Sure, no problem.'

Vincent

When Vincent got to the Kasper Angel Station, he found himself doing a lot of waiting around.

First, there had been a slow crawl out from the moon to the Oort Angel Station, out in the loose halo of cosmic debris orbiting Sol, far beyond the edge of the planetary system. That meant having to take an orbiter out from Luna to one of the high-speed cargo cruisers that fell in a constant stream from the Oort Station in a vast, elliptical solar orbit, for him there to be dropped into deepsleep and shipped out the rest of the way. He didn't dream, which was good, since he'd now become infected with Eddie's sense of urgency. Every day that it took to get himself out to Kasper seemed a day wasted.

He now toured the Station, feeling what he was sure was a typical sense of psychic shock at suddenly finding oneself somewhere remarkable one had only ever read about or viewed on a screen somewhere. It didn't take long to walk around the whole structure. It was a lot further into the Kasper system than the distance from the Oort Station back home to the Sun. And instead of orbiting the star itself, it orbited the next planet out, which was just a cold ball of iron and ice, the Kasper Angel Station being its only moon.

It really is Kim, he decided, having spotted her there in the distance: that small, heart-shaped face framed by unruly dark brown hair cropped short, on top of a long-limbed body. He started towards her.

She stared at him, a frightened expression on her face. She was passing at the far end of a crowded corridor, too narrow for him to squeeze through quickly. By the time he had worked his way past the throng of people, she was gone. But Kim was definitely on board the Angel Station.

'I need to see the Commander,' Vincent demanded. He had reached an office near the cargo bays; it was a refitted fuel tank jutting out from the side of the Station. Vincent had needed to pass through at least three layers of security – mandatory scans, security men with barely concealed weapons and hostile expressions – to get this far.

'Commander Holmes is busy right now,' said the man behind the desk. Vincent had found out that the military used this office as an administrative buffer between themselves and the Angel Station's civilian population.

'I appreciate that,' said Vincent. 'He knows why I'm here.'

'Can you tell me the nature of the enquiry?' asked the man behind the desk.

Vincent shook his head. 'Classified.' He handed over the smartsheet he had found waiting for him on his arrival. Perhaps Vincent had been hoping people here would suddenly jump to attention, usher him through, apologizing for the delay. That didn't happen.

The desk man nodded politely. 'I need to check this with Commander Holmes's office. Come back at seventeen hundred hours. We should have something back by then.'

'It's already been checked.'

'Well, I'm sorry, but it's procedure. I don't have any notification otherwise here.' The desk man shrugged his shoulders and gave him a friendly smile. Vincent wondered how many people were responsible for manning the desk; this was the third person he'd found here in as many days. 'We can't do anything without the appropriate authorization.'

He was being stalled; he could feel it in his bones. But why?

The answer came within twenty-four hours.

He woke up in the middle of the night to find the mail light on his quarters datacom blinking. He sat up groggily, found the right button, and a fresh smartsheet slid out of the datacom's printer. It was a message from Eddie.

Not just a regular message, but an encrypted data-file locked to the security code he'd been handed by Eddie before his departure from Luna. After entering the code, he found himself watching a maximum-compression video in which Vincent could just see an amplified image of the Earth over Eddie's shoulder. He must have recorded this at home, Vincent thought. He realized months had passed since they had last talked, but to Vincent it seemed barely a couple of weeks. Eddie really did look older, worn out.

'Things are not good, Vincent. The news of the burster event should have gone completely public by now. There've been leaks, of course, and a lot of questions, but nobody above a certain level is either talking or taking any kind of stand.' Note to self, Vincent thought: pay more attention to the news feeds.

'I've been hearing a lot of stories,' the video continued. 'Some of them are verging on the extremely paranoid, but there's a couple I'm not sure I can discount. I keep on hearing the same story from different sources. You'll know about the Blight? Well, it's spreading. It might even be out of control now.'

The Blight? Product of Angel technology, thought Vincent. A corrosive, destructive nano-organism. The bug that ate India.

'. . . talk and more talk. But you're talking about a disaster, a global disaster, Vincent. No other way to describe it.' Vincent saw that wild look in Eddie's eyes, the same one he'd seen that time Eddie had come to visit him in Antarctica. 'Where do we go if we don't have Earth anymore? Where do we go if we manage to devastate our own world?'

Kasper, Vincent thought immediately. *Where else could we go?* A genuinely Earth-like world. Even the higher orders of life there had a DNA not far removed from that found on Earth, almost certainly thanks to the aliens everyone called Angels. It was, of course, a deeply paranoid reaction. The Blight had been a problem for decades, and wasn't likely to go away soon, but surely it wasn't about to ravage the planet? Surely things hadn't become so bad?

'All I know is that, for some people, letting the Kaspians die off wouldn't be such a bad thing because, after the radiation's passed, they'd leave behind a world free of higher-order creatures,' Eddie continued. 'Which means, in the face of this global disaster back on Earth, it would be very hard to raise any serious moral objections to turning Kasper into a human colony. Now I know,' Eddie's pixellated features spoke quickly, one hand raised, 'just how paranoid and ridiculous this sounds. But I have to consider all the options. All we can do here is raise the stakes, make people aware of it before it actually happens – if it does happen. Bring things out in the open. But keep doing what you can, Vincent. We need you out there. Do what you can.'

But how? thought Vincent. What was he supposed to do – stand in the middle of a crowded passageway and tell everybody the end of the world is coming, like some of the wild-eyed crazies in tattered pressure suits he'd already seen wandering the corridors here?

I can't even get hold of the people who run the Station. And, what do you know, I try to get hold of some of the scientists running the Kasper Deep Space Array, and the whole thing is under temporary military jurisdiction. Refer to Holmes.

Despite himself, Vincent found he believed Eddie's theories. The only bit he hadn't known about was how serious the Blight had become. Back in Antarctica, there'd been talk about how far it could spread. How bad it could get. But all the available information then seemed to suggest it was containable, within acceptable parameters. Could that information be falsified, distorted? Perhaps it could, but it seemed so symptomatic of some dizzying descent into out-and-out madness and paranoia, where everyone was your enemy, or potential enemy. Could the sheer worry of it have affected Eddie's mind?

If it had, it was now affecting Vincent's too. He decided to check the public news feeds. The service in his quarters was too limited, so he went out to a coffee bar and hit the feeds there, feeling tired and fuzzy from too little sleep.

The news feed was linked to the Grid back home by dense packet bursts fed through every time the Station's singularity was powered up. Since ships came through only a couple of times a day, it meant he was several hours behind on the most recent events, drawing instead on a localized Grid-image updated with each burst.

That was all he needed, in the end. He went looking for information about Eddie. A news item said Eddie had retired from his post, several days before. No reason given.

Vincent looked around and saw there were only a few other people about. He shook his smartsheet until it became rigid, then leaned it on one of his knees as he tapped his way through information.

I am getting very paranoid, thought Vincent, studying those few other people nearby. None of them appeared to be paying any attention to him. *Nobody here is a spy*, thought Vincent. *Nobody here is out to get you.*

Eddie sends me a note, next thing I know and he's disappeared. There was no information, on any of the mainstream news feeds, about either the Blight or Kasper, or waves of radiation, or anything. Whatever crucial news Eddie had been trying to get out about what was happening, he seemed to have failed.

Vincent did find some related stuff in other parts of the Grid, however. Some people seemed to be paying attention, but there were the usual people proclaiming the end of the world, like the Primalists and a score of other crackpot religions. That made it hard to separate hard science from irrational preaching. And didn't the Primalists preach that Kasper was the new Eden?

Vincent thought about that for a moment. Perhaps . . .

No, Vincent thought firmly. *That way madness really does lie.*

Eight

Roke

Beyond the open flap of his tent, Roke glimpsed a hunched shadow flitting between tall marsh-roots that dangled their wide leaves down to touch the ground. Hesper's Crown was low on the horizon, hanging over the distant mountain peaks to the south. He stepped to the open mouth of his tent. Two guards stood there, both wearing the distinctive jewellery that marked them out as native to the city of Roke's birth. He asked them if they'd noticed anything, knowing that if it had been anything natural out there prowling on the edges of the camp, they would have seen it too.

When they told him they'd seen nothing, Roke nodded, then told them he would be leaving camp for some minutes. He needed time to think, which meant getting away from the camp.

But Seheren, the taller of the two guards, looked worried. 'Master Roke, we were charged by the Emperor to protect you. If something happened to you, the blame would fall on us, and we'd deserve it.'

'But I am still in command, and your orders are to follow my orders, Seheren. I don't do things like this lightly, and I'll only be gone a short while. If too much time passes, certainly come looking. But I assure you that that won't be necessary.'

The expedition was, by necessity, large: a consignment of troops, plus servants, cooks, even some wives, and a small herd of icebeasts which could serve as mounts, or as a source of food, or be traded if necessary. Roke carried papers that guaranteed them safe passage through any of the cities that now formed part of Xan's Empire. But now they had crossed the Northern Sea, a journey of two or three days by sail. Roke had not relished it, being trapped on one of several tiny vessels, whose constant swaying had not been good for his health. We were meant to be land creatures, he reflected, unsuited for the open seas.

Now they were here on the far northern shores, a long way from Tibe, and it was already considerably colder than the southern climes Roke had grown used to. Although his formative years had been spent close to these shores, revisiting this region failed to bring about any kind of nostalgic glow. Instead, it seemed merely bleak and forbidding.

Leaving the camp behind, Roke started walking towards the open land fringing the marsh-roots. When a small brown canthre came sniffing after him, he shooed at it. Looking old enough to be ready for its first embedding, he could as yet detect no glint of intelligence in its eyes. It soon gave up and wandered back to the camp.

He was alone now, the lights of the camp flickering distantly through the trees. He stared after the canthre. One day, he would die, and his flesh would be fed to other such canthres in what was known as the embedding ritual. His intelligence and his soul would flow into their receptive flesh, and they would learn to walk on two legs, and to speak.

After a few moments, a shadow moved from deep between the marsh-roots and slipped forward, hunched low. Roke could see the bright intelligence burning within its eyes, as if with some fever. The Monster opened its mouth briefly, showing, again, funereal rows of pitifully small black ruined teeth.

'Whatever it is you have to say, Monster, say it now,' snapped Roke. 'I have to return to the camp.'

– Call me Sam, it said. – It is my name, after all. Do you remember what I told you about the true nature of your gods?

Roke felt a deep chill spread through his bones. 'All too well.'

– What do you know of the city of Baul?

Roke stared at the Monster. It seemed even more ethereal, even less real, in this place of cold and shadows. 'A story, a myth – the lost city of the gods, where the world was created. It's a fantasy.'

– Baul is *real*.

Roke listened intently as the creature continued.

Ursu

Ursu remembered dying: he remembered the water sucking him down. He had no memory of spilling out of the deep tunnel caves and into the open air. He had no idea how long it had been before they found him by the river's edge.

His memory was hazy. He remembered a voice calling to him, urging him to leap into the well – an insane, suicidal act. The tribesfolk who found him told him he had actually been dead, but that he had come back to life, raised by the god they had found him clutching.

His rescuers were from one of the many thousands of nomadic tribal families who criss-crossed the icy wastes extending between the great city settlements of the north. The routes they followed were sacred, the same paths taken by the migrating icebeasts since long before the time of the cities. The routes were now marked by great stone pillars dotted everywhere. Some of these tribes were better trusted by city-folk than others, but they all embellished their sparse nomadic existence by trading goods from one city to the next. These ancient trade routes wound through valleys and through mountain passes.

At first, the effigy of Shecumpeh was nowhere to be

seen. He tried to mumble the god's name to the tribes-folk tending to him, but they said nothing in reply. Whenever they did speak, it was in their own language, of which Ursu had no comprehension.

When he had first come to, bound and sightless, he had poked out his tongue. When it encountered dry, rough cloth, he realized he'd been stuffed into some kind of sack. The ropes were tight around his feet and arms. Long hours passed, giving him plenty of time to speculate in the most negative ways on what had happened to him.

It was only with nightfall that his restraints were cut away. When released, the cold summer light of Hesper's Crown dazzled his eyes with its great pearly band stretching across the horizon. When he could focus, he saw he lay in the centre of an encampment, surrounded by tents, with small open fires dotted around in the semi-dark.

Somewhere far out on the tundra, he reckoned. He looked up, and saw a series of low hills extending into the distance. They were strangely familiar. Much closer were snow-apple trees scattered over their lower slopes, sufficiently ordered to show that they had once been carefully planted in long rows. Now wild roots clung to them, and sap-leeches, and he realized this was the city orchard.

He saw several adult females nearby with their newly embedded offspring tottering upright as they learned the unaccustomed art of walking on two legs.

Unembedded canthres also darted here and there on all fours, their long snouts quivering in the cold air. A distant rushing of water indicated the Teive, which also nourished the orchard. The tribe had probably followed the course of the river for part of their never-ending journey. Some of the females came to him and tended to his wounds, all minor scrapes and bumps. They told him the story of how he had been found.

While this was happening, a couple of adult males sat by him, watching him carefully, their deep-set dark eyes glittering in the starry dusk. They sat with their traditional tribal knives – short, serrated affairs with handles made from leather dusted with baked icewort, so that the handles glittered in the night – lying handy before them, in the dust.

'Where am I?' he croaked.

'Priest?' said a voice behind him. He turned to look into a pair of wary eyes. A young female, not much older than himself. She pointed at his chest. 'Are you a priest?'

'Yes. I don't know. No.' What was he indeed? 'I used to be.'

The younger of the males barked something in his own language at the young female, who hissed something back. She turned to Ursu. 'He wants to know if you're the one the soldiers are looking for.'

Ursu fought a powerful instinct to fold his ears flat against his head. As he felt them quiver above his scalp, he flicked them alert, trying to hide the gesture of fear. 'What soldiers?'

She eyed him unbelievingly. 'You're from the city,' she said firmly, 'and you had something with you. I think those soldiers want it badly. You were lying by the river when Eif found you.' She pointed to the young male who had spoken to her.

Eif was studying him intently, an unpleasant look on his face.

Ursu asked the question uppermost in his mind. 'Can I go?'

The young female seemed to find this amusing. She turned to Eif and mumbled something to him. Eif stared at Ursu with contempt, but what was it, Ursu wondered, that brought that glint of fear into Eif's eye?

He realized she was questioning him on behalf of their whole tribe, which consisted of perhaps a little over thirty individuals of all ages, from youngest to oldest, not counting the canthres. 'But you're our guest,' said the girl, and giggled.

'What are you going to do with me?' Ursu suddenly felt defeated.

'That depends,' said the female. 'My father hopes to trade you to the soldiers. He would have done so already, but he thinks he can drive the price up. He believes the thing you carried might be the god they are looking for, and they may be stupid enough to pay a lot of money for it – and for you.'

Ursu blinked. They had Shecumpeh? 'You still have it?'

'Yes, we have your little clay god,' said the older of the two males, his ears distinctively rich with jewels. The girl's father, perhaps? So she wasn't the only who could speak in a civilized tongue.

'You . . . intend to sell it to the soldiers?'

The older male slid forward quickly, in a fluid motion. Ursu felt his ears instinctively flatten in fear, but he forced himself to keep calm. It wasn't easy. The older male nodded slightly as if he approved.

'You know, the soldiers flayed some of your priests to discover its whereabouts.'

'I don't know what's been happening.'

'You knew enough to escape with your god.' The older male leaned back on his haunches, withdrew his dagger, and held it close to one of Ursu's ears. 'Here's what we're going to do, then. You know what it signifies if I cut off one of your ears?'

Ursu nodded. It was the sign of an outcast, a criminal, and he'd never be able to find shelter or aid, not even from others in the priesthood. 'I understand,' he said.

The sound of voices rose from the edge of the camp, and Ursu heard the distant, heavy whuff of an icebeast approaching. Xan's men, Ursu realized, seeing the sudden expressions of fear around him.

'Ree, Eif.' The older male gestured at the two

younger ones. Ree? So that was her name. The older male, he was sure, must be the chieftain.

Suddenly a couple of tribesfolk scrabbled forward, pushing him down on the mat he had been sitting on, one clamping a hand over his mouth as he started to protest. After tying his limbs together again, he was unceremoniously shoved back into the same sack he had woken in. At least he was not to be handed over to Xan's army just yet.

He wriggled around in the sack for a moment, until he heard another voice, loud and aggressive, in a strange, foreign accent. Just then an additional weight thudded onto his back, pushing his snout against the ground. They'd thrown a blanket or a carpet over him, he realized.

He listened hard, the fur on his skull prickling. Everywhere, voices chattered incomprehensibly amid the sound of icebeasts snorting, snuffling and braying.

Some time later, long after the unwelcome visitors left, they let him out of the sack again. This time he blinked in early morning light. Ree was standing next to him, a knife in her hand. Eif sat again by a fire, his expression still inscrutable.

Strong hands gripped Ursu's shoulders from behind, and he was propelled into one of the tents. As he fell onto rough furs still imbued with a faintly milky, rotten smell, the older male with the jewelled ears kneeled beside him, turning his knife over and over in his free hand.

'You did good, keeping quiet like that. And I want you to understand that we don't want to harm you. But we won't let you go either.'

'If those soldiers suspect you have the god, they'll slaughter all of you and take it anyway,' Ursu said as the other got up to leave, sounding a lot braver than he actually felt. The other studied him for a long, cool moment, then shook his head.

'You Nubalans were always a pitiful lot,' he said. 'Imagine using someone like you to steal their god away to safety. Didn't they teach you anything about life outside your walls? The soldiers won't touch us. If they did, every other tribe between the ice and the sea would shun them, harass them, steal their cattle and their supplies. The tribes are greater than any army of city folk. Remember that.'

And then he left, leaving Ursu on his own. Ursu waited a few seconds, then crawled to the entrance of the tent and peered out.

Two or three pairs of watchful eyes sat within several metres of him, their owners' wickedly long knives clearly visible in the dull morning light. Ursu slowly pulled his head back inside the tent.

Ursu woke again with a start, and listened to two voices arguing. One of the voices was an incomprehensible gabble of words.

221

'I don't trust him. Why does it have to be you, any-way?'

'Shut up, Eif, and leave me alone.' The harsh reply was barely above a whisper. So Eif could speak the Nubalan tongue, Ursu realized; although he had chosen not to before.

'I'll tell Yé.'

'Go shit in your own bed,' came the reply, and then he knew it was Ree. So Yé had to be the one with the jewelled ears. A shadow fell over the door of the tent, and Ursu dropped his head back, pretending to be asleep as she came in.

'Wake up.' She kicked him hard in his side. He rolled away from her, in case the knife was next. Instead she knelt to set a plate of desiccated fruit on the furs where he had slept.

'I heard you arguing with your boyfriend,' he wheezed.

He was pleased to see the spark of anger in her eyes. 'Eif is a worm-headed idiot,' she said. 'He stinks worse than you do, and he tries to touch my fur when nobody's looking. I told him I'd cut him, but he still won't leave me alone. Not that you care. They'll soon sell you to Xan.' The girl stared at him wildly, then ran out.

He drifted into sleep after a while, more from bore-dom than fatigue. He had given up watching his guards, whose attention seemed unwavering.

The orchard was ripped apart, blasted, dark.

Immediately he knew that Shecumpeh was with him, and he tried to turn, not knowing what he would see. The same small clay statue sitting in the dirt? For some reason, that thought frightened him.

– *Turn*, Shecumpeh seemed to say. – *Turn and face me*. The voice was like the milky smell of the ragged furs beneath his cheek, like the pale light of Hesper's Crown reflecting off the irises of an icebeast, like the scent of his mother's fur when he would wake in the night, the gift of knowledge still lingering as an aftertaste on his tongue.

No. I can't.

– Turn and face me.

He turned to face Shecumpeh.

There was a brief glimpse of something terrible, monstrous, withered and scarred. A mouthful of broken teeth, and eyes that glinted with enormous intelligence within a face like nothing Ursu had ever before imagined.

Then Ursu descended into a dense mist, sparkling with light.

Not mist, stars, he realized, not understanding where this awareness came from. Some invisible force was dragging him at tremendous speed through the stars . . . through Hesper's Crown itself, a voice explained, in that same language of images and sensations.

Am I in heaven? Ursu wondered. No answer came, but it was the most beautiful thing he had ever seen.

There were whirlpools of smoky gas, great pillars of dust that rose around him like mountains, seeming to stretch from one end of eternity to the next, stars burning red deep within them.

He tried to find his fingers, but realized his body had simply vanished, like morning mist. He was awareness and thought only, drifting through . . . through . . .

The images came faster, and somehow Ursu knew what they meant, what he was being shown. He saw Nubala, as if he was a glider bird, high in the clouds, looking down on it. Nubala fell farther away below him, in seconds, his world becoming a great orb. He saw seas, rivers and great mountains laid out below him, all so fast he could barely comprehend. Then even that sight fell away below him.

He saw the blazing sun, his world now a little ball flying around it. Then that fell away too, and he was back amid the light of Hesper's Crown. For an instant, he saw his world and the star it circled as tiny motes, less even than that, floating in the majesty of innumerable stars.

His perspective then appeared to rotate, and he felt fear at what he might see next. But, understanding came, from nowhere – as if he was simply an empty vessel, and knowledge and comprehension were being poured into him.

There was something beyond the stars of Hesper's Crown; no, inside it. A light, a terrible light, an explosion of furious, incandescent energy.

There – a tiny mote upon the face of that light. Something small and dark, floating there in the vastness of the heavenly firmament.

He floated closer to it, staring, seeing . . .

– This is where the killing light comes from, Shecumpeh informed him. – It was sent by creatures like gods, yet not gods. All that lives, from one end of the universe to the other, is their enemy. So they seek to destroy your kind and mine.

But what is it? asked Ursu, and though the words had only half formed in his mind, the answer came.

– Think of it as a kind of reconnaissance. Your gods – or those who created them – trapped those inimical to life deep within Hesper's Crown. There are ways to contain them there, far from natural life forms, in a place where no true life could possibly exist. But they are now using the stars of Hesper's Crown as a weapon. They can destroy stars in a way that makes them radiate the killer light that is currently racing towards your world.

The creature I saw? thought Ursu. He was hovering over the world now and he could again see the Great Northern Sea far below him. *Are you Shecumpeh? Is that what you look like?*

– I am not Shecumpeh.

Then what are you?

Ursu looked down to see the lands that lay beyond the northernmost Teive Mountains. Something black and massive sprawled there, like a canker.

– The gods are not gods, said the voice. – Look below. Do you see that city beyond the mountains?

Ursu could see the canker-like shape more clearly now. It was unlike anything he might have recognized as a city.

– That is Baul.

Baul is a legend, thought Ursu. *Isn't it?*

– No, said the voice. – It is real, and you must go there.

Nobody can go there, Ursu protested in his thoughts. Not beyond those mountains.

– Nonetheless, you must, said the voice. – You must go to Baul.

The visions suddenly faded – along with the voice.

Ursu smelled him even before he opened his eyes again.

A totem-reader, although Ursu did not realize that at first.

He was old, his fur patchy, his ears badly mutilated with poorly healed wounds. He wore brightly coloured rags, however, and Ursu was sure he detected a glint of madness in the old one's eyes. Ursu froze still where he lay, watching as the old one squatted down on his haunches, staring at him intently.

He had the god, the effigy of Shecumpeh, cradled in his arms. But something was different about it, and Ursu stared at it, trying to work out what.

There was a crack running across the body of the effigy, and something shiny glinted deep within.

The totem-reader barked something at him. 'I don't understand,' protested Ursu.

More nonsense syllables; the old one appeared to be agitated. Ursu lifted himself up slowly, wishing Ree or even Eif were there to translate the mad old fool's ranting.

'Make it speak!' the old one shrieked, his words suddenly comprehensible. 'Make it speak!'

Ursu didn't know what to say. And then he realized . . . something had happened to him while he slept. As the totem-reader's lips moved, the words that came out of the old one's mouth were more of the incomprehensible tribal gabble Ursu had no understanding of. Nonetheless, he found he understood the old one perfectly.

'I don't know how to make him speak,' he said carefully.

More nonsense syllables followed, that somehow translated into meaning in Ursu's mind. But not words themselves, he thought, just meaning, comprehension. The old one was asking him if he came from Nubala, though he pronounced it like a foreigner.

'Yes, I'm from Nubala.'

The old one's ears were cocked towards Ursu. And then it dawned on him: *I can understand what he's saying, but he can't understand me.*

The totem-reader spat out another jumble of words, but Ursu just stared back at him, tired and weary. The old one twitched his ears and bared his teeth, then retreated out through the flap of the tent.

They came for him again a few hours later.

He'd heard increasing whispers from outside as dusk began to fall. The food provided earlier hadn't been enough to sustain him, and a powerful hunger filled his gut. He heard something that sounded like their word for Nubala, and some other words that they spoke in hushed tones. Even though he could not quite make out what was being said, he heard two words repeated over and over. *Shai*. Again, *Shai* – the word always spoken in a harsh whisper. The other word was Fidhe.

Shai? In Nubala, of course, the Shai were the mythical Pale Ghosts, the icy white phantoms that roamed the ice in stories and legends.

Suddenly Ursu heard the rapid movement of leather-clad feet across the icy grass outside. Then his two guards burst in, seizing him by the arms while a third came up behind him and slid a bag over his head, pulling it tight behind him so that his protests were reduced to a slurring mumble. Cold air nipped his fur-clad flesh as Ursu was suddenly thrust out into the open air. He struggled desperately, convinced they were about to kill him.

He hit the ground hard, feeling heat near his face. The bag was wrenched off his head after a few minutes, and smoke stung his eyes, flavouring the air with its thick scent. He peered into half-darkness and realized he was now in a much bigger tent, with a hole at the top

228

through which drifted much of the smoke from a great central fire of dried grasses. Perhaps the entire tribe surrounded him, facing towards the fire, conversing in low mumbles. But there was no mistaking the sounds of pain from some of the tribesfolk, stretched out on furs.

There were more tribesfolk than he'd previously realized. And Ursu recognized the smell of Blackface fever. When he was very young, two of his uncles as well as his brother had died of it. His skin now crawled, wanting to be far away from the source of it.

Yé knelt by him, stared into his eyes. 'Tell me that your god is real.' There was a curious urgency in his voice.

'Our god?' said Ursu. 'Shecumpeh is the soul of Nubala.' He remembered the most recent vision, where the voice had declared it was in fact *not* Shecumpeh. It had also declared that the gods were not gods. But that didn't make sense. If the gods weren't truly gods . . . then what were they? And what had spoken to him?

'Without it, you are nothing,' Yé paraphrased the sacred lines. Ursu licked his lips nervously. Yé was perhaps no stupid barbarian after all. 'You stole away the god of Nubala, and your fellow citizens would, I'm sure, be delighted if we skinned you alive for doing what you've done to them.'

'It's not so simple,' protested Ursu.

'I don't believe you. You're a thief, the lowest of the low, and your ears should be sliced off. You should be cast out onto the ice, for the Shai to eat.'

'Shecumpeh is real,' insisted Ursu. 'I told you I was escaping because Shecumpeh commanded me to take him to safety.'

'I need you to do a Raising.' Yé spoke with a new authority, which reminded Ursu of Uftheyan's voice.

'Why should I help you?'

Yé glared at him, and Ursu eyed the long, tribal knife clutched in one clawed fist.

'You're a city priest who's never known real toil, who's never understood what it means just to survive from day to day, or to be responsible for the lives of so many others. But I don't have any choice in what I must do.' He now spoke in a low semi-whisper, as if he didn't want the others to hear. 'I need you to help us.'

Ursu stared at him for a long moment. 'I can't agree to anything unless I know you'll let me take the god to safety.'

'I can't let you take the god,' said Yé carefully, 'but I'll let you yourself go. I swear it. But you will never have the god.'

'You'll let me go?'

'You, yes, but not the god. That belongs to us now – or to Xan, if negotiations are satisfactory. I'll fetch it back to you for the Raising ceremony alone.' Yé put one hand on Ursu's shoulder. 'I am asking for your help, boy. You're a priest, and are bound by holy practice to assist any who ask for your help.'

Unfortunately that was all damnably, sadly true. Ursu had been brought up by rules ingrained in his mind from the first day he had set foot inside the House of Shecumpeh, as a barely sentient acolyte still learning to walk on two legs, but that House was far away now and nothing but a smoking ruin. He might well be the last surviving priest of the House of Shecumpeh, and it was not a happy thought.

I have carried Shecumpeh this far, he thought. *If I don't obey the Rule of Assistance, then why even contemplate carrying him farther?* But he instinctively didn't want to help them, would rather leave them to rot with their foul smells and worse manners.

'Listen,' said Ursu, 'if I tend to these tribesfolk,' he pointed to those lying sick in the smoke-filled tent, 'it is solely with the power of Shecumpeh that I restore them to health. You understand that much?'

Yé nodded.

'Shecumpeh is our god, and has brought me here for a reason – perhaps even to help you. But when Shecumpeh heals these people, it is because *he* has chosen to, not you. And when you see the power of the god of Nubala, you would be well advised to be humble towards that which you have kidnapped, for legend warns that Shecumpeh, when affronted, is a god of righteous wrath and anger.'

Yé stared at him. 'Are you saying that Shecumpeh brought this Blackface plague to us?'

Ursu hadn't thought of that.

'Perhaps. And perhaps he has decided now to be

merciful by allowing me to help you. But you will have to give me the effigy if I'm to perform a Raising.'

Yé's left ear twitched with a life of its own, a rapid, insect-like flicking. Ursu suspected he wasn't aware of it doing so. 'We'll speak of that later,' said Yé. 'Assist them first.'

Ursu sighed and stepped towards the first of the sick.

Kim

'Calm down. Take it easy.'

'I'm not mad at you, Bill, I just need to know more about those Books. You have to tell me.'

'Come on, Kim,' said Bill, 'you know I can't. The people . . . see, where I get things from, I don't just get them one at a time. They get hold of lots of different things, and I keep my mouth shut so they don't lose their jobs. And some of them . . .' He sighed. 'Let's just say they'd be extremely unhappy if they thought I'd betrayed them.'

She stared at him for a long moment, and he flinched.

She cocked her head, curious. 'What's up with you?'

'I – nothing,' he said. 'Just like—'

'What?'

He shrugged, laughed. 'I don't know. Like someone else was looking at me, through your eyes, you know? Weirdest damn thing.' He shrugged, smiled gamely.

'Bill. Listen carefully. Are you listening carefully?'

'I'm listening, Kim.'

'You don't have the bioware, so you don't know what it's like to take one of those Books. It's not just happy memories or family snapshots in 3D. It's complete immersion in another person's mind: everything they feel, whatever they see, how they react to it.'

'I thought you were able to move around, and stuff, of your own free will. That's more than just a memory, though, isn't it?'

Kim closed her eyes for a moment, then reopened them. 'Yes, you can. You yourself can interact, just a little bit. You can explore, but you're just exploring someone's memories. Except if you do that too much, some of it will be coming from you, not from them. That's what it's like, Bill' – she raised one finger, as if signalling for attention – 'if you eat a Book made from human memories.'

'Ah.' Bill nodded sagely. He'd heard of such things: animal memories, stuff like that. 'Run with the wolves, that kind of thing.' Then comprehension kicked in. 'You're talking about those Books I gave you. So what happened?'

'Listen, Bill,' Kim licked her lips, 'you said anything's addictive.' Bill nodded slowly and she continued. 'That's sort of true, but I don't have that kind of need. I have a specific aim. Do you understand what I'm saying? Addicts don't think things through, then go out to deliberately become an addict. Because that's what I did. I set out deliberately to do what I've been doing. But something happened when I ate one of those Books you gave me. I . . . I almost can't find the words to describe it. I need you to tell me the name of the person who found them.'

Bill shook his head slowly. 'Kim, I already told you I can't do that.'

'Yes, you can, Bill, or I don't say anything about what happened. You'll have to try someone else if you want to find that out.'

Bill looked pained, stared at her for a long moment. 'Okay,' he sighed. 'It was Pasquale. Word's been getting out, anyway.'

Pasquale. He'd been running his tiny one-man ship through the asteroid fields of the Kasper system longer than anyone else Kim had ever met. She felt good for him, as he was getting old, needed to retire. With a big find like the one Bill had described, Pasquale could end his days in luxury.

'I ate the Book, okay?' Bill nodded for her to go on. 'I was somewhere else. I mean beyond space and time, somewhere else.' She could see Bill had no idea what she was talking about. The words somehow weren't right: language wasn't adequate to describe what she'd seen, what had happened to her. 'I felt as if I lived for a billion years, and I fell right outside the universe' – she winced involuntarily, having been avoiding thinking of that deep, terrible abyss – 'and finally something came to me and spoke to me – but not in words. And then I was back here.' She wasn't ready to talk about the horrors of the Citadel.

Bill's shoulders heaved in a sigh, and he leaned forward and carefully clasped her hands in his. 'Kim, I think, in all seriousness, you have been out in that Goblin for far, far too long without any company.'

She swatted his hands angrily. 'I am *not* crazy! I'm *not* joking, Bill. I saw things, things that sort of spoke to me, that went through my head, that were—'

Alien?

She leaned back in her seat, suddenly silent, a coldness welling up in her.

'Pasquale,' she said, her voice suddenly small. Her eyes drifted far away for a moment. 'You said he found Angel Books. Right?'

'Sure.'

'You were right, Bill. I think I saw inside an Angel's head – or something like that.'

Bill shook his head. 'I gotta be honest with you, I didn't think there was anything at all in those things. But somebody wanted me to find out in case it turned out to be lucrative. You sure you saw all this stuff?'

Kim stared at him for several long seconds. 'Yes, I am,' she said quietly. 'What else did Pasquale find?'

'Did you feel that?'

Tomason glanced towards the security door, then at the monitors that showed what was behind the door.

She had been thinking about the artefacts. In several weeks of research, she and her research team had come to two conclusions: the blue glow of the artefacts was an unknown form of radiation, and it was the by-product of some internalized power source. In other words, they didn't know anything.

She looked over to her co-researcher. Lindsey was staring at her with a frown.

'I didn't feel anything . . . Oh, there it is.' There had been a faint tremor. Or was there?

'Could be a blow-out,' said Lindsay nervously. She had the corner of her bottom lip pinched between her teeth.

Tomason shook her head. 'Not a blow-out. Every siren on the Station would have gone off if that happened.'

'But I did feel that. Did you feel it?'

'I did.' She glanced towards a large-sized smartsheet, this one wall-mounted. They'd turned the sound down low, and left it running on the default settings. A montage of images from one of the news channels played across it, the Station's own standard text feed running below that. Nothing looked out of the ordinary. All seemed normal.

'It was probably nothing.' Tomason looked back towards the steel door. Could it be the artefacts?

'I'm going to take a quick look.' Tomason went over to the rack where they kept the lab suits and pulled one on, now peering out at Lindsey's alarmed face from behind a plastic visor.

'Hold on a minute,' said Lindsey. 'You really think the tremor came from those things?'

'One way to find out.'

Tomason had been running old records of other major technology finds, looking for clues, any correlation. She despaired at the amount of information that was still classified, and had already put in for clearance – how else could she do her job? – but had been warned the process could take months. By then, the artefacts would likely have been shipped through the singularity to somewhere with real facilities.

The steel door was merely the entry to an original airlock. Beyond the airlock was a hastily bolted-on accommodation unit converted into a makeshift lab for studying and storing the artefacts Pasquale had stumbled across. Tomason looked back at her co-researcher's worried face and hit the button that opened the main door. After a few seconds it lurched open with a dull, bass click, and she stepped through. She hit the button on the inside so that it clicked shut behind her, then repeated the process with the door on the far side of the airlock.

At first, nothing looked out of the ordinary.

The artefacts had been stored on steel shelves, with half a dozen cameras studying them constantly from every possible angle.

There were also instruments to monitor vibration,

temperature, sound and the entire electromagnetic spectrum. So far, the artefacts had done nothing to draw attention. With her limited resources, Tomason had thus been reduced to being really not much more than a glorified caretaker, until they could be shipped out.

Noticing one of the artefacts was missing, she frowned. Then she saw a shadow flit against the far wall. Something scuttered out of sight. An icy shiver ran down the length of her spine.

She realized the far wall was rippling and she froze, waiting. The steel wall of the lab was undulating very softly, like a bedsheet flapping gently in a summer's breeze. She backed away slowly, realizing she had no idea if her contam suit would be of any use in a vacuum, if the wall suddenly ripped open. Not likely. She thumbed the door switch without looking and counted the long, long seconds before she could slip back through it.

Nine

Pasquale

Pasquale could not sleep.

When he dreamed, mostly he dreamed of the blue light from the artefacts that had seemed to seep through his body, even, he imagined, his soul. He came from a long line of Chilean Catholics and often, as he slept, his hand would reflexively reach out to the tiny silver cross he wore around his neck. This had been his one personal trait that had remained endearing to his ex-wife during the turbulent two years of their marriage. Shortly after a less than amicable break-up, he had blown all his savings and a lucky gambling streak commencing a life in the stars.

During the four subsequent years he had spent in a cramped, second-hand Goblin amid the asteroid fields of the Kaspian system, it had often occurred to him he might actually have been better off continuing to work the nightshift back in Chile: humdrum tele-operating work for some conglomerate. The work had involved peering through goggles while a four-wheeled robot trundled through Blight-devastated Indian villages and towns, looking for anything salvageable. After three months in that Goblin, he had come to the weary conclusion that the only reason living humans were needed inside the Goblins was to decide what went wrong in case of instrument failure. Assuming they weren't killed by that same failure.

The gambling streak had proved the one occasion in his life when he'd been really lucky, and he hadn't expected that to happen a second time.

His training in operating the Goblin had taken a little under two weeks, but most of that had involved emergency procedures: how to signal to the Station or the nearest ship that there was a problem. There was also idiot stuff, like don't open the hatch when you're in deep space, but apparently it had happened. Pasquale suspected that wasn't always unintentional. Most of the other people he'd met wanting to be Goblin pilots were crazy or twisted in some way, or clearly just looking to disappear for a while.

But when the Goblin's sensors had zoomed in on the underside of a certain crater, somehow some sixth sense told Pasquale he'd struck lucky a second time in his life.

The crater had been located on a ferrous asteroid travelling on a highly elliptical, wildly eccentric orbit that the astronomers said had probably looped around Kasper's sun for most of forever before finally being sucked into Doran's gravity well probably not long before the arrival of humanity. It was sliding closer and closer to the planet's surface, so in maybe another year it wouldn't be there. The weirdest thing was that the rock had been surveyed before, yet nothing had turned up.

Every week or so the Station authorities beamed out to all the Goblins a list of rocks viable for investigation – meaning stuff, usually, that they had finally assigned a category number, or that had only just turned up on standard telescope sweeps. After that, it was up to one-self. Pasquale had found himself by chance only several million kilometres away from this particular rock, so decided to skip opening the airlock hatch for another day and take a looksee. Just for the hell of it.

He really hadn't expected to find anything.

At first it looked like he'd found your standard ferrous space-borne rock: the usual ratios of iron, nickel and cobalt. Pasquale had been tapping this info into an operational database when a light started blinking on the Goblin's systems board. Oh, happy day.

His discovery glowed with a strange light. At first he'd assumed it was radioactive, but everything on board the Goblin said no. So he brought it in, and studied it. Machinery? Pasquale wasn't big on imagin-ation and finding himself in another solar system on the other side of the galaxy hadn't seemed that big a deal somehow. But for the first time since his lucky gambling bonanza, Pasquale got excited.

There had been other stuff beside the machinery,

including a frozen block of something that got the scientific types orgasmic. None of this much interested Pasquale, but he knew how much it was worth.

Pasquale could not sleep, so instead he got up. Like Kim, and most of the people who found themselves living on the Angel Station, his home was tiny, barely large enough to stand up straight and stretch out your arms. There were cheaper quarters available, literally coffin-sized, that you could only slide into horizontally, and some people seemed to be happy enough with that. But Pasquale – who had once seriously considered a life as a professional poker player – relied on a pack of cards to keep himself afloat when all else failed.

This was one of the Quiet Times. Shift patterns were synchronized to match day and night back on Earth, and that meant there were periods of each daily cycle when the numbers of people in the twisting corridors were far fewer. Pasquale drifted downwards until he came to one of the spots where the raw construction material of the Station was allowed to show through all the human-added units clinging to the alien torus like some hi-tech mould. He got a kick out of touching the raw surface of the Station, although he couldn't say why. And if he'd ever been asked, he'd feel uncomfortable, maybe get a little angry.

But deep down he knew he was touching something old, *really* old. Other hands had once touched this, or something like hands. Hands that never saw blue skies or tasted Chilean peppers or eyed sweet-bodied hookers during long wild nights in the favelas on the outer edge of town.

He reached down to touch the alien stuff. It felt warm.

Something dropped to the ground behind him. Pasquale froze, then looked round. Nothing there except something that looked like a child's toy.

But it wasn't a toy. It got up, waved tiny feelers at him, and scuttled on its little metal legs over towards the exposed Angel material.

It sank into the raw fabric like a rock dropped into mud. The Station stuff flowed over it, absorbing it whole.

Without thinking, Pasquale reached up and touched the tiny crucifix hanging around his neck. He glanced about and saw more of the things – insects? Machines? – drop from a rip in the wall of the corridor which he could have sworn wasn't there a few moments before. They too headed straight for the Angel material, ignoring him.

Pasquale fled, heading to the higher levels, never looking behind him.

If he'd had the words to describe his feelings at that point, he'd have mentioned a feeling of primordial dread. He wanted to go hide himself in a cave somewhere, and the Goblin was a good enough substitute.

Kim

Kim found Pasquale packing his stuff. He looked like he was heading out for the long haul.

'Joseph,' she began, standing at the open door to his cabin. The old man jumped as if a ghost had tapped him on the shoulder. He turned and regarded her with wide, frightened eyes, then seemed to will himself to relax.

Pasquale looked the same as he always did, old before his time. 'Kim, good to see you.' He was fingering the tiny cross that nestled against his breastbone. The lights were dim behind him as he came forward, but in the semi-darkness she could see a whole host of Catholic paraphernalia: a crying Jesus, and postcards depicting the Pope in what looked like some South American city. 'How you been?'

'The usual,' she lied. 'I heard you got lucky.'

'Yeah, well, here's hoping my luck holds out.' Pressure cases lay on the tiny bunk behind him, one or two of them half-open, with clothes and personal belongings spilling out of them. 'I'm going back out for a while.'

'I heard you—'

'You hear a lot of stuff in this place,' he said, a little too abruptly. Then he signed. 'Look, sorry, but . . . you seen anything strange round the Station recently?'

Kim looked puzzled. 'Like what?'

Pasquale picked up one of the cases and moved towards her.

She stepped aside, for the first time noticing a luggage palette sitting across the corridor, stuff already piled onto it. He walked over to it, lugged the case on top, then turned. 'Like, like . . . bugs, you know what I mean?'

She stared at him. 'No, I don't know what you mean. You mean insects? Something escaped from the hydroponics? But that happens all the time, right?' His obvious anxiety was infecting her now.

'No, not like that. Like . . .' He smacked his forehead with an open palm. 'Like little silver bugs, is what it is. They look like insects, 'xcept when you get close to them, well, they don't.'

'Pasquale, I don't have a clue what you're talking about. What look like *what* close up?'

'Like your worst nightmare,' he breathed. 'I know, 'cause I seen them. I've been telling people about them, but they don't believe me. See, I was just out seeing a friend, he jockeys stuff all over the Station from the outside, gets bits of scrap and sells it on, right? He's an engineer. He's seen them too, on the outside of the Angel Station. Little silver bugs.'

'I've never noticed anything like that.'

'Lady, I hope you never will. Listen, you want my advice, sign up for anything going and get the hell out of here.'

She shook her head. 'I have some things to sort out. I heard you found something really special out there. I need to talk to you about it.'

'The Angel stuff?' he said. She nodded. 'If that's what it actually is,' he continued. 'I don't know, I just found stuff. So maybe I'm a rich man, I don't know.' He walked past her, grabbed another case and hauled it over to the palette. 'They won't let me go back through the singularity for "security reasons".' He put extra sarcasm into the words. 'And trust me, I don't feel too safe staying here right now. So that leaves just one place, and that's out *there*,' he said, stabbing a finger at the corridor ceiling.

'You're really worried about this, aren't you?'

'Kim, when I see little silver insects running around when they don't even have any right existing, I get very worried.'

'But what about security – Mayor Pierce or the Commander? Surely—?'

'I tried all that, but they've got some kind of emergency on, and I'll take a big bet it's got something to do with little silver bugs. Seems they don't want to talk to me or anybody else.'

Well, thought Kim, *I guess I know where I'm going next.*

'So you're just upping sticks and heading out?'

Pasquale came up close to her and put one hand on her shoulder, making sure to look her right in the eyes. 'Kim, I like you, really. I'm not crazy, and I don't think aliens are beaming signals into my head or anything. But some very weird shit has been going on around here the past day or two. So take my advice, be a good girl, and get the fuck out of here while you still can.'

'Something weird happened to me already, Pasquale. I think it had something to do with those things you discovered, maybe. I'm not sure.'

Pasquale just shook his head. 'Nothing to do with me anymore. I gave it all to the science bods, and I'm just waiting for 'em to credit my accounts with the rest of the money they promised me. In the meantime' – he shrugged – 'take care of yourself, Kim. But don't say I didn't warn you.'

Sam Roy

He almost didn't recognize Matthew when he saw him. He was different in some undefinable way. And then Sam realized: he'd mistaken Matthew for his father.

Whenever Sam reached the top of the steep path leading to the top of the cliff, he found food and water left on a shelf within a stone cairn that had been built specifically for that purpose. He ate and drank what he could as fast as possible, knowing time would be short. While he did so, he could look around.

The plateau stretched for a couple of miles, a high rocky shelf with a steep slope. From space, the Teive Mountains looked like a double row of teeth, a narrow valley lying between the two chains, which broadened out two or three hundred kilometres further east, before the land dropped towards the sea and became an island chain.

On the eastern flank of the plateau stood New Coventry, the name Vaughn had picked for their settlement. A dozen narrow streets, with a tiny town square paved with blocks of dark marble. Beyond that, the plateau fell rapidly away to steep cliffs. On the other side of the town, and below the cliffs there, were situated the deep caves Vaughn intended to hide in, along with everybody else, when the radiation came.

'Who's watching us?' asked Sam as Matthew came up to him, his face partly hidden behind the fur trim of a parka.

'I've got someone I can trust on duty today,' said Matthew. It had been several years since they had last spoken to each other. The boy Sam remembered was gone. There was bitterness and anger on the face of the man who had replaced him, and a narrow scar ran along the edge of his jaw.

'I don't believe your father's suddenly become so complacent,' said Sam. 'Perhaps you've forgotten what happened last time?'

'I haven't forgotten,' snapped Matthew. 'I'm sorry,' he said, his tone softer. 'I'm a little nervous.'

'If he had any idea we're speaking to each other, he'd kill you. And I wouldn't be so lucky.'

'He doesn't have any idea. He's caught up in preparations for . . . for what's going to happen.' The shadow of a smile crossed Matthew's face, then vanished in the darkness under his parka's hood. 'You know what he calls it? God's Holy Light.'

'Matthew, you'd better tell me what you need to tell me, then get out of here, for your own sake. He only let you live as an example. Remember that.'

'I hadn't forgotten. Don't underestimate me, Sam. I know what I'm doing now. There's nothing like the desire for revenge to get you motivated.'

How true, thought Sam. How true.

Sam glanced behind Matthew. 'You've brought the truck with you. Are you taking me back down the slope?'

Matthew grinned this time, and Sam saw a brief shadow of the boy he remembered. 'As far as you're concerned, I'm Luke.' Luke was one of Vaughn's most trusted soldiers. 'So yeah, I'm taking you down.'

Sam was suitably thunderstruck. 'What happened to Luke?'

Matthew's grin got wider. 'Let's just say Luke's not been quite the good little Primalist that Vaughn thought he was.' Matthew glanced at him curiously. 'You mean you didn't foresee that? I thought you could foresee everything.'

'The general events, yes; the specific details not so often, but sometimes. I know how most things are going to turn out, but the exact mechanism isn't always clear.'

'Well, anyway, Luke's going to do what *I* tell him

from now on, because if Dad ever has any idea what he's been up to, Luke is a dead man.'

'So what should I say next time I see him? Luke, I mean?'

Matthew shrugged. He gestured at the truck – a large, prefab snowmobile with an open trailer behind it – and walked towards it. Sam watched as he climbed into the truck's cabin and reversed it next to where Sam stood with the great stone ball.

'Here, let me help you,' said Matthew, flipping down the tailboard of the trailer. He started to lay his hands on the stone.

'No, don't,' said Sam hurriedly. He grappled with the sides of the stone, heaving and pushing until it rolled up the dropped down tailboard and into the trailer. Matthew had stepped back, looking slightly puzzled. 'It's just . . . a personal thing,' said Sam, not sure why he'd felt so uncomfortable with it. 'I need to do it myself.' *Because I've forgotten how to be any other way?* Sam wondered. *How strange.*

Sam hunkered down by the stone. 'So what do you intend to do now, Matthew?'

'Tell me, Sam. You're the one who can see so much. Can you really see so much more of the future than my father?'

'Of course,' said Sam. 'That's why he's happier with me well out of the way of the rest of you.'

Matthew stood by the open trailer, his hands stuffed deep into the pockets of his parka, against the bitter, freezing cold. 'But he doesn't kill you – or take you somewhere really far away, where nobody could ever find you.'

'We've been over this already, Matthew, a long time ago.'

'Because he's terrified of you. Because if he can't see you—'

'And he can't kill me either.'

'He could drop you in a volcano?'

'Careful there, Matthew. You don't want him getting any ideas. He doesn't because he knows he won't. He can see that much. He can see *me* there, at the end. His greatest talent lies elsewhere.'

'The far-casting.'

'Yes, he can do it across astonishing distances, you know.'

'Tell me what's going to happen.'

Sam shook his head. 'I won't do that. Trust me, Matthew, there are some things you're better off not knowing about until you get there.'

'Then we need to talk – about the Plan.'

'So you'll help me? Help me make it happen?'

'My God, yes,' said Matthew, fervour filling his voice. 'I want to hurt him so badly, Sam.'

'Take me back down now. Do we have enough time to talk once we're there?'

'A little while, yes. There are things you should know. He found something inside the Citadel . . . some kind of reproductive machine. I think he's intending to use it against the Station up there.'

'Angel tech?'

'Yeah. Sometimes I hear things, even things Dad doesn't want me to know about. You know how most of the shuttles had their orbital capacity disabled? He put one back together, a while back.'

'Who went off planet?' asked Sam.

'I'm not sure anybody did. I think it was done by remote – like he meant to plant something up there.'

Matthew pushed the tailboard back up and locked it in place. Sam watched clouds drifting between the distant mountain peaks as Matthew ferried him back to the bottom of the path.

Ten

Vincent

It had been some years since Vincent had experienced zero gravity. Okay, not quite zero gravity, since the exotic material the Station was constructed of had a tiny, almost imperceptible pull, but it was close to zero. He was here for a purpose, but he knew he needed an ally. Except the last time he'd encountered anyone who seemed like a potential ally, she'd run away from him as fast as she could.

There were maybe several dozen children on board the Station. At first he'd assumed they were all here with their families, but one or two had this weirdly feral look about them that made him wonder. When they propelled themselves through the tunnels, they did so in a way that brought the words *animal grace* to mind. They literally sailed through and around the crowds of adults all around them. He saw one girl, in a heavily customized jump-suit, work a kind of corkscrew pattern through a roughly circular tunnel with plenty of hand-holds, using them to boost herself up to an astonishing

253

speed. She had flickered past Vincent in the blink of an eye.

Vincent watched them carefully. He'd always been a fast learner.

He'd never understood what it meant to feel power-less until now. He'd managed to speak to Commander Holmes on just two occasions, each time catching him briefly outside of his office. Holmes had listened with patience for a few moments, clearly distracted, before excusing himself by saying they were in the middle of an emergency. The armed soldiers accompanying him had made it clear that a few moments was exactly as long as Vincent was going to get. Holmes hadn't reacted the way Vincent had hoped.

Vincent had certainly noticed an increased presence of armed military in the corridors over the past forty-eight hours. Something was clearly up. The problem was, every time he tried to speak to someone, anyone, he sounded completely crazy. *The end of the world is coming!*

It was surprisingly difficult to get through to even the scientists on board, and it became depressingly clear the Station lay on a kind of interstellar lunatic's highway of seers and prophets, all inflicting their own religious visions on their fellow Station-dwellers. The problem was the absence of Eddie. Eddie had clout. If Eddie had been here, it would be impossible to ignore him. He could pull too many strings, knew too many people for that to happen.

If only Eddie had been here.

So Vincent spent time watching children shooting down the corridors like bullets down the barrel of a gun, sometimes several moving at once, their bodies describing a peculiar airborne ballet as they sailed by.

It was another few days before he saw Kim again. This time he wasn't going to lose her. Once more, she was at the far end of a crowded corridor, at a kind of nexus where several gutted hulls had been welded together to create a kind of pedestrian highway. Vincent had practised a little during the Quiet Time. He kicked himself effortlessly up in the air, and slapped both his feet off a cushioned projection with a thump. This sent him sailing forward, and he grabbed another handhold to propel himself forward even faster.

He'd been worried about crashing into people, but they moved out of his way without seeming entirely aware he was there, so he needn't have worried. Kim looked up and spotted him, an alarmed expression appearing on her face. *It's been years and she still looks beautiful*, thought Vincent.

She didn't try to run away. *How do I stop now?* thought Vincent, panicking. It had been easy during the Quiet Time, when he'd had near-empty corridors to practise in. Then he'd sort of skidded to a halt, braking himself by bumping along the walls until he could grab on to something. *She's definitely not going to run away this time*, he realized with alarm. In fact, she looked rooted to the spot. *What's going to happen when I get to her?*

He found out a few seconds later, as she ducked.

He hit the wall behind her hard enough to hear a faint ringing in his ears, finally ending up in an ungainly pile at her feet. The inhabitants of the Station seemed to have an uncanny ability to avoid airbound astrophysicists. People just cut around him, many casting amused and slightly superior glances. He blinked, and thought, *Hope I didn't hit my head too hard.*

'Vincent! For God's sake, are you all right?'

Kim pulled him to his feet. 'I thought you were going to run away from me,' he said, feeling a little unsteady. She looked away from him for a moment, then turned back just as he was about to speak again.

'Don't say anything. I know,' she said quickly. 'Really, I know. I just panicked when I first saw you.'

'I'll have to admit I did wonder why—'

'Things have been difficult,' she interrupted tersely. 'I'm sure you understand.' He did, all too well, and it hadn't changed his opinion of her one bit. He'd been entirely aware of the pressures on her. 'So,' she said, with what sounded to Vincent like false levity, 'what brings you all the way out here?'

At last, someone he could talk to.

Elias

On the surface, the Angel Station seemed the focus for a cross-political power-sharing. This was a way of guaranteeing that no one nation held absolute power over any one Angel Station, and thereby gaining potentially unlimited military superiority through any Angel tech discovered. Which was the reason, Elias had discovered, why security gave every appearance of being incredibly tight, enough so as to make him feel nervous.

He was therefore reassured, upon further enquiry, to discern high levels of corruption just below the well-polished, regimented surface. His introduction to Bill, by Eduardez, had indeed proved only the tip of the iceberg.

It had been years since Elias had last worn a space-suit. He had a plan already worked out in his head, and the closer he got to his goal, the more excited he felt. He breathed deeply, staring out through the curving glass of his helmet, calming himself, focusing. He reached out, touched a button. A door slid open just in front of him. Somewhere, Elias could hear a hissing, something like a brief whisper or a sharp intake of breath, then he was in vacuum. He waited to see if anything went wrong, but there was nothing but silence. He gazed beyond the open airlock door and saw only blackness.

A radio crackled. 'Hey, Murray, you there?' It was Eduardez.

*

A few days earlier, Eduardez had shown him an external view of the *Jager*. The photograph was blurry, out of focus. 'Aren't they going to realize the instant someone comes near?'

'Sure, but the point is making certain they think you're a friend, not foe,' explained Eduardez. 'They got guys buzzing all over it just now, making repairs. Security ain't so tight as they'd like.'

'I don't want to take any more chances than I have to.'

'Sure, I understand that. Things are fine. Me and Bill go back a long way. I do him little favours – share and share alike, right? Otherwise life gets pretty boring out here. Look at this little gizmo here. You see that?' A slim black box, roughly soldered. 'This contains the same software used to run automated security routines on the *Jager*. This identifies you as a member of the repair crew, so you keep it on the back of your suit and you'll be fine.'

Elias eyed the little black box with suspicion.

'What if anyone asks what I'm doing there?'

Eduardez chuckled. 'Man, nobody going to ask you that. Little box does that for you too. Isn't a security routine on or around the whole Station hasn't been cracked some time or other.'

'What's with all the security, anyway? I thought the aliens were just primitive or something.'

'The ones down on Kasper, yeah, but they ain't the

ones built the Station. And what do you mean, why security? Don't you know what happened here?'

Elias frowned. 'I read some stuff about the Station on my way here.'

Eduardez stared at him in unfeigned amazement. 'Like when everybody disappeared? Elias, the whole crew that used to be here before the Hiatus, they just upped sticks and vanished centuries ago. Nobody found 'em, no trace of 'em anywhere.'

Elias looked blank. 'I thought that was just bullshit.'

'You serious, telling me you don't know about this? Ain't nothing going to happen now after all this time, but, still, what kind of back and beyond you been livin' in anyway, Elias?'

Elias stepped forward. 'I'm not paying you to insult me, okay?'

'Okay, sorry.' Eduardez raised a placating hand, giving Elias an up-and-down appraisal at the same time, like he was trying to see if he was armed. Elias had a couple of ceramic pistols hidden in the back of his jacket, the kind that weapons scans didn't usually pick up. Just in case.

A couple of hours before, Eduardez had guided him to one of the outermost reaches of the Station's human-habitable section, a complex latticework of tubes and supporting struts. Mostly hydroponics, Eduardez informed him while leading him down long corridors

259

filled with heat and plant life. There was even a kind of petting zoo with a couple of dogs and cats. Gerbils floated in the zero gravity like fat, furry bees, watching the men's passage with tiny eyes from behind wire mesh. The scent of the animals, of the plants, was furious. By the time they'd emerged beyond the hydroponics, Elias was sweating from the heat.

'What I don't get,' said Elias, 'is why they don't just rotate the Station and get some kind of gravity. They did it with some of the big military ships I've been on, so why not here?'

'You kidding? Could be that's what blew the Oort Station up in the first place.'

'I thought that's because they jerked around with the circuitry or something.'

'Yeah, that *and* they tried to spin the thing. Nobody's going to spin any more Stations to see if they can find out the real reason. So zero gravity it is, for evermore, or until somebody figures out how to make our own singularities. Besides, the place is a mess in every other way that needs to be fixed before they can get around to anything else. They tried using these 'ponics to make the place more self-supporting, but almost all the food and air still gets brought in from outside. Whole thing leaks atmosphere faster than we can breathe it. Here, see that?'

Eduardez pushed through into yet another hydroponics pod, preceding him in. Elias watched as Eduardez scrabbled at a hatch in the plate-steel flooring, under rows of tables covered in biogenetically adapted plant-life. The air smelled sweet and moist. He pulled the hatch up, and Elias reached down to help push its lid to one side. There was a space inside which Eduardez wriggled into and out of sight. After a couple of moments' hesitation, Elias followed him.

There was more room underneath there than he might have expected. Even enough to stand up in. 'What is this?' Elias asked, looking around what appeared to be some kind of storage space. It looked dark, unpainted bulkhead; the only light shone down through the hatch they had climbed through. Elias could see what looked like an airlock door set into one wall.

'My little hideout,' said Eduardez. 'I sometimes keep stuff here I don't want anyone else to know about.' Smuggling, Elias guessed.

Eduardez went over to some crates, and pulled one open. It was filled with medical pressure punches, the kind that shot stuff in without using a needle when you pressed it onto your arm. Eduardez pulled one or two out, and turned to Elias like a bon vivant offering a glass of sherry to a friend. 'Want a shot?'

'No, thanks. I want to keep my head clear.'

'Suit yourself. Don't mind if I do?' There was a tiny squeak as he pressed the punch against his arm and hit the button. He shook his head. 'Woof. Needed that. You're missing out, you know.'

'You have a job to do, and I'm paying you for it.

That means you need to keep your head clear.' Elias pointed at the crate. 'Touch any more of that stuff before I go over there, and I swear I'll kill you.'

Eduardez turned red and looked away. 'Okay, okay. Jesus.' *Can I really trust him?* Elias wondered. *But maybe I don't have any choice.*

'Let's go over this again,' said Elias, trying to keep his voice light and conversational. Every instinct in his head was yelling: *Get out of here. You can't trust this man. You don't know anything about him anymore.* Instead, he said, 'I'm going over in some kind of shuttle, right?'

'It's a stripped-down Goblin. Gets used for hull repairs, moving stuff around between the Station and nearby ships. Unpressurized, which is why you need a suit. Remember, all the usual safety codes and routines have been stripped out of it, otherwise we wouldn't be able to get it anywhere near any ship without being automatically hailed. Okay, here we are.' He opened another crate and pulled out a pair of spacesuits that, even to Elias's untrained eye, looked like they had seen better days.

His reservations didn't get any less. Elias stepped outside the airlock, trying to remember his military training. The Goblin was right there, only a few feet away. It had been reduced to a jumbled platform, with a series of cargo palettes arranged around its rear circumference.

The palettes were currently empty, but he'd need to use at least one of them.

'Secure yourself,' said Eduardez, his voice crackling over the intercom. Elias found the console and the pilot's seat. There were straps for his feet just below it.

A wave of pain washed over him and the universe seemed to spin for a moment. He tasted bile in the back of his throat, and knew it was the Slow Blight eating at him.

'Remember, Murray, you can also run this thing by remote control, you got that?'

Elias nodded to himself.

'Hey, Elias, wake up. You all ready for this, man?'

'I'm ready,' said Elias, feeling anything but.

'Everything you need is on the smartsheet, man,' came Eduardez's voice. 'You do like I said, you'll be able to waltz in there and waltz right out. Nobody'll even know the difference.'

Elias looked at the controls of the Goblin, remembering what he'd been told. *Ignore them. Use the remotes built into the suit.* All the suits and transport in use around the Kasper Station employed exactly the same protocols, designed for use by people possessing a minimum of skill or knowledge. *Just tell it where to go, and it'll take you.*

Elias had already taped the co-ord code for the cargo ship onto the arm of his suit. He punched it into the screen in front of him. With a jerk, the stripped-down Goblin moved off, performing what looked like a series of complicated manoeuvres with a variety of tiny jets studded around its body. The cargo ship soon hovered into view on a console screen.

The *Jager* was of the same class as the ship that had brought Elias in, usually filled with travellers in the suspended animation of deepsleep. But there was at least one passenger not on the official manifest.

Minutes passed, and the Station shrank behind him. Then more minutes. As he got closer, the *Jager* just got bigger, and bigger, and bigger, until it looked more like a great grey-white cliff extending from side to side of his vision. The universe seemed filled with the sound of Elias's breathing.

There was a small lever just in front of Elias's mouth. He reached out his tongue, and a tiny 3D image of a section of the ship ahead appeared on one side of his visor. A cargo-bay entrance in the side of the *Jager* was outlined in red and the Goblin guided itself in towards it with the minimum of fuss.

He could now see other figures, moving around the exterior of the *Jager* like minnows caught in the wake of a whale. A couple of other craft looked like the one Elias was riding in. He could see where patches of the hull had been peeled back, exposing the bare skeleton of the ship in parts. The *Jager* was clearly undergoing major maintenance work.

The radio crackled again. 'Okay, Murray,' said Eduardez's voice. 'I'm going offline now. Don't want anybody to eavesdrop on you this close, right?'

Elias found the switch for the radio and tongued it off. *Not that they'd get any clues from what you just said*, he thought, *asshole*. He drifted forward in silence towards the enormous ship, and suddenly his perspective shifted so that he felt like he was falling slowly towards the ground.

There we go, he thought. He could now discern the hatch with his naked eyes.

A few moments later, he parked the Goblin a few metres from the exterior of the *Jager*, untied himself from all the straps, and pushed himself over gently to make a soft impact on the *Jager*'s hull, right next to the same hatch that, Eduardez assured him, would gain him entry.

Elias reached down and pulled some tools out of the hip pocket of his spacesuit. One of them was like a spanner crossed with a spatula, a stubby metal arm with one end vaguely resembling a geometric half-crescent. It fitted perfectly into a slot in the hatch door and, as Elias turned the metal arm anti-clockwise, the door rose up and open. A puff of air passed him, escaping into eternity, as Elias fell inside.

He found himself in a corridor with nobody else around. Eduardez had got him in. Now the rest was up to him.

Trencher was here somewhere. Over the past few days, Elias had felt a certain attitude on his part drop

away like used skin: an ingrained feeling of grey hope-
lessness that had characterized his life for some years
now. For a long time, he realized, he'd been merely
existing, biding his time. No great purpose in life had
revealed itself to him. Now he felt a new confidence,
and for the first time in his life understood why some
people weren't afraid of death. As long as you went out
fighting for something you actually cared about, it
really was possible to die without fear. As long as it
didn't make you careless.

So far, there was no sign there was anyone else on
board – anyone awake at least. According to Eduardez,
there was a skeleton crew operating somewhere far away
on the other side of the ship. Elias pulled out the
smartsheet Eduardez had given him; it provided a deck-
by-deck layout of the ship, acquired, according to
Eduardez, at great cost. He flicked through the decks
rapidly until he found the section he'd marked earlier.

There.

He glided along the zero-g corridors, braking himself frequently with his gloved hands against the walls in
case he flew into someone who didn't want him to be
there. This had the advantage of allowing him to move
quietly. He had peeled the security code off the arm of
his suit, removing his helmet and putting it into the bag
he carried over his shoulder.

The corridor branched into two, so he consulted the
smartsheet, picked the one on the right. That one split

into three. Again, the smartsheet. This time he picked the middle one. He heard voices coming towards him.

No sense in taking chances.

He found an open door, ducked in, looked around. He was in a toilet, the kind built for zero-g: a row of enclosed grey cubicles. He stood just inside the door, listening to the voices approach. He tried to make out what they were saying, but there were several voices speaking all at once. Fearing they were on their way to take a leak, he ducked inside one of the cubicles and discovered something.

Graffiti?

But not just any graffiti.

There were several scrawls on the inside of the door, and Elias studied them until he was sure the voices had passed on by. Mostly it was just names: people that had worked on the ship, presumably, or passengers out of deepsleep. A small, crude drawing of an engorged phallus and a list of things its owner would like to do with it, almost exclusively to the detriment of someone Elias was pretty sure was some kind of commanding officer. And then another cartoon – drawn by somebody who had a little talent – of a flaming sword.

The Primalist symbol.

Elias felt the hair on the back of his neck prickle with excitement. It was just graffiti, so seeing it here might just be coincidence.

Vaughn, he thought; *Vaughn has something to do with this*. Vaughn was the one loyal to the Primalist creed. It occurred to Elias that he still had no idea how many people on board had been responsible for placing Trencher there.

Two? Three? A hundred?

When the voices had faded completely, Elias sneaked back out once he was sure the corridor was empty again.

His smartsheet plans showed a series of vents running parallel through the ship: service shafts that provided easy access to sensors and something called shielded-exchange nodes. He found his way to one, a low grey door that came up to his knees, with a warning marked on it: DANGER. UNAUTHORIZED ENTRY WILL BRING AUTOMATIC PENALTIES AND A POSSIBLE CUSTODIAL SENTENCE. Eduardez had told him that they linked different parts of the ship together. Elias reached out for the handle and the door swung open easily. He climbed inside.

He pulled/pushed himself along a series of rungs that lined the inside of the shaft. If the smartsheet was anything to go by, this ship was huge. All he need worry about now was whether getting Trencher back out of there would be as easy as getting himself in so far.

He pushed another entry hatch open, and peered out into a corridor that looked more or less identical to the one he'd left. Still no one around, but there was a sign on the far wall reading CRYOGENICS, with an arrow pointing to the right. Elias pulled himself through, thinking that this was almost too easy. Where was the crew?

He stood and listened. Nothing.

He then followed the sign, treading as quietly as he could. Maybe it really *was* this easy.

He heard his assailant before he even saw him.

Elias turned, ramming his right elbow backwards as he span around. There was a satisfying thud as it connected with somebody's face, though tendrils of pain shot up his arm with the impact. A man with smooth skin and short-cropped hair staggered away, blood flowing from his suddenly ruined nose. Unfortunately, he hadn't come alone, and Elias noticed the zap stick coming for him too late to evade it.

The zap stick was a modified taser shaped not unlike a mace, which delivered a powerful shock on impact. Assailant number two had thrown it at Elias's head. He brought his other arm up, and the mace bounced off it, but the shock it delivered sent him flying backwards.

He was unconscious for only a few seconds, then coughed himself awake, tasting blood, and realized he'd bitten his tongue. Something hard impacted with his face. As he opened his eyes, he saw a blurred figure withdrawing his fist for another punch. Elias kneed him hard in the groin. The blur fell back, howling.

'And screw you, too,' Elias mumbled with a swollen tongue, through a mouthful of blood. His ears were singing. He managed to right himself after a few moments, grabbed a handhold jutting out from the corridor wall, and kicked his collapsed assailant hard in the guts, the force of the blow sending the man sailing away from him.

Which still left the other one.

The first assailant, whose nose Elias had broken, had drifted further along the corridor, leaving a trail of blood globules hanging in the air. Elias kicked off from a wall until he caught up with him, grabbing the other man's arm and punching him on the face until his eyes rolled up in their sockets.

It wasn't hard to figure out that somebody had known in advance that he was coming. He thought about Eduardez, but he also thought about the zap stick. He went back along the corridor, dragging his captive with the broken nose after him, shedding blood everywhere. As potential assassins went, these two hadn't been too good. Unlike Elias, they hadn't been trained for zero-gravity combat. And zap sticks were the kind of soft weapons favoured by the public-relations departments of police forces: non-lethal but good for immobilizing people. So maybe they'd wanted him alive . . .

He pressed a couple of fingers against his captive's neck, found he was still breathing, then searched him. He found a couple more zap sticks and a more traditional taser, also some vials and needles. Either he was a junkie or he'd intended to shoot something into Elias. Make that *definitely* wanted him alive.

The one whose balls he'd kneed was muttering something, his eyes still glassy with pain. Elias would have to figure out what to do with them both. Elias floated back over to him and kicked him hard in the guts again for good measure.

Then his eyes fell on something shiny pinned on the inside of the man's lapel: a tiny badge, barely larger than a fingernail. It looked like it was made of silver, and represented a flaming sword.

The sound of running feet. No time to do anything with them now. Elias left his assailants where they lay and ran into the cryogenics room, sliding the door shut. There he hauled a cabinet over from one side until it blocked the door, tipping it back so that its rear edge wedged a heavy bar lock halfway up. That would have to do until Elias could figure out what to do next. He looked around him.

The cryogenics chamber was vast, its ceiling curving high above his head, following the contours of the hull. Great racks rose around him, stacked high with body pods. He went over to one pod at eye level, and peered through its tiny round window. The pod was vacant, as expected. Whatever passengers had been kept in deep-sleep onboard would have been decanted some time ago, and these pods wouldn't be filled again until the ship was ready to make its return journey.

As someone started hammering on the door behind him, he retrieved the smartsheet, studying it with shaking hands. His head still felt light, unfocused. He tapped the zoom panel until the section of deck he'd ringed previously sprang up, showing clearly the layout of the cryogenics chamber. The ring he'd marked shifted to outline a section of the vast chamber adjacent to one wall. Elias crumpled the 'sheet up in one hand and ran.

He encountered a blank wall, and stared again at the smartsheet, frustrated, then studied the pods stacked all around him. If Trencher was stored in one of these, it would take Elias hours to find him, and he didn't have hours to spare. A hissing sound echoed distantly off the chamber's metal wall, the kind of sound made by an oxyacetylene torch. Elias didn't know how long it would take them to break through, but sensed it wouldn't be long.

He smoothed out the smartsheet, moving his view of the deck outlay from side to side, ignoring the sheen of sweat growing on his upper lip, and the rising panic inside of him. Where was he now? Was Trencher here at all? The map made no sense to him, and he wished he'd taken the time to study it more carefully. So stupid of him. He zoomed in to maximum magnification.

When he'd received the diskette from Josh, it had contained precise information about where on the *Jager* Trencher was stored. Yet, according to the same information Elias had uploaded into the smartsheet, Trencher was just here. But *here* was a blank wall, a section of bulkhead.

A sudden thought occurred to him. He went over to the wall running alongside one of the tall stacks of body pods and spotted several service hatches. He felt a blossoming of hope.

Maybe they hadn't wanted to take the risk of storing Trencher with the regular passengers. Perhaps they had opted for more traditional smuggling techniques instead.

A clang of metal rang through the cryogenics bay. They were through. He heard voices shouting to each other, as they spread out. Surely this was the first section they'd come to investigate?

Elias picked a hatch at random. It opened as easily as the first one had.

Several feet further in, all the service tunnels connected together via a single passageway running parallel to the chamber wall. He crawled along it, hoping his hunch was correct.

He found a panel that didn't look quite right – or to be more precise, someone had glued a plastic panel over a steel hatch, but with apparent haste. It wasn't difficult to pull it to one side and peer into a space beyond, which looked like it had once contained equipment of some kind.

Instead, there was a body pod, and Elias's heart rejoiced. He wondered how much time he had left as he crawled inside. Then he remembered the ceramic pistols, and reached behind himself. To his relief he found they were still there safe in the pack over his shoulder, underneath his loose helmet.

Looking through the pod's tiny viewing window, he

recognized the face of a man he'd given up for dead several years ago.

There was the sound of a hatch being opened behind him.

Shit, thought Elias, and scrabbled back. He saw shadows around the hatch he'd crawled through.

'In here!' someone yelled. Then the voice faded, as its owner stepped back from the hatch to give the alert. Elias clambered back and proceeded further along the service tunnel on all fours. There wasn't time to study the 'sheet and see where else the passage might lead from here. He had to go deeper and hope they didn't know the layout of the ship any better than he did.

Pushing himself along the tunnel as fast as he could go, after fifteen metres he came to a blank wall. Dead end.

Shit again. Elias was starting to feel desperate. The only way out was back the way he'd come, where they'd be waiting for him. He lay low on the tunnel floor, allowing just enough room to reach behind him and extract both of the pistols. Gripping one in each hand, he worked his way back towards the hatches leading into the main pod bay. He listened for the voices.

Then he remembered he was still wearing his space-suit, the helmet hanging loosely over his back. Eduardez had warned him that all the safety protocols on the Goblin had been disabled. What else did that mean?

Time to find out.

A head showed itself through one hatch, peered his way, and caught sight of him approaching. A hand reached in, gripping something shiny. Elias lifted one of the tiny ceramic pistols and fired. The figure fell back out of sight, howling.

Elias swiftly shifted around in the tightly confined space of the service corridor, and tapped into the control pad on the front of his suit. He tried to picture the current position of the Goblin but realized that was useless, as he'd proceeded through so many twisting tunnels.

He reached into a pocket for the smartsheet, keeping his eyes firmly fixed on the open hatch ahead. They'd now dragged their comrade away, and Elias figured he had just a minute or two before they decided what to do next. Elias suspected they would try very hard to kill him, regardless of what orders they'd originally been given. Trapped in here as he was, Elias realized they had the upper hand, unless he could come up with something soon.

Keeping one gun trained on the hatch, he quickly smoothed out the smartsheet with his other hand. He glanced at it. Wasn't there something . . .? Ah, *there*. The smartsheet displayed a row of buttons next to a schematic of the cargo ship. He flicked through a series of options until he found what he was looking for.

What Elias had briefly forgotten was that he could view information about the *Jager* in realtime. Of course

– like any standard smartsheet, it could hook into the local Grid and update automatically.

He hit up what he needed, and watched as the schematic updated. He tapped rapidly through the decks until he got an external schematic. It showed tiny dots moving in realtime around the body of the ship.

Bingo.

He located the ID code for the Goblin he'd come in on and noted its coordinates, relative to the *Jager*, from the information running in columns next to the schematic. He next found the remote-control panel on his suit and started tapping information into it. He watched as the Goblin's icon shifted position on the smartsheet, now moving rapidly from one side of the cargo ship to the other.

He had not failed to notice that the cryogenics chamber in which he was trapped sat next to the hull. The realtime display – as Eduardez had cheerfully pointed out – showed where the repair work was being carried out; the hull's outer layers stripped back, leaving inner walls exposed. Accordingly, it was clear to Elias that the section of inner hull directly over the cargo bay was remarkably vulnerable at present.

The tiny dot of the Goblin was now directly above the cryogenics chamber. He tapped further commands into his control unit and watched as the Goblin shifted position again, this time moving further away from the cargo ship while its nose remained pointing towards it.

Another head hovered cautiously by the service hatch. Elias aimed a shot at it and the face disappeared. Elias swore; he was now out of ammunition. Each gun had been a one-shot disposable, the best Eduardez had been able to get him at short notice. It sounded like there were several men out there, and he knew they could wait him out, or just drain the atmosphere out of the cargo bay.

Unless.

He halted the Goblin once it was half a klick from the hull of the cargo ship. Once he figured the Goblin was at a good ramming distance, he set its engines to maximum burn, watching as the blip indicating the Goblin on his smartsheet hurtled forward, directly towards the exposed inner hull over the cryogenics chamber.

He waited anxiously, long, long seconds.

'Murray, you're—' boomed a voice from the service hatch.

It sounded first like paper tearing, then like a tornado let loose within the body of the *Jager*. There were sudden screams from beyond the hatch, which suddenly became faint and distant. As Elias heard his helmet snick into place, he thought about the men he'd just killed, trying not to feel remorse. *It was you or them*, he reminded himself. These weren't just normal security personnel; they were something else, and they'd been waiting for him.

He let himself slide forward into the cryogenics

room and found the men were all gone, along with all the air. An emergency door had slammed down, sealing off the chamber from the rest of the *Jager*.

Some of the body pods, tugged loose by the instant hurricane, were now caroming slowly around the vast interior space. Above him, part of the roof had been rent open to the endless night. He could see stars beyond. The whole bay had depressurized in maybe fifteen seconds.

He remembered Trencher, and realized there wasn't time to get him out, not this time. Right now, he had to get himself the hell out of there, before the emergency crews came looking for him. Elias hit the Goblin's homing button and, a couple of seconds later, saw it descending towards him through the huge bay's airless interior. It looked like it had had the shit battered out of it.

He pulled himself into the pilot's seat, surveying the damage. Looked bad, but the little Goblin was tougher than he'd thought. He guided it carefully upwards, past jagged spears of steel jutting into the hole it had torn in the side of the *Jager*. As Elias rocketed past the jagged edges of the *Jager*'s wound, he thought he caught a glimpse of something and frowned behind his visor.

He could have sworn he'd seen bugs swarming around the breach in the hull.

Little silver bugs?

*

'I didn't tell them a thing! I swear, man! For Christ's sake, let me the fuck out of here!'

It took Elias a minute to find the intercom button on Eduardez's home-made airlock's control panel. All the buttons were marked by strips of tape with Eduardez's illegible scrawl on them, and it took a while to decipher each. In the meantime, he'd shot an occasional glance at the two-way screen that let him see Eduardez cowering inside the airlock, and let Eduardez see Elias standing menacingly outside of it.

'So what does this button do?' Elias probed a little flick switch, making sure Eduardez could see what he was doing.

Eduardez screamed over the intercom, high-pitched like a woman, 'No! No! Don't touch that one! I didn't tell anyone anything! Please—'

'Doesn't seem to do anything much,' said Elias, keeping his voice matter-of-fact. 'What about this one here, then? Here at the bottom? It doesn't say anything on it.'

There was a thud, and Elias looked up from the switch to see Eduardez's face pushed up against the screen's camera lens. His fingertips pressing hard against the glass were turning almost as white as Eduardez's face.

'Listen,' said Eduardez, his voice sounding hollow over the intercom. 'Listen, I mean it, I don't wanna die. That's why I'm telling you the truth, okay? I don't know what the fuck happened to you out there, but it didn't have anything to do with me.' Elias made sure Eduardez could see him reaching down for the unmarked switch with a look of concentration on his face. 'Man, that's the override switch! In the name of Jesus, don't touch that!'

'Override switch?'

'Opens the outer door! Don't – please don't touch it!'

'Right, I'd forgotten about that,' Elias lied. 'But I can't help wondering why you would want to open the outer door from way back here,' he said. 'You've already got an internal switch for opening the outer airlock door, so why would you need two?'

'That's an override you've got your goddamn hand on! Be really, really careful, okay? Please!'

'Override, huh?' Elias pondered for a couple of moments. 'So let's see. If somebody's in there and, say, you want to help them get into vacuum quicker, then that's the button you hit?'

Eduardez nodded furiously. There were now tears in his eyes.

He's such a lizard I think I'm actually going to enjoy this, thought Elias. Some of the epoxy he had recently been using had stuck to his hands, and the skin had peeled away when he'd tried to remove it. The sore patches were now itching furiously.

'I'll just bet that's what it's for,' he snarled. 'Maybe you just thought you'd set me up, sit back and see what happened, right?'

'Murray . . . Elias, please, I swear to God I said nothing.'

Elias thought there was at least a reasonable chance Eduardez was telling the truth here. But he couldn't be sure, so he hit the switch.

Eduardez screamed loudly as the outer door opened. Elias watched with satisfaction as the pressure drop sucked him out of the door.

Still screaming, he bounced around inside the large bag Elias had epoxied over the airlock exit an hour earlier. It had taken quite a while to glue it into place.

But it now seemed worth it.

'You can stop your screaming now,' Elias growled over the intercom, 'and stop thrashing around. The glue holding that thing on is pretty strong, but I wouldn't take any chances with it.'

It was a modified escape bag, a last-measure pressure balloon you could throw yourself into in the hope of rescue arriving before the bottle of air attached ran out.

Eduardez was still thrashing around like a madman. He was not good in a panic situation.

'Listen, Eduardez, here's the deal. Tell me the whole truth and I won't leave you in this thing until the glue gives way.'

Eduardez had pulled himself back into the airlock compartment. 'I can hear air escaping! I ain't kidding!'

'*Tell* me, Eduardez.'

'I didn't do it, fuck you!' Eduardez screamed at the

top of his voice. Elias finally decided he was telling the truth. Shit.

He'd thought maybe Eduardez had some kind of link to the Primalists, but that was starting to look unlikely, which meant Elias was running out of leads. Vaughn was in there somewhere, for sure; it was clear he'd known in advance Elias would be coming here, even back in London. And Trencher was still out there, on board the *Jager*. The whole situation was making some kind of impact on the Station's news feeds but, from what Elias had seen, the owners of the *Jager* weren't talking much. It looked like the whole thing might get written off as some kind of accident. And then Elias was right back where he started.

Elias cracked open the airlock door and looked inside. Eduardez stared back at him warily. 'I told you the truth,' he stammered.

'I don't like the look of that unmarked button, Eduardez,' Elias replied. 'Can't begin to imagine what kind of nasty things a man could get up to with a device like that.'

Eduardez stepped out of the airlock, stared at him evenly. 'Shouldn't treat a man like that.'

Elias smiled. 'I could care less. Oh yeah, see this?' He held up one of the airpunch syringes Eduardez had used on himself. 'You think of doing anything bad where I'm concerned, I'll make sure to find a way to let whoever's in charge of the Station know that you keep a big pile of these for sale.'

Pasquale

Sixty thousand klicks out from the Station, and slowly building up velocity, Pasquale guided his Goblin in the direction of the inner asteroid belt. A message blinked on the screen, a legal notice reminding him not to allow the ship within a certain distance of Kasper.

'Goddamn big-eared flea-infested shitheads,' Pasquale muttered to himself. All this trouble just for a bunch of furry cavemen. All that shit back home, and here was a planet just ripe for the taking. Pasquale had Mayan ancestors, and his maternal grandmother had sworn blind that the family could be traced back to the ancient Mayan kings. He fingered the cross at his neck. Well, that was so much horseshit as far as he was concerned. Maybe those conquistadors had been pretty rough, but life all round was a lot better for progress and real civilization.

Something glinted in the corner of his eye.

He looked round, unsettled. *Imagining things now*, he thought. He'd felt worried ever since he'd left the Station only a few hours before. What if things got really bad there and there was no Station to return to?

You're such a worrier, he thought to himself, but it was easy to get paranoid out here. Maybe he should get on the Kasper Grid and talk to some of the other Goblins.

There it is again, he thought, jumping up from the pilot's seat. He put one hand on a ceiling rung and peered behind him. He leaned over the console and turned the lights up more – he preferred a kind of cosy semi-light when he decided it was evening – and moved into the rear of the ship.

A bug.

One of those little silver bugs, he thought, feeling sweat form on his brow. *Just the one, though. Stick it in the airlock, cycle it through. Run it through the recycler, see if it likes that. Just the one. Over . . . there.* He moved back, saw it disappear through a grating that led to one of the manual-override fuel-control panels.

When he lifted the grating up, a thousand pairs of shiny metal eyes looked up at him. The Goblin shook, almost as if something inside it had come loose.

'Oh fuck,' groaned Pasquale.

Eleven

Pierce

'Sir, they're everywhere.'

Pierce had just stepped into Commander Holmes's office, to be greeted by a wall of military. In the confined space they were standing almost shoulder to shoulder, at least a dozen of them.

'That's not the news I want to hear,' said Holmes, looking grey. 'What about the escorts? The military ships?'

'A couple of the cargo ships look to have been infected, sir. The military escort *Pyongyang* is definitely infected.'

'Excuse me,' said Pierce, pushing gently against some of the uniformed shoulders in front of him. 'Excuse me.'

Someone wearing the stars of a military commander turned round and glared at him. 'Who is this man?' he demanded, looking back to Holmes.

'He's Mayor Pierce, Commander Johoba. I'm sure you're familiar with his role in life on the Station.'

'What we're discussing here,' said Johoba to Holmes, 'is not a civilian matter.'

Pierce finally pushed his way past Johoba and saw two people he recognized: Rachel Tomason and Lindsey Mansell, both science types. 'I wouldn't say that,' he said loudly. 'I've been talking to people, too, and there's sightings all over the place. I'd say this is very much a civilian matter now.'

Johoba was mentally hurling daggers at him, Pierce could sense. 'I'm hoping the Commander is considering an evacuation order,' Pierce continued politely.

There was a burst of angry conversation amongst the men squeezed into the small room and, if anything, Holmes looked a little greyer. 'This situation is containable!' somebody shouted. 'We don't need to evacuate anyone.' Pierce traced the voice to an Asian man in uniform. *Holmes must have every Escort Commander in the Kaspian system in here*, he thought.

'I thought it might help clarify the situation if Professor Tomason could say a word or two,' said Holmes. 'Mr Pierce,' he glanced in his direction, 'please remember that, until any official decisions are made through this office, everything you see or hear in this room is confidential.' Pierce nodded acknowledgement.

All eyes went to the two scientists. 'As uh, some of you know,' said Tomason, clearing her throat, 'some artefacts, undoubtedly Angel in origin, were recovered a few months ago and have since been held in a secure facility on board the human-habitable portion of the Angel Station. The artefacts went missing three days ago, about the same time as the first sightings of these, uh, bugs.'

Missing? Pierce stared at them. Tomason glanced in Mansell's direction, as if seeking encouragement. Mansell nodded, and she continued.

'Were they stolen?' asked the Asian Escort Commander.

'No, not stolen. In fact, we're not too sure exactly what happened, but we can make some guesses. We had the artefacts under visual surveillance at all times. Commander Holmes?'

Holmes nodded, and Lindsey Mansell stepped forward with a rigid smartsheet. She set it up on a little stand and tapped a small panel printed on it. An image of a room inside the secure containment facility sprang up, a date appearing in the top right corner. It showed various objects stacked neatly on shelves and on the floor, held in place in the low-g by adhesive pads. The date in the corner showed it had been recorded three days before.

'This comes from our surveillance systems. What you're seeing here is a laboratory where we stored the artefacts and made such tests as were possible within the limited resources available on the Station. The artefacts were due to be shipped soon to a better-equipped secure facility back in Sol System. However, something unexpected happened.'

Understatement of the century, if this has anything to do with the bugs, thought Pierce. Mansell was fast-forwarding the display, then stopped it. 'Watch that tube-like container over in the left corner. Just there.' She pointed. 'About now.'

Pierce watched along with the others as the tube appeared to fracture, its smooth, metallic-blue surface rapidly developing a series of cracks. It looked like the cracked mud of a dried-out riverbed, except rendered in metal. 'This is in realtime. The whole transformation took only a minute or so.'

The cracks deepened, then suddenly the cylinder crumbled to pieces.

Pierce stared in horror and he heard others around him gasping, or muttering under their breath. The pieces were *moving*. Moving like something living.

Pierce realized he was looking at the metal bugs everyone had been hearing about – seen by somebody they knew, or by somebody who knew somebody they knew. Pierce had heard a hundred stories in the space of only a few days, but hadn't seen anything himself. Until now.

'We don't know what triggered the change,' said Mansell, shrugging. 'But there are theoretical precedents for this kind of thing.'

'Like what?' asked Holmes, an appalled expression on his face.

'What I think we're looking at are viral machines,' said Tomason, stepping forward to stand next to Mansell. By now, on the screen, the bits of cylinder had scurried off out of sight into different parts of the laboratory, moving, it seemed, on tiny metal legs. 'Self-reproducing cybernetic organisms.'

'What the fuck are you talking about?' said one of the Escort Commanders, a heavy-set man who looked like he'd started to sweat a lot. These were professionals, used to commanding thousands, but they all seemed out of their depth on this one. Pierce noticed one or two others casting occasional worried glances at the floor or at the corners of the room. It took Pierce a second to realize why. They were looking for bugs, and the realization sent a thrill of fear down his spine. He even glanced down at his own feet, wondering if anything could have scurried by without his noticing.

'Machines that replicate,' said Tomason, looking weary. 'The idea's been around for centuries. There's even the possibility that the Stations themselves are self-replicating, although of course nobody really knows – can know, yet. Mayor Pierce is right, people are seeing them everywhere. The footage you've just watched shows perhaps a dozen individual bugs at most. Everywhere you go now, people are talking about them, and from the way they talk there must be hundreds of them, if not thousands, by now. All happening in only three days.'

'Commander Holmes, sir, I appreciate the limits of

my role on the Station,' said Pierce, 'but the fact is, I must insist that you now have no choice but to abandon the Angel Station, at least temporarily. We don't know if these things are a threat or not, whether they mean us harm or not.' Pierce turned to look at Tomason and Mansell in turn, looking from one to the other, his voice rising as if to a question.

'Professor Tomason, do these things mean us any harm?' asked Holmes. *He's out of his depth*, thought Pierce. *This isn't the kind of thing he ever expected to deal with. But that's the problem, isn't it? We became complacent even after returning post-Hiatus and finding an Angel Station abandoned by its original crew, vanished, with no trace of them anywhere in the system. And now it's happening again.*

'Sir, I don't know,' said Tomason. 'All this is brand new. What I can say is that if these things are replicating – and I believe that they are – then they must be obtaining their raw material from somewhere else. That means either the original Angel Station itself, or else the human-habitable portion of it.'

'They're eating the Station?' said Johoba.

Tomason shrugged. 'Maybe. I don't know. I don't have the resources—'

'There is one other matter to consider,' said the Asian Commander, stepping forward. 'Abandoning the Station may not be a choice we're able to make.'

Holmes stared at him. 'Can you explain that?'

'Okay, put it this way. We – or rather the Station,

plus hopefully only a few of the escort vehicles guarding the Station – are infected with some kind of plague, possibly alien, possibly even intelligent. That's as much as we know, and apart from that we're in the dark. For the majority of people living and working on board this Station, the only immediate alternative is to return through this Station to the next Station in the chain, the one at Hellas. That would almost certainly mean infecting that Station as well, and so on, until finally these creatures would be delivered to the Sol System. And if they do turn out to be non-benign, and if they somehow arrive on Earth—'

Pandemonium erupted.

People were yelling all around Pierce, and he was surprised at how calm he felt. He wondered why, and then he realized. It was too late already.

He'd glanced down once more at his feet, and noticed something that hadn't been there before. There was a tiny little hole in the floor, right next to his shoe. Something small and shiny was pushing its way through. And it did look like an insect, at least at first glance.

There was something almost endearing about the way it probed and heaved its way through, its tiny legs – at least a dozen of them – waving and scraping at the hole. Had that hole been there before? Unless his foot had been over it, Pierce certainly hadn't noticed it before. The thing pushed its way right through, then seemed to orient itself by turning in a full circle, something like an insect's feelers waving at the front of it.

On closer inspection, of course, it wasn't really an insect: more an artefact, or a machine with insect-like properties. It looked strangely half-formed, as if it had been assembled carelessly in a hurry.

Another insect machine next pushed its way through. This one joined the first in looking around itself. Then they scurried off alongside one wall, destination unknown.

Pierce wondered how he could get his hands on a Goblin at short notice.

Vincent

They had gone down to the arrivals bay, near the hub of the Angel Station. It looked as if it had originally been designed with pomp and circumstance in mind, for the arrival of dignitaries or politicians or such. Seats were bolted to the floor (this area being near enough to the Station's central core for its curious pseudo-gravity to exert a gentle but not insubstantial pull), and a wide viewport through which the complexity of the Station's human-built add-ons could be viewed in comfort. They were alone here, although Vincent kept expecting someone to walk in on them at any second. He had folded his arms and crossed his legs, prey to a permanent vague uncertainty of how he should arrange his limbs when at rest.

'So when did all this start?'

'When do you think? It was just after . . .' Kim waved a hand at him without actually looking at him. She stared out of the viewport instead. 'I had a hard time. A really hard time. I didn't think I could cope. In fact I couldn't.'

'Perhaps the money would have helped,' said Vincent gently. 'I know how much money was due to you after your discoveries were catalogued, studied. You'd be amazed at what's been achieved but, of course,' he said with a grin, 'I can't really tell you that.' She turned to him with a frown. 'It's a secret,' he continued, thinking of tiny starships flitting about the galaxy, all without the aid of the Angel Stations. *The universe is really ours now*, he thought for maybe the millionth time. *We'll be able to go where we want*. He looked at her.

'I *will* tell you, but just not yet. When this is all over.' He would, since she deserved to know, had to know.

'Thanks.'

He'd told her everything he could about the radiation now approaching the Station. In turn, she'd told him about Pasquale's claim of seeing some kind of artificial insect. Now it seemed that lots of other people had seen them.

What you were doing, he wanted to say to her, was

293

suicide. She had told him about the Books, about her attempts at exorcizing the knowledge of her lover's death by becoming her, albeit only for a little while. A long, protracted suicide of the mind.

He remembered Susan, for he had known them both when they had been involved in post-graduate work at the University, a long time ago. It had been an interesting time, and they had crossed paths time and time again at interdepartmental parties and also through mutual friends. There had been . . .

But this was all so long in the past now, and after Kim had travelled here with the woman who had become her lover, to study the ruins that Vincent knew had fascinated her since she was a child, he had heard of them only through professional connections as his and their personal lives had diverged. And then, finally, only through the main news channels on the Grid, as early triumph had rapidly dissolved into disaster.

You were the love of my life, he wanted to say to her, realizing, even as he thought it, that it was indeed true. He had not expressed himself well enough at the time to communicate this either through deed or word, and he had – he suspected – paid the price. And now here they were again, both so far from home.

'About the bugs,' he said, casting for something else to think about. 'If they're real, I think I know who might have something to do with them.' Kim stared at him. 'There's a woman called Tomason.'

Kim nodded like she'd heard the name. 'She's head

of the exoscience research facilities on the other side of the Station. I met her a couple of times.'

'Well, I went looking for her. I knew her name through some academic papers she'd published, and I'd even requested research material from her directly at different times while I was still back home, so she also knows who I am.' Kim nodded, watching him with interest. 'Of course, we'd never actually met, but I have all my requisite credentials with me.'

'None of which have actually helped you get any-where since you arrived here,' she said.

'Exactly. So I thought, if there's anyone I can talk to about this stuff, it's Tomason. She's high enough in the scale of things to have the ear of the Commander here, or at least that much I was hoping.'

'And?'

'Nothing. They've locked down that secure facility you mentioned.' He gave her a significant look. 'Neither Tomason nor any members of her core research staff are currently available, and the only place they could be is—'

'The Central Command facility,' Kim finished for him. 'That's the centre of everything around here. That's where all the decisions are made. You can't get in with-out a pass.'

'I don't have a pass,' said Vincent, 'and it doesn't look likely I'll acquire one.'

'You really think the Kaspians are doomed?'

'I'm not a defeatist by nature,' he said after several

seconds, 'but I don't know what can be done to help. They obviously have their own emergency to deal with here. Maybe it's got something to do with what happened post-Hiatus, when the Station was abandoned the first time.'

'The first time?' said Kim, raising an eyebrow.

'As opposed to the second time, yes. But we should be making plans.'

'There hasn't been an evacuation order. I haven't even seen any of these bugs myself, so I can't quite believe they exist. I can't help thinking they're the product of some kind of mass hysteria, or . . . oh.'

She fell silent and followed Vincent as he took her gently by the wrist and led her closer to the viewport. It provided a realtime display of the environs of the Station. Three of the military escorts were visible, far beyond the Station's boundaries. There was a set of controls next to the viewport that allowed you to zoom in on different sections of the Station. She had just noticed something that looked like mercury flowing across the outer surface of a habitat pod, one of the big ones housing part of the Hub. Vincent played with the controls, finally bringing them to focus at extreme magnification.

'I came down here the other day,' he said. 'Not many people seem to pass through this part of the Station nowadays, and I find I can think here. I started playing with the controls. They really are everywhere, I'm afraid.'

She could see them clearly now, flowing across the outer surface of the Station. They were small and shiny, their carapaces rough-hued. For the first time in a very long time, she felt truly afraid.

'Where the hell did they come from?' she breathed.

'Well, what are the two places I can't get into just now?'

'Central Command and – oh, right.' The secure facility, where they'd brought the Angel artefacts. Great. Where else would they have come from?

Or not so great. *I don't know who I am anymore*, she thought. *I don't feel ready to be Kim, to deal with – the things that happened. I want to be Susan, strong, capable Susan.* But the Books – her supply was running low. She ached even to think of them. She could be Susan again with them, could feel that strength and clarity and courage in her.

Just being herself, Kim thought, seemed something of a disappointment. She walked over to the memorial plaque set into the far wall. It was silver and huge, measuring six feet high by maybe ten wide. It listed the names of all the disappeared: the original crew of the Angel Station. *There are people much worse off than me*, she reflected.

There had to be a plan of action. As first the rumours and then confirmed sightings of the insects had spread, she had expected some kind of an evacuation order to be announced. There were military escorts on permanent patrol, of course, for exactly this kind of eventuality. To transport people from the Station out to them would require no great feat of organization. There were a couple of hundred Goblins as well, not even counting the ones currently out in the depths of the Kaspian System, hoping to become the next Pasquale.

Vincent joined her, standing next to her to study the plaque. He'd examined it several times himself already, on previous visits. Somehow, sharing this moment with someone he knew made it seem all the more real. 'It's strange to think it really happened.' She looked at him as if she didn't understand what he meant. 'What I mean is, it's one thing to know what happened here in the abstract. It's another to come here and stand in front of real, solid evidence that something so bizarre could really take place. It beggars the imagination, you know what I mean?'

'Oh, yes, very much so,' she replied. She suddenly thought of stars like clouds of mist drifting past her, of a great and eternal darkness swallowing her until she fell forever. It did, indeed, beggar the imagination that more than a thousand individuals could simply up and vanish, all, it seemed, within the space of a few hours, leaving a mystery that might remain unsolved until the end of time.

'I wonder what it was like to be here when the Station shut down but nobody could go home. They must have thought of going to Kasper. It would have been the most obvious place.' She shook her head. 'You know, every year or two, another documentary team arrives here to try and dig up something new, and all they ever find is the same as everybody else did. There's no sign of anyone human on Kasper itself.'

Vincent didn't look convinced. 'A planet is a big place.'

'Not when you've got surveillance satellites like Central Command do. They'd know.' She leaned in closer to study one particular entry. 'Imagine being him.' She was pointing to a name at the beginning of the list, which was accorded particular prominence along with several others. 'In charge of a place like this, and the whole world falling around your ears.'

Falling indeed, thought Vincent, leaning in closer. The name had been inscribed clearly and carefully.

The words inscribed in the silver read: *Commander Ernst Vaughn.*

Vaughn

'Sir?'

Vaughn turned. The air cut like a knife at this time of year: a chill blast of wind that sliced through the mountainous pass that extended below him, spilling like an invisible river from the high peaks behind him to the fallow grasslands far below. Half a mile or so distant, on the edge of a craggy cliff, rose one of the great shield generators that hid them from lens and eye alike.

Strange, he'd never quite got used to the smell of

the air here. The rest of them, though, they were born here, so they knew nothing else. They were the true inheritors of God's purpose. *But I'm still luckier than Moses*, he thought. *At least I got to see the Promised Land.*

He turned to see a young man, perhaps in his mid-twenties, standing a short but respectful distance behind him. A path stretched out beyond, leading down to the streets of New Coventry. Jonathan, that was his name. And wasn't he due to be married off to that girl Elizabeth? Ah yes, that was the one. Strange, but he remembered well the time when he had automatically known the name of every individual in their little colony. But times had changed, Kasper was changing, with the glaciers retreating and the long millennia of ice already fading into the native Kaspians' ancestral history.

'Sir, we're intercepting reports from the Angel Station, sir. It looks like the replicators have self-activated.'

'Details?'

'We picked up several transmissions, on both the Goblin frequencies and the encrypted military channels. It seems the Station itself is riddled with them, and the military channels have raised a lot of speculation about abandoned Angel weapons. They seriously think it's to do with the Angels, sir.'

Interesting, thought Vaughn. Events really were moving at quite a pace now. 'Thank you, Jonathan. Keep me informed. And tell Ann I'll be down within the hour to take personal charge of the monitoring operation. In the meantime, I don't want to be disturbed unless it's news of equal importance, understood?'

'Yes, sir.' The young man started to turn back down the path.

All they needed now was to locate the last god. And then, and only then, could Vaughn be assured of the cleansing fires that would sweep the aliens away and leave the new Eden fresh for God's children. For he had foreseen it, and it would come to pass.

Ursu

When he had attended Raisings in the past, it had been more as a witness than an active participant. The learned ones of the House of Shecumpeh had believed early demonstration of what the god could do for them was a good way of capturing an acolyte's heart. There were words to be said, rituals to be observed, and then, if the god looked into the hearts and minds of the dead or dying and saw sufficient goodness in them, it might just deign to bring them back.

He leaned over one of the bundled figures lying in the great tent he had been brought to and saw it was only a child. He didn't ask where its mother was. *I need the god*, he thought. *I can't do this without Shecumpeh.* What would he need to say to make them understand?

Ursu heard voices behind him as others entered the tent. They then stepped aside to let their totem-reader enter, cradling the god in his arms like it was a baby. He seemed to walk with difficulty, his limbs perhaps seizing up under the influence of the plague.

Even the air in here smelled diseased, thought Ursu. But it was better to see Shecumpeh here, even amongst barbarians and enemies, than to think of it lying at the bottom of some pool. The totem-reader carried the god over to him, and laid it reverentially at the feet of the last remaining priest of the House of Shecumpeh.

Ursu awkwardly nodded thanks. They all watched him expectantly. He felt like an actor about to perform. What if nothing happened?

He picked up the god, and studied the side of it where a crack had appeared. Again something glinted from inside. He feared to look too closely, afraid of what he might see. It had never occurred to him before that there might be something *inside* the god.

Then he saw something he had not spotted earlier, when he had first noticed the damage to Shecumpeh. A glow, so faint as to seem almost imaginary, and tinged with blue, was emerging from the crack. He looked up and saw expectant eyes watching him, then he turned to the child.

Ursu laid one hand on the god seated on the ground before him. He recited the ritual words, repeating each verse three times. By the second recitation, he began to feel slightly dizzy. By the third, his lips moved, but the words themselves had turned to internal sense impressions, much as the god's voice became whenever it spoke to him. He next saw something that he had only heard of, never experienced.

The child coughed, its lungs labouring hard under his hand. Ursu closed his eyes and recited the verse of Raising over and over again. Someone – one of the other acolytes, who was given to whispered blasphemies? – once told him that he had overheard two of the elderly priests confiding that the words really meant nothing, that their ritual only made it seem as if the priests were taking part, when in fact they were entirely surplus to requirement.

However, Ursu had in his mind heard the words translate into the language of the gods. He now felt as if he could understand anything anyone said, anywhere in the world.

The sick child already seemed – how to put it, Ursu wondered? – more *connected* to this world again. Ursu hoped that meant it was saved from the Blackface. The child's spirit – or whatever it was Ursu registered – fluttered in his mind's eye, but with renewed vigour. Below it lay a dark place, a place where—

Ursu reeled back, both physically and mentally, from that glimpse of some great abyss, a place of forever darkness falling away into eternity. *Shecumpeh*, he enquired, *is that where we go when we die?* He would rather live a thousand times a thousand years than ever face it.

The shaman lunged forward, putting one hand on Ursu's shoulder, and reached past him to touch the child's forehead. He then stared at Ursu, his long snout quivering.

Yé came forward, gesturing the shaman to move back. He picked up the child gently. 'Ythe?' he said. 'Ythe, can you hear me?'

Tiny eyes opened, staring up at Yé's broad face, then closed again. The child was soon asleep. Ursu registered the conflicting emotions in Yé's face.

Let me go, Ursu wanted to say, but Yé's face darkened as if he could see the plea forming in Ursu's mind. He turned away, still clasping the child in his arms.

A few hours later, Ursu was allowed to retire to his own tent. Despite having saved the lives of several members of the tribe, he was still to be kept under close guard. Now he was too valuable to them to be even given to Xan, he thought sourly, feeling exhausted and mentally drained. He tumbled back onto sour-smelling furs and slept. He woke again shortly before dawn, sure that he had heard someone calling his name.

'Ursu? Priest Ursu?' The voice sounded familiar. It's Ree, he thought, and looked up to see her head poking through the tent flap. As he glanced beyond her, into the dim approaching half-light, for a moment of elation he realized his guards were gone.

Ree produced a knife from her sack-like shift. It

glittered in the dim light filtering into the tent, and Ursu felt his throat go dry.

She crawled in through the entrance, then stood over him.

'Tell me how you did that – made the disease go away.'

Ursu licked his lips. 'The . . . power is in the god. It doesn't come from me.'

She stepped forward, with a glassy look in her eyes. 'Even my father Yé can't do that, and they say our tribal leaders, they're like gods.' Her face screwed up. 'But if some filthy, flea-ridden city type can heal someone, just by touching them, that can't be true, can it?'

'I told you, *I* didn't do it,' Ursu protested, feeling desperation creep into his voice. What in Shecumpeh's name did she intend to do with that knife? 'Where are the guards?' he said.

She stared at him for a moment as if he were a complete imbecile. 'They're all off celebrating and getting drunk. It's because you cured all the sick. They're all recovering. Even my father is getting drunk.'

Ursu stared at her. Only she now stood between himself and freedom.

Then he remembered Shecumpeh. He would still have to find the god.

'Are you frightened of me?' she asked. 'When they found you by the river, you were dead, did you know that? That makes you holy, doesn't it?' she said, holding the knife out in front of her.

There was a crack of thunder on the horizon. It faded, echoing across the great, icy plains. Something about it . . . didn't sound right.

Ursu realized Ree had heard it too. She wasn't looking at him anymore, glancing over her shoulder at the tent flap behind her. She turned, fumbled her grip on the knife, and it fell between them.

He made the tiniest gesture, like a minute jab of his hand in the direction of the weapon.

Ree squealed, and dived for the knife.

He kicked her in the head as hard as he could. She collapsed, making an *oof* sound. Ursu stumbled to his feet, and fled into the night, the sounds of her cursing floating in the air behind him.

He looked around to find himself surrounded by tents, their campfires burning, but the wastes of the tundra lay moments away. It would be dawn before long, which would make it easy for them to track him. This was hopeless, thought Ursu. He didn't stand a chance. A great crack of thunder reverberated across the plain, drowning out the last of the drunken revelry.

'You!'

Ursu whirled around, to look into the face of one of his absent guards. He came staggering towards Ursu, much the worse for some rank barbarian wine. 'It's you they want!' he slurred, before falling face down in the ice.

Ursu gaped down at him. He could hardly believe he'd once been afraid of these people.

There followed another crack of thunder . . . but then Ursu realized what was wrong with it.

There was no lightning.

He glanced up to see the skies were perfectly clear, the sun almost ready to rise and cast its light over the world.

So where was the noise of thunder coming from?

The drunken guard's fingers were twitching feverishly where he lay face-down in the snow. Blood pooled in the snow around him, flowing from a crater-like wound in his back. Ursu heard shouts and screams in the distance.

Ursu stepped back, his heart pounding. What in Shecumpeh's name was going on here? Then he remembered the god. Nothing else mattered. He had to find the god.

He glanced down one final time at the guard, who was making little gasps as if trying hard to breathe.

More thunder pealed out across the ice. More screams could be heard. As Ursu ran between the tents, several of the tribesfolk ran past him, ignoring him completely. He had not failed to see the terror in their eyes.

It had to be Xan's men. Ursu heard the sound of braying icebeasts. Running towards a fire, he realized it was a tent blazing in the dim light. A body lay sprawled half out of it.

Find the god, and then he could leave.

As he hurried on between the tents, tribesfolk went running past him, heedless of his presence. Another crack like thunder, but much closer, exploded somewhere nearby. Was this Shecumpeh's doing? In his search, Ursu dived inside a tent to find a group of frightened children huddling there. As he entered another, a figure lunged forward, snarling. Ursu yelped and lashed out.

Another tent contained a bundle wrapped in furs. The furs had a distinctive pattern to them. He realized they were Yé's furs, discarded. He pulled them aside to reveal the effigy lying on its side. With a huge surge of relief, he gathered the god into his arms.

Back outside again and, at the next thunder clap, he at last saw a spit of lightning. But not like any lightning he had ever seen before. Through the gap between two tents, a hundred steps away, a bright flash stung his eyes and Ursu sensed something hot zing past his ear. He ducked and ran at a low crouch, the effigy still cradled in his hands like a baby. He skirted the final tent, heading for the open tundra – and, he fervently hoped, freedom.

But the god was heavy in his arms, and he didn't notice a hand snaking out to grab at one leg. Ursu lashed out with his other foot, but the restraining hand merely tightened its grip. Ursu looked down and straight into Yé's maddened eyes.

The tribal leader half lay against a tent wall. 'You brought them on us.' He was panting hysterically. 'You and your damned god, you brought the demons down on our heads, I hope the Shai make a meal of you!'

He released his grip and Ursu ran, fleeing the village of tents. He kept on running until sheer fatigue forced him to slow his pace. He could still hear voices floating across the half-frozen grass, sounding nearer than they really were. Not so far away, their outlines clear against the night sky, trees extended across the hilltops.

Then sounded the familiar slap-slap-slap of an ice-beast's progress, its padded feet stamping heavily across the rough soil somewhere to his right. He ducked to the left, heading towards the trees at a slant that would take him longer to reach them, but further away from the voices.

Then came the sound of clawed feet drumming on the earth and splashing through pools of icy water. Terror drove him on faster, faster towards the tree-line. At first, he couldn't be sure they were riding for him, but now he was certain. The shelter of the trees was only seconds away now. He heard further shouting, soldiers calling to each other. He cursed himself for still wearing the distinctive robes of a priest. He would have to find other, less conspicuous garments whenever he next found the chance.

The god was so heavy that his arms were aching. Again there was the sound of that strange thunder, and something heavy splashed somewhere far off to his right. Ursu whined in terror, but he was almost there.

The din of the riders pursuing him sounded closer now, but the trees now loomed on the slope directly ahead. They grew in a tangled mass, their roots snaking over low ridges towards the pools of brackish water which lay below. Again, something zinged past his head, splashing ahead of him into waterlogged earth.

What had Yé said, that he hoped the Shai caught him? Those Pale Ghosts who forever wandered the ice in search of the unlucky and the lost. But surely that was just a legend, a story . . .

Finally reaching the trees, Ursu was nearly at the end of his endurance. He did not dare look back to see how close his pursuers were. He could only hope the terrain ahead was too dense and impenetrable to be navigated by mounted soldiers. There was just a chance he could still get away. His head thudded as if a hammer beat within it, and the arms that gripped the god were numb.

He pulled himself up between a tangle of ancient gnarled roots, barely able to hold onto the god with just one hand. Some kind of missile splintered the wood next to his hand. Ursu yelled with fear, hauling himself up onto higher ground. The ceaseless thunder followed him, under still clear skies.

There were ruins up here, great piles of stone that had collapsed long ago, gaping holes amid the walls which still stood, but Ursu didn't have the time to stop and look. The whole desolation was overgrown, and infested with plants and trees so thickly entangled Ursu had trouble picking his way through them. Not much further, he thought, and then he could rest, just for a little bit. It was dark and dense up here, but the shouting and braying sounded more distant now. Perhaps they had turned away.

He collapsed against the side of a great tree, fungi sprouting from its half-rotten trunk, and waited, listening intently, as the sun slowly rose above the horizon.

After he had rested for a while, he moved on.

Elias

The Station corridors were in pandemonium. Elias steered a difficult course through them, thinking this must be what it was like on a sinking ship. He had a name, and a door number – but where was it?

He pushed down a narrow passage leading off one of the Hub's main thoroughfares. He'd already witnessed a couple of fistfights during the several hours since he'd dealt with Eduardez. People were panicking, and the silver bugs were everywhere. They infested the Station on both the outside and the inside. He'd accidentally kicked one when it suddenly scurried out in front of him, but it had merely picked itself up and continued on its way. Some kind of machine, he realized, like the things he'd observed on his escape from the *Jager*.

He had to get back out there, rescue Trencher, whatever the hell they were intending to do with him. Elias was worried they were going to send Trencher back through the singularity. Why they'd brought him here in the first place was a mystery but, now that the shit was really starting to hit the fan, the only logical course of action for the Primalists was either to send him back to Earth or to move him further along the cosmic daisy-chain of Angel Stations. And if they did that, Elias knew the chances of him ever finding Trencher again measured roughly slim to zero.

He couldn't allow that to happen.

His skin itched constantly, the sensation occasionally blossoming into something more akin to a dull pain. His left hand had developed a minor twitch, and he knew it was all brought on by the Slow Blight.

He found the right door number and pressed a pad in the centre of it. A small dull light illuminated next to the door, and Elias was aware he was being studied from within. 'Miss Amoto?' He waited another moment. 'I need to hire your Goblin, Miss Amoto.'

A few seconds later, the door clicked open. Behind it was visible a narrow cot, a tiny chair and a desk, and beyond them a paper screen that probably hid the toilet or maybe a kitchen. Most of the available space was buried under luggage cases and scattered belongings. Kim Amoto – assuming he had come to the right place – stared back at him. Tall and gangly, in that weird way people who had been born in low-g environments tended to be. Though far from unattractive for all that. She wore soft loose trousers and a utilitarian-looking shirt that, nonetheless, seemed to show off her figure quite well. He could see a man, maybe in his early thirties, balanced precariously on a low stool in one corner.

He risked a sideways glance at the man, whose gaze, Elias had noticed, tended to wander to Kim when he thought she wasn't looking. More than just friends, thought Elias. No, used to be. They weren't that close now, perhaps.

Kim studied him carefully. 'The Goblin's not for hire, I'm afraid. In case you hadn't noticed, everyone's getting themselves off the Station.' There was a sarcastic edge to her voice that almost made Elias smile.

'I'm aware of that, but I'm in a hurry too. I'm prepared to pay well for it.' Elias pulled out a credit chip and held it up so she could see. He then tapped a little blue square in one corner of the card, and made sure she could see the numbers scrolling across it. 'That's how much I'm prepared to pay into your account, Miss Amoto.'

Her eyes got bigger, but she stayed cool. 'This job, how long is it going to take? And is it legal?'

'It won't be long, no more than a few hours. And I don't really know if it's legal or not. I suspect it depends on where you're coming from.'

She looked at him sharply. The man – a studious-looking type – was watching their conversation with interest. 'Who sent you?' she asked, after a pause.

'Bill did.' And that had cost Elias too. After this, he wasn't going to have much money left. 'I think you know him.'

She breathed sharply. 'Yes, I do. All right, then.' She stuck her head out into the corridor and assessed the people hurrying past. She looked back at Elias. 'Vincent comes with us,' she nodded at the man behind her, 'or the deal's off.'

Elias examined him for a moment. He seemed harmless enough. 'Whatever.'

'Okay, here's the deal. I want a drink in the Hub first. We can all talk there. Then you can tell us what you want to pay us for.'

Elias glanced down the long corridor, towards the Hub. 'Those little silver things are everywhere now. I heard some people saying the Station might not survive more than another couple of days.'

'Before it loses its integrity and starts venting atmosphere? Yes, I know. But I didn't catch your name.'

'Elias Murray.'

'Okay then, Mr Murray, I don't know how long it's going to be before I get a decent drink again, so I want one last one in case there's no more Hub by next week, all right?'

Elias shrugged. It made no difference to him.

Most of the drinking establishments along the main stretch of the Hub had already closed down, and it was clear that those proprietors left were grabbing what little business they could before they themselves abandoned ship. The three of them pushed off along the corridor without saying anything. The panicking expressions around them, the sudden disruption of so many people's lives, said more than words might ever say. Elias felt some of that same fear clutch at him. The walls surrounding him could no longer be trusted to protect him, or anyone else, from the cold, vicious vacuum that lay beyond them. Maybe they only had minutes left, and he'd die without ever finding Trencher again. Maybe . . .

No, every smartsheet on board the Station seemed to be broadcasting emergency relays containing information about the 'infection', how the insects didn't seem to be aggressive towards people: but the safety of the Station had been compromised, and people were being advised to find a way to get off or else subject themselves to a rigorous evacuation procedure designed to make sure this infection didn't reach any ships still uncontaminated by it.

Elias had no intention of being taken anywhere on a military transport, unarmed and unprotected, if he could possibly avoid it. That meant spending money on hiring his own ship – and finding Trencher, whatever it took.

Elias felt ill at ease sitting there in an almost empty bar, watching the Station residents who had become refugees overnight hurrying past, sorting out the final details of their lives on board. Elias wondered if they'd ever have a Station to come back to.

He looked down at his hands, and saw they were

both shaking. As he willed them to stop, the tremors eased just a little. Not much time left, he thought, but if he could do one thing right, just one thing, he would find Trencher.

He thought again of that face he had glimpsed through thick, shielded plastic, and he shivered.

As he glanced at Vincent, he realized the man had been staring at him the whole time. Not in a challenging way, but in a . . . in a way that suggested he knew more than he had been letting on. Maybe he was her business partner?

'This is a strange situation.' Vincent continued looking at Elias.

Elias nodded, not sure how to reply.

'This job,' Kim said. 'Tell me about it.'

'Okay, I need to retrieve a friend of mine from one of the ships out there near the Station. He's on board a cargo carrier, or he was the last time I saw him. I need you to take me out there so I can fetch him back.'

'Hold it.' She put up one hand. 'Perhaps you aren't aware of the quarantine rules they've imposed since this emergency started.' Elias looked over her shoulder to see a tiny silver head squeeze itself out of an air duct. It dropped to the floor, and scurried away. Another followed it, and then another. Elias unclenched his jaw muscles and tried to force himself to relax. 'No ships are allowed anywhere near any vessel that hasn't already been hit by the infection. They'd shoot us out of the skies if we approached.'

'The *Jager*?' he said by way of explanation. 'I believe it was infected fairly early on. I saw the bugs swarming across it myself.'

'Okay.' She looked thoughtful. 'Okay, if it's already infected, we might not have so much of a problem. Next question, why doesn't your friend just get on board one of the regular shuttles and come over here himself?'

'He's being held there against his will,' said Elias. 'He's been kept on ice for a number of years, and though he's unconscious, he's still a prisoner.' He saw the disbelief on her face, and held up his hands. 'It's a long story – and I mean a *really* long story.'

'It's not the veracity of your story I'm concerned with,' she said. 'It's whether the people who are holding your . . . friend against his will are prepared to let you just take him away. I'm not very keen on finding myself in the middle of a shooting match.'

'You won't, I promise. Look, all I really need is transport – transport there, then back again.'

'Like catching a taxi ride?' she said.

'Exactly.' He nodded.

'Except a taxi ride where some types we'd rather not meet might just start shooting at us because they don't want your friend up there to take a taxi ride with you.'

He shrugged. 'That pretty much sums it up.'

She sighed. 'Give me a minute.' She got up, tapping Vincent on the arm, and they walked together across the Hub's main corridor, to where the bar area resumed on the other side. Most of the tables on that side were empty too. Elias watched and waited.

'I'm not sure. Is this the kind of thing you get up to these days?' Vincent asked her, a quizzical look on his face. She was starting to remember how difficult it was to tell when he was being serious or not.

'No, it's not, but . . .' She sighed. 'I can't even get to my Goblin right now. I have to pay a fine first, Vincent. Don't ask me what I did. I just screwed up, all right?'

'Surely the bureaucrats aren't going to prevent you from regaining your ship during an emergency like this?'

'Yeah, you'd think so, wouldn't you?' she said bitterly, feeling her cheeks burn with anger. 'I had gone to see Central Command with just that in mind.'

'And?' Vincent realized that must have been the point at which he'd spotted her in the crowd.

'If they'd only let me have it, I probably wouldn't still be on the Station right now. You know what they said? They said I'd have to wait until after this emergency before I could get it back. So I said, how the hell am I going to get off the Station, then?' She raised her hands in frustration, then dropped them to her sides. *God bless Bill*, she thought, knowing he must have been thinking of her when he sent this man Murray to contact her. He'd known just how badly she needed the money – and he was right.

'They told you to get in line with all the other refugees on board the military ships?'

She nodded. 'And leave my ship behind? Not if I can avoid it, Vincent.' She looked back at where Elias was still sitting. 'Not at all.'

'Okay,' said Vincent. 'One other thing, though. He mentioned the *Jager*, and we both know something happened to it a couple of days ago. Some kind of accident was reported.'

'Yeah, so?'

'So maybe he had something to do with that?' suggested Vincent, also glancing over at Elias. 'And if he did, are you so sure you really want his money?'

As Elias watched them come back over, he could already tell the woman was willing, but that didn't make it a done deal. Her partner certainly didn't look so happy. They both sat down opposite him.

'I want certain things understood,' began Kim. 'If we go out there with you – *if* we go – we don't know *anything* about what you're up to, not officially at any rate.' Elias nodded to that. 'We take you up there, but we're not coming on board with you. Is that clear?' Elias nodded again. 'We take you out there, we bring you back, and if we even begin to think people are likely to shoot at us, we're not prepared to endanger ourselves, and we still know nothing about what you were up to. I need you to agree with that, otherwise you can keep your money.'

Elias pondered for a few seconds, but he really didn't have much choice. In fact, if this woman had any idea how much of a last resort this really was for him, she might think about asking for more payment. On the other hand, the fact she seemed happy to take whatever he offered her suggested that maybe she wasn't in the best financial circumstances herself.

'All right, then,' he said slowly. 'Does your friend want to add his ID as a witness, and I can transfer half of the money now?'

'And the other half after the job is done?'

He nodded. Kim tried not to show her exultation. She had just got her Goblin back.

Twelve

Ursu

After some hours, Ursu realized he was totally lost.

The woodland seemed to go on for ever, and he had encountered more ruins, stumbling into them rather than locating them. The foliage was so dense that the only daylight fell directly from above.

It had been close. After he had carried the god into the woods, he had lain hidden in one spot for the next few hours, trembling with cold and fright. That had been uncomfortable enough, but a curious realization had come to him, that he had not felt nearly as scared as he had just before Nubala fell to the invaders. It was as if his ability to become frightened had been diminished by a process of either constantly evading capture or effecting escape once captured. Now he felt his senses numbed to the world around him. Now, he merely survived, whatever that might take.

After an hour or so of hiding, he had heard the sound of others thrashing about the dense woodland all around him, and had struggled on through the undergrowth, finding a deep, dark nook in the hollow left by a fallen tree. Soon after, a freezing rain had begun to fall, and as he sought shelter beneath the tree's mighty roots, he had heard voices calling to each other, some nearer, some farther, until finally they had faded away. Eventually he had pulled himself up, and forced himself to move further into the woods.

While stumbling through the forest, alone and afraid, he had felt the presence of Shecumpeh by him. Ursu looked up and, amid the harsh winds whistling through the foliage, heard words being spoken to him which were like the rustling of a breeze.

Look to that star, the voice seemed to say, but as Ursu peered up through the branches, he could see very little at all. He then looked around and saw a great rock rising in the distance, whose upper surface rose almost as high as the trees around it. He hiked his way towards it, through the undergrowth, then pulled himself up a steep natural ramp of earth that had accumulated behind it until he was standing beneath the wide, uncluttered expanse of the night sky, the forest now spread out beneath him.

Look to that star, the voice repeated. Ursu looked this way and that and spotted it. It lay far to the south, far from Hesper's Crown, and back in the direction he had come from.

Ursu looked around further and, though it was deep into the night, he thought he could detect glints of light some considerable distance off.

Keep the star to your back, the voice seemed to urge him. That way he would be always travelling in the right direction. *Go to the water*.

What water, Ursu wondered. When he looked again, he realized that the glinting light he had noticed was actually starlight reflecting off water. A river must cut its path through the forest.

Ursu knelt down beside the effigy and tilted it over to one side so that he could again see the faintest blue glow emanating from the crack in its side. There was definitely something inside it. What would happen if he dropped the god, and it shattered? Could that destroy Shecumpeh? The more he considered it, it hardly seemed possible that a deity so powerful would entrust its spirit to a lump of dried clay. There must be something else to it.

He listened again to the gentle hiss of the wind, expecting a voice to rise up and warn him against what he was contemplating. But the sound of the wind remained only the wind.

Ursu slid a fingernail into the crack and tugged at it until a chunk of the clay fell away. Suddenly Ursu felt a cold sweat slicking the fur under his robes. Inside the effigy was some kind of metal which was smooth to the touch. In a surge of apprehension, he broke away the rest of the god's clay covering until he could see what lay underneath.

The revealed artefact had a wide, square base, out of which rose a short column, also square, but twisted slightly. It narrowed slightly at the top. A made device? Ursu's fear began to give way to anger. This, he thought, was no living thing.

'This is no true god,' said Ursu, and it was as if a life-long spell had been broken.

But someone – or something – *had* spoken to him.

– I spoke to you, said the voice of Shecumpeh.

Ursu looked around, but failed to notice the hunched shadow that watched him from the shadows below the rock.

'Show yourself,' said Ursu, trembling. 'Show me who you really are.'

– Everything Shecumpeh has told you is true. But I am not Shecumpeh.

'Then who are you? Tell me the truth! Is Shecumpeh a god?'

– No. Shecumpeh is no god.

It was too much for Ursu. He fell onto all fours, and howled to the stars like a beast – or a canthre.

After a while, sensing that the mysterious presence had gone, Ursu lay down by the god of his people and studied its new contours, tracing a fingertip along its smooth metal surface. It seemed impossible, somehow, to connect that overwhelming sense of presence with this *object*.

He pulled himself upright, found his way down from the rock, and wandered amongst the roots and trunks until he could again see the star far above him. Then he turned his back on it and started walking.

A few hours later, he came upon an abandoned camp with the river just beyond it, probably one of the many tributaries of the Teive that flowed south to the Great Northern Sea. The land had become rockier and hillier as Ursu had progressed, and occasionally he thought he could discern great, dark shapes on the horizon. The Southern Teive Mountains, perhaps? If that was the case, at least he was moving away from Nubala and Xan's army.

The camp itself looked as if it had been hurriedly abandoned a long time ago. There were only a few tents left, almost all appearing to have been trampled by some manner of wild beast. A rusted sword lay by the ashes of a long-burnt-out fire. When Ursu investigated one of the collapsed tents, he found several leather sacks secured with straps. When he opened one to find boots and clothes, his heart rejoiced.

He looked at the dead fireplace, then went and gathered some dry wood. Next he searched for a flint, and discovered a couple marked with the sigil of Hesper, the neighbouring city to his native Nubala.

After several abortive attempts at raising sparks, Ursu finally managed to get a fire going. He inspected the satchel and found the god fitted neatly into it. After adjusting the straps, it sat comfortably enough on his back. Meanwhile he relished the warmth rising from the flickering flames.

Then a thought occurred to him and he reopened the satchel. Taking the god back out, he set it in his lap and studied it. Not a god, he realized, just a carefully shaped lump of metal. But at the same time, surely something more than that.

But his thoughts still roamed, even as his belly ached from hunger. Then another idea popped into his head. He knew now how to find some food.

Having found a suitable stick to sharpen, he headed towards the river just as the sun rose over the treetops. He felt Shecumpeh guiding him farther and farther along the river's edge.

He was about to turn back when a sudden urgency surged within him, even though all he could see around him was mud and water and steep, slippery embankments. Then he almost fell over a wooden boat pulled halfway up onto the dry soil and concealed with bracken. Again his heart leapt, for a boat meant travel. It could carry him down this tributary and into the great river flowing south.

He stared uncertainly at the surging water, then determinedly began pushing at the sides of the boat, rocking it from side to side until it came loose from the confining undergrowth.

It was only then that he noticed the corpse, with a wound in its side.

Whoever he had been, he had belonged to Xan's

army. His clothes were of the superior quality worn by mercenaries and soldiers. Clearly, he must have travelled downriver before stopping off here. Perhaps he had got badly injured further upriver – near Nubala?

I must do an Embedding, thought Ursu. He fetched a sharp knife back from the camp. *This is a holy thing I do*, thought Ursu, and he began reciting the litany of Embedding as he cut into the dead soldier's flesh.

This is how we begin, thought Ursu. You had to eat the flesh of the dead before you could become a sentient person. Only then did you acquire the skill of walking upright, and of communicating with speech. To eat the flesh of the dead, after all, was to honour them, and most especially to preserve their memories and their strength.

Fatigue was starting to overcome him, and he realized he had to get some sleep before he next moved on. The correct rituals had to be performed, however. The dead had to be appropriately honoured before they could be remembered.

He spoke the incantation, then slid the sharp point of the knife into the rear of the skull. This proved difficult, so in the end he fetched a rock from the riverside and used it to break the skullbone as he had seen a Master once do. Then he was able to cut away the parts tradition said contained the last thoughts and memories of the dead, and proceeded to chew them raw.

Finally he lay back and closed his eyes. As sleep came to him, so did a dead man's memories. He remembered the sequence of death first, the sword that struck into his side as he entered the city of Nubala with his comrades, then being carried off and abandoned somewhere to die. He could remember crawling away, finding his way down to the river, where they had been building boats to ferry supplies to support the siege.

He remembered back further, fleeting images of the court of Xan. For the first time now, Ursu knew what the Emperor looked like. The visions continued in fits and starts, and with them came knowledge: a deep foreboding as he came to realize that the Emperor consorted with demons, with Shai, glowing, hairless figures. They reminded him at once of that crouching figure he had glimpsed, indeed something out of a nightmare.

The dead soldier had clearly been someone important, a commander-in-arms of the armies besieging Nubala. As knowledge filled Ursu's mind, there came with it horror.

Elias

'Cramped, but it's home,' said Kim, ducking through a tiny airlock.

Elias pursed his lips. This might be better with just the two of them, he thought, glancing briefly at Vincent. He could see, even from the outside, that the Goblin was going to be a squeeze for all three of them, plus Trencher.

He glanced around the docking bay, where identical heavy airlock doors carried signs indicating if there were any craft on the other side of them. He then watched Kim's small, tight butt wriggle through the connecting tube between the Station and the Goblin itself. He looked again at Vincent, who just shrugged.

Kim turned and gestured from the far end of the access tube. 'Come on through,' she said. Elias climbed in and crawled along on his hands and knees. Once inside the Goblin, he could barely stand up straight.

'These things always look bigger from the outside,' he said.

Kim looked surprised. 'You've been in one before? I thought you said you'd come straight from Earth.'

'I did military service, had to learn a lot of things fast – usually by compression learning' – he tapped the side of his head – 'where they cram it in.'

'Oh, right.' She shrugged. 'Well, most of it's taken up with engine, but I guess maybe you already know that. Plus the life support, of course.'

Elias glanced around the tiny cockpit, seeing where a narrow crawlspace led through further, probably accessing just enough space for a single bunk and some storage. He'd already noticed a cargo pod attached to the rear of the ship, connected to the Goblin itself by a pressurized tube. 'I thought these newer types dredged oxygen and nitrogen out of the vacuum.'

'Sure, ramscoop – plus an Angel drive for hard acceleration. But that means having shielding for the electronics on board, and it takes up most of the rest of the space. Plus emergency backups, in case those don't work, and a body tank in case those don't work either.'

'Listen, I don't mean to be rude, but why do you need him along?' asked Elias, jerking his thumb at the airlock tube and, by implication, Vincent. 'You're the pilot, surely. Or is he your co-pilot?'

'No, he's not my co-pilot, he's a friend. I'd just like to have him along for the company,' she replied coolly.

Elias nodded. She obviously wasn't completely sure about him, or simply didn't trust him. It would only be for a little while anyway, he reminded himself.

He heard scrabbling through the tube and turned to see Vincent emerge. It was definitely getting crowded here. Elias was not prone to claustrophobia but, even so, his throat tightened involuntarily. Fortunately, one-man craft or not, the Goblin was equipped with a co-pilot's seat. He sat down in it quickly while Vincent gazed around, carefully not looking at Elias. Well, trust and friendship all round, thought Elias. It would be good to get this trip over and done with.

Kim looked flustered. She was not used to having anyone else in here, he thought. It couldn't be easy for her. Elias slid around in the seat until he felt comfortable, then locked the web restraints over his chest. He watched the woman slide into the pilot's seat beside him, and took a sideways glance at Vincent.

Kim closed her eyes for a few moments, took a deep breath, then exhaled. Set in front of her and Elias was a series of screens which fed visual data from outside the ship. 'Okay.' She tapped some buttons. 'Everything's online,' she muttered, then turned around. 'Vincent, close up the airlock and lock it off, will you?'

She hit some more buttons and sat back, blowing a few loose strands of dark hair out of her face. 'Okay, now we wait for departure confirmation. That might take several minutes.'

Vincent floated around behind them, examining almost everything with curiosity. Elias felt the minutes pass very slowly, and registered the look of relief on her face when confirmation finally came through.

Kim

She guided the Goblin away from the Angel Station. The screens showed only stars and the blackness of space beyond, but various other displays revealed the positions of every ship in the vicinity. She charted a course toward the *Jager*.

Kim did not want to know what Murray was intending once he reached the *Jager*. She did not believe his story, and doubts had niggled at her incessantly since he had appeared. *I am doing the wrong thing*, she had thought, over and over. *Whatever he's paying me, it's not worth any more trouble with the law.*

On the other hand, she had reminded herself, the authorities on the Angel Station currently had their hands too full to think of anything else. She hadn't allowed herself to think further what that might mean in the long run. Whether there might be anything to return to, for instance. If it hadn't been for Vincent's sudden appearance, she might well have headed deep into the Kasper system until things blew over.

And if it didn't get sorted out, if something drastic happened to the Angel Station? But there were other ships out there, capable of keeping a lot of people alive for a long time.

After that, well, there was always Kasper itself, if it came to that. She wondered how the military transports would react, under those circumstances – if contact with Earth was lost. Shoot people down for getting too close to the forbidden planet? Under normal circumstances, the military were legally entitled to do so, but these were hardly normal circumstances.

Later. She would think about these things later.

She excused herself, got up and went through to the aft section, the closest place she had to a real home, leaving Vincent alone with Elias.

When she eventually came back into the cockpit, Elias was still in the co-pilot's seat, chatting quietly to Vincent. It was small-talk, mostly from Vincent, about academic life back home. She wondered if he'd mentioned anything to Murray about what he feared might happen to the Kaspians.

Kim climbed back into the pilot's seat and made some minor course adjustments. They were almost there. She pressed a button and a screen to her right, just above Elias's forehead, sprang to life. It revealed a grey-white shape floating against a sea of darkness. It was the *Jager*.

She glanced at Elias, who was watching the screen intently. There was a look of . . . of hunger on his face, an expression of such intense desire it made Kim feel voyeuristic to watch him. Elias glanced across at her, smiled awkwardly, then turned back to the screen, his expression a bit more guarded.

Kim glanced up at the overhead screens, just in time to see the *Jager* explode.

Or rather, it seemed to come apart as if being unfolded by an invisible hand. The cargo transport simply shattered into a cloud of silver fragments that blossomed towards them, moving fast. Kim gaped at the screen, watching the cloud approach. It was as if her eyes couldn't quite register what they'd just witnessed. As the cloud came closer, it resolved itself differently. She reached over Elias's shoulder and touched a screen to increase the magnification.

Silver bugs – millions of them – drifting straight towards the Goblin. She put her hand to her mouth. *Oh my God*, she thought, *what if there were people on board? What happened to them?*

Larger sections of the fragmenting *Jager* were becoming visible. She could see the naked engine core, and that too was coming apart. She knew how she would describe this scene for the rest of her life; it was like a child unwrapping shiny metallic paper from around a gift, and the paper being reduced to a blizzard of fragments. Except it was a cargo ship coming apart. She felt a dull heaviness in the pit of her stomach.

She glanced at Elias to her right. He looked shaken and pale, but he was studying the screen closely.

After a few minutes it became clear the components of the expanding cloud were now streaming towards the Angel Station. The Goblin lay directly between the Station and the *Jager*'s prior location.

'Is there any way we can avoid them?' asked Vincent from behind her.

Kim was about to answer, but just then the Goblin shuddered, as if making its own response. For a moment they heard a sound not unlike the patter of rain against a window pane.

'They're not stopping,' said Vincent with relief. She followed his gaze to the screen displaying the scene behind them. Far behind them now, the bugs were moving towards the Station.

She wondered what would happen when they eventually got there.

Thirteen

Pierce

As the Station started to come apart, Pierce thought: *If I make it through this, I'll have such a story to tell.*

The whole Station was getting quieter, quieter than Pierce had ever known it to be. He'd been assuring everyone he met this evacuation was just a temporary measure, that the authorities back on Earth knew what was happening. The news of the invasion of silver bugs had finally gone public all across the Grid, and constantly updated reports were running on all the public datafeeds. Headlines and videos blazed on smartsheets everywhere, held anxiously in the hands of refugees waiting for rescue, or lying discarded in the abandoned corridors of the Hub.

Other reports were coming through, too, about a wave of radiation moving towards the Kaspian system, and only days away. It wasn't hard to guess someone somewhere had been withholding information, almost certainly someone high up in the chain of command.

Pierce was located in Central Command, a bundle of

habitats and office units, watching the coordination of the rescue effort. There were going to be a lot of questions asked about delays in the evacuation effort. For the moment at least, no traffic was heading in or out of the singularity. Avoiding the bugs anywhere throughout the Station was no longer possible. They were even infesting Central Command.

Pierce heard a loud clang, and the operations room around him shook. A klaxon sounded, then came a crunching noise like a steel girder being bent double in one instant by some huge malevolent hand.

He had already abandoned the idea of looking for a Goblin to escape in, finding a streak of integrity within himself he'd never suspected existed. He acted as the Mayor for the people who lived on the Angel Station, even though that in itself was a kind of joke. Somewhere along the line, however, he'd come to believe in his role. There was no one else between the military administrators of the Station and the civilians who made up the bulk of its population, so he'd decided to stick around to help as best he could, and accept a military evacuation when the time came.

And because he was officially an employee of Central Command – being a civilian as well didn't seem to make a difference – he was obliged to go last. Like the captain of a sinking ship, he thought, with less bitterness than he would have thought he'd feel.

One of Holmes's aides ran through the door. 'That's

it. Out, everybody, *now*. We're losing atmosphere. Get down to Bay Green Seven.'

Pierce watched as everybody else got up from their consoles. *Well, what are you waiting for?* he thought, and ran for the door.

Along the corridor, silver bugs coated the walls and ceiling. Huge holes had been eaten out of the bulkheads. Emergency lights now functioned in many parts of the Station; communications and power had been shut down in several sections. But thankfully most people were out of harm's way. *Can't they shut the damn klaxons off?* he thought.

Oh, not good, he thought, when they got to the corridor connecting that part of Central Command to the rest of the Station. The corridor had sealed itself off, swinging the emergency airlock down from the ceiling on its enormous hinge. Pierce and the others peered through the tiny viewing window set into it.

Only stars visible. No sign of the connecting corridor beyond. He wondered if that was the loud noise he had heard – that they had all heard. No access to Bay Green Seven, then.

He looked at the sweating faces all around him. 'Six?' suggested someone wearing the uniform of a lieutenant. 'It's back down this way. If we go back down here,' he pointed down another passageway, 'and cut right, that connects to the Hub.' The lieutenant didn't wait to see if anybody disagreed and took off at a run. Pierce ran after the lieutenant. They all ran.

The corridor leading to the Hub and Green Six was still intact, but it was getting hard to breathe. 'That's the atmosphere dropping low,' he heard somebody explain. Pierce turned and recognized Holmes's aide. He could not remember the young man's name. The bulkheads shuddered around them. Pierce glanced back the way they had come, and saw the whole corridor behind them twisting out of shape.

Any pretence at order, at military discipline, went out of the window as they scurried down the corridor connecting into the Hub.

Kim

Kim increased the magnification on the rear viewscreen until they could see the whole Kasper Station in all its glory. Something was wrong with it too. Sections of the human-habitable portion had come adrift, were floating near the mouth of the singularity. Other sections were twisted and bent.

'You know,' said Vincent, 'when all this started, I even wondered if those bugs were intelligent.' Kim and Elias stared at him. 'They're artefacts, obviously. Machines. So, even if they're not living creatures as such, they're definitely programmed to perform certain tasks. The question is,' he said, 'just what it is they're programmed *for*.'

338

'Do you think they were intended to destroy?' asked Elias. 'Some kind of weapon?'

'I don't know. Maybe. But the main factor that's been obvious all along is that they consume metals in order to reproduce, no, duplicate themselves. Like Von Neumann machines.'

How does he do that? wondered Kim. He just talked away in that calm voice, and somehow the tense atmosphere had been defused. They were all still frightened, unsure what was going to happen next, but they were now thinking about other things too, like the whys and the hows. 'Machines that make copies of themselves?' she asked.

Vincent shrugged. 'It's pretty obvious that's what they are.' He pursed his lips. 'You know, there's one thing I've been wondering about. I mean the Angel Station – the main body of it that isn't human. They don't seem to have been eating that, do they?'

'What in God's name are you talking about?' Murray scowled. 'Just look at it. The whole thing's coming apart.'

'No, the human-inhabited bit of it is, those sections added on to the original alien Station after humans arrived in this system. The original Angel Station – the part that encircles the singularity – they haven't touched it.'

Kim was thunderstruck. 'Do you think they've got some connection with the Station, the bugs?'

A hint of a smile twisted the corner of Vincent's

mouth. 'I don't know – nobody does – but I've got an idea. What if they're some kind of defence mechanism?'

They stared at him. 'I mean, think about it,' he said. 'We don't know what happened to the original human crew of the Angel Station when the Hiatus started. Something else might have attacked them. Something from the original Station itself.' Vincent looked pleased with himself, but Kim noticed Murray was staring blankly into some place inside himself. He looked bleak and miserable. She remembered. Of course.

'Your friend. I'm sorry,' she said, moving towards him until he could see her properly. 'Do you think he was on board?'

He looked up at her. 'I have no reason to think he wasn't,' he said at length, clasping his hands helplessly in front of him. He looked like a man who had just found out that someone very important to him had died.

Pierce

The Station trembled around them. Something banged explosively far around the curve of the Hub, followed by a moaning, sucking sound that sent a freezing chill down Pierce's spine. A gentle wind tossed his hair. Then the wind became stronger, then began to suck at him. It was getting much harder to breathe, or to think.

'The Hub is breached. Green Six is this way,'

pointed the lieutenant. But everyone knew where Bay Green Six was and was already running. They were close to it, very close. Pierce knew there were military shuttles docked there ready for departure by the last remaining crew. The wind had become a hurricane.

Someone had reached the bay door, and punched in a security code. Each tap of a finger on a glass screen seemed to take an eternity. Then the door slid open. Slowly.

Black spots began appearing in front of Pierce's eyes. He was panting for air; they all were. They squeezed and crushed their way through the door, giving way to blind panic. Pierce turned and glimpsed the lieutenant behind him. Something happened to the Hub behind the man. A strip seemed to peel away from one of the bulkheads, and Pierce saw blackness beyond. Then something invisible reached out for the lieutenant and the two men behind him, pulling them through the air towards that blackness. The door slid shut, cutting them off.

'Come on.' Someone tugged at the Mayor's shoulder, as he stared through the reinforced glass in the door at the spot where the three men had last been seen. He'd never seen someone actually die before. He turned to see the other survivors boarding the shuttle. He followed, feeling numb.

Inside, he stood near the rear of the cockpit, watching the Station disintegrate from the outside. As they moved away from the docking link, the fat torus shape of the construction became visible. The human add-ons looked as if they had been shredded.

'How could that happen in just a few hours?' someone whispered.

Pierce knew what he meant. A few hours earlier, you could have harboured the notion that the bugs were a containable problem, that a solution still lay within reach. But they had won, he realized, whoever – or whatever – they were. Entire sections of the Hub and of Central Command were floating free now. To his surprise, Pierce realized that he missed the place already.

Elias

Elias had been watching Kim carefully as she worked the Goblin's console. It looked easier to operate than any other Goblin he'd encountered, so he suspected this particular vessel was less versatile as a result, more limited in what it could do. She was standing up, facing away from him, studying some piece of information scrolling down a screen mounted high above the console panel.

He was still in the co-pilot's seat. He studied the section of console before him until he found a set of controls for the viewscreens. Things had changed, he realized, but not that much.

'Excuse me,' he said, turning to Kim. 'I need you to take a look at something.'

She glanced down at at him. 'What is it?'

'Before the *Jager* . . .' He searched for the right word, but couldn't find it. 'Before it exploded, we were watching a high-magnification image on one of these screens. Is there any way I can see it again?'

She looked at him quizzically, shrugged. 'Sure, here.' She leaned over him, touched more panels on the console. The *Jager* magically reappeared on a view-screen, intact again. This time a date readout appeared in the lower right-hand corner. 'Ten minutes before it came apart. What about it?'

Elias stared at the screen in fascination. 'Can you fast-forward it, just a little?'

She touched the console again. The time on the screen shot forward, to just a couple of minutes before the ship finally dissolved. 'There.' He stood up out of the co-pilot's seat and touched the screen with his finger. 'Do you see that?'

Kim folded her arms and watched. It looked like a shuttle leaving the *Jager* seconds before her destruction. She grunted in surprise. 'I do.'

'Where did it go?' he asked. She shrugged, her expression saying *I don't know*. She then zoomed in so they could see the tiny vessel moving rapidly away from the *Jager*. Seconds later, the cargo ship again blossomed into spinning fragments.

'Whoever's on board that shuttle made it out by the skin of their teeth,' she said. 'It must have been very bad there in the last moments.' She looked at Murray. 'You think your friend might be on that shuttle?'

'I'm sure of it,' he said.

'What makes you feel so sure?' asked Vincent. 'It could be anybody on that shuttle.'

'I know things,' Elias replied, 'that you don't. I was on board the *Jager* myself, and found people there you really wouldn't like to meet.' *I've already told you more than I should have*, he thought. There was something too convenient about it all: Trencher being here, so far from home; then these bugs, the *Jager* exploding.

'As I said before, I'm not interested in your reasons for visiting the *Jager*,' snapped Kim. Elias noticed her lips were set in a thin line.

'So what now?' said Vincent. 'Everybody either on the Angel Station or on the transports must have witnessed what happened to the *Jager*. Do we go back to the Station, if there's anything left of it, or head for one of the transports?'

Kim, Elias could see, still had that tense expression on her face, and was deliberately trying not to catch his eye. *She's wondering what I'm going to do*, he thought. And then he realized just what it was that he might need to do.

'Mr Murray, I'll be frank with you. The only reason I accepted this job was because I had to pay a fine to get my Goblin back. But whatever you're involved in, I really don't think I want a part in it. I don't think you're telling us enough,' said Kim. 'I've fulfilled half of the bargain. We came this far.'

She thinks I'm responsible for this in some way, thought Elias, seeing the look in her eyes. 'The return journey is free,' she continued. 'I'll reimburse the remainder of your money outside of the fine once we're back under Station jurisdiction. I think that's fair under the circumstances.'

She's worried she's in way over her head, Elias realized. An idea was forming in his mind. 'Before we come to any conclusions, I want to trace the trajectory of that shuttle we just observed.'

'Pardon?'

'The shuttle. The one leaving the *Jager*. Every ship – even one as small as this – keeps a log of the trajectory and estimated departure and arrival points of every other ship its sensors pick up on.' Kim blinked, looking upset. She hadn't known that fact, he realized. How much training had she received before she'd been allowed to use the Goblin? How much training had any of the other miners wandering around this system?

'Here.' He leaned forward, tapped a code into the console. New images sprang up on the overhead screens, web-like lines of trajectory spinning out from the *Jager*'s former location. One line spun right back to the Station, the cargo ship's own point of origin. Another line described the approach of their Goblin to the *Jager*. Yet another line described a gentle arc, moving away from the *Jager* – the shuttle Elias had noticed.

But it did not lead back to the Station, or even to the singularity. Instead it arced out in an entirely different direction altogether, towards some point deep in the Kaspian system. Elias heard Vincent swear softly behind him.

'That doesn't mean anything,' said Kim, sounding flustered. 'The system is full of freelancers working the two main rock belts.'

'That's not where they're headed,' Elias said carefully. 'Shuttles are only intended for very short trips. If they were only intent on escaping, they'd have headed for a transport. Nobody willingly takes short-range shuttles on long-term trips.'

'If that shuttle can only travel so far, then it must have headed for somewhere nearby.'

Elias was thinking hard. 'Maybe – unless it was unmanned. It could go a lot further without a crew or passengers on regular life-support. Just point it in the right direction, and off you go.'

Elias could see the other two were staring at him like he was crazy. 'Remember what I told you, my friend was iced, in a sleepbox. Listen, I'm going to make you an offer. I'll pay you twice as much again to take me deeper into the system. Along the same trajectory as that shuttle took.'

By way of reply, Kim slid back into her seat and tapped at the console. The Goblin had continued on the course intended to bring it to the *Jager*. Elias could see she was changing the course of the Goblin. But not to follow where the shuttle had gone. Back towards the Station.

'You said you intended to go deep into the system once this job was concluded,' reminded Elias.

'On my own,' she said. 'Not with anybody else. *On my own*. I prefer it that way, Mr Murray. I'll drop you off with one of the military escorts, and they'll see you're taken care of.'

Elias pulled out his credit chip and placed it on the console in front of Kim. It skidded slightly across the console's smooth surface, its motion seeming liquid and slow in the zero gravity. Numbers blinked up at Kim as she looked down at the chip.

'That's not an option, not under any circumstances.' His voice was calm but he could feel himself tensing.

Her voice trembled. 'And what if *we* don't want to follow your shuttle?'

'That's not an option either.'

He sensed Vincent's hand reaching for his left shoulder, almost before he felt it. He turned, grasped Vincent's arm just above the elbow with his right hand, pulling the man to one side. At the same time Elias turned in a motion almost balletic in the zero gravity. Elias snapped his left elbow up, impacting hard with Vincent's nose. Vincent made a muffled sound, and crashed into the back of the co-pilot's seat. Small globules of his blood span through the air of the cockpit.

Kim lunged at him, reaching for his face with her

hands. Elias grabbed both her wrists before she could get to him, and pushed her down against her chair. She grunted, sliding back against the console as she tried to wrestle out of his grip.

'I'm sorry about this.' He meant it. 'I have to find that shuttle. You don't understand how much is at stake here.'

'Bastard,' she spat, 'this is my ship. Get your own ship.' She twisted, kicked at him.

'I don't have one,' he said, evading her blows with ease. 'I'm sorry, but I'm doing the right thing.' *I am*, he thought. Nonetheless, he could taste sour bile at the back of his throat.

Elias now sat at the controls of the Goblin, studying the data-streams coming in from a variety of sources: from the local Grid, updated constantly by packet bursts fired through the singularity; from the Station itself, where pressure-suited investigators were studying the wreck of the human-built sections of the Station; from the military escorts, but relatively uninformative and mainly brief statements updating what everybody already knew.

He did not feel good about taking Kim's ship from her, but neither could he see any alternative. He especially did not want to come to the attention of the military. Yet he had remained in the designated co-pilot's seat, out of a sense of deference to the Goblin's owner.

Kim had taken the injured Vincent through to her cabin. They hadn't appeared since, and Elias assumed they were discussing what to do next.

Meanwhile he busied himself at the ship's onboard computer. A chill rushed through him as the ship estimated the long-range end of the shuttle's trajectory; straight towards Kasper. The craft had an hour's head start. Reorienting the Goblin, he aimed it deep into the heart of the Kaspian system. Around him, screens filled with computational analysis translated into diagrams, and the estimated fuel consumption of the Goblin's Angel drive. Finally, Elias settled back in his chair. From here on in, the Goblin could fly itself. It was only when he arrived there that he would have to worry about his options.

Kim

'Just keep the gauze in place till it stops bleeding,' advised Kim.

Vincent mumbled something about that *bastard*. 'Do you think he's seriously dangerous?' she asked.

Vincent stared at her until her face began to colour. 'He wants something very badly, that's what I think,' replied Vincent. 'I can't judge his veracity, but the first thing I noticed was how edgy he was.'

'I know what you mean.' She paused for a moment. 'But I needed the money.'

'Your friend Bill passed him to you, as I recall. Can you still trust Bill's judgement?'

Kim sat back and stared out into space. 'I don't know. I don't really think Bill is such a great judge of character, and he certainly deals with some lowlifes, but I don't think he'd have sent Murray to us if he thought there was any chance something like this might happen.'

'The next question,' said Vincent, 'is what do we do about him?'

Kim looked him in the eyes. 'Unless you've got any great ideas, I don't think there's very much we can do.' She saw him start to protest. 'Listen, let's just ride this out – and see what happens when he finds that shuttle.'

'And if he kills everyone on board it? And decides he doesn't need any witnesses?'

'Think, Vince, what happens when he catches up with the shuttle? He's going to have to leave the ship then. At least this way, we can wait safely for an opportunity. We're two to one; and that might count for something.' *Or it might just leave us both dead*, she added silently.

But it would take days still before the Goblin caught up with the shuttle, wherever the damn thing was headed. Which meant they were headed far from the environs of the Angel Station, deep into the Kaspian system.

*

'Kim,' Vincent spoke from somewhere behind her, 'can you take a look at this, please?'

She turned around. He wasn't looking at her, but staring at something else, out of sight. It had been two days now since Elias had taken control of the Goblin, and the weight of acceleration had grown rapidly during that time. Kim had enough experience to tell that Elias had set the Angel drive to maximum burn. That would carry them for a considerable distance across the Kaspian system in a relatively short time.

At one point she had found him sleeping, still sitting absurdly in the co-pilot's seat. A tiny gun was held loosely in the hand resting on his thigh. She had emerged from the crawlspace as quietly as she could, intending to warn him that, at the kind of velocity they were moving at, the Angel drive would burn out all its fuel within hours. That would make the return journey a long and hard one, moving at a bare crawl.

She had studied him for a long moment, then one eye had slid open as he watched her, for just a few moments, then closed again. Unnerved, she had retreated back through the crawlspace, without saying anything to him.

Vincent and she had agreed to take turns at sleeping, since neither liked the idea of both being fast asleep while Elias was at the controls. The confined space they shared stirred old memories, but memories that carried pain with them, at least for Kim.

Now Kim was barely awake. The stress of the past several days had been building up on her.

She lifted herself from her bunk and looked round for Vincent. He was squatting with his back to her by the other crawlspace, to the rear of the cabin, that led back past the side of the engine core to a cargo bay little larger than the cockpit. She floated over until she was beside him as he peered along the crawlspace.

'What is it?' she whispered quietly.

'Thought I saw something move down there,' he said.

He pointed, but she saw nothing at first. The passage was lit by tiny panels embedded every few feet. Then something passed in front of one of the corner lights, casting a brief shadow.

Please don't let it be, she thought. *Please don't let it be.*

But she already knew it was.

'I think we've got stowaways, if you know what I mean,' said Vincent unnecessarily.

Kim watched for several moments more, then bent down to crawl through. She hesitated. *They're not dangerous to people*, she thought. *To the Station, yes, but they don't eat human flesh. They ignore us. Remember that.* She crawled onwards.

She emerged into the rear cargo bay. They were everywhere, clinging to every surface. She couldn't even find a handhold.

They hadn't been there a few hours before, when

she'd last looked in here. She looked around, searching. They totally ignored her. Then she spotted it: an access panel floated in freefall, a gaping hole where it had previously been fixed to a bulkhead. The silver bugs were swarming through it. She pushed away from the crawl-space to peer inside the hatch. There should have been a range of electronics and a readout, a backup monitor for the engine core in case of general systems failure. There was now only twisted wreckage, chewed and torn.

There was a faint hissing noise, and the tiniest breeze tickled her nose, coming from somewhere behind her. She tried to trace its origin, but with the bugs swimming from bulkhead to bulkhead, she couldn't see.

'We're going to have to turn back,' she said, coming back to explain to Vincent. 'I'll go and speak to him now. He'll turn back when he understands the alternative.'

Vincent nodded. 'You should also tell him about the radiation. If nothing else convinces him, maybe that will.'

Elias was awake again as she crawled into the cockpit. 'You'd better not be lying,' he said, after she had told him the situation.

Or what? You're going to shoot us all? She almost

said it, but held her tongue. 'Go take a look for yourself.'

For a moment he looked indecisive. 'All right. Go back through.'

She turned, pushing herself back through the crawlspace. Elias emerged warily into the cabin a few moments later. He carried the tiny weapon again.

'I know you don't have a very high opinion of me,' he said unexpectedly. 'I wish you could understand.'

'Does that mean you'll give me my ship back?' asked Kim.

He just looked away from her. *I wonder what's going on in his head*, she thought. He was no mere thief; something bigger was at stake here. Although trust wasn't on the agenda, she sought understanding.

He knelt down by the crawlspace leading back to the cargo bay and peered through.

Kim had boosted herself into a corner, as if giving Elias room to pass. Now, while his attention was momentarily elsewhere, she aimed a kick towards the back of his head. She pushed off from the corner, a few moments passing like an eternity. He still hadn't looked up, still gripped the tiny weapon in one hand as he gazed down the narrow tunnel. She was just behind him now, falling towards his unprotected head.

He jerked back instantly, and she thought: *He knows what I'm trying*. Her boot caught him hard on the back of the neck. He made a sound of surprise, but still held on to the pistol. His free hand reached up, gripping her ankle like a steel vice.

Once Vincent realized what she was doing, he grabbed one of his discarded boots from the corner and smacked Elias hard across the head.

Elias kept hold of Kim's leg as Vincent hit him again. Kim's heart leapt into her mouth as she saw Elias point the pistol straight at Vincent. He didn't pull the trigger however. Instead, he turned pale and began to sweat, his hands shaking. There was something wrong with him, she realized.

Vincent struck again, now with his fist, catching Elias on the mouth. Kim still had one foot free, and now battered the back of Elias's head with it, bracing herself against a bulkhead to give her the leverage she needed.

Suddenly, Elias went limp, and at first she thought he was unconscious. Her leg slipped from his grasp.

'Vincent, get the gun,' she said desperately, then realized he already had. He held it awkwardly, clearly unused to handling weapons.

He could easily have killed Vincent, she realized, and wondered why he hadn't. She felt she should feel pleased with their small victory. But strangely it didn't feel like that.

'We weren't lying about the bugs,' she insisted, as if justifying herself, having pushed a safe distance away from him. She hoped Vincent would be capable of using the weapon if necessary.

Elias said nothing for a moment. Then he raised

himself a little, and looked over at her. 'I may have a damaged tooth. I need access to the medical program.'

'Fine. Vincent, just make sure you keep that thing aimed properly.'

'Where are we going to put him?' asked Vincent.

'The cargo bay, I guess.'

'Is it safe? I mean, all the bugs—'

'How many?' Elias interrupted.

Kim looked at him sharply. 'I'd rather you kept quiet.'

'You saw what happened to the *Jager*,' he said. 'How long before this ship goes the same way?'

Kim opened her mouth, and closed it again. Unfortunately he was right.

'We've only been away from the Station for a few days. We still have time to turn back.'

'By the time we decelerate and reverse course, it will be almost fourteen days before we reach what's left of the Station. Kasper is much nearer.'

She stared at him in shock. 'You can't be seriously suggesting —'

'There's no alternative, not if we have those bugs on board. It's also where the shuttle's headed. There are people on Kasper – humans.'

'You mean at the North Pole? The research station at the Citadel?'

'I mean *other* people. Primalists, maybe, hiding out somewhere on the planet's surface.'

'You're crazy,' said Kim, flabbergasted. 'They've

done aerial and satellite surveys of the whole planet, watching their culture from a distance. If humans were down there, or interfering, we'd know.' This was ridiculous, she thought. They needed to find some way of restraining him until they could get back to the Station.

Then she remembered the tiny air leak in the cargo bay. She would not admit to Elias that he might be right about not turning back.

'There has to be a reason why that shuttle is going there.'

'You don't even know where the shuttle's going!' she yelled. 'You're crazy! One thing I do know, those things have emergency protocols hardwired into them, and just maybe that's the real reason the thing left the *Jager* when it did. Maybe its heading this way was just an accident, maybe this is its onboard computer's response to the *Jager* coming apart. Elias, maybe there's nobody on board. Did you think of that?'

'Unmanned shuttles running on random algorithms don't make course corrections,' Elias argued smoothly, 'unless they've been programmed with a destination in mind. Flying to Kasper isn't the obvious destination for a short-range shuttle of that type. You may have noticed it hasn't been giving out any distress signals either. It's running silent.'

Kim glared at him. 'Here's what we're going to do. You're going to stay here, while Vincent and I go through to the cockpit. If you try to enter the cockpit,

I'll make sure at least one of us uses that gun to good effect.'

Elias said nothing more, his expression disturbingly smooth and untroubled.

Back in the cockpit, Kim busied herself at the familiar console.

Elias had set numerous datastreams running across half the screens, some from pockets of human life on the Angel Station that had, against all odds, survived the onslaught. The majority of the bugs, it seemed, had now disappeared from there. The emergency, for the Station at least, was almost certainly over.

'Keep that gun aimed at the crawlspace, Vince,' she warned, as he came and stood by her, leaning over the co-pilot's seat and peering at the screens.

'Look at this!' he yelped. 'That's the cloud of bugs that came off the *Jager*.'

'What about them?'

'Says here they kept on going until they reached the singularity. Know what they did when they got there?'

Kim tapped at a control. Something was wrong, but she wasn't sure what. Some codes she could access easily, others seemed . . . locked off. She then tried to access the navigation system, but was blocked at every attempt. 'What did they do, Vincent?' she hissed in frustration.

'They flew straight through it.' Vincent's voice was full of wonder. 'Flew straight through, but didn't emerge at the next Station in the chain. My God, I wonder where they went.'

'Vincent, I have other things to worry about just now. I can't control the Goblin. I can't change our course!'

The gun felt slippery in her hand. It was an uncertain weapon, partly because she had never fired a weapon, partly because even though it seemed simple enough to operate, she could not be sure if she had the nerve to use it. She had emerged into the cabin to find Elias still sitting in a corner near the cargo-hold crawlspace, arms folded neatly.

'Tell me what you did to my ship, or I swear I'll blow your fucking head off.'

'Some things I learned in the military. Override procedures they don't mention in the manuals. The army's good for that kind of thing.'

'Tell me where we're heading.'

'Kasper.'

She stared at him. 'And just what the hell do you think we're going to do when we get there?'

He shrugged. 'Find that shuttle.'

'Elias, I'm not even sure this ship could make it down to the surface of a planet.'

'Neither am I, but it's an option. The Goblins were all designed with such an eventuality in mind.'

'How can you be sure?'

'For a start, the details are listed under the emergency protocols contained in the console. The Goblins are derived from a very functional military design. Some of them are ex-military, in fact, which is one reason people like you can afford them, being surplus to needs, decommissioned. They can handle re-entry if they need to.'

'Elias,' she protested, feeling desperate, 'in case you hadn't noticed, this thing is hardly aerodynamic in shape.'

'It can make it,' he replied. 'All these kinds of ships have the necessary shielding. As I already told you, I came here looking for a friend of mine, who was brought here against his will. Why they would bring him here wasn't initially clear to me, but now it is. Somebody wants him back, and that somebody is on Kasper. It's the only logical conclusion, the only possible conclusion.'

'Or maybe you're insane, and you're imagining all of this.'

He smiled without humour. 'You're welcome to believe that if it makes you feel more comfortable.'

'Tell me how to access the Goblin's navigation systems,' she said, raising the gun threateningly.

'No, not ever. I'm sorry.'

'For God's sake, I can't even radio out a distress signal. We'll die if we can't . . .'

He stared back at her calmly. Her hand was shaking, she realized.

'Elias, listen.' She then told him about what Vincent had said, about the radiation coming from somewhere near the centre of the galaxy. Maybe he'd understand now, she thought, if he even believed her.

'Look on the public news channels if you don't trust me,' she said. 'It's just starting to break.'

He continued staring at her, but after a moment his focus shifted, so that he seemed to be gazing at some faraway place Kim could not imagine. 'You know, it's all starting to make sense now,' he said after several seconds.

'So you'll turn us back?'

'I told you.' His voice was strangely calm. 'It's too late for that. We'd never make it.'

'We have to try,' she said, hearing desperation growing in her own voice. 'We could send out an emergency signal, and someone might be able to meet us halfway.'

To her horror, he shook his head from side to side. 'Things make sense now,' he repeated. 'Kim, I'm not trying to get any of us killed. We'd have a better chance by maintaining our course to Kasper anyway. Even if it comes to the worst, we can find a deep cave somewhere . . .'

An idea came to Kim, making her start. 'The Citadel,' she said.

Elias looked at her blankly.

'The Citadel,' she said again.

Elias shook his head; clearly he didn't know what she was talking about.

'It's a place on Kasper, the biggest Angel artefact of them all. It goes deep, Elias. Very deep.'

Fourteen

Vaughn

Vaughn slid his shirt off, revealing a well-muscled chest criss-crossed with tiny long-healed scars. He dropped the shirt into a basket. A girl called Ann came into the room and handed him a cup of what the Kaspians, roughly translated, called green wood tea. She left with a vague smile.

Matthew knocked a few moments later, and entered Vaughn's office. The room was low and wide, with windows that looked across at the Northern Teive peaks. The Kaspians rarely ventured this far into the mountains, and even if they did make the attempt, there were ways to dissuade them. Mists hid the valleys far below. Some of their nomadic tribal peoples still travelled up to the foot of the Northern Teive peaks, but Vaughn wasn't worried about them being able to scale those heights just yet.

Vaughn's home doubled as a kind of city hall, and the surveillance systems were run from a room directly below his office. It was the other backup systems that

Vaughn was concerned with just at that moment. They would be required when the fire came and the world was made anew. Those other systems would be stored in the Retreat, as the deep caves had come to be known. Preparations for the catastrophe that would wipe out the native civilization were under way, and if it wasn't for the loyalty and the patience of the people around him, Vaughn didn't know how they might have managed it.

'Father,' Matthew greeted him, then went to stand by the blazing log fire Vaughn had stacked that morning, shortly after he had materialized before the Emperor in Tibe. 'I don't know how you can drink that stuff.' Vaughn's son nodded towards the green wood tea.

'I like it.' Matthew grimaced, but in a humorous way. 'It's strange,' Vaughn continued, 'how it isn't the young who take to these things. This is the tea of Eden, of a new world. Young as she was, even your mother . . .' He caught himself: no use digging up old memories. He smiled, showing his teeth. 'It's not so bad, actually, and the natives certainly seem to like it.'

Vaughn picked up a fresh shirt and put it on. *Not long*, he thought, *not long*. And then they could abandon their mountain retreat forever. He would miss it, but there would be so much else to look forward to. He studied his son. He was sure he'd burned the fire of rebellion out of him. And yet . . .

'We've run an analysis on the nanocytes,' said

Matthew. 'I thought I ought to let you know. The majority of them have departed en masse through the singularity. Including the cloud originating from the destruction of that transport ship.'

Vaughn looked up. He hadn't anticipated that. Still, they were dealing with an ancient alien technology; it was bound to be unpredictable, though it had served their purposes well enough so far. 'What happened when they emerged at the next Station along the chain?'

Matthew eyed him with a grim expression. 'That's just the thing, Father. They didn't.'

'They didn't re-emerge? They were destroyed?'

'Possibly.' Matthew shrugged. 'Or . . .' He hesitated, knowing the importance of what he was about to say. 'Or they went somewhere else.'

'There is nowhere else for them to go,' Vaughn said firmly. 'I didn't see any of this.' *But then it's so damnably unpredictable*, he thought. *Sometimes you see it there, the future laid out as clear as day, almost. Other times, it's like staring into a void, not knowing how certain events might turn out.*

For the moment, Elias was lost to him. He was now the closest he had ever been, but Vaughn could not detect the other man's presence in his mind. It was frustrating and worrying, in one sense; Elias was a force to be reckoned with, as was Trencher. Only Trencher realized how great a force he was. But Trencher was taken care of, for the moment at least.

'Matthew, did this information come through regular channels?'

'Standard decryption of intercepted military and public datastreams. Everyone in the vicinity of the Angel Station saw it.'

Vaughn shook his head, as if he could shake off his worries. They were so close now . . . 'Do we have an estimated time of arrival?'

'Another day,' said Matthew, knowing who he meant. 'Twenty-eight hours, give or take a window of fifteen minutes. Ray and Thomas say everything is operating as normal, all the onboard guidance systems are fine. So it should achieve touchdown with no problems.'

'You have excelled yourself, Matthew. Tell Ray and Thomas they have my thanks. You've all done an excellent job. Now leave us.'

Matthew departed. He was a good boy, thought Vaughn, despite his earlier faults, his former lack of commitment to the path of light and knowledge. Burning it out of him had been necessary, but heart-rending, terrible. However, the boy's vicious anarchic streak had needed to be crushed. Vaughn remembered well one clear, bright day when Matthew had found out that his friends were all to die.

Vaughn had made sure Matthew was present to witness every death.

Vincent

They were going to have to break out the pressure suits.

Sleep or rest of any kind was becoming impossible for any of them, thanks to those now all-pervasive machine bugs. Elias no longer had control of the Goblin – because as Kim now knew, despite all her frustrated attempts otherwise, he didn't need to.

Vincent could see how hard it was for her to be effectively locked out of her own ship. Vincent still held the gun, but they were going to have to ride things out in stalemate, if they didn't think of anything first.

In the meantime, at normal magnification the planet Kasper had grown from a point of light to a wide disc. One of the displays showed two great continents straddling the northern hemisphere, almost touching in one or two places, otherwise separated by an ocean.

The great stony spines of mountain ranges were visible, particularly twin chains that spread to the furthest northerly points. The Citadel became clearly visible at maximum magnification, a dark stain across the planet's north pole. Further south there was a band of green and blue vegetation extending to the equator, but much of the planet was still locked in the vestiges of an ice age, now receding.

'How long before we get there?' Vincent had come into the cockpit to stand behind Elias, who had again taken the co-pilot's seat. Kim had decided to let him back in, not without reservations, although Vincent had been against it. A state of detente seemed better, she had decided, than to somehow keep him prisoner.

Elias looked at Vincent for a moment before replying.

'The shuttle's about to enter the atmosphere. It's already making braking manoeuvres.' A silver bug dropped from behind a screen and landed gently on the console in front of Elias. There were scratch-marks and other signs of damage on the walls all around them. Vincent watched the bug as it used its mandibles to slowly dig a hole in some steel casing to one side of the console. He saw the faintest spark of light as its mouth parts gouged into the metal. Horrifying as it was to watch, it was also strangely fascinating. These things seemed able to cut through the toughest metal like butter. He kneeled down and tugged at the thing's rear legs. It made no attempt to defend itself, merely returned to its destructive feast. Then he picked it up, again making no attempt to resist, and batted it through the air, away from the console.

'Elias. We're not going to make it there before this ship comes apart, you know that?'

'I don't know that. We're less than a day away now, and I need to plot a landing trajectory. If for any reason we can't land within range of the shuttle, we should aim for somewhere far away from any populated areas. We don't want to have to deal with the natives if we can avoid it. Cross your fingers that shuttle doesn't decide to land too far north or south either, or it's going to be seriously cold.'

'Elias, Kim is sealing off the cargo bay now, as we've lost most of our air pressure back there. I don't know how long our air can last in this part of the ship either.'

Elias turned slightly. 'That bad?'

Vincent nodded carefully. 'Possibly worse. Only time will tell.'

An uncomfortable silence fell, and Vincent waited. He knew if he waited long enough, Elias would feel compelled to say something. Vincent was a very patient man.

'Look,' began Elias, 'about what happened.'

'There's nothing to say, Murray. You took control of the ship. The real question is, what happens next. That's what's worrying me most, not whether or not you gave me a bloody nose.' It was curious, but Vincent found himself feeling strangely sorry for Elias. There had been a brief tide of hatred, fuelled by testosterone and anger, but that had ebbed away now, faded. It made it easier for Vincent to think more clearly, to try and imagine what would happen when they reached where they were going.

'Well, you know where I'm taking us. I've already talked this over with your girlfriend,' Elias said gruffly.

'That's not the question I intended to ask.'

Elias stared at him pointedly.

'Assuming we survive,' said Vincent. 'Assuming we don't get slaughtered by the natives or freeze to death or starve because we don't know what we can or can't eat locally, what happens then?'

Elias frowned, folding his arms in a vaguely defensive gesture.

'What you and Kim do is up to you,' he said at length. 'I have to find that shuttle.'

'On your own? On a world that, unless what you say turns out to be true, may never have had more than a few dozen pairs of human feet touch it, and then only within a restricted area inaccessible to the natives? And what will you do if you manage to find that shuttle, all on your own?'

Elias became tight-lipped, looked away from Vincent and back towards the console and its permanently scrolling datafeeds.

'You don't have any idea what you're doing, do you?' continued Vincent. Still, Elias didn't answer. 'Something you should know,' Vincent spoke to the other man's back. 'When it comes to survival, nature almost always get it right. Cooperation, Elias, is the key to survival. Cooperation, remember.'

Vincent turned away and returned to Kim's cabin.

Ursu

'Here, bring him here.'

The merchant was hurt, dying. The knife wound was deep, and his bright red tongue lolled feebly out from a muzzle full of carefully sharpened teeth. They had made a mat out of the heavy green water-reed infesting the marshlands that blurred the contours of the land abutting these northernmost waters of the Great Northern Sea. Ursu looked around, towards the Southern Teive Mountains, now far behind him.

The village stood within the ruins of an ancient walled city breached during some long-ago war. The city, like the land, was called Ibestresan. Ib-estr-e-san – meaning land of the reeds.

Great wooden ships had sailed far down the river that skirted the ruined city, their sails rippling with gold and black, the colours of the Emperor. The soldiers they carried were camped not far from the little settlement. There was little law here, save what the imperial soldiers brought with them.

'There isn't time to move on,' said the female who had fetched Ursu to the merchant. 'We have to help him here.'

'Not where we might be seen by the soldiers,' said Ursu. 'Let's get into that building there.' He pointed towards a crumbling villa. Its lower level was open to the elements, the floors scattered with straw and animal droppings. Ursu took one edge of the mat and together they dragged the victim out of sight.

'Soldiers came looking for him at home,' said the female. 'He managed to get away.'

Ursu thought better than to ask why, having drawn far too much attention to himself already. There was an air of rebellion here, of a kind that Ursu had not found in other places during his travels. The tribes close to the sea seemed to have a greater independence, as if they gathered succour from the vastness of the ocean itself.

One or two other townsfolk had appeared. Word would get out, he realized, that someone with the means to carry out a Raising was travelling north. But he couldn't turn away. His backpack held something more valuable than any empire. It contained the future of everything that had ever existed.

The boat he had found deep in the forest, now many days behind him, had carried him away from immediate danger, but several times he'd barely avoided colliding with military supply ships. Abandoning the craft eventually, he crossed steep hills until he found the coast that curved north towards the edge of the world, where the seas became solid ice.

The further he travelled, the more his past had seemed to fade behind him.

'I need to be alone now. You must all go,' he said, waving them away.

He then probed the edges of his patient's wound. The merchant jerked slightly at the touch as the power of the Raising flowed into him. His breathing seemed steadier now.

After a few moments, Ursu realized he was not alone.

He could sense the figure crouching behind him, but did not turn to look. Not Shecumpeh, but the other one: the Shai. He did not wish to see again those terrible lacerations across its unnatural pink flesh, those staring eyes set deep in a snoutless face.

– The soldiers have heard stories about you. They will connect you with the disappearance of the device you carry. The Shai leader wishes to prevent you reaching Baul, and he will stop at nothing to do so.

'Last time you said he would destroy the world.' As Ursu pinched the edges of the merchant's wound together, the flesh began to knit with astonishing rapidity.

There was sudden shouting in the distance, and Ursu yanked up the backpack containing Shecumpeh and pulled its straps over his shoulders.

– Yes, confirmed the Shai. – Or will allow it to occur without his intervention.

Ursu stood and forced himself to turn. 'Don't you have anyone to tend to your wounds?'

– I can attend to them myself. There is much for you to learn. The answers lie in Baul, down in the deep caverns.

'There is a machine there.'

– As I told you.

More shouting. Was it closer? There were still so many questions he wanted to ask the Shai.

'We need to speak – but not now. When will you come again?'

– Soon.

The creature seemed to fade back into the deep

shadows from which it had risen. 'Wait,' cried Ursu, in frustration. It might be days before he could speak with it again.

The Shai had come to him several times over the past few weeks, telling him secrets of the world at large, helping him understand the visions he had seen. He had even seen this city of Baul in his mind's eye, as if from far above, and now knew it to be real. He had also seen visions of impossible places high in the sky, places filled with countless Shai.

It seemed not all Shai were the same.

He wanted to run, and hide, far away from the soldiers. And once he had reached Baul, whatever it was that the fates or the gods or strange visions of demons wanted him to do, he would do it, and then he would walk, until he was in no place he could recognize, in a land as far from Nubala as he could possibly be, and there, just perhaps, he might find himself a life of peace.

Kim

'We're not going to make it, Elias.'

'We'll make it,' he replied tersely. 'What's happened back there?'

'The cargo bay is now in vacuum, and we had to repair the seal on the connecting crawlspace because the bugs were starting to eat through that too. I'm going to move as much stuff as we can through here and seal off the cabin.'

She could see how much the stress of the past two days had been affecting them all. She also knew how slim their chances were, as Kasper loomed large ahead of them.

That they had even come this close to the world that filled their viewscreens struck a note of paranoia in Kim's mind. The international military force that supported the Kasper Angel Station was prepared to go to considerable lengths to maintain the no-go zone that surrounded the alien world. But, within a few days, the Station itself and every vessel in the system had been threatened or attacked by an unknown, unstoppable enemy. For Kim, the main question – apart from whether or not they would survive the next few hours – was whether it was all just coincidence.

There seemed nothing to tie these events together, but some part of her mind kept playing over the details of what she knew, wondering if there might be something, anything, in amongst the few disparate facts she knew that might suggest some element of predetermination.

Elias shook his head. 'Leave it. This close to the planet's surface, that isn't going to make any difference. We're less than maybe an hour from a touchdown.'

Only an hour? They might be dead in an hour. Kim didn't like the idea of dying without knowing a few things first. 'Elias, you haven't told us anything about this man you're looking for.' He hunched his shoulders and ignored her, just staring at the screens.

The truth was, Kim had a feeling they might make it. Although she could no longer personally control the Goblin, she could still read the encyclopaedic information stored within its databases. Elias was unpleasantly right about a lot of things: the Goblin was, indeed, capable of atmospheric re-entry – once. But it had to enter the atmosphere at the right angle, at the right speed, using up almost all of its available fuel to brake.

They were going down there, but they weren't likely to be coming back up again.

'His name is Trencher,' Elias said eventually. Kim blinked, realizing he'd actually spoken.

'Who is Trencher?'

Another long pause. 'You should know, I suppose. I met him after I finished my military service. We had . . . certain things in common. I didn't then understand why. Something happened to me,' he was looking at her now, 'during my military service. It had something to do with Angel technology. I took part in a secret research programme: bio-genetic experimentation, augmentation.'

I was right the first time, thought Kim, alarmed. *He is crazy. There is no Trencher*. It was just blind luck that he arrived at the Station when he did, that so many things seemed to happen together just then.

'What did they do to you?' she asked quietly, thinking she must humour him.

'I'm not sure. I wasn't the only one. They wanted to enhance us by using gene treatments, make us better soldiers.' He smiled ruefully. 'I volunteered – so did the others. It seemed . . . it seemed like the right thing to do.' He shook his head, looked away again.

'Is this true?'

'Of course it's true,' he snapped. 'You said you wanted to know.'

'This man Trencher, was he part of this programme?'

Elias shook his head. 'No, he was born that way, but it was due to the same basic approach: he was made, created. We found each other because I needed someone to show me how to live with what I now had, what I couldn't give away.' He glared at her. 'You don't believe me, do you?'

'You haven't really told me much, Elias. What did this research programme do to you?'

'If I told you,' he said carefully, 'you'd have every right to think me completely insane, so I'm not going to, okay? But I will tell you this: Trencher knew something was going to happen. He didn't know exactly where or exactly when, but that certain events were going to take place, and that when they did he wanted me to do something for him.'

'Is this what you had to do – follow him here?'

'Yes.' He stared at her. 'You still think I'm crazy, right?' He nodded gently, turned his attention back to the screens. 'Can't say I blame you.'

'Elias, do you have any real idea of the kind of people who wind up on Angel Stations? There are about fifty lunatics for every one person with a legitimate reason for being there. I'm not necessarily saying that's true of you, but—'

'I heard about those experiments,' said Vincent from behind her. Kim turned with a start; he'd come through from the cabin without a sound. 'I resealed the crawlspace, but I don't think we have long,' he said to them both.

Elias looked at Vincent. 'What did you hear?'

'Nothing ever got put on public record, but there've always been stories floating around the Grid concerning experiments with Angel-based gene treatments. Crazy stuff, but no way to prove any of it's true.' He shrugged. 'But I do know it's not the first time it's happened, either.'

'Who else?' asked Elias.

'Take your pick. Once the Angel alterations to human DNA were identified, it didn't take a great deal of investment or equipment before pretty much anyone could start tweaking the appropriate genes to see what happened.'

'Oh, come on,' groaned Kim. 'We don't have time for this. These are fairy tales. Nobody believes this stuff.'

Vincent squinted at her. 'Don't you remember the big biotech bust a couple of years ago?'

'I don't know what you're talking about. I—'

'Some South American biotech firm, with labs in North America and Europe, turned out to have strong financial links with the Primalist religion. There were enough financial irregularities for the authorities to end up raiding a couple of facilities, where they found illegal biotech work was being done using Angel gene sequences. The whole thing blew up into a huge scandal, when a bunch of governments were caught dabbling in very black biotech research. So finding out that someone like Elias had a bunch of shit pumped into him while he was in the army doesn't surprise me, or anyone else. Now do you understand why I might be rather interested in what Elias is saying?'

Kim shook her head, confused. 'I'm lost, Vince.' She raised her hands, then dropped them down by her sides in a gesture of defeat. 'I've been out here for a while, remember? I wasn't paying so much attention to the news.'

'Because you keep punishing yourself for something that wasn't your fault.'

'Let's not get into that – not here, not now,' said Kim, holding up a warning hand.

'Look here,' said Elias suddenly. He tapped at the console and they saw a bright flash of light at the edge of the Kaspian atmosphere. 'That's the shuttle in re-entry.'

Vincent leaned over his shoulder. 'Where's it going?'

'Looks like it's heading for that mountain range,'

Elias said, 'there, at the edge of the continent. Big, too, like the Alps, or the Andes.'

The Goblin shook just then, and there was the sound of screeching metal. Low vibrations rippled through the ship's hull, building in intensity for a few seconds. Vincent grabbed the edge of Elias's seat and held on for dear life.

'Okay, that wasn't good,' said Kim, her face pale. She'd retreated across the cockpit by grabbing on to handholds.

'This is what I'm going to do,' said Elias, urgency in his tone. 'There are set emergency landing procedures the Goblin can follow. That means the ship can take itself down with minimum or no intervention from us. However, that doesn't necessarily take the bugs into account.'

'You don't say,' said Kim.

'I'm setting the ship to take us in now,' said Elias, tapping at the console. 'Thing is, I don't have too much control over where we land.'

'How come?' asked Vincent.

'I've only ever done this in a training simulation,' Elias said. 'The Goblin can take certain things into account, second to second; things like air pressure, wind speed, the terrain, that kind of thing. As long as we don't land in the middle of one of their cities, we should be okay – I hope.'

The ship shook again. 'Elias, I hope you're right and I hope we're down soon, because those little things are going to tear this ship apart,' said Kim. The planet filled the screens now, and Kim felt damp sweat on her shoulders and hands. Her teeth hurt from clenching her jaw. She thought longingly of the last few Susan Books, still in the cabin.

She'd realized, soon after much of the Station had been destroyed, that the one distillation unit in the whole System had probably been destroyed with it. She had no remaining distillate outside of the few Books that remained in her possession. All that remained of Susan, of her mind, her memories, was contained in a tiny plastic cylinder just a few feet away. She had to preserve it at all costs, until more could be made.

In the meantime, she might be able to draw some extra strength by eating just one. Enough to get her by, until she acquired more – assuming they came out of this alive.

She glanced at a screen, and saw that clouds now filled all the displays. They were on the edge of the atmosphere, she realized. Elias started to strap himself in. 'Screens are going to go blank in a minute. Strap yourselves in. It's going to be a rough ride.'

She pulled herself into the pilot's seat, gave Elias a long, hard stare. 'If we ever get out of this, don't expect either of us to help you.'

'I won't.'

I'm back, Kim realized with a start. *I spent years keeping away from the Citadel, only remembering the things I wanted to remember. But now I'm back.* She remembered the air at the Kaspian north pole, cold and clean and sharp. It occurred to her that if they survived, they would have automatic responsibilities: avoiding contact with the Kaspians was a priority. She had to believe they might be rescued eventually.

There was a research station at the Citadel, she reminded herself. If they could get there, they would have a chance of rescue. *They'd probably soon know we were here anyway.* Kasper was ringed with surveillance satellites that would have little difficulty detecting their passage.

And if they were finally rescued, there would be boards of enquiry, complex legal issues to be dealt with concerning interference with a culture that was regarded as untouchable. She tried to imagine how their situation would look to such a board: a pushy scientist who'd previously managed to get people killed through her professional incompetence.

Once the matter of how they had come to be on board the Goblin with Elias, and the precise circumstances of their business arrangement, came to light, they would be excellent candidates for becoming scapegoats, whatever happened to Elias himself. Kim wanted to make sure their chances of surviving Kasper without a criminal record were as high as possible, and that meant playing things by the book as far as she could.

'Okay,' said Elias, 'make sure you're buckled in good and tight.'

'Kim,' Vincent said, 'we're going to need booster

shots before we go down – something to help us deal with the gravity. I don't have so much of a problem, but you've been in zero gee for a long time. I want you to come through to the medical unit now.'

'I will, Vince.' She had been worried about that too. She had kept up taking regular treatments in case she found herself in the deep end of a gravity well, and was now glad she had. She stood up. 'Let's get this done, then we're going to have to all strap in.'

They returned fifteen minutes later, just in time to see the screens flare red for a moment, before finally going completely blank.

They all stared at each other. 'That wasn't it,' said Elias, studying the flickering icons and images in front of him. Kim locked herself into her seat, and Vincent did the same behind her, hooking himself into protective webbing. She scanned the console, then her eyes widened in alarm.

'Elias!'

'What?'

'It's an integrity breach. Look!'

'What does that mean?' asked Vincent, his voice strangely high. The view on the screens had begun to change. The smooth curve of Kasper had begun to slide to one side, the screens showing an increasingly larger area of space and stars. They were preparing for re-entry, she realized, a thrill of excitement and terror rolling down her spine.

'It means something's happened to the ablation

shield,' explained Kim. 'We can't land, Elias. We're going to have to think of something else.'

'There is nothing else,' said Elias. His voice sounded deliberately controlled and calm, but there was a brittleness there that betrayed him. He was staring at the console as if he could summon forth renewed hope by sheer force of will.

We're going to die, Kim realized.

'Okay,' said Vincent, 'listen. When you say integrity breach, you mean that's it? They've eaten through?'

'The cargo unit has an ablation shield that inflates outside of the aft hull,' she said. 'But something's affecting it. It could be the bugs.'

'How can we be sure it's the bugs?'

She looked at him with a hopeless expression. 'We can't. Not without actually going out there and looking.'

Vincent had seen the bugs, the way they worked at things. If they were responsible for the breach, it wouldn't take them long to cause it irreparable damage. 'But they're not through it yet.' He was already out of his protective webbing. 'Until then, we can still use the ablation shield to get through the atmosphere, right?'

'Yeah,' said Elias, 'but only if we can figure out a way to stop them now. Jesus, I really hope you've got something in . . .' Vincent was gone. Elias could hear him pushing through into the cabin behind. Kim jerked around in alarm.

She unbuckled and followed him through, nervously eyeing the seal they'd put over the cargo-unit crawlspace. 'Vincent, what are you doing?'

Vincent removed a wide panel flush with the cabin bulkhead. Then he yanked out the Goblin's one pressure suit and started to put it on, adjusting it for his smaller frame. 'We've still got twenty minutes before we actually hit the atmosphere, right?'

'Yeah,' said Kim slowly. 'You're not going out there, Vincent. It'd be suicide.'

'Tell me you've got a better idea?'

'Just tell me what you've got in mind.'

'Nothing that's a big deal. I won't be in any danger. The bugs won't attack me. I'll just brush them off the shield. I'll stay hooked to the hull. Then I come in. Then we meet some aliens. Then we get rescued. No problem.'

She was thunderstruck. She had wondered if, in some screwed-up subconscious way, she herself had enabled all this to happen, because of the way she had lost Susan. She lived every day with the memory of people who had died under her leadership.

But it wasn't the same now. This time there was no easy way out, no obvious path to safety. She could think of no other solution.

'Let Elias do it,' she said. 'He's a soldier. He knows how to deal with these things.'

'Kim, shut the fuck up!' She blinked, staring at him with a frightened expression. 'This is serious. If we don't do something now, we're all going to die. We're not going to draw straws, we're not going to argue.' He already had the suit on, started to lift the helmet over his head, then paused. 'I'm not trying to be a hero. I'm just trying to get out of this mess alive. Feel free to make alternative suggestions.'

She said nothing, just stared at him.

'Good,' he said, clamping the helmet over his head. Moving numbly, she turned him around, checked his pressure seals and got an 'okay' from the computer readout on the suit's backpack. She wasn't sure if he had his radio on, so she gave him two quick slaps on the shoulder to say *You're ready now*.

He crawled back through to the cockpit, on hands and knees, briefly startling Elias, who nodded, seeming to grasp the situation immediately. 'You've got fifteen minutes, Vincent,' he said. Vincent nodded, and unlocked the inner door of the airlock. Kim followed him, sealing it shut behind him.

Vincent

Vincent didn't allow himself time to think, once the inner airlock door was sealed behind him. He used the airlock's console to open the outer door, and stared out into infinity as it swung open. *I know what I'm doing*, he thought. *No time to hesitate*. He clipped his line onto a hook in the hull, and pulled himself out.

The ship was rotating even as he clambered. He

reeled, dizzy, then remembered the tricks they'd taught him the first time he went space-walking. That had seemed like an outing, at first, in near-Earth orbit, the kind of bold thing you did after you'd surfed in Hawaii or climbed the Andes.

Vincent had indeed surfed once, badly, while spending a couple of weeks at Mauna Loa. He'd never climbed the Andes, though he had spent a weekend in the foothills at a resort when he was still barely into his twenties. After that, he'd undergone more serious near-orbit training in vacuum when he'd thought he had a real chance of working directly, hands-on with the Lunar Array. That opportunity had never materialized.

He'd always meant to go space-walking again. He'd just never quite envisaged it being under circumstances like these.

Aside from the limited time they had, he didn't foresee any real problems. He just focused on the issue at hand, and allowed himself a brief moment of wonder at what people were capable of, given the right circumstances. A few weeks before he'd have laughed at the notion of being caught up in such a foolhardy situation, as if such things were avoidable. But nobody could have predicted this particular sequence of events. And when you needed a solution to your problems, you didn't seek it out of a sense of bravado, or a desire to appear brave; you did it because you had no choice, because somebody had to do it, and that happened to be you. He let that simple truth occupy his mind while he pulled himself around the bulge of the Goblin's cockpit section.

The Goblin comprised three separate sections: the cockpit at the front, the living quarters in the middle, the cargo hold and engine core in the rear. Each bulbous section was roughly circular in shape. The craft's surface had a series of rungs embedded into the hull. He guessed these were to assist pressure-suited miners from the airlock to the cargo section at the rear. While clinging to one of these, he looked automatically for the planet below. As he saw it, he realized his mistake. Cold terror gripped him as his perspective shifted suddenly. The Goblin had oriented itself so that its nose was pointing outwards, away from the planet's atmosphere. Its ablation shield was already inflated for atmospheric re-entry, blossoming out from aft of the cargo bay.

The surface of Kasper now seemed to fill half of the universe. Vincent could clearly see mountain ranges spread out below him, and the great sea separating two massive continents. Much of the land surface was still white with ice and snow.

His guts clenched, and he froze. It seemed like he was falling, falling through an ocean of air. Like he was squatting on the top of a tower thousands of miles high.

This had happened last time, too, he reminded himself, during that first space-walk, seeing the Pacific Ocean spread out like a great blue diamond far below his feet.

Get it done, he urged himself. His throat feeling dry as parchment, he somehow managed to slowly work his way along the length of the craft. He reminded himself over and over again, that he was not going to fall . . . at least no faster than the craft. He kept the fear in its place.

As he got to the shield, the cable that spun out from the airlock floated behind him like a thick silvery rope. He'd run out of rungs now, but he still needed to get underneath the ship, and onto the ablation shield itself.

He forced himself to let go of the last handhold, and floated free. It was the hardest thing he had done in his entire life.

He gently pushed himself along until he could see the bugs, about two dozen of them, which had barely started working on the shield. He touched gloved hands to the ablation shield until he stopped sliding forward. He managed to brush at one of them and it simply floated off into space, its tiny metallic legs waving help-lessly. Like all the others he had seen over the past few days, it had a haphazard, home-made look to it, as if assembled from entirely random pieces of junk found lying around. Which of course, he suspected, was exactly what they did when they reproduced.

He gradually pulled himself around the surface of the ablation shield. He couldn't see any clear sign of damage, so perhaps they'd been lucky after all. There were signs of destruction on the hull itself, particularly around the cargo-bay section. But as long as the ablation shield held out, it should protect the ship.

He was floating directly underneath the Goblin now. They were close, so very close . . .

He then noticed a tiny red light blinking rapidly, to one side of his mouth, inside his helmet. He stared at it for a few short moments, then ignored it long enough to brush several more bugs away from the metal ring that connected the base of the shield to the hull. He pushed himself further around the shield's circumference, finding more bugs. He pushed them away from the shield, watching as they spun lazily away, like tiny metal partners in a zero-gravity waltz. Meanwhile, he tried to ignore the vast onrushing landscape below him.

Once he was sure they were all gone, he remembered the blinking light, but ignored it and with both hands took hold of the cable tying him to the Goblin like an umbilicus, and started to haul himself back around the surface of the ablation shield.

As he glanced towards Kasper, the planet looked a lot closer than only a few moments before. Spread out below him he could see great rivers, and what might be forests. The sight of it sucked him in, rich with terrible beauty, and for the briefest of moments he was lost to the world.

He tongued the switch next to his mouth and the red light changed to green. Kim's panicking voice came over the intercom. 'What's happening there? You have to get back inside, Vincent! Right now!'

Shit! He glanced at the information constantly scrolling across the bottom-right corner of his helmet's visor. He saw that he had about forty-five seconds to get himself back inside.

'We're going to make it, Kim,' he yelled, pulling himself away from the ablation shield until he grabbed on to a rung on the hull of the Goblin. 'We're going to be fine.'

'Okay. Just get yourself back inside in one piece, Vincent.'

His momentum as he launched himself away from the ablation shield had caused him to skid sideways across the hull, losing a valuable few seconds. He happened to glance down and saw a red tinge to the edge of the shield, and realized his suit was heating up, becoming uncomfortably warm in only a few seconds. Then he pushed himself back up along the length of the Goblin towards the airlock.

I should be dead by now, he thought; the Goblin was entering the upper limits of the Kaspian atmosphere at tremendous speed, fast enough that he should have been burned up by atmospheric friction. It took him a moment to understand why he hadn't. Once the ablation shield had inflated, its diameter was somewhat greater than the diameter of the Goblin itself. As it plummeted downwards, the shield acted almost like an umbrella, sheltering Vincent from the unimaginable heat of re-entry so long as he remained no more than a few inches from the Goblin's hull.

Nonetheless, the heat inside his suit continued to increase dramatically, dangerously so. His visor display gave him ten seconds, nine. Vincent hauled himself up over the curve of the cockpit section, while the ship fell rear-end first towards Kasper. Then something happened, a curious sensation of weight pulling at him . . .

He hauled himself on top of the cockpit section and looked around. In those few precious moments, he saw the vast geography of Kasper spread out below and around him, the Goblin's ablation shield white with heat.

Swiftly he pulled himself down into the airlock hatch and hit the control panel, feeling every second, every fraction of a second moving slowly, too slowly . . .

The tug he had just felt became almost imperceptibly greater, the slowly increasing pull of a gravitational mass. The door he had just entered was no longer a door, but a ceiling hatch. He tumbled down onto the inner airlock door, watched the outer one slam shut.

The inner door opened, and he fell inside, yelling. He hit the wall nearest the cabin crawlspace.

Kim

She made to unbuckle her webbing, but Elias reached out to restrain her. The ship began suffering terrible vibrations, enough to make the teeth rattle in their jaws. An enormous bass rumbling filled their ears. The cockpit had become a vertical tube, their seats fixed high up on one side. Kim could see Vincent lying in a motionless crumpled heap below her. His head seemed bent at a strange angle.

'I need to help him.'

'Don't,' Elias said firmly. 'I don't know exactly how this is going to go.' The Goblin had begun to shudder extremely violently now. First one screen and then the next was filled with hissing static. 'Stay in your seat. If we're going to get through this at all, it'll be because he went out there.'

She pulled her arm away from him. Elias reached out and touched the console. A screen of static was replaced by an outline image of the Goblin, one end more distended with the ablation shield. She hated Elias for knowing about that when she herself hadn't. It made her feel stupid, ignorant. He had stolen her ship from her, but it didn't give him the right to outguess her, outmanoeuvre her. Lines showed the angle of the Goblin as it rammed through the upper reaches of the Kaspian atmosphere.

Things I know about Kasper, thought Kim. *It's like Earth. Uncannily so.* There were people who claimed the habitable worlds found through the Angel Station network had been specifically re-engineered by the Angels to be similar to each other. It was accepted by the scientific community that the Angels had interfered with human DNA somewhere in humanity's dim ancestral past, and the same seemed to be true of the Kaspian species. *So, on some level, we're related*.

The Goblin chose that moment to shake so violently that she let out a cry, thinking, *This is it, this is it*, but they were still alive, still falling, and Kim thought, *After this is over, because it will be over, I'll never be scared of anything again, because I think I've used up three lifetimes of scared so far, and they're not going to let me have any more*.

What could they eat, she wondered. The last time she'd been here on Kasper, her team had been far from any flora or fauna. They'd brought their own food with them. Yes, the Goblin had supplies, too, but they were finite.

What would be poisonous? Would the local diseases kill them? And then there were the natives – they were everywhere. They weren't an advanced species, true, but wobbling on the edge of an industrial revolution. If they had landed the Goblin on sixteenth-century Earth, they would have been burned at the stake, no questions asked, she thought. Unfortunately she didn't know enough about Kaspian society . . .

And then she realized who did, and hope flared up within her – bright, incandescent hope, even as they hurtled downwards.

'Now.'

Kim looked to Elias. Had he said something? She saw his hand on the console next to a control panel. A smaller viewscreen situated between them now carried one phrase: *burn initiated*.

The Goblin slammed about as the ablation shield was jettisoned and the engines fired at full capacity, counteracting the craft's rapid descent, preventing them from slamming into the ground at several thousand miles per hour. 'We should aim for water,' Kim yelled at Elias, but he didn't respond. He was doing something else at the console.

She leaned over as far as the webbing of her seat would allow and realized he was trying to control the Goblin's descent. Lines of vector pointed away from a body of water towards a mountain range. The same mountain range the shuttle had aimed for.

'Elias, no, head for water.'

'Either we drown or we crash,' he yelled back. 'Might as well try and get closer to our target.'

Your target, she thought. *We're flying blind, and our pilot is a madman*. Everything would have been different if he hadn't come to her with money that was worse than useless now. She held on grimly, and waited.

The Goblin tore through the upper reaches of the Kaspian atmosphere, trailing a line of incandescent fire. It had automatically adjusted its angle of entry so as to come in at a slant. Because the Goblin hadn't been designed with aerodynamic properties in mind, outside of any emergency landing algorithms designed to compensate for this, it needed to burn up all its fuel in one long blast in order to slow its speed and prepare for some kind of landing.

When the Goblin's protocols had first been designed, the engineers had programmed in a contingency for *emergency crash-landing*. After consultation with military psychologists and public-relations firms, this nomenclature had been changed to *controlled re-entry procedure*.

And as the Goblin fell, and as the natives of Kasper – and a lost colony of humans hidden in the high Teive Mountains – looked up and saw a second trail of smoke and fire across their sky, without their knowing it, their world was changing irrevocably, forever.

Emergency lights were beginning to flash at different points around the console. The ship was taking too much strain, she could see. She tried not to think about Vincent lying crumpled near them. He could be dead, and it seemed wrong for him to die only a few feet away, while they sat strapped into chairs and waited.

'We just lost two propulsion jets,' said Elias. 'I think this is going to be rough.'

Fifteen

Sam Roy

His skin looked smoother, less blemished from wounds he had received than it had done in over a century. Ernst was paying remarkably little attention to him, and Sam could understand that. He couldn't imagine what it must be like for almost every human alive: not knowing what would happen this day or the next, or the week after. For Sam it was all a foregone conclusion.

He waited a few moments more for Matthew to appear at the top of the path. The boy glanced behind him with a grim expression. Sam knew exactly what he was going to say – as if he had already said it.

Which, in a sense, he had.

Sam looked up, hoping to catch a glint of the shuttle in descent. *Trencher, my old friend*, he thought, *it's been such a long time. Perhaps it would have been better if we hadn't known, even then, and under just what circumstances . . .*

Sam was back at the bottom of the slope. If he wanted to eat or drink, he would again have to force the ball back up the path leading to where the food and water was. He had forced himself to rest, even as his belly ached and his throat cried out for moisture, for sustenance. There had been little snow in the past several days, and he could not rely on what little he could find to assuage his overpowering thirst.

What would happen, he wondered, if he merely dragged himself to the cliff's edge, and threw himself off? Would he finally be free, with his head caved in and his brains scattered across that alien mountainside?

He would recover, unfortunately, as happened the last time he had tried that. Vaughn had punished him, of course, once he had recovered well enough to receive the punishment.

'I hope you know what you're doing,' warned Sam, as Matthew got closer. 'You've been down this way a lot recently. Someone might notice.'

Matthew shook his head emphatically. 'He won't know. The others will alert me the instant he deviates from his schedule.'

'I've known your father for a long time, Matthew – since long before you came into the world. He's capable of many things. It takes a special man to engineer' – he raised one manacled hand and encompassed the valleys to the east with a sweep of his arm – 'all of this. His plan.'

Matthew stared at him with an expression bordering on the contemptuous. 'Sometimes you sound too much like you admire him for me to really be sure we can trust you.'

Sam raised his eyebrows. 'Take a close look, kid. See the manacles? Know how long I've been confined here on this mountainside? Know the one thing that's kept me sane all this time?'

Matthew scowled. 'Yes, yes, I know. But the way you talk about him sometimes—'

'In some ways, Matthew, your father is a great man. But history is littered to the gills with great men doing bad things. We were born into – created by – the Primalist religion whether we liked it or not. Try and imagine what it's like, Matthew, to be told that you or one of your brothers was born specifically to lead some tiny portion of humanity to salvation. When you seem to have powers normally attributed to gods and legends. To be told that you and your brothers are the progenitors of a new age.' Sam listened to himself, thinking, *What a bore you used to be, so given to grand speeches and cheap philosophy. You never quite got out of the habit, did you?* 'All your father has done is fulfil the expectations of those who brought him into this world. That doesn't mean we don't have to try our damnedest to stop him.'

'You said something big is going to happen soon,' said Matthew. 'The shuttle is already on its way, everyone is in place. This is no time to be mysterious, we need to know.'

Sam chuckled. He almost felt free, as if these chains were now made of paper and he could shrug them off easily. It was strange to think it was almost over. This mountainside was all he had known for a multitude of lifetimes. He couldn't imagine what it might be like not to live in searing pain, every second of every day, not to suffer unquenchable hunger without the blissful release of death.

'I couldn't be absolutely sure Elias was going to make it here along with the others,' said Sam. 'That's what I was waiting for. The probability he'd survive this far was extremely high, and the fact of my observing his arrival in the future will have tipped the balance. But I've been surprised before. Remember, Matthew, some of the things your father and I foresee are still only probabilities, not inevitabilities. It's up to us to work together to choose the outcome we want.'

'What do we do with Trencher?'

Sam sighed. 'You do what you're supposed to do. Just get him out of there, and away from Ernst.'

Matthew stared at him, his face full of uncertainty and anger.

Matthew was becoming like his father. 'Maybe we should just leave you here on the mountainside when this is all over,' said Matthew. 'We need certainties, not maybes. We need to know this is going to work.'

Sam squatted in the freezing dirt, flexing his knees. What Matthew had said was exactly the kind of thing Ernst might have said. 'Trencher, your father and me – remember what I said about us. We can tap into something which the Angel DNA put inside us before we were born.' Matthew's irritated glance indicated that he knew all this. But it was important, now more so than ever before, to repeat it. Again, and again if necessary. Sam continued: 'There are things that are going to concern us greatly when all this is over. The Angels were ready to bring dangerous predestination into the universe, but did you ever wonder why?'

Matthew cocked his head. 'And you think *you* know the reason?'

'I don't *think* I know,' Sam said softly. 'I *do* know.'

Matthew gazed at him in consternation, as he couldn't possibly understand. The powers that derived from the gene alterations didn't seem to pass themselves on through subsequent generations. Sam and Trencher and Vaughn had each had their embryonic DNA altered in a lab, before being reimplanted into the wombs of three loyal Primalist women whom each had learned to call mother. He wondered if the Angels had deliberately wanted to prevent these abilities passing on from generation to generation. Perhaps he could understand why.

'The wavefront of the explosion will reach this system within a few hours,' said Sam. 'That's all that matters right now. And when your father opens the door of that shuttle, he's going to get the biggest surprise of his life.'

Kim

Kim watched as their fuel reserves plummeted ever closer to zero. They were flying blind as re-entry had stripped the Goblin of most of its exterior sensors and data feeds. Elias had explained to her the Goblin was flying according to an internalized map of the terrain they were traversing, pieced together before and during their descent.

Her hands itched to guide her own ship, but she had no experience of flying in atmosphere.

As they waited for the end, Kim watched their fuel reserves sink further, so close to zero that she wondered how they were still airborne.

'We're just about down,' said Elias, his voice strained. 'We're only a couple of hundred metres up.'

'Any idea where we're landing?'

'No.' Elias cursed. 'All I know is, there isn't enough fuel to make it as far as the shuttle.'

You don't say, Kim thought to herself. *And there was me just worrying about getting out of this alive.*

The Goblin dropped lower, lower. It shuddered, dropped again.

'Fuel's all gone,' observed Elias.

Now the Goblin dropped like a stone. Kim screamed, feeling herself become suddenly weightless again.

It seemed to Kim that a world fell on her, and consciousness fled, leaving only blackness.

Roke

'Master Roke, Master Roke.'

It was so bitterly cold here. Roke turned, glanced out through the flap of the tent. He could see the Teive Mountains rising far to the north. A young guardsman entered the tent, and Roke set down his writing implement.

'Master Roke. You should come outside. There are flames up in the sky.'

Roke frowned. Then, as he heard a low hubbub of commotion, a sudden stab of fear ran through him. Perhaps local rebels were intending to attack them? He looked quickly around, feeling reassured when his eye fell upon the case in which his armour was stored.

Roke stepped outside into dim twilight and glanced up towards the band of stars that had recently been renamed Xan's Crown. A line of smoke cut across it. Roke dropped his gaze and looked around him. There were three hundred warriors in this expedition, plus half that number more of attendant smithies and random camp-followers.

The trail of smoke was very far up indeed but, despite his age, the old Master's eyesight was still clear and sharp. He had never seen anything like this, nor ever heard of it.

His eyes followed the direction of the smoke trail. It faded out at great distance over the sea, as if a burning arrow had flown across the horizon in the far west, beyond the point where the Great Northern Sea became uncharted ocean.

At the opposite end, it pointed to the midst of the distant Teive Mountains. *On our way*, thought Roke, looking around at the members of his expedition, gathered in loose knots around camp fires burning in the wide spaces between tents.

Then a second miracle happened. Something new passed overhead; roaring like a west Tisane volcano containing a bellyful of angry gods. Trailing flames and smoke, it passed only a thousand or so imperial measures above their heads, heading for the forests that coated the shores of the Northern lands.

We are being attacked by demons, thought Roke. The fiery object passed far into the distance, dropping into the distant forest which was perhaps no more than a half a day's march away.

As Roke waited for something else to happen, he noticed the camp had fallen silent. Even the exuberant wildlife of this northern wilderness had fallen quiet, as if the world and its gods had paused mid-breath.

Luke

'Storm coming in.'

Luke glanced up and saw white cotton-wool clouds tumbling down a distant peak. He reached up and adjusted the hood of his thermal suit. They all wore white, thus fading into the gleaming, snowy landscape. He scanned the sky nervously, looking for shuttles, any sign that Vaughn was yet on to them, had anticipated what they were going to do.

It had taken time for Luke to accept Matthew's heresies, but he was smart enough to know the seeds of rebellion had been planted when he had been black-mailed into concealing Matthew's meetings with Sam Roy. It had been so hard, at first; Matthew had dis-covered Luke's affair with Elizabeth, a girl intended for another under Vaughn's complex breeding programme. Now Luke was a willing co-conspirator, but in the past several days he had woken many times during the night to find his teeth chattering loudly, his fading nightmares full of the fear of discovery. 'What have we got, ten, fifteen minutes before the bad weather reaches us?'

'Something like that,' said Michelle. He glanced over and saw the troubled expression on her face. Luke had some idea of what she was going through. Her parents were deeply loyal to Vaughn and, although she disagreed with them to the point of betrayal, he knew she loved them dearly. But here she was, and they were – what had Matthew said? – doing the right thing.

The three of them had travelled overnight, coming on foot into the foothills lying far below the plateau where they had spent almost their entire lives. They were all familiar with this territory through regular hik-ing trips, as they worked at maintaining and checking the shield generators dotted across the surrounding peaks. The regular patrols also helped ensure that none of the native Kaspians had wandered too close. It gave them a legitimate reason for being where they were, if questioned.

Luke scanned the skies above their heads. Nothing. What if something had gone wrong? Either way, their past lives were finished, over. They'd never be able to return home. He forced himself to think about other things, to remember how things were supposed to go.

The flight path for the *Jager* shuttle had been put together by a few Primalists outside of Kasper, who still believed in Vaughn's incipient godhood. Apparently they were willing to believe this after Vaughn had manifested himself to them a few times. And, thanks to his relatively privileged position within Vaughn's home, Matthew had found a way to remotely insert a command routine into the shuttle's flight path that would cause the shuttle to land here first before continuing on to its rendezvous with Vaughn. The deception would be worth, at the most, a few minutes, and Jason had helped carry out the tricky and complex programming that was necessary. They'd run a considerable risk of discovery, timing being very much of the essence.

Vaughn might not trust his son any more, but Luke and Matthew and Jason were the ones who understood best how the computer systems operated.

The *Jager* shuttle would drop onto the floor of the valley where they waited, touching down for barely 120 seconds. That was risky, very risky. But just long enough to enter the craft, open the deepsleep coffin, and drag Trencher's comatose form free before the shuttle lifted off and resumed its course.

Luke looked up, saw a flash of light, far up. A sudden sense of elation filled him, surprising him with the strength of it.

Come on, Matthew, thought Luke. *Get out of there, now, before he comes looking for you.* If Vaughn hadn't already figured it out, he would soon, and Matthew would need to be far away by then.

Kim

She dreamed a great weight was crushing her.

Kim woke up, tried to shift, and a blazing agony of pain ran across her chest. *I'd rather stay here forever than go through that again*, she thought. She felt leaden, made of stone, the near-Earth gravity crushing her into her seat. She'd survive it, but she wouldn't get used to it.

Still strapped into her pilot's seat, she lay there for what felt like an eternity. The Goblin was still, quiet and dark.

But we're alive, she thought wonderingly, then looked around and realized she couldn't see anything. For a bone-freezing instant, she wondered if she had gone blind. She twisted her head round wildly until something glinted in the deep shadows.

We're down, but no power. She was suddenly glad Elias had ignored her, and not aimed for water. How the hell would they have escaped? The Goblin would have sunk to the bottom like a stone, with them all trapped inside, slowly suffocating.

In interacs, she'd always been bad at playing the heroine and, to her disappointment, she wasn't now proving much better in real life. Despite his tendencies towards piracy, Elias, she realized to her annoyance, was probably better cut out for this kind of situation.

Flexing one arm, pain shot through her again, but this time not quite so bad. She remembered how to speak. 'Elias?'

No answer.

'Elias?' *Please, dear God, don't let me be the only one left alive. I can't do this on my own.*

Vincent?

Shit. She couldn't believe she'd almost forgotten about Vincent.

She knew she had to be careful as she unbuckled herself from the safety webbing. Wherever the Goblin had landed, it tilted at an angle. She was already half hanging out of her seat. She used her good arm to untangle the straps from across her.

She tumbled out of her seat with a yell, sliding along the cockpit's rear bulkhead. Breathing hard, her heart hammering in her chest, she felt out with one hand, touched the rim of the crawlspace.

After a couple of minutes, she felt able to lower her

head enough to peer through to what had once been her cabin. It was faintly illuminated by daylight.

As she gazed around the cockpit, faint shapes started to reveal themselves. She reached up gingerly and touched the top of her head. Her first worry was that the intense pain indicated she had damaged her neck, but if that had been the case perhaps she wouldn't feel anything at all.

Pain is good, she thought. *It reminds you that you aren't dead yet.* Elias seemed to be gone. Gone for good? she wondered.

A wave of depression washed over her, almost overwhelming in its bleakness. She would be lucky to survive for a week, she realized. Even if something did not try and devour her, she would have to hide from the Kaspians. She didn't want to think about all this.

She peered through the crawlspace, toward where her cabin was still visible. At least the whole structure didn't shatter on impact. Then she worked her way through, grunting with pain every time she jogged her left arm against the wall. Gradually she could discern that one wall was cracked open. Real sunlight – it was years since she'd seen any – poured through a great rip in the side.

Through it things like trees were visible. She could hear strange sounds beyond. Animals? Birds? She caught a glimpse of clouds beyond the trees, far overhead, and faltered. Until she had first come to Earth, she had never walked under a naked sky before. So many years living in the Goblin had made it easy to forget what being on the surface of a world was like. And thank God for modern medicine, otherwise she'd have barely been able to crawl, let alone walk.

The securing locks on most of the storage cabinets had broken, spilling out their contents. But where the hell were Elias and Vincent? They must have already gotten out. Or perhaps something else had happened to them. No, she wouldn't allow herself to follow that train of thought.

She kneeled and started poking through the debris. Food? They'd have to have a food supply – at least until they could figure out what was safe to eat outside.

But if she was right, she had a way to find out. The knowledge they needed to survive, she was sure, was quite possibly contained within the remaining Books of Susan's memories. She hunted around until she found them, groaning with relief when she did so.

The Goblin seemed utterly destroyed. Kim climbed up on top of an open storage door, pushing herself up to the rent in the hull. She saw grass – or something like grass – and peered at it, squinted. Was it moving? But there was no wind blowing . . . and her skin crawled. Up at the Citadel, in the North, there had been nothing living. It could have been the Arctic up there. This wasn't the same.

Or perhaps it was just the wind. The trees nearby looked more like bundles of black snakes gathered together and thrust in the ground, with wide, spade-like leaves fleshy with veins. She tried to push her head through the rent in the hull, but something gave way beneath her. She grabbed at a piece of buckled metal, slashing the palm of her hand, then managed to boot herself over the edge. Falling to the ground, she landed with a loud *oof*.

Her arm filling with furious pain, she rolled over to near the roots of one of the trees, and looked up through its branches. She settled herself on one knee, then the other, and stood up unsteadily. The Goblin had carved a wide gouge through the forest. Its cargo section had split off and shattered altogether. The central cabin section was badly warped but intact. By some miracle, the cockpit seemed to be relatively undamaged. She looked around, saw Elias. He was kneeling over something, in a glade just aside from the wreck, sunlight illuminating his shoulders and his head. She walked over towards him.

'Elias?'

She came closer, to see he was kneeling over Vincent's supine form. Elias looked up at her, saying nothing, with a frightened expression.

'Elias, what's happened to Vincent? Will he be all right?'

'I didn't anticipate this,' said Elias, his face deathly white.

'You didn't what?'

She heard a sound from the forest on her left, and turned. A face like a nightmare rushed towards her from between the trees, eyes burning bright and its teeth bared in a snarl. Something flew through the air towards her, and for the second time that day, all consciousness fled.

Matthew

Within the great caverns, they had been digging since before Matthew was born.

When you stood at the entrance to those deep caves, you could look up to a high rocky ceiling that reminded him of pictures of cathedrals. This cave was only one of a linked series that ran deep beneath the mountains. Until Sam Roy had found a way to utilize the Angel technology he found deep within the Citadel, creating a shield that could hide them from view, this had served as the home for the Kasper Primalists.

He recalled what Sam had told him once about the war that had taken place amongst the orthodox Primalists, who had become appalled by the lack of control they had over Vaughn and his two brothers, Sam and Trencher. Vaughn and Sam had remained faithful to the basic Primalist edicts, but accused those who had created them of betraying the principles of their own religion. Sam claimed they had wiped out half of the Primalist leadership in a bloody putsch, forcing Primalist-controlled corporations with offworld interests to seed the first Kasper Station crew with Primalists who had declared their loyalty to Vaughn.

The surviving Primalists who had instigated the genetics programme that had created them were only too glad to see them go, and happier still when the Hiatus came and sealed them off, seemingly forever.

Matthew was old enough to find some irony in being brought up to believe his father was the Son of God. But whatever it was that had been unleashed in Ernst Vaughn's genes, it was genetically recessive. Matthew himself had been born an entirely normal human being, to his father's disappointment – or perhaps relief.

He listened for any sound. So quiet here. History had happened here; events he'd only learned about, too young to understand the hardship of those early years. He could see nearby the rapid-assembly makeshift homes the First Families had originally lived in, almost lost in the cavern's deep gloom; and the transport shuttles, similar in design to the one that had flown Trencher down from the *Jager*.

Vaughn's plan, of course, was to make use of the caverns again once the gamma radiation arrived. But Matthew felt troubled by something Sam, his uncle, had said, when Sam had told him the burster might not be natural in origin.

There were times when he did wonder about Sam's sanity; however, the fact remained that when Sam declared something was going to come to pass, it came to pass. What had happened that morning had been the first real demonstration Matthew had seen of the man's power. It had frightened him, making him wonder what it would be like to be imbued with such power – and thankful he'd never have to find out.

The cave where they kept a few shuttles in a ready state of repair was just ahead, and he walked rapidly through the caverns, eerily silent but for the faint echo of his boots. He suddenly sensed a presence forming just behind his shoulder, and for a brief instant feared it was his father. Freezing sweat erupted on his brow, and he thought he might faint from the terror. No way would Vaughn let him live this time.

It was only Sam, appearing in mindform, and Matthew almost moaned with relief. But the man's form seemed warped, twisted.

'He knows,' said Sam, his voice strangely out of synch with the movement of his lips. 'Get out of here, Matthew. Get out of here immediately.'

'I'm on my way,' said Matthew, breaking into a run. He could see the shuttles now, the same ones that had brought Vaughn and the others down into the mountains during one single, long night, mere months after the Hiatus had begun.

He found the ship he'd long been preparing for his flight. It hadn't been easy finding the time and opportunity to sneak down here regularly, but one thing Matthew had inherited from his father was his cunning. There were only a dozen of them standing between

Vaughn and his plan involving the gods of Kasper, but that was enough. They were all well trained in their separate skills, skills they'd have needed in Vaughn's brave new world. Skills they could also use against him. No turning back now.

He climbed into the shuttle and within a minute felt its engines growl before it shook and lifted up from the floor of the cavern. He guided it forward into the sunlight, and took off into the clear skies.

Elias

Elias was mildly surprised to find he was still alive.

The creatures – the Kaspians, he should call them? – had come pouring out of the forest in their dozens, swarming over Kim's prostrate body. He'd thought she must be dead at first. They'd then flung themselves onto him, binding him tight with something that looked like pale blue reed. He'd expanded his chest as wide as he could while they held him to the ground.

Just before they'd attacked, he'd looked up from Vincent's body, to notice two of these creatures watching him from within the woods. Strange eyes which were curiously blank, long, wolflike snouts, and legs that bent the wrong way.

For all their alienness, they carried what were recognizably weapons. One of them had what looked uncannily like an old-fashioned flintlock strapped across its shoulders. They were garbed in heavy clothes dyed a deep brown and black, with some kind of pattern inter-woven into the material, colours which made them seem to almost vanish amid the earth and trees.

He'd turned to see Kim edging towards him, and tried to say something to her. But the sudden shock of the landing had chased all sense from his tongue. Just then, one of the creatures had come running out from the woods, twisting something round its head like a bola. As the creature released it, it slammed into the rear of Kim's head, and she dropped like a stone.

After that the three of them were dragged off and thrown into a wagon, its wheels bumping and lurching across rough ground. Elias shifted against the reed bonds constraining his arms and shoulders. It was much tougher than expected but, by sucking in breath and wiggling his torso, he managed to manouevre the bonds further up towards his shoulders. It then took only a matter of minutes to free himself.

The slatted covering of the wagon was loose and crude enough to allow a fair amount of light in, striping the three prisoners in alternate shades of light and dark. The enormous beasts hauling the vehicle looked to Elias vaguely like hippopotami, with wide, splay-toed feet. There were maybe forty of the Kaspians in attendance. Most were on foot, but a few of them rode three or four each on the back of some of the beasts drawing the wagon.

He kneeled down and touched Kim's head. He'd

already tried to do something for Vincent, but wasn't sure his administrations would work. The Kaspians had interrupted him too soon. Even in this dim light he could see how badly bruised Kim was. But she stirred at his touch, and an eye flickered open.

'Kim?'

She replied with a moan of pain. He tried to help her sit up, leaning her against one side of the wagon. It was so low-roofed he couldn't stand, in fact could barely crouch, as it bumped and crunched over the rough terrain.

'Kim, wake up,' he urged. Her eyes opened again, but unfocused. She snorted, pushed him weakly away, then leaned over to vomit in a corner of the wagon. Elias held her arm steady until it was over.

'What's my name?' he asked, after she had managed to right herself.

'What, you've forgotten?' He could feel her shaking, and hoped she hadn't gone into shock. 'Your name's Elias.'

'I just needed to check. You've been knocked unconscious twice now. It can cause serious brain damage.'

She shuddered suddenly. 'That thing that came at me . . .?'

'Was a Kaspian,' said Elias.

'God, I've seen pictures, but . . .' She shook her head.

'Yeah, I know.' He helped her struggle out of her

bonds and, once she was free, she tried unsuccessfully to find a more comfortable position inside the wagon.

'Vincent?' she enquired. 'Is he—?'

'He's alive,' said Elias. 'I've been trying to do something for him, but he needs the kind of medical attention he's not likely to find around here.'

She fell quiet after that.

'Listen,' he said, 'we're a long way still from those mountains the shuttle was heading for. Maybe hundreds of kilometres? I know we didn't exactly discuss this before, but you're going to have to decide what you're going to do now. As Vincent will take a while to get better, you might have to decide for him in the meantime. You suggested this Citadel would be a good place to hole up in?'

The expression on her face changed to one of horror. 'Only as a last resort,' she protested. 'Things are . . . they're strange in the Citadel. I was there a long time ago, doing research and artefact recovery. That wasn't a good experience.'

'But it's still an option, right?'

'Yes, but . . .' she shuddered, 'it's dangerous.'

'How?'

'Hard to explain. Let's not worry about it until we get there. If we ever do.'

She leaned over Vincent, listening at his mouth. 'I'm no doctor,' she said, 'so I've got no way to tell if he's getting better or worse. I think we need to find some way to communicate with them. Maybe the Kaspians can help us with Vincent.'

'These creatures don't want to help us. Talk to them if you like, but I already told you where I'm going.'

'Look, maybe *you* have a chance of getting away,' she said, 'but Vincent doesn't. I'd better stay here with him.' She let out a long, low sigh. 'I wish I had the medical kit from the Goblin.' Her eyes widened. 'But we've still got smartsheets, haven't we?' Joy filled her face. 'Elias, we could send a distress signal!'

He smiled grimly and produced the one he'd used only a few days before to guide him through the *Jager*. 'I already tried it. Remember, the local Grid's databased on the Station. So no Station, no Grid, at least for the moment. Could be days before the whole thing gets online again.'

Kim looked crestfallen. 'We should keep trying anyway. It's one way out of here.'

'Yeah, we should,' Elias agreed.

He shifted, moving closer to Vincent's crumpled form. Something was wrong. He splayed out the fingers of one hand, placing them over the other man's cheek. Kim moved towards him, alarm on her face. 'What are you doing?'

'He's fading,' Elias said. He closed his eyes, trying to see what couldn't be seen . . . but there was no other way to describe it to her. Like something on the edge of his memory, a hint of a shape or a concept just out of his mental vision, always refusing to come to the fore. But there, nonetheless, a spark of life, of knowledge.

Vincent was fading fast. Elias couldn't be sure just what the injury was: most likely his long and anguished tumble across the cockpit as they accelerated towards the surface of Kasper. Fate now suggested Vincent was going to die for lack of medical attention. Elias might be able to do something for him, but good results weren't guaranteed. If all three of them were to escape, they'd have to carry Vincent with them, and the process would almost certainly worsen his condition, quite likely kill him.

Elias, on the other hand . . . what if he moved on his own? He glanced quickly over at Kim, then back again. That would mean abandoning them.

But he'd made a promise to Trencher. Trencher, who had always been able to see so much further into the future than Elias could, and so much more completely. For Elias, the future was usually just a hint, a flash of something or other that sometimes didn't reveal its significance or its meaning until it actually happened. But if Trencher was truthful in what he had said, then for him the future was a clear and open book, full of little in the way of surprises. He'd made it clear to Elias that this talent was much more of a curse than a blessing.

But abandoning Kim and Vincent . . .? He despaired of finding a clear path of action. Those two were innocents, bystanders, in the war between Trencher and Elias on one side, and Vaughn on the other.

He kept his fingers and palm pressed on Vincent's face and neck until the skin of his own hand tingled. He closed his eyes, imagining there was something still there in the darkness.

Something yielded, and a soft groan escaped Vincent's lips.

Trencher once said that people like me and him aren't really human any more, he thought. Sometimes Elias wondered just how many others might be out there who'd been blackmailed or cajoled, bribed or beaten or ordered into accepting gene treatments, and who had come out of it something more than they had been before, but no longer quite human.

Luke

The weather worsened rapidly, as visibility dropped to no more than a few metres. They could hear the distant hum of the *Jager* shuttle's engines long before it hovered into view. Luke swore as the craft suddenly appeared above them, dropping rapidly. They scattered as it dropped onto ancient ice, kicking up a cloud of superheated steam. Freezing hail pelted them as they ran forward.

'We were lucky with the ice storm,' yelled Michelle as she hammered the security code into the shuttle's airlock door. 'If it screwed up the radar, then maybe they won't have noticed anything at all.' She talked rapidly, almost stumbling over her own words. Luke could understand why she sounded so nervous.

No, not nervous, terrified. He wondered if she would be able to handle the strain; after all, they were risking so much. Regret about his own family began to flood over him, but he pushed it away, thinking, *This is the right thing, this is what we have to do*. And with any luck, they too would all see that . . . once Vaughn had been dealt with.

As the airlock door slid open, Luke jumped in first, glancing back over the heads of the others. What if Matthew hadn't been able to make it? What if Vaughn had stopped him? What if their reprogramming of the flight path had been discovered? He listened anxiously for the sound of Matthew's shuttle approaching, but it was impossible to discern anything over the wind howling through the open airlock.

'Move!' yelled Jason, behind him. 'We've only got a couple of seconds.'

Luke pushed open the inner airlock door, and the other two jumped in behind him. The shuttle was much, much smaller than the ships that had originally brought their families to Kasper. It was clear the life-support systems and much else had been stripped out. He wondered about the great cargo ship it had come from, the people who walked its echoing corridors.

More people than he could count, perhaps, or

imagine. From a world beyond a snowy wasteland; beyond a great spinning Station, the gateway to a whole universe. It was out there, and real, but so damnably out of reach. It wasn't *fair*; they had the right to choose their own destiny – not to have it decided for them by someone else.

Next through to the bay storage area, and there it was. The deepsleep coffin, a man from another world inside it. 'Michelle, you've got the access code,' he said. She nodded and stepped up to the coffin.

Jason eyed his chronometer. 'There isn't enough time to do what we need to,' he warned. 'This thing's going to take off again before we can get him out of here.'

'Shut up,' growled Luke. Just then a light blinked on the side of the coffin, and a faint *snick* told them that a lock had been released. Together, Jason and Michelle heaved the lid up hurriedly. Trencher lay inside, barely visible amongst the tangle of wires and tubes, and a strong antiseptic smell flowed out of the coffin's interior. A nasty business, thought Luke, having to keep a human being like this for so many years.

Though Trencher was old, Luke could still see the resemblance to Vaughn – a resemblance that unnerved him considerably. He stepped quickly forward and helped them lift the body free.

'Let's get the hell out of here, *now*,' urged Luke.

The shuttle's engines had already started their ascending whine, a vibration rolling through the floor beneath their feet. If they weren't quick, the craft would take off with the three of them and Trencher still on board. The old man's naked body was slippery from the chemicals, and it took all three of them to manhandle him out of the shuttle door and down onto the ice. The shuttle's whine built up to a roar, just as Michelle flung herself out of the airlock, and the ship began to move. Jason grabbed her arm to steady her, and then they fled, dragging Trencher's body unceremoniously across the ice as superheated steam again shot out from under the shuttle's belly. They watched silently as the craft rose high into the sky, the airlock door closing as it ascended to its original flight path.

'Remember,' said Luke, 'we now keep strict radio silence. If anyone back home tries to contact us and we reply, they might be able to figure out where we are. Got that?'

The other two nodded. They would have to get him into clothes or he could freeze to death in seconds, thought Luke, before he remembered: the genengineered ones, Sam and the rest, they were all something different now. They didn't die.

Trencher was still unconscious, his bare flesh assaulted by the vicious hail. Luke and Michelle held him up while Jason dropped his backpack to the snow and pulled out a sleeping bag and some thermal sheets. After all, he might be invulnerable, but there was no reason to let him suffer extreme discomfort. Then they waited.

Come on, come on, thought Luke. Long, tense minutes passed, but none of them had the will or the energy to say anything. Matthew should have been here by now. And still the icy wind whistled along the valley's length.

He's not coming. Luke felt panic begin to rise in him. He tried not to let the others see just how relieved he was when, moments later, another shuttle fell out of the sky, setting down a hundred metres or so away from them. It was impossible to see who was at the controls, but it could only be, had to be, Matthew. They half-carried, half-dragged Trencher's limp form towards the waiting craft as the airlock door opened and Matthew jumped out.

Having pulled Trencher inside, and onto a diagnostics palette, all four watched as the shuttle's medical unit took over. His skin felt like ice, thought Luke, and they were out there for only, maybe, two minutes. A normal human being could die in half that time in this environment without adequate protection. Trencher's chest now rose and dipped with greater regularity, his eyes moving regularly beneath their lids, his lips parting. Luke glanced at the others to read their expressions.

Good, he thought. *They all look just as scared as I feel.*

Sixteen

Kim

She'd never known anything like it.

She had watched Vincent die. What she had seen Elias do to revive him had nothing to do with any medical textbook available anywhere in the galaxy. The performance had filled her with an odd, almost supernatural, dread. Vincent had actually died there, in Elias's arms, a death rattle slipping from his throat, the life leaving him forever. His features had smoothed out, becoming a mask.

And then, somehow, he had come back.

Kim was a rationalist. There had to be, as in all things, a reasonable explanation. Blowouts and tunnel collapses were not uncommon in the tiny Hellas colony she'd been born in, and it still happened occasionally. She already knew from unpleasant experience what a dead body looked like, felt like. Once you'd been there, once you'd witnessed something like that, a dead body held no mystery.

Although there might be techniques for reviving

the apparently dead seconds, or even minutes, after apparent demise, she did not believe such techniques could possess such a *hallucinatory* quality. That deep sense of dread that had filled her, an almost instinctive horror at *something*. She almost believed she'd seen a shape flickering in the air, an uncanny sensation of being on the edge of something vast and deep and unknowable of which, if she squinted in just the right way, she might just catch a glimpse.

Vincent's eyelids had flickered, showing the whites of his eyes. Then his chest began to move again, erratically, for the first time in many minutes. By this stage, the convoy they were part of had left the edge of the forest behind. Now, they seemed to be passing through a wide, grassy plain.

Elias looked at her, shrugged. 'He's getting better.'

She couldn't keep the wobble out of her voice. 'I know when someone's dead. Vincent was *dead*.'

'Not dead enough, then,' said Elias, with the faintest hint of a grin. 'I told you how they experimented on me.'

She swallowed. 'So anything else you want to tell me? Maybe about communing with the devil?'

'Yeah, I guess, something like that.'

Even in the slatted darkness of the wagon, Elias could sense her expression was icy.

Sam Roy

'You had something to do with this, didn't you?'

The lash cut through the flesh of Sam's back, ripping fresh wounds. Red, human blood glistened in the Kaspian sunlight. Freezing air blew across the mountain-tops, adding fresh pain to the raw edges of the new wounds.

'I knew it would happen,' said Sam. 'Don't you know that?' His lips pressed together in a snarl as the pain descended again. His hands scrabbled at rock and snow and earth, the sinews beneath his ruined flesh standing out like steel cords, almost fleshless.

Vaughn stopped the punishment for a moment, panting heavily. 'Don't think I don't know what you're up to,' he growled, 'you want to ruin *everything*. But we have a purpose here – God's purpose.' His voice became almost pleading. 'Sam, why did you turn against me?'

Sam Roy muttered something under his breath, which in itself was strange, because, for decades now, he'd grown used to not giving Vaughn the satisfaction of any answer. He could hear Vaughn somewhere behind him, by the edge of the cliff.

Vaughn came closer again. 'It's still not too late. We'll have a world to ourselves before long: fresh and clean of the sins of the old. God's world. I can forgive you, Sam. You used to be my right-hand man. You used to be my brother.'

Sam somehow found the strength to turn and glare

blearily at Vaughn, whose lash hung limp towards the broken earth. 'Ernst, it's over. You can't see what I can see. You're right: we *should* be working together. But . . . but not towards the destruction of an entire world. That's not God's plan, Vaughn. It was never my plan, either. There are greater things involved here, Ernst, believe me.'

And Sam almost told him, then, it being so hard not to share what he knew – what so few could possibly have guessed. After all these years of wondering if there was a way to amplify the power that already lay within him: and it had been right there all along.

Pain.

Sam Roy was now a connoisseur of pain, having known little else for over two centuries. Short of throwing him down into the core of a star, there was little that would kill him. Vaughn knew this, of course, and used it to prolong Sam's suffering indefinitely. Pain in itself was a source of power, and when Vaughn came to punish Sam for doing what he was destined to do, the pain itself drove Sam to new levels of precognitive ability. As his flesh opened to bleed beneath the freezing sunlight, the clarity of his visions grew and, with it, came understanding. An understanding of which Ernst Vaughn, with his relatively limited vision, could only ever grasp a fragment.

But what little Vaughn did know was still enough to incite him to murder an entire world.

'I'm going to tell you something you don't know,'

said Sam, carefully twisting his head around to look at Vaughn. 'Do you want to hear it?'

Vaughn said nothing, merely stood there gazing at him. 'Go on,' he at last said quietly.

Sam spoke with growing certainty. 'You can't win – and do you want to know why? You know how they used to say everyone makes their own future? That's all we ever did, Ernst. It doesn't become real until we see it there, in the future; and that's when we, here in the present, simply become that point's past, rushing towards what is suddenly inevitable, unalterable.'

Vaughn scowled. 'Nonsense, that's an insult to the divine plan. We don't create the future, God does. You're becoming arrogant, Sam.'

But Sam knew it to be true, and wondered if that was fear he could see in his brother's eyes.

'But the point is, it depends on how well you *can* see, doesn't it? And Trencher and I could always see much further than you could.'

'This is sounding old, Sam. You're wrong, I've heard all this before. You're starting to repeat yourself.' Vaughn's eyes were blank but murderous.

'When I see the future, I see much more – and in more detail than you ever possibly could. We both know it, however much you deny it. I spent years studying the Citadel, and it gave up its secrets to me. The salvation of this entire world is there. I can foresee every second of what will happen here in the next few days, all laid out like chess moves described in a textbook. And the more clearly I see, the more that future becomes real, while your imagined conquest becomes nothing more than a figment of your fucked-up imagination.'

Vaughn came towards him with a snarl, his hands clenching, ready for further brutality. Sam continued quickly. 'Anything that happens here happens largely because I see so much of it. Yet I think we both know who else sees more than either of us.' Vaughn moved behind the great boulder to which Sam was tethered, near the cliff edge. Sam spoke on: 'Trencher could always see so much clearer, further than you, Vaughn. I certainly could, too. I know what's going to happen. I know where it's going to go wrong for you, but you'll never know until it actually happens.'

Sam and his rock stood near the top of the path. He'd managed to wolf down some food before his brother had come looking for him. Sam knew what was going to happen next: had known since Vaughn had chained him here. He knew every word that would be said, every deed that would be done, so he fulfilled his lines like a good actor, or perhaps because he simply had no choice.

But there *was* a way out. If only he could grasp it, he could defy eternity, and the certainty of his fore-knowledge. That was the true secret of the Angels, of what they were, and of where they had gone.

'It's too late now, Ernst. You should have thrown me into the heart of a star while you had the chance. Maybe that would have changed the way things worked out, if you'd done it early enough – but not now. Not now.' Vaughn pushed at Sam's rock until it started to shift. Sam could see how much effort it was for Vaughn, not having Sam's centuries of practice. The shape and the surface of that rock was like a lover's skin to him now, something so utterly familiar.

He was dragged along, his body limp and pain-racked, as Vaughn started to roll the rock closer to the edge of the cliff. The manacles around Sam's thin, skeletal wrists became taut. 'Of course, it's not me you're really afraid of. You thought that if you could at least bring him here, where you could see him, you could then contain him, stop him interfering. Bad mistake, Ernst, really.' Sam clawed at the soil with his fingers, as the great boulder rolled slowly closer and closer to the cliff edge. It was a long way down. But Sam didn't fight it, because it was going to happen, as surely as the sun set in the evening and rose again in the morning.

He'd warned Matthew how long he and the others would have, timed it to the last second. *Trencher is the one who sees all*, thought Sam. *The one for whom reality coalesces around whichever path he chooses through the fog of quantum probabilities that is all our futures. The one whose eye truly is like the eye of God. The unwilling messiah. Who always knew he would be here, in this time, in this place, and for all his incipient godhood – for all our incipient godhood*, he thought, as the great ball of stone teetered on the edge of the cliff, over the snowy wastes far below – *is as trapped by his fate as any of the rest of us.*

Our curse was always to know it.

The great stone toppled over the upper edge of the path that wound its way far, far down the face of the cliff. It dragged Sam Roy after it and, as his bones shattered and his body ruptured, he screamed, not so much because of the pain but because he'd always known he would scream when this time came.

A few hours before, Vaughn had watched as the shuttle from the *Jager* appeared, zooming low over the Southern Teive range, dropping onto a stable ice-field less than a mile from the New Coventry settlement. It kicked up a furious cloud of superheated steam that burned away millennia-old permafrost in an instant. Vaughn stood at his favourite place – where he liked to stand on mornings like this – watching the craft settle down, the powerful whine of its engines dropping to a loud hum.

Even in this age of technology, it was still a wonder to know that you could reach out, even across half a galaxy, and trigger a sequence of events that would deliver someone to you with what seemed the minimum of fuss.

The whole town had turned out to watch.

They had lowered the shield long enough to allow the shuttle to find its way through to them. It had been only for a few minutes, so it was an acceptable risk. The military authorities who administered the Kasper Angel Station were still in considerable turmoil, and did not benefit from knowing the purpose or the nature of what had attacked them. Although, of course, there had been some unexpected results.

Vaughn could smell the excitement in the air – in all his people. The Endtime was approaching, which would finally liberate mankind from the shackles of the past. Young men and women, the inheritors of the world that would be their Eden, their fresh beginning under the eyes of God, stepped forward onto the ice-field. They were dressed in the uniforms of the Coventry militia, all fiercely loyal to the Primalist cause. More specifically, they carried equipment that would allow them to isolate any nanocytes that might have hitched a ride this far down the gravity well.

There was an air of ceremony in the way they moved towards the shuttle, because they had been taught to understand the nature of the Adversary. They had been taught that Trencher was the only one with the power to thwart God's plan. Part of that teaching had also been that Sam Roy had aided the Adversary, and was to be punished eternally for that sin – or until he repented and joined them in the world that lay ahead.

After the fire came, and they had retreated into the caverns deep beneath the Teive Mountains, they would re-emerge into a world renewed. New cities would be built for future generations, as the cosmic fire spread further on through the galaxy, destroying base, unholy life as it proceeded. The Kaspians would become merely a story told to children, something half-forgotten, unworthy, and God would smile on the righteous and bless them all. This was a good thing, a holy thing. Vaughn stepped forward just as the shuttle's hatch opened with a hiss, some of his militia entering first.

He sensed immediately that something was wrong.

Running up to the ship, he stared into the dark space beyond. He could not find words to describe the sensation he felt: a cold, dark feeling, of loss and failure.

Before he slipped inside the shuttle, Vaughn glanced back to see a sea of several hundred anxious faces.

He thought again about the Primalists back on Earth, and the way they had tried to cast him out so long ago, but now all rotting in their worm-filled graves, sleeping the sleep of absolute death. A few had believed they could gain salvation by helping him, and his miraculous appearance to those few back on the homeworld had secured their loyalty. He could not countenance the possibility that one or more of them had now betrayed him.

The shuttle rang with hollow footsteps. Then he found three of his people standing around a single deep-sleep coffin. It was open, and empty.

As Vaughn stood there, flexing and unflexing his fingers, he reached out with his mind, looking desperately for Trencher, but it was impossible. The farseeing was . . . difficult, at times unpredictable, particularly if he couldn't picture the place in his mind's eye. Sam, damn him, was the only one with any real talent for that kind of thing. It didn't seem right to be given so much by God, but to be able to use it so ineffectually . . . A low moan escaped his lips as he realized the impossible had happened.

Trencher *had* been on board.

But now Trencher was very, very gone.

Seventeen

Elias

It came upon Elias like a storm: like a great wind had blown up, and he himself was somehow receiving its undivided attention.

'Elias, what's wrong?'

'Trencher.' A sense of the future rushed through Elias's mind, but it was a storm of conflicting images. He envisaged one of the aliens hefting some kind of effigy in its paws, a briefly snatched image of Vaughn in some high mountainous place, then he saw . . . an end, the void; the same one he had seen before, but this time different.

'Trencher's alive,' said Elias. 'I need to find him.'

The wagon had come to a halt, and Elias peered through the slats. They had arrived at some kind of vast encampment, and he wondered if they had been taken to one of the Kaspian cities. But he couldn't see anything looking like solid buildings; all he did see had an air of impermanence.

Ursu

He'd found a place to stay out of sight for a few days, while he waited for a ship that could take him further north. He would head upstream, along a great river extending almost as wide as the seas further south. He'd learned that this was one of the best routes north: it meant he could cut east once he was back on dry land, thus avoiding many of the intervening mountain peaks. The worst of his journey, he suspected, was behind him.

The inhabitants of the village were barely distinguishable from the tribesfolk who had captured him soon after his flight from Nubala. But their ways seemed considerably more peaceful, thankfully.

This far north, he'd expected to be out of reach of the military forces of Xan, but even in this benighted twilight land the Emperor's soldiers made their presence known. He understood, now, why they wanted Shecumpeh so badly – the object he had once regarded as a god.

He was surprised at how oblivious these people seemed to the military forces invading their daily lives. But in time he came to realize that they continued to lead a life otherwise undisturbed, and would likely continue so long after both he and the soldiers were gone. Like the tribesfolk who wandered the ice, they had no god jealously guarded behind city walls.

Ursu had found himself a day's work with some fishermen who worked the river, earning him enough food to keep his hunger at bay for one night. He had woken up in darkness, to find the Shai addressing him.

He didn't enjoy the knowledge he had been regularly given. He now realized it had not been Shecumpeh speaking to him, so long ago, in the depths below the House of Shecumpeh, but this malformed Shai, speaking through Shecumpeh, the god somehow amplifying the creature's thoughts.

It was his role now to carry Shecumpeh back to the place from which it had been removed so long ago, from a cavern lying deep within the city of Baul.

Once he had gone upriver, the Shai had told him, he must start moving west along the coast, and then he would be able to find a path that would lead him to Baul.

Kim

She watched Elias crouching in a corner of the wagon. He was staring out through the slats, his eyes bright with the starlight.

'I'm beginning to think we should try and make a break for it,' Kim suggested, after a long silence. Vincent was breathing much more steadily now, but he still hadn't woken up.

'I've been watching them,' Elias replied softly, 'and there are always at least three of them guarding us. They're armed.'

'Maybe we should figure out what they're going to do with us,' she said. 'We haven't had any food in over twelve hours. We're going to starve if this goes on.' She showed him her precious vial. 'These are memory Books.'

'You need Observer bioware to use those things, surely?' Realization dawned in his eyes even as he spoke. 'I see' – he hesitated – 'you're an Observer?'

'I had the bioware implanted illegally. Don't ask why, but I had my reasons.'

He looked at the vial uncertainly. She could read his mind; they didn't look like much.

'These contain the memories of someone I was very close to, someone who happened to be an expert on this world.' He looked at her, surprised, and for the first time in a long while, she felt she had the upper hand.

'So you're saying,' he said carefully, 'that everything we need to know about surviving on Kasper will be in these things?'

'There's certainly a chance that some of it is.' Seeing the scepticism on his face, she continued, 'Put it this way, if what we need to know now is by any chance contained in these, I'll need to find it soon.'

'So were you planning on doing this sometime soon?'

'I'm not sure if I should while we're still here. I think it's too dangerous. I need the right time to use the Books. If I'm distracted by other things, I won't get the full benefit.'

Something else was happening outside. A glimpse confirmed that a dozen or more of the alien creatures were approaching, some of them carrying burning torches. For a blood-freezing moment, Kim wondered if they intended to burn the three of them alive inside the wagon.

But the vehicle shook as one side of it was lowered.

They stood up slowly, and stared down at the assemblage of heavily armed aliens standing around them, ears flicking gently against their fur-covered skulls.

The wagon was tethered to a trio of monstrous creatures, with wide mouths and slab-like teeth, their heads swaying gently back and forth in the night air.

After a few uncomfortable moments of appraising each other, there was commotion as another group appeared. Rough, sharp-clawed paws reached out and pulled them to the ground. Kim watched in alarm as some of them sniffed and prodded at Vincent's prone form, but to her relief they decided to leave him where he was. She noticed Elias had a bright glitter in his eyes.

The clothes worn by the newly arrived group of Kaspians seemed more ornate and richly coloured, and several had jewels pinned through their ears.

Elias glanced at her. 'Don't suppose you speak the language?'

She stared at him for a few seconds, then realized it was a joke.

'We couldn't speak their language even if we tried. Our mouths are constructed differently.'

The Kaspian with the jewelled ears came closer, emitting a series of sounds like rapid clicks and multi-pitched barking.

'It's trying to say something to us,' she whispered. 'And it expects us to answer.'

Elias and Kim stared at each other for a moment before he turned back to the alien.

'Hello,' he attempted. This had the effect of merely producing further clicking noises all round. The Kaspian leader shook its head in a gesture, so naturally human, of resigned defeat. A reaction so familiar only accentuated the utter strangeness of the situation.

Paws tipped with long black claws reached out to tug them forward again.

They were then pushed and shoved deeper amongst the tents, to an open space surrounded by pavilions with strange, looping designs painted on them. A faint memory triggered in Kim's mind, a memory that wasn't even hers, but something relating to the power structure on this planet. She thought of the vial of Books in her pocket, reaching a hand in to touch them for reassurance.

In the open space lay a pile of metallic junk that inspection revealed to be interior parts of the Goblin. The jewelled Kaspian gestured first at the debris, then at Kim and Elias. They had no idea what it was asking them.

His attention drifting, Elias stared towards the distant horizon, wondering what had happened to Trencher.

Ursu

'These creatures that live in the heart of a star,' said Ursu, 'what are they?'

– Not the heart of a star, the monstrous Shai spoke inside his head. – In a galaxy, a cloud of stars.

Ursu shook his head. He'd been travelling inland away from the river for several days now. Whenever he slept, he kept the Angel device well wrapped in a ragged cloth; otherwise the otherworldly blue light it radiated became too visible in the night.

When this is all over, Ursu thought to himself, *I'm going to go home. I'm going to see if there's anything left of the city. But I won't be a priest this time.* Perhaps Xan's soldiers had already killed all the priests of Nubala in their desperate hunt for the Shecumpeh device. And perhaps that was just as well, since he couldn't imagine Uftheyen or any of the other priests accepting what Ursu now knew to be true.

The picture of a galaxy arose in his mind as he trudged along. Clouds of stars, thought Ursu, but that was all too much to take in. He shook his head, feeling irrationally angry.

'All right, they live in the heart of the galaxy. And

you've told me about them, but only that they oppose these creatures you call—'

– Angels, yes, who imprisoned another race within the singularity that lies at the heart of the galaxy we inhabit. As the creature mentioned *singularity*, the word was translated in Ursu's mind into something close to a comprehensible concept. A ball of rock, but the size of an entire world, being squeezed by enormous hands until its own internal heat ignited it into a star, then being crushed again, and again, reducing to the size of a mountain, of a house, until finally it sucked in all its own light.

Then the Shai revealed the image of a great cloud of stars drawing rapidly closer to each other, eaten up by their own heat and density, squeezed together until they became something else – something terrible and dark that lay beyond the veil of stars Ursu saw nightly in the sky above him . . .

But this was too terrible a concept to think about. He shook his head, as if to free his mind of it. It reminded him of the well he had been trapped in, but bottomless, so that you could fall forever, and ever, and ever.

Ursu was now climbing upwards, nearing the crest of a steep hill that granted him a view of the distant ocean, now reduced to a thin silver line on the horizon behind him. He imagined he could make out ships pushing through blustery winds, on their way to distant ports. Nubala had been cold, but Ursu was here experiencing an intensity of cold that required an entire, undiscovered vocabulary to describe.

The inhabitants of the last little town had been strange, small folk distinguished with broad, flat ears who spoke some dialect Ursu could barely make out. They had directed him inland to the east, towards the Northern Teive Mountains. They thought he was crazy, to travel alone so far into such a hostile land. It was the land, they warned, of white, icy death.

'Why were the Angels at war with these other creatures?' he pressed the Shai.

– A philosophical disagreement. They did not communicate with anything you might recognize as a spoken language. Instead they communicated their ideas between themselves soundlessly, mind to mind.

Ursu struggled to understand. 'You mean mind-readers?'

– Nothing so crude. They used technological means – directly.

'I still don't understand.' Ursu watched his breath clouding in the crisp morning air as he came to the top of the craggy hill, and caught his first glimpse of the Northern Teive Mountains, those cruelly jagged cousins of the Southern Teive range.

– Remember how the effigy spoke to you, when you still believed it was in itself a god. And how I speak to you now drawing on your memories and sensations. So much conflict on your world and mine arises from misunderstanding: a misheard word, a misinterpreted action. Breakdowns in communication can lead to wars and injustice, because, for all our skills at communicating with each other, we do not always do it as well as we should.

– Well, the Angels recognized this fact, and found a means to communicate intent directly, in such a way that the recipient understood not only the message, but also the context of the message from the specific emotional or even social circumstances of the communicant.

Ursu was struck by this. 'You are saying the gods were created as facilitators, as a way of avoiding the possibility of misunderstanding.'

– Yes, but they have other purposes too . . . as guardians, caretakers. The Angels realized an attack was coming.

'They saw into the future?'

– Something like that, yes.

Ursu thought for a while. 'You told me earlier that they had no free will.'

– When the future becomes the present, in that eyeblink before it becomes the past, it becomes set, unchangeable. Nothing can alter it then. But if you look into the future, that act of seeing itself fixes the future in place. In a sense, the future is determined by the one with the greatest ability to perceive it. Sometimes, the mere act of looking at something is to change it.

'And you can see the future?'

– Yes.

Ursu thought hard. 'And just because you see it, it *must* become what you see?'

– That is the essence of it, yes. However, I am not the only one with the ability, and that is where matters begin to grow complicated.

There was a sparse forest in the valley ahead. It looked dark, forbidding, but he'd have to traverse it to get anywhere near the mountains.

'So what will happen after all this is over?' asked Ursu, finding his way down this side of the hill's more gentle incline. In the distance, he could see tribal totems rising from the plain beyond the forest, great stone pillars maybe half as old as the world.

– Ursu, as long as I and people like me exist, free will is gone from our lives and yours. To remove us completely from this existence is the only way to recover that free will. The Shai who is my enemy wishes to be a god. But I should think otherwise, and you are going to save your world.

'And am I going to succeed?'

This time there was no answer.

Sam Roy

He opened his eyes. The vision of the Kaspian ex-priest faded, to be replaced by the shelter he had dug from the snow. He had managed to drag himself away from the bottom of the cliff he had fallen down, a considerable journey still from where Ursu tramped north towards the Citadel.

After he had initially betrayed Ernst, it had rapidly become clear to Sam that the man would have had a higher calling as a medieval torturer. When he wasn't in too searing agony to think, Sam had been almost impressed with the range of carefully deliberated cruelty of which Ernst was capable.

As Sam had landed at the bottom of the cliff, most of the bones in his body were smashed. He was still alive, however. Neither he nor Ernst ever knew just what it would take to actually kill them.

After centuries of torment, Sam was sure his pain threshold must be as high as any in human history. It had become, by this time, merely a state of being.

At least he was no longer manacled to the ball of rock. Though it had shattered on the long drop down, he was still left with the heavy steel chains fitted tight around his scrawny wrists. He painfully gathered them into his arms.

Of course, he had known in advance for all these decades that this would eventually happen. Worse still, he had known that he would be dismayed and horrified by the even greater damage to his ruined body. Nor would this foreknowledge negate the fear and the doubt he would feel.

When it occurred, his communication with the Kaspian god-machines had led him to certain conclusions suggesting why the Angels were no longer present in the universe. Except those self-same conclusions led to yet further questions, such as why the Angels had deliberately booby-trapped human DNA with the key to incipient godhood.

He suspected the answer lay with the intelligence now imprisoned within the heart of the galaxy. In his farseeing conversations with the sentient machines, the Kaspian gods had seemed unclear on the precise nature of that intelligence. But that the answer lay in the Kaspian's fabled city of Baul was a conclusion he had drawn for himself.

Sam hadn't ever lied to the young Kaspian priest, but the awful truth was that he didn't really know how things would finally turn out. Had never known that, couldn't know, however hard he tried to probe the future . . .

He lay whimpering there, deep in his snowy cell, and waited for his bones to knit. His skin was blue with cold, but he still could not attain the luxury of death. In a few hours from now, he'd struggle forth again . . . and then certain things would inevitably happen. But in Baul itself – the vast artefact that humans had named the Citadel – he didn't know what would transpire, could only be vaguely sure of events leading up to the crisis.

Beyond that point, he saw only a blackness, a void more terrifying, more innately disturbing, than any knowledge of the future he carried within himself.

Roke

When Roke had first set his eyes on them, he had been terrified of these creatures, the Shai.

Communication was proving impossible with them, as they did not appear to have one of those small metal boxes the Shai Vaughn possessed, allowing them to respond back in one of the Kaspian tongues. When Roke addressed them, they reacted only in confusion.

Roke had therefore gained the distinct impression that these three Shai were not connected to Vaughn, or at least were not nearly as powerful. Were there conclusions to be drawn from their sudden dramatic appearance? Roke had seen the ruins of the craft that had flown blazing over their heads, and the swathe of destruction it had cut through the forest. Were they fleeing from something? Roke couldn't begin to guess. But the unexpected factor was their substantiality. They felt real to the touch: made of flesh and blood, not phantom creatures.

He gave up pondering and decided to retire for the night. Roke had ordered a dozen of the guards to construct a holding pen for the creatures. Perhaps, if he persisted, he might still get to understand the role these three had to play in the Shai Sam's plans for all of them.

Kim

'Now might be a good time to try the Books,' said Elias.

Vincent was showing more signs of life. He'd mumbled a few words, and he'd looked up at her for a few seconds, before seeming to drift into a more natural sleep. It was maybe a good sign, but he wasn't out of the woods yet.

'I was thinking that,' Kim said quietly. It had been awkward, even strangely embarrassing for them, standing there with some kind of eminence amongst the Kaspians attempting to communicate with them. *Hello, take me to your leader*, she imagined his clicks and soft barks might be translated; but they had stood dumbfounded, unable to reply.

'You understand, though, there are no guarantees,' she said. 'I might not be able to get anything out of it. And if anything sudden happens during the night—'

'I don't think it will,' he replied. 'They sleep at night, just like we do. That's why they've got us in this . . . cage.' He peered around in disgust.

'If only we could figure out a way to talk to them, they might even be able to help us.'

Elias looked at her incredulously. 'Jesus, think about what you're saying. Imagine if some of them had landed in medieval Europe. How long do you think it'd take before *we'd* stuck them on a bonfire.'

'They haven't yet shown any sign of intending us harm,' she replied tightly.

'Which makes them rather better than us, I guess, unless they're thinking of eating us eventually.' He shrugged away the hard look she gave him. 'Okay, maybe not that bad, but they're primitives, and forget that at your peril.'

Kim pulled out the vial, and shook one of the last precious Books into the palm of her hand.

She put it on the tip of her tongue, felt it began to dissolve, soon filling her mouth with that familiar sour taste. As she swallowed, she noticed Elias watching her with a curious expression. His eyes flicked away, and he sat in silence, crouching on the bare earth in a corner of the little wooden box confining them.

Kim closed her eyes, daydreamed . . . daydreamed through another person's eyes, in another time. She was seeing the world through Susan's eyes. She was back in the Citadel again, far away. No, not so far away, now.

She concentrated harder, trying to draw the Susan memories away from that time, that place.

Back on Earth now; random, dream-like images flitted before her mind's eye. She again experienced being Susan, learning about becoming an Observer, about the bioware technology. She sat in a comfortable room with a dozen others, a soft-screen writer by her arm.

'Let's be frank,' the lecturer was saying. 'There are a

lot of ways to describe the process when an Observer consumes a Book, and how their bioware interacts with the complex molecules, and the information encoded on them. But let's be frank.'

The lecturer – a name came to Kim, but it meant nothing to her – surveyed the men and women seated in front of him. 'Every such theory amounts to bullshit,' he continued. 'But it's part of the human condition to give even the unknowable a rationale. By quantifying it, we give it the illusion of fitting it into some compartment of human knowledge. Yet nobody really knows how the implants work. And because they shouldn't work, they are technically,' he said with a broad grin, 'an impossibility.'

Kim frowned inwardly. Wherever the knowledge she was looking for was, it wasn't here. Yet it was proving extraordinarily difficult to extricate herself from this scene. The lecturer was now looking at her directly.

'The reality of what the Angels were, and what their bioware itself was, or is, lies somewhere with the secret of why the universe seems so silent of communication – of those alien radio signals we once assumed were flying between star systems.' Kim/Susan stood and walked to the door. As she glanced back at the lecturer, he seemed to be in pain now. She was sure she could see blood staining his shirt and trousers, but his other students appeared to be oblivious to his distress.

'So why the great silence during those long, pre-Angel years when we searched the skies for signs of

extraterrestrial intelligence – while all the time it was
right there, beyond the orbits of Pluto and Charon?
Perhaps that was because we could not share the
aliens' concept of what it means to really communicate.
Kim?'

But before she could react to him addressing her by
a name he should not have been using, she was already
somewhere else. She was back on Earth in Susan's private apartment – a place Kim remembered with the
fondness of lost love tinged with regret.

She knew instinctively that *now* she was in the right
place. She recognized instantly all the printed books,
the loosely stacked ream of smartsheets, packed with
information about Kasper: information about its flora
and fauna; observation and speculation about the
Kaspians' civilization.

Now, crucially, she could taste that knowledge,
letting it flood from the Book into her mind. Yet, at the
back of her mind, she wondered what had happened
earlier: at how she had experienced the illusion that
something within the Book itself had spoken directly to
her . . .

She looked up and caught sight of herself/Susan
in the mirror. Susan's mouth was moving, speaking
silently from the reflection.

But there's no one else here, thought Kim, her blood
freezing in her veins. She looked around, feeling
panicked, then back again to the mirror. To her horror,
she now saw another figure reflected in the glass.

Lurking in the shadows behind her, it was the same lecturer, but his body was now horribly distorted: his skin blue and waxy, criss-crossed with dozens of scars. All his teeth were blackened and broken, and a wave of nausea flowed over her.

'But what does it mean to truly communicate?' the mutilated image continued, as if still addressing his class. 'Words are not enough, for to truly communicate ideas, you must first remove the barrier of spoken language, the barrier of our different experiences. To truly communicate, you must first become the other person, to gain a full understanding of them. Without that enhancement, communication – as the Angels understood it – is impossible.'

Kim walked towards the door, too terrified to look behind her in case there really was something there. She had been under a lot of stress recently, and maybe hallucinations and make-believe were encroaching on her reality. She stepped out into a busy corridor, feeling lighter and stronger than she remembered experiencing on the homeworld. But then, as a native, Susan had no problem with the gravity.

Then she noticed a mouthful of broken teeth grinning at her from along the corridor, and the lecturer's monstrous form came loping and dragging itself towards her. She felt nauseous, and in the real world dropped her face against the strange-smelling Kaspian soil. She became distantly aware of Elias watching her, tight-lipped and tense.

Her mind was filled again with the lecturer's loathsome image. 'I've had centuries now to study what remains in the Citadel,' it continued unstoppably, 'and that's how I uncovered a tragedy. Those Books were a means for the Angels to understand each other – and other species – from a multitude of unique perspectives. The memories are not actually contained within the chemicals themselves. Instead they trigger something – not universal consciousness, not God, not anything that crude, but something for which no words exist.'

She was running now, under the great bright spaces of an arcology's vast atrium. Arctic sunlight spilled down from above, reflecting brilliantly off distant snowfields. She swallowed her fear. *This is only a Book*, she thought, *not something real.*

She stopped, turned. It came closer. She felt her horror replaced by something more like pity mixed with revulsion. It was a man, but his injuries were so horrific it was like looking at some product of interac-generated imagery rather than anything that could be alive.

She swallowed her panic. 'Who are you?'

'My name is Samuel Roy Vaughn. I live in the mountains to the north.' And suddenly she was there too, in this man's own memories, piloting a shuttle down from the Station in the hectic weeks after the Hiatus began, filled with a sense of holy purpose, of manifest destiny.

'We came here because some of us had been created

to foresee the course of the future.' She suddenly remembered a childhood spent with other siblings, the regular tests that were carried out, the feeling of loss when one of them would fail a test and would be gone the next morning from their sunny dormitory, never to be seen again. 'Like Elias, my genes were altered through experimentation with Angel biotechnology. But I, more than all but one, have seen the path of the future. Please understand.'

Then a sense of desperate terror, the blood flowing in yet another suicide attempt. But the release of death never came. Feeling faint, she swayed in front of the ruined figure crouching before her, its lips obstinately unmoving even as it spoke within her. This experience was like eating a Book, but a thousand times more powerful, more full of sensations and information. How could so much information be contained in one dissolving molecular package? And then she remembered the creature's words spoken when it had still appeared human. *It can't, it doesn't.*

'I, I don't . . .' she faltered. 'I don't understand.'

'You *do*. Accept the information. You *know* now. Before the Book fades, reach into Susan's memories. All of her is in there. Go to the Citadel.'

I can't, she thought. *I won't go back. There must be other places we could shelter from the radiation. Every nightmare I've suffered for ten years is in there.*

The Book was indeed fading. Awareness of the rough soil beneath her hands was becoming more vivid;

she could hear the everyday sounds of the camp around her. She gagged as an ocean of knowledge poured into her mind, so vast and so deep she feared she might drown in the flood of memories and accumulated knowledge.

She was back completely in the world again. Dawn light criss-crossed the interior of their cage with stripes of dusty brilliance. It took several moments for her to realize that Elias was not there – simply no longer in the cage with her. She reached out, touched Vincent's still form, and somehow knew, in that instant, that he was finally, truly dead. His cold skin felt like marble under her fingertips.

Elias had left her a note on a folded smartsheet lying by Vincent's shoulder, its pixels glowing faintly in the morning light. Desperately, she willed Vincent to wake up, his head hanging loosely in her arms.

She finally let the tears come, because there was no one there to hear her, and for a little while she blamed Elias for Vincent's death, and wished vengeance upon him.

After a while, she unfolded the smartsheet and smoothed out the creases. The words shone out at her brightly from the sheet's tiny paper screen.

Vincent died 1 hr after you ate Book. Got him to tell me some things first. Told me more about radiation. All fits together, some, anyway. Sorry about Vincent, was nice guy. We'll know if we won if we're all alive next week. Elias.

She let the smartsheet fall to the ground. Vincent had been in a coma the last time she was conscious of him. Had he woken up since? How else could Vincent have told Elias anything? And then he'd died? The horrible thought that Elias had speeded his death occurred to her, and she examined Vincent's body for any signs of injuries she hadn't noticed already.

Finding none, she realized he had just got sicker and died. She could now see where Elias had scrabbled into the hard dirt by one corner of the cage, digging with a broken-off section of plank, and somehow doing it all without drawing attention to himself. The cool air beyond beckoned her. She wanted to be out, away from Vincent's corpse, out amongst the living, whatever kind of creature they were. But what would she do, once she was out there? Follow Elias wherever he had gone? She wouldn't kid herself that she possessed that kind of resourcefulness.

She wiped Elias's message from its screen, just in case the Grid was back online. To her delight, on hitting update, she was presented with a packet that had arrived through the singularity within only the past few hours. The smartsheet had automatically updated itself meanwhile, and they had not even realized.

A plan of action began forming in her mind. But,

while thinking it through, she noticed a new message alert was flashing in one corner of the smartsheet.

The message was addressed to Vincent. She'd assumed the smartsheet had belonged to Elias, but on closer examination the 'sheet was good quality, not merely designed to be used for five minutes and then thrown away. Vincent had personalized it.

The message itself was from somebody called Eddie Gabarra. The name rang a bell – some friend of Vincent's?

She read the message, swearing occasionally at what it said. This was a day for revelations. She could hear movement outside, and wondered how long it would take their captors to realize one of them had got away. She decided not to worry about how they might react to that discovery. *Two days*. Elias was right: they only had two days, then half the existing species on Kasper – including the one that had built this cage – would very likely be wiped out.

She ran a Grid search for the information she needed, drawing the locations from Susan's memories. Normally, the memories gleaned from a Book slipped away within hours, but after eating only the one Book, she experienced an unprecedented clarity of recall, the information it contained taking up residence in her long-term memory with no prompting. That made it hard to dismiss the dialogue she'd experienced with the – whatever it was that called itself Sam Vaughn.

Papers and studies regarding the Kaspians, information derived from those clandestine searches under-taken far from the secluded icefields of the Citadel, researchers and soldiers being dropped down in uninhabited areas under cover of night, to retrieve what they could without danger of accidental intervention. Samples of their language, too. Some of this body of knowledge, she was aware, had come from Susan herself.

So there they were: samples of the language, place names – a fountain of information. What was the name they used for their lost city of the North? Baul. Nobody was sure if they meant 'the Citadel', but that didn't seem unlikely.

She then came across software that translated human language into the sigils and symbols of the Kaspian language, based on samples found and some extrapola-tion. She heard further movement, then rapid chittering and clicking just beyond the cage. *They've found Elias's escape route*, she thought. *Now they're going to come in here. Then what happens?*

More chittering, shadows flashing through the spears of light criss-crossing the cage, as the Kaspians moved about.

She was as ready as she'd ever be, when the door was yanked open and a long, fur-covered face with pale scarlet eyes looked in at her. She stood up, her legs feel-ing weak and shaky, and held the smartsheet, with its bright pixellated screen facing towards the Kaspian, the single word *Baul* blazing on it in each of the three main Kaspian tongues.

It studied the 'sheet for several long seconds, then let loose with a long sequence of chittering sounds. It stepped aside, and she saw the one Elias thought might be their leader, standing watching her with wide, blank eyes.

Eighteen

Sam Roy

Sam pushed his way out of his snowy cell, after waiting for another twenty minutes or so. Ernst would be out looking for him. He had the manpower, and the technology, to sweep the mountains thoroughly, although that would take time. Sam was unarmed and, for the moment, alone.

There! A bright silver gleam passing between two great jagged peaks. It shot closer, coming from the opposite direction to New Coventry. Soon it resolved itself into a shuttle, before dropping down to the snow with a roar. Matthew jumped out, followed by three others. Sam had met none of them before, had never even known the names of most of Matthew's co-conspirators. They stared at him now with a mixture of awe and horror. He was, after all, the brother of Ernst Vaughn, the man who had ruled their community vigorously since long before any of them were born. He was also, by the tenets of their upbringing, the Devil made flesh.

To Sam, Trencher's mind seemed to come shining through the landscape like an invisible sun – still unconscious, but powerfully alive.

'Luke,' said Matthew, breaking the brief silence. 'Fetch Sam some clothes. We're getting out of here now.' Luke nodded, came forward and took one of Sam's arms, helping him to hobble aboard the shuttle. Sam pretended not to notice the revulsion on the boy's face.

The heat inside the shuttle hit Sam like a wave of fire. He stumbled and almost collapsed, but Luke helped him back upright. 'Are you all right?' asked Luke, his eyes full of alarm, as the others followed them on board.

'Too . . . too hot,' said Sam, his throat dryer than he ever remembered. He could not comprehend this sensation of being *not cold*. His ruined skin seemed to contract around his body painfully in response. However, he was healing rapidly. 'Get him through to the bay,' ordered Matthew as the shuttle door clicked shut. Sam still reeled from the heat, but supporting hands helped him through to the rear of the craft. The bay section of the shuttle had been converted into a makeshift hospital. Two fold-down cots had been bolted to the floor and one of them was already in use. They tried to coax him onto the other one, but Sam shrugged them off and, with what seemed to be the last of his strength, staggered over to study the frail, thin figure that occupied the other cot.

Trencher. It had been so long – more than a few life-times. Sam peered down at the old man, and saw a face not unlike his own, lined but unscarred.

Trencher's eyes opened and Sam, looking into them, seemed to see great whorls of stars in their unknowable depths. *Where were you really,* Sam wondered, *while you were hooked up in that coffin? Did you live in one place and yet another, both at the same time like I did? Or did you just dream the years away there, in your steel and plastic coffin?*

'No.' Trencher spoke, his voice thin and fragile. 'I talked with them too.' Just a few words, but a universe of meaning within them.

'Sam,' it was Matthew, 'what now?'

'Exactly what I told you. You must head for the Citadel, but we need to do something else first.'

Roke

One of the Shai prisoners had escaped during the night, and Roke wondered if the Monster had been aware this would happen. Another of them had died. When he had sent men to scout out the forest in the wake of the burning craft, he could not forewarn them about what they might find, for fear of coming under suspicion for being so well informed about the apparently unpre-dictable. He had his future within the Emperor's court to think of.

He had ordered the scouts to bring back anyone, or anything, they found alive, for interrogation. The scouts had looked uncertain at that. Why should there be anyone to find within the forest, even after that vast object had crashed through the air above them? The place was far from the traditional routes of the northern tribes, and filled with nothing but ghosts and forest beasts.

Roke had fretted, unable to totally trust in the Monster, fearful he had cast in his lot with demons who meant the Emperor ill. Maybe he should simply fulfil the task Xan had given him: survey this unknown territory and report back. But, of course, the dramatic descent of the flying ship would not go unreported . . . Roke had pulled his ears tight about his head in frustration.

There were mutterings amongst his ordinary soldiers as well, about how Roke appeared to be attempting to communicate with the monsters they had captured. And now one of them seemed to have vanished into the night, managing that without disturbing the guards. That it might be prowling vengefully through the forest even now chilled Roke to the bone. He wished to be gone from this area as soon as possible.

But then something remarkable had happened.

This last remaining Shai did not try to speak. Instead it held up some strange glowing sheet. And the familiar word for the city of Baul was emblazoned upon its surface, in letters clear and readable, yet somehow composed of light.

Now in Roke's quarters, the alien smoothed the glowing sheet out upon a slab of wood, then guided Roke's long fingers to it, so that one of his thick black digits pressed against it. As if in response, letters in Roke's own language appeared.

Roke understood immediately. As he touched one panel and then another, more letters appeared. The alien guided his hand until he understood how to organize the letters into coherent words. As he wrote *My Name is Roke*, other, unfamiliar sigils appeared on the glowing sheet next the sentence he had written. These must be the creature's own language, he guessed.

The alien turned the sheet around to face it. *I am Kim*, she wrote. *One of us has died.* A sentence appeared below her rapidly tapping fingers. The syntax was wrong, the order of words confusing, but Roke could understand, or make reasonable guesses.

He realized he was communicating with a creature from another world. It was a dizzying sensation that seemed to chase all his former doubts away.

You are all in terrible danger, the creature wrote.

Fire from the sky, Roke wrote in reply. The creature twitched, as if it hadn't realized he knew.

Ursu

At first he'd been wary of this tribe, remembering previous bad experiences. But he soon discarded the wide blanket of his instinctive prejudice. Not all of the tribes reacted the same.

This tribe was called the Deshugevvit, like all tribal names a compound of the names of the spirits inhabiting the great stone markers that defined their eternal trail across the northern wastelands. The Deshugevvit were dying out, it seemed, but not from disease, starvation or warfare; they were losing their younger members to the ports and cities of the south, as they married into city-bound families, or joined city guilds, or became part of the new breed of merchant-tribes who facilitated trade between the city-states of the newly founded empire lying south of the Great Northern Sea.

So when he found them, or rather they found him – huddled by one of the great stone pillars lost in this empty white wilderness, with the great mountain range to the north the only thing to distinguish sky from land – they had taken him in and fed him.

They were mostly old folk, their numbers clearly dwindling. They seemed polite, but extremely superstitious, rituals seeming to fill much of their time between eating and sleeping. Time seemed to stretch out into vast eternities amid the deep white coldness surrounding them, and it wasn't hard for Ursu to imagine these folk might think this was all there was to the world.

Ahead, the mountains drew slowly closer: great forbidding crags that stabbed upwards into a pale sky.

The Deshugevvit were not the only people who journeyed so close to the mountains of the far north.

The land had curved back in until for a few days Ursu had found himself following a stretch of coastline. In the few hamlets encountered along the way, flood-endangered towns that had once perched on rocky prominences, Ursu had heard many stories about explorers and travellers meeting their doom in these icy wastes, while attempting to find a sea passage north that simply wasn't there.

But he had heard other tales, that there was now indeed a land passage somewhere ahead that hadn't existed before; caused by the melting away of the ice, affording a way through to the most distant points north.

For the tribe itself, there was no end of portents, signs and demons to persuade them that the end of the world must be coming. If he hadn't known better, Ursu might have joined them in their prayers. He had seen something silvery flash overhead only the previous night, as if some great bird with skin like water-dazzle nested there in the frozen mountains.

But the fire from the sky would be coming all too soon.

The next day, the tribe informed him that they had reached the very last standing stone before the great mountain peaks of the north. They had held a council, believing he might have some great purpose beyond the mountains, and decided that Ursu should scout ahead, with some of their younger tribesfolk, to see if the way north was now clear.

Vaughn

Vaughn assumed mindform and hovered on the edge of a humanly inaccessible crag, staring towards the peaks to the north.

He could be tricked, but never defeated. That just wasn't in the cards for him. The wind sliced through where his body should have been, while his real flesh twitched in its chair some miles distant. He watched as a shuttle flew low across the landscape, and wondered if the Station authorities had managed to get their orbital observation satellites up and running again. Disabling them had been hard enough work in the first place. Effecting it a second time would attract too much unwanted attention, and they wouldn't be able to cover up another failure.

Which meant there was a fair chance for anybody observing to spot the shuttles suddenly appearing, in the region of the Teive Mountains, as they slipped from under the protective blanket of the shield generators. It was a necessary risk, however, if he was going to locate Murray or, more importantly, Trencher. He wondered if this was how it had been for other great leaders throughout Earth's history; that moment when random circumstance forced strategy to deviate from its original plan, to evolve and – for better or worse – become something else.

But ultimately it was a matter of expediency, of cutting one's losses. They might lose their anonymity, the secrecy of their existence, but would speed that much more quickly to absolute victory. But now his son had disappeared. Was he being tested by God, he wondered? The awful possibility that Matthew was insane enough to turn against him a second time seemed unbelievable, but who else would have had the audacity to steal Trencher from under his nose? A tide of anger overwhelmed him. Matthew would have to be punished.

Someone was calling to him. Vaughn opened his eyes, as the distant crag faded. Someone was standing over him.

'Wake up, sir, wake up. We've managed to locate one of them. It's Murray.'

There were six of them in all: two women and four men, all mid-twenties, all trusted. People whom Ernst Vaughn felt sure would not turn renegade. He supplied them with arms and a shuttle, and sent them off to find Elias Murray.

Tracking the Goblin that brought Murray to Kasper had not been difficult. It meant flying over occasional small settlements populated by tribal Kaspians, who might wonder for a few days, but that hardly mattered.

They'd all be gone in a few days anyway, ushered into history by the inexorable will of God. The shuttle flew on.

The forest stretched for dozens of kilometres beyond the point where the Goblin had crashed. At one point they flew high above some kind of Kaspian military camp, which was obviously investigating the crash site. They took pictures of this, and reported back over the radio. They also activated onboard detection systems that could pick up traces of body heat.

These instruments could be fine-tuned to discern the difference between human beings and Kaspians, because of variant body temperatures. They had already picked up one figure conforming to the right body-heat index moving rapidly north, some dozens of kilometres north of the crash site. One other human possibility was soon located immobile within the alien encampment.

On again reporting to base, they were ordered to apprehend or kill whoever was moving through the forest, and only then deal with the static alternative inside the encampment. As their pilot guided the shuttle down to a forest clearing, their hearts were filled with joy while unwrapping their recently fabricated weapons and checking them. They were the soldiers of the New World, and their mission was blessed by God.

Moments after they had landed, a rock was thrown at the shuttle just as they prepared to disembark. Their leader, an earnest and devout young woman called Katie, ordered a red alert and passed out live ammunition. Jones, their technical officer, youngest of them all at nineteen, reported picking up a man-sized heat trace less than fifty metres away.

Their objective was clear: they would attempt a clean kill. Katie strapped on her comms helmet and recoil armour, then led them in a quick prayer before hitting a button to open the shuttle door.

The empty forest clearing stared back at them.

Using hand signals, and maintaining radio silence, they fanned out towards the nearest trees, the shuttle entrance a bright rectangle of light behind them.

Elias watched the naive youngsters deploy from behind one of the shuttle's landing struts. Once they were far enough away, he stepped out from his meagre hiding place and jumped up into the shuttle's airlock. Sudden yells of protest from outside were cut off as the outer door slammed shut. The only sound now was a faint pinging, as bullets ricocheted off the hull.

Elias strode through to the cockpit, and within seconds had activated a console command blocking external access to the ship's computer. This would ensure that the previous occupants could not run an override to reopen the airlock from outside.

He was now very hungry, so went looking for the mess, which was tucked into a narrow space between two bulkheads. It was stocked with enough food for several days, so he grabbed himself a sandwich and went back through to the cockpit.

He ignored the figures jumping and yelling outside,

and the occasional ping of a missile bouncing off the exterior. The shuttle looked like it had seen much better days, but it was sturdy and well maintained.

He fired up the engines, watching the crew outside scatter for the trees as they built up to a whine and then a roar.

Trencher, here we come, he thought, as the forest dropped away below him. With a sudden thought, he turned south first.

This shouldn't take long, he hoped.

Ursu

The whole world was reduced to white, and Ursu reflected that it wouldn't take long to go crazy out here. The tribe's thousand and one odd little rituals – so simple and crude compared to the beautiful complexity of Nubalan rituals – now came to make a great deal of sense to Ursu. They grounded the tribesfolk in the real, the here and now, for all that their culture seemed to avoid dealing with issues of space and time. For them, the spirit paths took precedence over everything, even the concept of existence itself.

There were three of them now: Ursu himself, a pathfinder called Telidante, and Telidante's son, called Desker. Ursu had undertaken an astonishing amount of walking since he had left Nubala, but compared to the pathfinder, he was a mere beginner. Telidante's fur was streaked with white, his features hardened by a lifetime of scouting.

Desker was close to Ursu's age, a little younger perhaps, but appeared so effortlessly resourceful that Ursu felt like the hopeless town-dweller he thought he'd left behind.

The rest of the tribe wasn't going any further. The stone pillar here marked the end of their spirit path – as far as they were concerned, it marked the end of the world. But it was good that Telidante and his son were prepared to help Ursu on towards the mountains. The foothills surrounding the mighty peaks were clearly visible, though the tops of the mountains themselves were wreathed in drifting clouds. As they approached the range, Ursu thought he had never seen anything so impossibly beautiful.

'Another one,' said Telidante, while stopping to take a piss in the snow. The spirit pillar had long vanished into the white horizon behind them.

'What?' Ursu had been blankly following them, his thoughts lost in the vastness around them. But then he saw what Telidante indicated: a silvery streak gliding between the summits like some great bird. It was no more than a speck reflecting sunlight, but despite that would, close up, be clearly of enormous size.

'Bad omen,' muttered Telidante, picking up his pack again. 'We'll take you as far as the pass, then you're on your own. We should be there in a few hours.' His eyes flicked around the landscape constantly, though Ursu couldn't see anything out there to draw his attention. He never looked directly at Ursu for more than a fleeting instant, and seemed to prefer just one or two words where most might use a dozen.

Telidante continued, staring off into the far distance as they trudged on. Ursu's legs constantly ached as he struggled to keep up with the other two.

'Has anyone ever traversed this pass before?' he asked eventually. Minutes or hours might have passed since last anyone spoke, but it was hard to tell. They were now passing some great stony outcrops half-hidden under ice and snow. The ground seemed to be rising slightly, as if changing gradually to a newly minted landscape.

Telidante just snorted, so it was Desker who replied. 'Anyone passing through there dies, or the Shai soon get 'em. Snow and ice blocked the way for a long time now, but things're changing.' The boy said this with audible regret. 'Heard folk might be able to get through now, but we Deshugevvit don't know if any succeeded. None ever came back, if they did.'

Ursu could elicit no further information from them.

As another silver streak shot across the distant landscape some hours later, Ursu glanced at the other two and noticed their grim expressions and down-turned faces.

They came finally to the foothills and stopped to rest. There was something on the other side of these mountains, thought Ursu. Something that lived only as a legend, a story. He slept fitfully for a while, as the others started building a fire. He woke to see one of the silver bird-things hovering far overhead with an audible roar.

Desker and Telidante seemed to freeze, as they sat warming their hands over flickering flames, this time watching as the *thing* passed overhead. Telidante began to mutter some kind of prayer under his breath, the rapid syllables blending together. His son began to pack up their belongings.

'You're on your own now,' announced Desker, as his father turned back the way they'd come. 'We can't go any further, and we don't want to know what's happening here.' Ursu tried to reason with them, but Desker was already running to catch up with his father. They headed off into the snow without another word, even a farewell.

Ursu stood still as the great silver bird circled far above him. *I can't turn back*, he thought. *And how could I ever escape from such a thing?*

Several minutes later the silver bird seemed to drop suddenly, plunging down into the snow covering the foothills. Ursu could hear a strange high-pitched whining sound. He stood transfixed, listening hard and staring into the distance, but a high wind had picked up suddenly, blurring the defining line between sky and horizon, whipping the surface snow into the air in a frenzy. The silver bird had disappeared from sight. He picked his stuff up and continued trudging towards the foothills.

A little while later he felt sure he could see something: a tiny, mobile dot in front of him. But it vanished, obscured by the blizzard howling around him. He concentrated only on putting one foot in front of the other, till eventually the wind subsided, and the sun again shone harsh and bright upon the world.

What he had noticed earlier resolved itself into a figure, but one that stirred up a vague disquiet in Ursu's soul. As Ursu kept walking, the figure came ever closer.

With stunted ears, and its legs bent the wrong way, it was swaddled up in unfamiliar clothing. Soon Ursu could hear the sound of its feet crunching through the snow, and a short distance behind it was the silver bird, close enough now for him to see it was something manufactured.

Ursu halted, staring at the strange creature approaching him. *Shai*, he thought instantly, though the stories he had been told in the House of Shecumpeh described nothing quite like this.

Yet he recognized it as that thing he had only ever seen hovering at the edge of his vision, or lurking in shadows, though it did not appear as badly mutilated as previously. It stopped right in front of him, casting curious eyes over this last remaining priest of Nubala.

Ursu gazed upon the creature that had guided him here, so far from home.

Roke

Roke heard the whine first, as from some mythical beast, increasing in volume and pitch as it drew closer. He stepped rapidly to the flap of his tent and peered outside. A terrible wind had whipped up from nowhere, and the air was filled with the sound of frightened ice-beasts braying and soldiers running for their weapons.

There appeared to be no enemy, however. Until Roke looked up.

Kim stepped up beside him and carefully laid tiny fingers on his long arm, causing him to look up at the Shai's bizarrely hairless face. Roke interpreted her action as meaning: *There is nothing to worry about.*

Roke stepped outside and caught the attention of a senior guard who, despite his evident confusion and fright, managed to come to some kind of attention. In the meantime, the enormous flying craft – the second such that Roke had seen within only a few days – dropped onto half-frozen grassland at the edge of the encampment, dwarfing everything around it.

Roke felt his terror dissipate, replaced by deep fascination. He had been aware for some time through his dealings with the Monster that there was much more to his world than he could ever have guessed. But now he felt that realization deep within him, now saw solid and clear evidence somehow more potent than when that first craft had hurtled into the forest, bringing these alien creatures to his attention.

He told the guard to assume command for the moment, to gather men and weapons ready, but not to attack. As light appeared on the side of the craft, the Shai stepped towards it, then stopped, looking back at Roke.

The alien studied her uncertainly. It was so tempting to gather up his followers and order them to return to Tibe.

Kim beckoned him with some meaningless noise. Roke thought hard for a few seconds, then decided to follow the Shai. She walked rapidly ahead of him, climbing into the opening in the side of the craft.

He had considered earlier that this would be his last adventure. It would hardly do, therefore, not to see how it ended. Roke stepped forward to join her.

His own people seemed too dumbfounded to do anything but watch as Kim guided him upwards and inside the machine. He found himself in a world he could never have suspected existed.

Vaughn

Katie had reported back in about their plight. His son Matthew was still untraceable, as was Trencher. The members of a survey team sent out on a regular maintenance mission had also disappeared. It all combined to drive Vaughn insane with anger.

Of course, the gamma wavefront would arrive here

within mere hours, slamming its way through the inner Kaspian system at the speed of light. The entire community was in pandemonium as last-moment preparations were being made. Half of the population was down in the Shelters already, and would remain there for several weeks, until the worst of the radiation had dispersed. After that they would emerge, to a New World awaiting them.

Vaughn hurried out of the Centre, walking past the now-abandoned homes of his people. Faces nodded in greeting as he rapidly passed them. Goods, equipment and food supplies were being shifted down the steep earth ramp that led to the Shelters. On the surface it looked like chaos but, as far as such things go, all was proceeding to plan.

Sam was out there somewhere too. Ernst Vaughn realized the mistake he'd made by playing into his brother's hands.

Somewhere deep inside of him, a tiny thought of defeat struggled to be recognized. He clamped down on it, hard. Failure was not, could never be an option. That would be to deny centuries of planning by himself as well as the Primalists back on Earth; it would also be to deny God, and such a catastrophic crisis of faith could not be countenanced. *I am doing only what is good*, he thought. *Something holy, blessed; a total cleansing.*

Ernst Vaughn glanced down at the rifle in his hands, as if aware of it for the first time. It gleamed in the sunlight, freshly fabricated for him by one of the automated industrial units. It nestled in his grip, quiescent – not truly a killing thing, he thought, until serving for that purpose.

He thought of the pain it would bring him, to kill his son, the one he had believed would stand by him in the world to come. No matter, now. He gazed along the narrow thoroughfare that cut across the plateau, bisecting the community. There had been other wives over the long years . . . and other children, but none had betrayed him like Matthew. He could see his people waiting for him, a few dozen men and women, the sunlight glinting on their freshly minted weapons, waiting by a shuttle.

So it's come to this, he realized. But, even without the benefit of precognition, he'd always known it would.

Nineteen

Sam Roy

Sam watched with interest the reaction of the younger men to the alien.

Ursu stood quietly blinking on board the shuttle. These creatures' faces always appeared expressionless, but Sam had come to realize that they had other ways of showing their emotions, broadcasting them so graphically that they had difficulty hiding them from others of their kind.

A gentle flick of the stubby triangles that were Ursu's ears telegraphed his fear and anxiety. Sam had guided him into the shuttle's mess, situated halfway between the cockpit and the rear cabins. Matthew and the others stood around tight-lipped, looking thoroughly uncomfortable with the Kaspian's presence on board.

Sam had investigated their unease. 'It's just an

animal.' Michelle shuddered, looking embarrassed by her own response.

'An animal maybe, but one which is a member of a civilized species,' argued Sam. 'With a long and rich history – rich as our own.'

Michelle and a boy called Jason had exchanged looks. 'That doesn't make them properly intelligent,' said Jason. 'Look at those things they worship, produced by some alien race. It's clear that any civilized elements in their society were directed externally.' Sam knew he was referring to the Kaspian gods; the Facilitators.

'So what. If they've been influenced by the Angels, it's no more than we were once.' For all their current rebellion, it seemed to Sam that Ernst Vaughn had brainwashed them from birth. They were like those early Americans who wanted freedom for the slaves, so long as none of them came to live on their street or slept with their daughters.

But then, he reminded himself, it wasn't for the sake of any Kaspians these kids were rebelling, it was for their own. They simply wanted to rejoin the human race, but perhaps it was best to let them find out for themselves just how hard that might turn out to be.

Feeling a prickling at the back of his neck, Sam turned his attention back through to the cargo bay. There he could see Trencher sitting up awake, looking stronger, recovering rapidly.

'Can you see anything of the Citadel?' Sam asked

him.

'Glimpses, nothing more.'

Sam licked his lips nervously, stepped closer to Trencher. 'Will we succeed?' he asked, out of earshot of the others.

'Possibly. Who knows?'

Sam nodded. This lack of foreknowledge was strangely exhilarating.

Kim

'I'm telling you, Elias, if you're right about your Primalists, we're not going to find any welcoming committee up in those mountains.'

The Kaspian landscape flashed below them in a blur. 'I'll deal with that when I get to it.'

'Did Trencher ever mention a man called Sam Roy?'

Elias's hands stopped flicking across the shuttle's controls. He looked at her carefully. 'What happened after I escaped?'

'After you abandoned me?' she corrected.

'I'm sorry. I just—'

'You just thought I'd slow you down,' she finished. A flash of anger crossed his face. She turned to Roke, who stood watching them, occasionally glancing curiously around the cockpit. She felt a pang of sympathy for the alien.

'How do you know that name?' Elias persisted.

'After I ate one of my Books, something happened,' Kim replied. It was hard for her to contain her excitement now, about the things she had discovered. 'He's connected in some way with Trencher, isn't he? While I was under the influence of the Book, Sam found some way of talking to me. The Books are – well, they're not just for recording people's memories and experiences. Their purpose is something much deeper than that, more like a . . . a shared experience, something like that.'

Elias looked away for several seconds, as if staring into some place deep inside of himself, before finally he spoke. 'Sam and Trencher are brothers. They were brought up together with another man called Ernst, all products of the same gene treatment, but it affected all of them in different ways. They rebelled. The people who had created them couldn't control them. That's what Trencher told me.' He looked her in the eyes. 'So if you're talking to Sam in your dreams, I believe you. But I'd believe pretty much everything just now.'

'He told me how he had studied the Citadel after the Hiatus began. And he told me that you and Trencher and he are all connected by the same thing.'

Elias raised a hand, palm outwards. 'Fine, all right. But this isn't the time and place. Now tell me why I shouldn't go find Trencher.'

'Why do you think Trencher ever wanted you to come here?' asked Kim. 'Just to rescue him?'

Elias looked at her. 'Sure. I guess.'

Jesus! she thought. How single-minded could the guy be? 'You left a note for me with Vincent,' she continued patiently. *And we're going to have to go back and bury him if we can still find him*, she thought. She didn't want to think of his body being abandoned in the middle of some lonely alien forest.

'Sam told me you can all see into the future, at least some of it. Don't you think perhaps your friend Trencher saw all this coming, in some way? Don't you think that he'd want *you* to help do something about all this, when the time came?' As she stared at him, his eyes flicked away. 'Given the choice between saving your friend, and saving this entire world, don't you think that perhaps the right choice is clear? Look. Trencher brought you here for a reason, but it's not the reason you seem to think it is.'

His face crumpled, almost as if he might cry, but then this flash of emotion was gone, replaced by a neutral mask. 'Trencher means a lot to me. I was on the run for a long time,' he said, his tone almost wistful. 'I couldn't have made it on my own – if he hadn't been there to give me some idea of who I was, what I'd become . . .' His voice fading, he shook his head, stared up at the screens showing the grey blur of the landscape below.

'Elias, I don't know all the reasons either of us are here,' she said gently. 'But I do think there *are* reasons. Vincent came here because he wanted to find some way, any way, of stopping what's about to happen. But I don't think he ever seriously thought there was any way to do that. Sam seems to think there might be a way. I'm not sure what exactly, but it's got something to do with the Citadel. Sam wants us to go there.'

'How much time do we have left?'

Kim glanced at the time display. 'A few hours.'

Sam Roy

Sam studied his naked flesh in the toilet mirror. The minor scars had now turned a livid pink. His teeth still looked like hell, but there was a tingling of life in his gums. He reached up and touched a jagged residue of tooth. It rocked gently against his forefinger, came loose with no pain. As it clattered to the floor, he angled his head up and saw what resembled a tiny bud of white porcelain deep in the cavity it had left.

When he returned, he found Trencher still sitting cross-legged on the floor with the Kaspian they called Ursu. The Facilitator stood in the space between them, looking so obviously an Angel artefact now it was free of its earthenware casing. It glowed faintly, a blue halo surrounding it. Trencher now looked remarkably lively, considering he'd been fished out of a deepsleep coffin only a few hours back.

The two were communicating with each other, Sam realized. Using the Facilitator, as he himself had done with Ursu. He knelt gingerly on the floor next to them, and studied intently the alien device which was the constant focus of their attention. He could distantly hear the discussions and argument of other crew, gathered in the cockpit. They were clearly unsettled by these strange old men they had thrown in their luck with, and more so by this creature they thought of as alien – even though they had grown up on the same world.

'Tell me what you know,' said Trencher, turning to look at him. The words had been expressed as a concept, something formless, beyond semantics, via the Facilitator which had become the technological hub of their three-way conversation.

'The Citadel is the key,' Sam replied by the same method.

The Kaspian had calmed down, despite continued alarm at its strange surroundings. It helped that through the medium of the Facilitator, he could share in their communicated thoughts and ideas. It was uncertain, however, whether the alien could properly absorb the information imparted to it. It didn't take the Facilitator, though, for Sam to empathize with what was going through its mind.

'Why am I here?' it asked. 'I have brought Shecumpeh to you, as instructed. Now let me go.'

Sam felt sad at what he realized was, after all, a kind of betrayal. 'We require your presence when we go to Baul. It is part of a compact between your species and the race we call the Angels, made a long time ago. We

can't do this without members of your race present,' he
said.

Ursu was silent after that.

Sam caught Trencher's eye, made a gesture with his
head indicating he wanted to talk to him alone.
Trencher stood up and approached the other man.
'Sam, we've got a lot to talk about.'

'Yeah, but—'

'We don't have the time, I know, I know. I see
you're healing well. I know how hard it's been.'

Sam shook his head. 'You left us – me. I *knew* you
were coming back – God knows both of us could see
that, even Ernst could see it – but why? Why did you
leave in the first place?'

Trencher smiled faintly. 'I would have thought you
could give your own answer to that – because none of
us has much choice in what we say or what we do, even
Vaughn. He's as locked into his actions by his own precognitive abilities as we are. Do we really want to get
into a philosophical argument right now?'

'We aren't going to get to the Citadel any faster than
we're going, and if things don't work out the way we're
hoping, I'd at least like to get some things clear before
we die. I used the Kaspian gods to understand the Angel
language. Once I had that, it led me to the proof, there
in the Citadel.'

Trencher nodded, anticipating Sam. 'If we look into
the future, whatever particular future we end up
seeing—'

'– out of a vast range of possible futures—'

'– the probabilities collapse to accommodate that one particular probability,' Trencher finished.

'It's hardly that simple,' said Sam. 'There are only a few of us with the precognition skill. If we all see slightly varying futures, the direction in which the wave function collapses is determined more by whoever has the greatest ability in precognition.'

'Which, fortunately for us, almost certainly isn't Ernst. But I fear I do not feel greatly reassured.'

Sam nodded. 'You could have come back, before the Hiatus, and helped me stop Vaughn before it got too late. Instead you ran away and hid on Earth.'

'Because I'd already seen that would happen?' Trencher shook his head. 'Maybe, yes. And perhaps because I wondered if things really would turn out the way we'd foreseen them, or if perhaps we could be wrong.'

'We weren't, though. Which brings us to another question. Why can't we now see what's going to happen next?'

'Perhaps,' said Trencher, 'because we're going to die.'

'Or perhaps there is a way out,' said Sam fervently. 'The Angels could see ahead, too, yes? And that's why they left.' Sam had spent enough time studying the Citadel to know. They exited this universe, he thought, because they had become something like gods, with all the attendant horror and infinite boredom of possessing absolute knowledge. So they had gone somewhere else.

'What I'm about to tell you,' said Sam, 'I don't recall foreseeing. I don't know whether you did. So you may be about to enjoy a genuine revelation.'

Trencher's eyes glistened with pleasure. 'Go on,' he said.

'The wave of radiation heading towards this world, it's not a natural phenomenon.'

Trencher stared. 'Then who?'

Sam explained what he had discovered about the second race, in the heart of the galaxy. 'At first I thought this was a faction of the Angels, separated perhaps for political reasons, perhaps religious, or more likely something beyond our understanding. But the more I learned about the Citadel, the more I realized there must be another species in the galaxy that shared in the knowledge and power of the Angels. There was a war between them, I think.'

'This is indeed a revelation. And you elicited all this in the Citadel?'

'There is machinery down in some of the lowest levels of the Citadel, something like those things.' Sam nodded at the Facilitator.

It was so much easier to communicate the raw concept through the Facilitator. *Here*, thought Sam, and a flood of knowledge entered Trencher's mind.

Perhaps the Angels had shared their knowledge with this mysterious other race; perhaps they had gained it solely by themselves. However that might have been, Sam was sure of one thing. There had once been a conflict, one that might not yet be over.

'The Angels won, of course,' Sam elaborated. 'They imprisoned their enemy – contained them? – within the heart of our galaxy, where there is nothing but light and heat. How they are held there, I do not know.' This information came through to Trencher almost as if he had lived through these things himself; the galaxy spread before him in his mind, ships composed of energy and space twisted together, diving towards the very core of the Milky Way in the blink of an eye.

'The species imprisoned by the Angels are using the galaxy just like a weapon, firing off incredible bursts of life-destroying energy,' said Trencher in a low murmur. 'A terrible thing, but magnificent also somehow.'

'But *we* can do something about it. The Angels provided us with the means.'

'Of course.'

'And then?'

'After? Why, my dear brother,' said Sam, 'we destroy the future, of course.'

Ursu

Ursu watched the two Shai talk between themselves but no longer communicate with him. He was surprised to find he could still communicate with the Facilitator separately, not just as a means of conversing with Sam Roy. He asked the device how they would save their world.

The words-pictures-feelings overwhelmed Ursu with responses. He learned that the Facilitators served more than one purpose. They also administered – controlled? – no, monitored the whorl of stars known as Hesper's Crown.

And when the fire from the stars came to burn his people away, something would save them. A mechanism – something that would shield them.

'Except that the shield isn't working.'

For a moment, Ursu imagined that these words had come from the Facilitator itself. He felt a presence beside him, looked around and saw the Shai Sam staring at him with those small, intense eyes.

'That's why we go to Baul,' he said to Ursu. 'We need your god to reactivate a device that will save your people, as well as your world.'

Kim

The Citadel reached towards the Kaspian sky with impossibly lofty black towers. Kim had led Roke through to the shuttle's cockpit.

She still felt slightly dazed by how quickly events had moved, particularly Elias's sudden appearance with a stolen shuttle.

Kim had come full circle, returning to the place that had become a familiar part of her dreams and nightmares for so many years.

'You know that I've been here before.'

Elias didn't look round. 'Yeah? I thought they didn't allow anybody down here.'

'Except for exploratory missions. I used to work in search and recovery, researching Angel sites for possible artefacts. The Citadel was always high on the list, before and after the Hiatus. It's far away enough from Kaspian civilization for us not to be seen as interfering with their natural progress.'

'It does seem pretty inaccessible. Maybe deliberately so?'

'Seems like a fair bet.'

They were over the mountains now, the last of the peaks slipping away behind them. Only the Citadel now lay ahead. 'So I guess if you've been here before, you know where to head for,' said Elias.

'I'm . . . not sure,' she said. 'I know where the main entrances are, but the whole thing is so vast. I—' They both realized that the message light on the console was blinking. They looked at each other questioningly, then at the light again. As Elias reached out and touched it, a message appeared on a screen, followed by a set of coordinates.

It was apparently from Trencher.

Elias stared at the message, thunderstruck. Maybe it was from him. Maybe it wasn't.

'What are those coordinates?' asked Kim, after a moment.

'Give me a second and I'll find out.' He looked down. 'Okay, straight ahead.' Straight ahead? It could be a trap, he thought.

What the hell, he figured. *If you're going to go, you're going to go.*

'So, you think it's really him?' she asked. Elias had already redirected the shuttle, aiming for the coordinates listed. The craft tilted until pointing at the eastern rim of the Citadel.

'Haven't a clue. Let's go find out.'

He's looking forward to this, she thought. *He doesn't care if he gets killed or not.*

Curious, Kim touched the console to bring up magnified images of the precise section of the Citadel they were aiming for. A great maw of an entrance appeared above a tunnel, leading far underground. There was movement there.

'Somebody's home, all right,' said Elias, intently watching the image. 'Any exploration teams still meant to be down there?'

'No, I don't think so,' said Kim. 'I would think they'd all have been called back.'

'I'd think so too, Kim. Do we have any weapons on board?'

'Weapons?' She stared at him.

'I want to stay here and keep an eye on things. It's pretty obvious our being here is no secret now, or we wouldn't have been able to get our hands on this shuttle in the first place. The crew who tracked me down were well armed, but clearly not very experienced. That suggests people unused to combat situations, which gives me some advantage. But they might have kept other weapons too on board this shuttle.'

'I've never used a gun before,' she confessed. *Before I pointed one at you*, she silently added.

'You seemed pretty enthusiastic a couple of days ago, but it probably won't come to that. But it's good to know we can defend ourselves, if it does come to that.' His tone was calm and reassuring, which worried Kim.

Elias had already described to her how he had appropriated the shuttle. This alone brought up many unanswered questions for her, concerning the nature of the human beings who had found their way here so long ago.

She glanced back, through to the cargo bay. 'You want me to look?'

He gave her a reassuring smile. 'That would be useful, thanks.'

There were arms back there. Mainly standard projectile weapons with clips attached, plus some atmospheric shock guns, like the sonic slammers Kim had seen the bad guys using in interacs. Plenty of ammunition too –

not enough for an army but maybe enough for a massacre.

She went back fore to give Elias the news. The Citadel filled the sky in front of him.

'Right,' said Elias. 'Keep an eye on things here while I go take a look myself.' She nodded, resting her fingertips on the back of the pilot's seat, while the shuttle propelled itself towards the coordinates Elias had entered.

Everything had turned around so fast. Not so long ago, she'd have looked on those weapons as a way to overcome Elias. She wasn't quite sure when she'd decided to throw her lot in with him, perhaps when Sam had spoken to her while she had been under the thrall of the Book. Hearing a noise behind her, she turned to see Roke still sitting quietly in the corner.

A pang of sympathy filled her. Despite the blank eyes, she imagined he felt lost, out of place. She got out the smartsheet and went over to the Kaspian. Explaining certain things wasn't going to be easy, but he deserved to be allowed some idea of what was about to happen.

Twenty

Sam Roy

Things were going to move fast now, thought Sam. So many decisive moments in history were decided almost in the blink of an eye, with most people none the wiser. Because that's what it sometimes came down to in the end: blood, and death, and pain – and possibly that great void he'd never yet been able to see beyond. Perhaps death was the only fitting reward he could hope for.

Sam and Ursu and Trencher had spent time going over what would happen when the moment came. The Facilitator was the key to everything: the only Facilitator which Ernst Vaughn had not prevented from reaching the Citadel, the place from which it originated.

The Citadel itself grew organically from the continental bedrock of Kasper. In external appearance it resembled a tree trunk severed close to the ground, with twisted roots reaching out to plunge into the ice and rock all around it. That geomorphic tangle gave them plenty of potential hiding places close to the spot where they had landed, near an abandoned base camp at the edge of the Citadel.

Unfortunately, Ernst Vaughn and whatever forces he'd been able to assemble would enjoy the same advantage. They were all now deep into that blank, empty void which none of them had been able to see beyond with all their precognitive powers. Sam could not even be sure Elias had received their message. Now he could only hope.

There were others there, barely a dozen, whom Matthew had trusted to side with them, and who had used the confusion of Trencher's disappearance to slip away in another of the shuttles. All were young, all eager to rejoin the human race – to travel to a home-world they'd never known. Sam felt stronger and healthier than he could ever have believed. Though his body still bore the marks of years of abuse, if he only had his freedom for a few hours longer, it would have been worth it to feel so healthy again.

Sam knew that Ernst would be on his way here by now; there was only one place the last Facilitator could go. Stepping out of the shuttle, Sam watched all the young people embracing and chattering around him, clearly amazed that they had come this far and still survived. Some of them, he suspected, might well soon be dead.

He buttonholed Matthew. 'You're going to have to arm these people – are they ready for that?'

'Of course.' Matthew nodded. 'I did everything you

said. We've got weapons and supplies, although I'm not sure they—'

'If we don't pull this off, and the radiation does come, the Citadel should be able to shelter us for some weeks at least.'

'It won't come to that,' said Matthew confidently, but Sam could see how pale and drawn he was. The youth seemed to have shrunk within the parka he wore.

'Matthew. Something on your mind?'

'He's my father,' Matthew said quietly, 'and I just wish there was some way we could settle this differently. Make him see this isn't right. Look, I know that seems—'

'Your father's been locked into what he believes for far too long for him now to accept anything else,' said Sam. 'I used to believe in the same things too. But I changed.'

Was it possible to avoid an armed contest? Sam hoped so, hoped there would be some way. It might be simple: they might just walk in, activate the shield, and that would be it. Or it might take a lot longer – and Ernst would do everything he could to stop them.

And then, so suddenly that it seemed wrong, it started. Sam felt almost betrayed, as if all this business were some kind of game with rules that had been broken. A shot rang out. People screamed, some yelled, most just ran for cover. Another shot.

Screw this, thought Sam, and walked out into the open, shielding his eyes against the harsh polar sun to try and locate where the shots were coming from. Somewhere higher up, he surmised. Somebody yelled at him to take cover, but he ignored them. He heard the distinct whine of a bullet ricocheting off stone.

Trencher came forward and pulled him to one side, joining several others crouching beneath a stone outcrop. Sam peered up, saw a distant figure retreating from a high vantage point where the ground rose to meet the nearest entrance into the Citadel. The shots ceased.

'Well, that settles it,' said Trencher. 'Ernst isn't in a mood for debate.'

'A couple of us have gone off to try and flush them out,' said a girl called Michelle. 'But we're going to have to keep our eyes open.' She looked pale and shaken, as they all did. These kids had rarely come into contact with real violence before. Perhaps they felt betrayed, thought Sam, that one of their own people would shoot at them.

'Okay,' he said. 'We need to get moving. We have to get the Kaspian in there before Ernst gets his act together.' Perhaps, he thought hopefully, Ernst was still on his way, having sent just a small advance contingent to guard the Citadel.

'We might have to take some chances, you realize.' Trencher was echoing Sam's own thoughts. 'If you don't mind risking the golden calf, that is,' he added. Sam knew he meant the Facilitator, and the Kaspian who had brought it.

'We'll take no more chances than we have to.' *I've learned so many secrets here*, thought Sam. *And now the Kaspian gets to find out too.*

Perhaps, he thought, it was best that the alien creature has no idea what he had in mind for it.

Kim

Kim watched as Elias brought the shuttle in for a final landing beside the Citadel. The whine of its engines dropped rapidly as the craft settled on a smooth patch of rock, near two other landed shuttles with people standing by them. People where people shouldn't be, she reflected. Somehow she felt sure none of them had anything to do with the research station here.

'Elias, do you know any of these people?'

He snapped out of his reverie. 'No, I don't. But I know Trencher's here. I can feel it.' He saw the anxious expression on her face. 'They don't mean us any harm, if that's what you're thinking, or they'd have started shooting by now.' He moved towards the airlock door. 'We need to get those guns ready now.'

Kim looked at him uncertainly. 'You really think we're going to need them?'

He shrugged. 'Better safe than sorry.'

Elias

He saw Trencher standing there as soon as he disembarked. The man was looking a lot older than he remembered.

Trencher looked past Elias towards Kim and the alien emerging from the shuttle behind him. 'There's some things here I didn't see in my mind,' he commented to another old man with horrific scars criss-crossing his face, where visible under Arctic-style survival gear.

'Trencher,' said Elias, his expression volatile. 'I . . .' He choked, not sure what to say. Powerful emotions warred deep within him. 'I came,' he said at last.

'You did good, Elias,' Trencher smiled gently. 'We've both come a long way from the streets of London. Now, do you understand what's happening here?'

Elias felt uncertain. 'Only what you told me before you . . . before you disappeared. I know that Ernst Vaughn brought you here,' he said. 'But I still don't know why. And I don't know who all these other people are.'

Trencher sighed. 'Freeing me wasn't the reason I wanted you to come after me. This is exactly where I'm supposed to be – where I should be.'

Elias shook his head, still confused. Trencher laid one hand gently on his arm. 'Remember what I said, Elias, one of the last times we spoke? I wanted you to do just what you had to – what you would do anyway. Come with me. We're both going to have a long, long talk.'

Sam Roy

Kim stood alongside the alien, Roke. Sam Roy saw her glance in his direction, her eyes suddenly growing wide in recognition.

'You're Sam,' she said, approaching. 'I – you don't look the same.'

'I've been feeling a bit better lately,' he admitted with a smile. 'I tend to heal very fast.'

'So, it's true? There's something there inside the Citadel that can protect us?'

Sam nodded. 'But we do have opponents. People who want to stop us. You should know that in advance.'

'Yeah. I sort of got that impression already.'

He motioned to her to follow him, and to bring Roke with her. Its ear-jewels sparkled in the bright crisp air, most of its frame barely visible under a voluminous parka designed for the human frame. He'd healed so much, Sam realized, that Roke hadn't recognized him.

Sam could see Trencher and Elias conversing off to one side. Ursu sat nearby, with the Facilitator, seemingly fascinated by this other Kaspian. Matthew was going amongst his people, huddled in tight little groups, explaining what was ahead of them, cajoling, encouraging.

It seemed to Sam that Matthew's people might, for all their initial spirit, be wavering. Sam could see it in their eyes. They wanted their own future, but he suspected not all of them were prepared to pay the price that might be asked of them.

Elias

Trencher gathered them all together: Sam, Elias, Roke, Ursu and Kim.

'Okay. So where do we head for when we actually get in there?' asked Elias.

'Inside the Citadel? Sam's the one who knows it best, him and your friend Kim,' said Trencher, looking over to where they stood beside each other. 'I'm under the impression either one of them could find their way around in there blindfolded.'

He turned back to Elias. 'But it's dangerous, Elias. There are precise routes to follow. Space and time . . . they don't operate the way they should, once you get in there.'

'I only know parts of the Citadel,' warned Kim.

'But I know almost all of it well,' said Sam. 'It's not going to be a problem.'

'And then?'

'We all foresee things, Elias – you, me, Sam, Ernst.

It's not completely accurate, it's sometimes misleading, but most of the time it's more than any of us can bear. You must know that by now.' Elias nodded grimly. 'We don't know exactly what's going to happen in there, but we do know what we have to do.'

Elias looked sharply at Sam. 'Someone else arrived here with me and Kim, but he didn't make it. He warned me about some kind of explosion that's coming.'

'The technical term is gamma-ray burster, but that information's correct.' Sam explained his findings about the war between the Angels and the other, unknown species. 'There's every reason to believe these creatures who fought against the Angels and lost are responsible for it in some way.'

Elias shook his head. 'What would they gain by killing everything in sight? This is a lot to take in.'

Sam nodded towards the Citadel. 'It starts to make sense when you know that whoever created the Citadel incorporated a means to protect it – and this entire planet – from the burster event. There are machines called Facilitators that act as watchdogs over the whole thing, intelligent enough to debate the actions that should be taken, depending on particular circum-stances. The Facilitators were removed from the Citadel a long time ago, probably by the distant ancestors of the Kaspians themselves. Now we need to get at least one of them – just one – back inside there, or else the shield won't activate, and everything above the local

507

equivalent of a snail is going to be incinerated within a few weeks.'

Trencher gripped Elias's arm with surprising strength. 'Vaughn stole years of my life, Elias, and now I really want to make him suffer. I'm sick of his taunting and his games. We won't let him win, do you understand me?'

'I understand you. How many stand against us?'

'A lot, and Vaughn is in charge of them. He's here, Elias, in flesh and blood.'

Elias looked uncertain. 'If he's anything like you, then he can't be killed.'

'That remains to be seen,' said Trencher. 'Remember what I said, Kim and Sam know the way in. At least one of these aliens needs to go with them. Make sure it does, Elias, and make sure it then activates that shield. Do the right thing, my boy. You always did.'

Elias glanced around at the men and women who gathered nearby. 'Are they all from the Station?'

'That's a whole other story,' muttered Trencher.

Elias studied the kids with guns and felt his heart sink. Civilians. Well-armed civilians, but how would they really feel when they came face to face, bullet to bullet, with their former friends and neighbours?

The best solution was to prevent things from getting that bad.

Elias climbed up on a landing strut of one shuttle

craft and waited until they noticed him. Gradually they all fell quiet, after Sam yelled for their attention.

'Hi, folks,' he said. 'I guess you all know why you're here. Listen, within the next few hours, a lot of people – including the Kaspians – are likely to die when the radiation strikes. Sam here has been investigating a way to stop it. That means we're all going into the Citadel, we're going to switch on a defence shield, and then we're going to come out again. All of us.'

Sam then came forward and addressed the small crowd. 'Ernst Vaughn has misled you for too long. He has put himself in the place of God, and aims to become a destroyer of worlds. God would not require such sacrifice as proof of love or devotion. Yet Ernst Vaughn does. That makes him the true Adversary. Those who oppose us are our friends and neighbours. But if we have to, we must defend ourselves, not only for our own sake, but for the sake of this world on which all of you were born.'

It seemed strange that the alien who had captured Elias and Kim should apparently choose to come to this far-off, desolate place. Most of the time the creature stood quietly with the other, slightly smaller Kaspian, both watching with those huge unreadable eyes.

The smaller one was the key, both Sam and Trencher had told Elias. He had to get it in there alive. But the older one with the jewels in its ears would also suffice.

Somehow the process wouldn't work without the presence of an alien.

Ursu

Ursu had entered a world he knew he might never understand. From talking to Roke it did not take long for him to realize that the other was, in fact, someone of considerable importance; an imperial emissary, no less. And although they were not overtly being kept prisoner, the prospect of enduring forty nights of ice by escaping in any direction was as effective as the bars of any cell. Though Roke was someone important in Xan's empire, here in this strange place, on the very edge of this empty black city out of time and legend, they found their roles strangely reversed. It was Ursu who had struggled to bring the Facilitator to this place, Ursu who had successfully evaded the armies of an empire – with, admittedly, some help from the Shai.

They were moving now. The female Shai came to him, speaking words both incomprehensible and alien. Out of habit, Ursu laid a hand on the surface of the Facilitator, and understood exactly what she meant. They were now going to enter Baul, and there would do that which needed to be done. Roke watched them both with old, tired eyes.

Ursu again found his way back to Roke's side as they started off. They moved quickly up a steep path that ran along the perimeter of the legendary city. The mountains that separated Baul from the rest of the world were visible on the horizon, their astonishingly high peaks cutting deep into the sky. The increasingly steep path led over the ridge of a long hill that extended root-like far out from the main part of the Citadel. Sheer black cliffs fell away below them, a precipitous drop.

If they were to be attacked now, they were in an extremely vulnerable position, but they passed on unharmed, unseen – for the moment.

Elias

Elias moved ahead of the rest of them, feeling as if he were leading a band of armed children. Coming over the top of the incline, he gazed down at an entrance to the Citadel. One of several entrances, Kim had explained but, according to Sam, this was the quickest access to where they needed to be. And with the burster wave only hours away, time was now everything.

There were several shuttles scattered along the wide stony ramp that led up to the entrance. Elias's heart sank; Vaughn was already here. He could see figures moving about down below, and wondered if one of them was Vaughn himself. His hand instinctively tightened around the barrel of his rifle. There were enough armed men and women visible to ensure that the people coming up the trail behind Elias would be outnumbered, outgunned.

He brought up his rifle and peered through the telescopic sight until he could pick out individual faces. Nobody that looked like Vaughn, however. Shit, he was probably already inside the Citadel. Elias scanned the whole area, particularly where the ground rose up on the far side of the ramp, in case Vaughn had positioned snipers.

He then studied the cavernous entrance through the rifle's sight. This far north, the sun sat low on the horizon, and in twenty minutes it would no longer shine directly onto the entrance and the path leading inside.

He lowered the rifle, noticing how Vaughn's shuttles were parked some distance away from the entrance. The path Elias stood on led down a perilously steep incline to a point no more than three metres from the entrance itself.

Elias retreated the way he had come until he rejoined the waiting column of his own people.

'I've got an idea,' he began.

The only problem was getting the precise timing right, since they'd be cutting things very fine. In a little over an hour, deadly radiation would begin creeping over the surface of Kasper, a silent, invisible killer.

Kim, Roke and Sam, with Ursu, still clutching the Facilitator, were to continue along the path, remaining out of sight. The rest of them, led by Elias and Trencher, headed back in the direction they had come, following a route that would take them in a wide circle, and into the rubble and boulders fringing the far side of the entrance ramp.

As they eventually moved in among the massive boulders there, Elias halted the young Primalist rebels, and explained to them what they must do.

Kim

Kim didn't understand the significance of the Facilitator until Sam explained it to her. It was still hard to believe until she then spoke directly with each of the two aliens. The flood of visual information and knowledge she received was not unlike that experienced by eating Books. Except this time, the information surged through the Angel artefact, not through her own bioware. Her understanding of the two aliens, why they were here and the role each played in their world, seemed to grow tenfold in seconds. Absolute communication, she thought; not verbal, not entirely visual, but on some deeper level. She was learning to see the universe through the eyes of aliens.

As they came to the topmost point of the path Elias had scouted out earlier, they fell quiet, and watched the activity around the shuttles parked by the entrance, but cautiously from a hidden vantage point. Kim studied the Citadel entrance, and the sheer rock face rising above it. Someone positioned up there would have a better view of what was happening below. Kim cast her eye over the myriad boulders scattering the slope that dropped away from the entrance, but could see no sign of Elias's group. She guessed that was a good sign, for if she couldn't see them, maybe nobody else could either.

Time was running very short. Whether or not they succeeded in reactivating the shield, they needed to be inside the Citadel when the burster wave hit.

'Now we wait,' said Sam firmly.

Elias

Even the smallest of the surrounding boulders was about half the size of a Goblin, so they had even better cover here than Elias had expected. He spoke quietly to Trencher, then they both looked around for good firing positions.

Unsurprisingly, few of the Primalists who had sided with them showed much enthusiasm for shooting at people they had grown up with. Elias watched as Matthew went amongst them persuasively, stiffening their resolve.

Kim

'There he is,' she said. Sam looked up quickly, as did the two aliens. She could just make out Elias's lonely figure walking out from between a couple of boulders, towards the Primalists still crowded around their shuttles.

Elias

As he walked slowly towards them, the Citadel entrance gaped beyond them like the mouth of hell. 'Hey there,' he called out.

Someone barked out something Elias couldn't make out. He continued steadfastly forward, conscious of the weapons levelled at his chest.

'My name is Elias,' he said, finally stopping. One of them stepped a little closer.

'If you're carrying any weapons,' growled the Primalist, 'drop them now.'

Kim

The curious Primalists had all shifted around to the far side of the parked shuttles, looking towards Elias with their backs to the Citadel entrance.

Kim glanced at the others, and realized she didn't need to say anything. They moved rapidly in a line down the steep path, towards the giant entrance.

Elias

'I'm unarmed,' said Elias. 'I want to talk to whoever's in charge here.'

'Who sent you? Who are you?' Various voices spoke at once.

Elias noticed with satisfaction that none of them seemed to be paying much attention to anything but him. The parked shuttles blocked most of the view towards the entrance, so if Kim and her party were coming down the incline, he couldn't yet be sure.

Don't fuck it up, he prayed, as two of Vaughn's men came forward and began checking him for weapons.

'Look, I just want to speak to the man in charge here. If he's who I think, we go back a long way.'

'Vaughn? You want to speak to Vaughn? You won't find him here. He's down inside the Citadel.'

'Shut up, Stephan,' growled one of the others. 'We're the ones asking the questions.'

Too right, thought Elias. *At least one of you has some brains.*

A shout came from somewhere and all heads turned. Elias saw a woman come running up to them, breathless. 'There's a whole bunch of people heading down by the side of the entrance. I think they must be with him.' She was pointing at Elias.

Stephan's eyes widened, and he swung his rifle like a club, aiming it straight at Elias's head. Elias reached up and caught the end of it firmly, holding it still, while he

516

punched his attacker hard under the chin. Stephan's jaw clicked ominously and his eyes rolled back in his head. Then several men grabbed at Elias, and he went down under a hail of fists and gun butts.

Kicking and punching, Elias kept trying to get back on his feet. *Shit*, he thought. *No good after all*.

A single shot cracked through the still air, and then another.

Elias heard a bullet ricochet somewhere nearby.

The men and women attacking him froze, as if in a brief tableau. As he looked past them, he realized some of Vaughn's people were already heading for the Citadel entrance.

Go, he thought. *Go*.

Kim

Damn! Somebody was shooting at them.

Sam hurried them on. 'Get in, get in,' he muttered, deliberately placing himself between them and the distant shuttles.

After the daylight outside, the gloom inside the colossal entrance was truly appalling. Sam urged them on, deeper and deeper into the vast tunnel that led downwards from the entrance. They hurried into deepening blackness while the Primalists who had sided with them supplied covering fire from the boulders nearest the entrance.

After a few minutes, only a vague greyness existed behind, to remind them there was a way out of there at all. Kim had forgotten that the entrance tunnel curved slightly here, in a long, gentle spiral into the Citadel's core.

They stopped for breath, listened and waited. There was no longer anything to be heard from above, but she didn't allow herself to be lulled into a false sense of security. She lowered a small backpack to the ground, and fumbled through it until she found one of the torches they'd brought from the shuttle Elias had hijacked.

Sam reached out to put a hand on her arm before she could switch it on. 'Not now,' he said. 'The light could lead them right to us.'

'Hell,' she said, exasperated, 'we won't be able to find our way through this place in the dark.'

'That's not a problem,' he said. 'You're going to have to trust me.'

'This place is dangerous,' she argued. 'It doesn't work the same as anywhere else.'

'I know exactly where we need to go,' he said. 'Trust me when I say I know what I'm doing.'

She felt him take her arm, then communicate with the two aliens. Kim felt furry hands, with hard rough claws, reach out of the darkness and grip her surprisingly lightly by her upper arms. The sensation made her momentarily dizzy with panic. Sam guided them on through utter blackness, Kim convinced every step forward might result in them all plummeting into some hidden abyss.

Kim listened as the aliens conversed with each other in clicks and whistles, and immediately she knew what they were talking about. She envisaged a city surrounding an outcrop of volcanic rock. And then the same city – no, she somehow realized, a different city – this one beleaguered, under siege. She saw the smaller of the two aliens escaping from the city, carrying the Facilitator.

She was getting drawn into something, she realized, where it would take too much time to understand the complex details. Sam began talking to her then, and even as he spoke, she could see his words being translated into images and concepts that she assumed made some sense to the two Kaspians.

'There's a chamber a couple of levels below,' he said, invisibly in the darkness. 'It's been a while, but I think I can get us there without any problems.' And she could see this chamber for herself, as clearly as if accessing her own memories.

The Facilitator and the bioware Book technology must both tap into the same thing in the brain, she thought.

'Give me your backpack,' said Sam several minutes later, and she passed it over. He opened it and pulled out a pair of torches. The sudden light was so bright that the aliens flinched away from it.

'So at last we're allowed to see,' she muttered. They had come to a fork in the tunnel. She saw a sudden image, in her mind, of a great fire sweeping through the galaxy . . . of her disembodied self flying at tremendous speed through clouds of stars, towards the heart of the Milky Way.

'That's the Facilitator talking now, not them,' explained Sam. He trained his torch down the left-hand tunnel and started forward.

'You mean that thing's sentient?' said Kim, as she and the Kaspians followed him.

'Sure. Although whether it qualifies as being alive in a sense we might understand is another matter. But it's certainly capable of thought and decision-making, within the parameter of its intended purpose.'

'So what I just saw, what we all saw, that was pro-grammed into it?'

'Something like that. Or perhaps they're Angel memories stored inside it like reference material. Did you feel the minds operating beyond the clouds of stars in the heart of the galaxy?'

'Yes, I did. I felt something.' The darkness beyond the reach of the torch's light seemed less oppressive now. But Kim still felt as if the blackness were some kind of liquid she could drown in. It brought back bad memories.

'Hang on,' said Sam. 'I know where we are now.'

Kim gazed around her and shivered. 'I really hope you *do* know where we're going, because if you don't, I can't imagine how we're going to find our way back.'

Sam looked behind them. They'd only proceeded a

little way beyond the tunnel's fork, but it looked . . . different. 'Typical topological warping for the Citadel,' he said. 'Nothing to worry about, as long as you know what to expect.'

Kim stared down the tunnel and shivered, remembering all too clearly what had happened the last time she had been in the Citadel.

Ursu

He felt the older alien place a hand on his fore-limb, slowing them both down until the two Shai had moved a little ahead of them, still intent on their conversation. 'We have to remove these outlandish creatures from our world,' Roke whispered, with a degree of passion surprising his companion.

'I believe they wish to help us,' protested Ursu.

'But to what end, to what end?' muttered Roke. Ursu saw the Shai called Sam glance over his shoulder, briefly showing them its teeth.

'It can hear our thoughts as well as we can hear theirs,' said Ursu, caution in his tone. 'We should talk about these things later.'

Roke merely blinked his eyes in acknowledgement.

Kim

'It's trying to deviate us from our course,' said Sam as they moved on down an increasingly narrow passage.

'If we're not careful, the Citadel's spatial topology could redirect us into some kind of dead end,' she replied. Like a Venus flytrap catching insects that wandered into its throat, she thought. 'Just make sure you do know what you're doing.'

There were more twists and turns still to come; the further in, the narrower the corridors became. But Sam navigated them all with apparent ease, leading his party of three who followed dutifully behind.

'We're almost there,' he announced, after a little while. The ceiling above their heads was much lower now. They suddenly heard a sound somewhere ahead: like the creak of a chair, or the scuffing of feet along the ground? Either way, they all four froze and listened.

Sam motioned to them to stay where they were, and stepped quietly forward. Light was evident from somewhere ahead, enough to now light their way, though Kim couldn't quite figure out the source of it. Several metres ahead Sam halted, turning his head first one way, then the other, listening like a bird.

'Ernst,' he said, disappearing suddenly around a corner Kim could have sworn hadn't been there a moment before.

No sound, nothing. For the first time in her life, she understood what people meant by a deafening silence.

She edged forward, beckoning the two Kaspians to follow.

Kim looked around. Had she blanked out there for a moment? She'd been walking towards where Sam had last been . . . now she was suddenly around a corner. *The Citadel strikes again*, she thought wearily, hearing the two aliens come up behind her. The smaller one was holding the Facilitator.

She looked the alien in the eyes, and spoke slowly as if that might give it a better chance of understanding her – even though she knew the Facilitator would make her fully comprehensible.

'Are you ready to use that thing when you have to?' she asked.

'Yes.' Ursu spoke in his own language, glancing over the room beyond. It was illuminated, but she still couldn't figure out the source of the light. 'But I'm not sure what I'm supposed to do.'

Me neither, thought Kim, turning away. The room was vast, circular, low-ceilinged. At its centre was a circular dais with a score of what seemed to be shallow indents around its perimeter.

There were tiny notches in each of the indents, and suddenly Kim understood that they must place the Facilitator into one of those notches. *How do I know that?* she wondered for a moment, before realizing it must come from the Facilitator itself. She turned and looked at the smaller Kaspian, gripping the object to its chest. She hoped it had delivered the same knowledge to the alien.

Sam was nowhere in sight. She cautiously stepped forward, regretted it immediately.

The room seemed to twist around her. Suddenly the Kaspians were at the far end of the great circular space. She stopped moving, every muscle in her body bunching. She now saw Sam a short distance away, kneeling on the floor. She hadn't been able to see him earlier because, from the opposite end of the room, he had been hidden behind the dais.

'I can't see him,' he said, his voice thin and weak. She realized he was lying in a pool of blood, and started towards him.

'No, don't,' he said. 'Stay where you are. Is the dais glowing?'

She looked to the dais. One of its indents had taken on a pale blue glow. 'Yes,' she said.

'Tell the Kaspian to walk forward,' Sam instructed. He had pulled himself most of the way upright, clutching at his side. He seemed to have stopped bleeding. Perhaps, she thought, it was only a surface wound. Kim turned and gestured to the smaller alien, and yelled for it to follow her footsteps. She noticed it hesitating for a moment.

Somehow just a few short steps seemed to carry the Kaspian all the way across the circular hall. Kim's mind couldn't make sense of that. *Don't think about it*, she thought. The alien stood quivering beside her, its fur reminding her of a dog. The second Kaspian stayed where it was. She could almost feel the Facilitator tugging itself out of the alien's hands. It stepped forward.

'Don't,' said Sam. 'Go left, not towards the dais. Now turn.' The alien turned carefully, its ears pressed flat against its skull. 'That's it. Forward now – carefully.'

Kim could see it was now next to the one glowing indentation; yet the dais was in the opposite direction from that which the alien had appeared to move towards.

Just then, someone Kim had never seen before seemed to drop out of a tear in reality. It seemed to her that he was just suddenly *there*, emerging from around some impossible corner. *How did he do that?* she wondered, even as he leapt towards her. She had been holding her rifle in one hand, now realized it was gone – taken from her before she had even reacted. She watched it slide across the stone floor, into some impenetrable dark corner.

Her assailant had his own weapon, she noticed: a sonic slammer. He shoved it against the Kaspian's back. She saw his finger begin to depress the trigger.

Suddenly Sam was there beside her. She had seen him move, out of the corner of her eye, in a motion so superhumanly fast she couldn't quite take it in. He shot past her again, all in the passing of a moment.

She saw Sam swipe at the sonic slammer, knocking it away from the alien's back. A ripple cut through the air towards the far end of the room, flipping the second alien onto its back. The smaller alien was left unharmed; Sam had just saved its life. Kim couldn't feel so sure about the other Kaspian.

She felt powerless and helpless without the rifle. Lifting the torch, she shone it towards the man whom Sam was now grappling with. The new arrival had grey hair, a deeply tanned complexion, and eyes that seemed to burn with the fires of hell. The torch light managed to dazzle him for a moment, then he scrabbled away, reappeared close to the smaller alien.

Kim watched him try to tear the Facilitator out of the Kaspian's grip. The creature squealed, but wouldn't let go. Kim leapt forward, without really thinking about what she was doing.

She had a sensation of eternity opening up below and around her, and for the briefest of moments her soul quailed at the place in which it found itself. But just as rapidly that sensation was gone, and her shoulder was slamming into the grey-haired man's side, sending him crashing into the dais. He came back at her, howling, tearing at her face with his fingernails.

She went down screaming as his fingers gouged at her eyes. Sam reappeared in a blink, pummelling at her attacker. The pair of them rolled away from her, struggling violently.

Kim did not waste any time.

'Now!' she screamed at the Kaspian quivering barely a few metres away from her.

She watched breathless as the creature lifted up the Facilitator and placed it carefully into the slot in the blue-glowing indent. The blue immediately faded.

Nothing happened.

Is that it? thought Kim. The world didn't seem any different.

Ernst and Sam were poised several steps apart from each other now, but Kim had the impression that, due to the Citadel's bizarre topography, they might as well be standing on opposite sides of a canyon. Both were panting, and Ernst looked distinctly the worse for wear.

'It's not over yet.' Sam suddenly turned to her. 'You have to put him in exactly the right place.' *What right place?* thought Kim, but then the precise meaning of his words flooded into her mind, via the Facilitator. She now saw the artefact as the centre of a vast network of glowing lines stretching through the crust of the planet. Some of these lines were broken, disconnected. One more element was needed.

She realized something had happened to the very centre of the dais. A hole had opened up in it, deep and black.

In an instant, she understood the dais was designed to accommodate a flesh and blood mind as well as the Facilitators. Any one of them – human or Kaspian – could control the Citadel from the dais, which was the hub of a vast planetary network of which the radiation shield was only one aspect. Whoever interfaced with the dais in this way would clearly gain enormous power. She glanced at Sam, and his thoughts flooded into her: even if they won this struggle, the worsening situation on Earth would almost certainly mean the eventual dissolution of the treaty that had up till now kept Kasper isolated. Eventually, this world would be conquered. Sam's gaze fixed on her for a brief moment, his eyes bright. If one of the Kaspians interfaced with the dais, such an outcome might be prevented. A kind of benevolent dictatorship, a—

No!

Kim was not sure if the cry of protest had come from her or from someone else. It took her a few moments more to realize it had actually come from the Kaspian standing nearest to her.

'I can't do that,' it communicated in clicks and whistles. And Kim could understand why. The Facilitator was showing them all a kind of living death: as powerful as a god, but alone, supremely alone. More than ever, the Citadel seemed a place of death, a vast and powerful tomb, much more awesome than somewhere conducive to life. Sam had planned a kind of supreme sacrifice. One maybe too great for the Kaspian to make.

Ernst and Sam faced each other in a wary crouch, an eternity between them. 'Make it do it, Kim. One of them has to,' Sam called out.

The sound of echoing voices came to Kim, and she glanced towards the entrance to the huge room. Torch beams flickered. As the voices came closer, one was more recognizable than the rest.

It was Elias.

'Don't,' she whispered, but he was already stepping into the room. Suddenly he was beside her, only inches away. There he stood frozen, unfamiliar with the Citadel's complex topography.

'Just stay exactly where you are,' she hissed.

Elias nodded slowly, remained rooted to the spot.

'Just don't move,' warned Kim. 'Not even an inch.'

Looking over at Sam and Ernst, grappling, Elias cursed under his breath. He raised his rifle, aiming for Ernst Vaughn. The bullet never seemed to reach him. 'I don't understan—'

'Don't try.'

Ernst and Sam leapt apart again; now Ernst appeared wounded. As Sam edged closer to where Kim sensed the invisible precipice lay, she started to voice a warning.

'We can't kill each other,' said Sam loudly, looking directly towards her. 'Only one other way to finish this now.'

Ernst retreated, his face crimson with effort . . . and reappeared right beside Sam. Kim heard a movement behind her. She reached back and gripped Elias's upper arm.

'Don't try,' she said. 'You'd never get there.'

Sam reached out and almost seemed to embrace Ernst. Ernst started struggling in desperation, as Sam locked his arms around his opponent's neck. It was almost as if he was welcoming home a long-lost lover.

When Sam leaned backwards, Kim moved forward a fraction despite herself. That was just enough for her to see the edge of the precipice, a space between spaces, yawning open just beyond her toes. She could see the panic grow on Ernst Vaughn's face, his expression now almost comical, like a clown losing his balance on the tightrope.

They fell backwards together, Sam still clasping Vaughn in a tight embrace, the momentum dragging them back until they fell into nowhere. Into a chasm the size of eternity . . .

Kim stepped quickly away from her position, wanting to get as far away as possible from that awful void. Her knees buckled beneath her, but Elias caught her as she stumbled.

'What happened to them?' asked Elias, puzzled.

'They're gone,' she said. 'I don't think they're coming back.'

Ursu

Ursu was relieved to find Roke still alive, though injured by some force Ursu could not begin to understand. The older alien kept clutching at his innards, as Ursu helped him back towards the entrance of the dais room.

'So this is the legendary city of Baul,' wheezed Roke. Beams of torchlight flickered around them, as more of the Shai appeared, halted at the entrance by one of their own, lest they suffered the same fate as the two Shai who had vanished. 'This is a place of evil. May it be swallowed up by the earth for ever.'

Roke flicked his ears, and continued. 'I heard the Shai explain how absolute power resides in that dais. That any one of us could . . . Ursu, do you realize what this means?'

'The Prophecy of the Fidhe,' agreed Ursu. 'Yes, I do.' The prophecy that one of their race might rise to rule the world like a god. 'You think Emperor Xan is meant to occupy that thing?'

Roke was silent in thought for a while as the Shai chattered around them. 'I don't know,' he confessed at last.

Trencher

It had occurred to David Trencher Vaughn, as he dreamed forgotten dreams during that long sojourn within his narrow coffin, that life was nothing more than the prelude to one final moment of existence, that only during that last second of living could you truly appreciate and understand the meaning and purpose of all that had gone before. Trencher himself had been in the unenviable position of always knowing how that last moment would feel. Even Sam had never comprehended just how complete Trencher's understanding of future events was.

Well, here I am, Trencher thought. *I've known this moment for so long it feels like I've always been here*. The shield had now been activated, but the Citadel itself remained a deadly weapon. He realized he'd always known about this moment, first as an infant's foreboding, then as nightmares of a great and dark place full of mystery and secrets. Now he understood what it meant. Now he was here, he understood why he had never been able to see anything beyond this point.

In his mind, Trencher always liked to think that the Angels had been compassionate beings outpaced by their own technology. Something terrible had been created when they had learned to touch the future: a kind of temporal devastation still wreaking its effects, untold aeons after they themselves were gone.

It was time to give free will back to the universe, he realized.

Spotting Elias, he went over to him. Trencher could see how the man's hands were shaking, noticed the greyness of his skin. The Slow Blight was eating away at him, and if Trencher had been able to see beyond one important point only moments away, he would have guessed that Elias Murray didn't have long to live.

'Elias, listen to me. You have to get all these people out of here, soon. Do you understand me?'

For a moment Elias stared at him as if he didn't recognize him. 'I – no, I don't. Where's Sam? Did you see what happened to him? And Vaughn?'

'Elias, I need you to do exactly what I tell you. Sam

and Ernst Vaughn are gone. You'll never see them again. But this isn't finished. I need to destroy this section of the Citadel.'

Elias stared at him now. 'Destroy it? How the hell do you do that?'

'Get them out of here, Elias. What Sam wanted from the Kaspians is too much to ask. I can only give you so much time.'

For himself, time seemed to slow down, so that he saw Elias's mouth begin to gape open in a question even as he turned and ran into the dais chamber.

Apart from Elias, whose precognitive skills were extremely weak, he was the only one left possessing the precog ability that had been so disastrously gifted to the human race. It was now necessary to remove himself from the universe. Trencher ran towards the dais, and towards the void that now opened at its centre.

Darkness glittered beyond the opening. Secrets lay beyond it, secrets beyond his imagining. He fell into it . . . and fell forever.

Kim

She watched from nearby as Trencher ran into the dais chamber, moving almost too quickly for her eye to follow. He had leapt up onto the dais itself, and was gone. She saw Elias blink in confusion; one moment Trencher was there, the next he had vanished. She could see the questions on his lips, a look of utter loss twisting his features.

A distant rumble rolled through the ground beneath their feet. She looked up, a sudden sense of déjà vu instantly drenching her in cold sweat – in time to see Elias himself start towards the dais.

'Okay, stop right there,' she yelled, running after him before he'd taken more than a few steps. 'Nobody's going back in there. I said *stop*.'

She knew he could have shrugged her off in a moment, but instead he did stop and look at her. 'I need to know where he's gone,' he explained, just as the ground trembled a second time.

She managed to drag him out of the huge chamber and back to where a few of the Primalist rebels stood muttering nervously. Kim really didn't want to think about whether history was going to repeat itself, but if it was, this time she was determined the outcome was going to be different. There was a lifetime, no, a thousand years' worth of secrets and research lying only a few feet away from her, but now she found she wanted no part of it.

She saw that a strange light was now emanating from the whole of the dais. It hurt the eyes even to look at it.

'Elias, we're going to have to get the hell out of here, quick. Please tell me it's safe now to go back outside.'

'What the hell are you talking about? I'm not going anywhere.'

'Just believe me,' her voice was shaking, 'when I say we really need to get out of here. I heard what Trencher asked you to do, and you don't even know what could happen now Trencher is in there.'

'He said to get everyone out of here.'

'Yes, well, get them out. I . . . I have an idea what's happening here. The Facilitator, it's still translating, barely, but I think I understand. Trencher's taken control of the Citadel so he can destroy it. And then he's going to . . . going to . . .' She moaned in pain. She'd seen where he was going to go. Someplace beyond death, beyond anything she could understand.

Removing himself.

She urged and harried them all on, running ahead with the torch to light their path. Somehow it seemed much easier to find their way back out than when coming in. It helped that they were heading back towards the light. More alarming rumbles travelled through the ground beneath them, and although the path wasn't steep, she felt fatigue driving shards of pain through her legs. Only the Kaspians seemed able to keep up a steady pace. But how to tell their thoughts, since the Facilitator lay far behind them now? At least she still had the smartsheet tucked away in a pocket.

And then they were out into a dim grey twilight. She could see bodies nearby. The rumbling behind her had grown to a terrifying roar, like some great caged animal

535

provoked. The ground tremble grew apace until it seemed the whole planet was shaking apart. Great clouds of dust and smoke swirled around them, cloaking the little group that had gathered, coughing, in the open.

Twenty-one

Eddie

'Would you like me to go over it again?' asked Eddie, looking around at the others in the reception suite. He had run through the computer records already. They were on board the *Num Chai*, a military frigate that had been turned into a temporary headquarters for the administrative government previously housed on the Angel Station. The *Num Chai*, like almost every ship in the Kaspian System, was parked in stationary orbit around a large enough mass to act as a shield against the gamma radiation still blasting through the System in a steady but now, apparently, decreasing wave. Another week, thought Eddie, and all that anybody human in this System will have to worry about is accidental asphyxiation.

Several thousand automated tracking and observation devices, whose purpose and attention was directly focused on the only known living civilization outside of mankind, watched as the radiation wave poured towards Kasper at the speed of light. The computer modelling sequence Eddie had just run showed that something invisible – a force field, for want of a better term – had deflected the radiation around the planet, leaving its surface unharmed.

To very little surprise on Eddie's part, Kasper very quickly became the focus for the attention of every physical scientist in the system.

Eddie Gabarra watched it all with mounting fascination.

'So far, Commander Holmes, it looks like you've come out of this with your nose clean,' he said. So many of the human constructions on the Station were ruined; would have to be rebuilt from scratch. The cost would, of course, be enormous, but the potential payoff from what had been seen, observed by a dozen different and independent sources, would make that seem a minor consideration.

Holmes's eyes slid away from the astronomer towards a view of the stars that had replaced the computer modelling sequence behind Eddie's shoulder. *Oh, but you were in so deep*, thought Gabarra. *Not that we can prove it, unfortunately.*

'So there really are people down there?' said a voice from behind him. Gabarra turned, to see Bill Lyndon. Beside Lyndon, standing at the rear of the suite, were Mayor Pierce and a woman called Teresa DeLinz, convener of the board of investigation assembled by the Earthside organization to whom the Station authorities answered.

'Yes, Bill, there really are people down there.' Lyndon had agreed to testify against a variety of key Station personnel in return for not being prosecuted on the basis of his own illegal activities. Indeed, Lyndon had managed to put himself across so adroitly as a concerned citizen during the past week's discussions that Gabarra suspected the man's true calling might have been in politics.

Gabarra was familiar with DeLinz from other meetings, other places. She had a thin, lined face that spoke of a lifetime of hard experience. The meeting was now over; an official statement had been decided upon. Holmes kept a tight-lipped silence, but DeLinz stepped over to Gabarra, and guided him to a corner of the suite well away from the others.

'I understand you believe a friend of yours may have come into contact with the illegal colonists,' said DeLinz quietly.

'Vincent, yes, he came here on my behalf, before the Station was attacked. The logs show he was on board a Goblin ship that surveillance satellites reveal crash-landing on the planet.'

'You think he knew something?'

Gabarra shrugged noncommittally. 'Maybe, but I don't know. I've seen long-range shots of wreckage down there, so I don't know the chances he even survived. If he did know something—'

'You should know,' interrupted DeLinz, 'that

certain matters are being discussed on a higher level, unofficially.'

'Such as?'

'Whether to make public our recovery of the descendants of the original crew,' said DeLinz. 'It might throw up too many questions.'

'Like why didn't we know about their existence there before,' said Gabarra. 'But did we?'

DeLinz's face remained impassive. *I'll bet you did*, thought Gabarra. *I'll bet you knew all along*.

Eddie Gabarra had been forced into hiding while he made his way to the Kasper system. His worst moment had come with the false news of his death. Not that they hadn't tried to effect it; there had been that time at the Oort Angel Station when someone had followed him down a darkened corridor and tried to kill him . . . That had been an unpleasant experience, and he knew he had been very lucky to escape with his life.

'Did we know?' he repeated. 'You understand I have a very personal interest in what's been going on.' A conspiracy stretching from Earth to Kasper? To keep knowledge about the wave of radiation spreading through the galaxy from the public, from anyone who needed to know it?

Gabarra knew now how bad things were getting on Earth. And as awareness of the coming catastrophe grew, the importance of Kasper came more and more to the fore – a world that, if it weren't for the native sentients living there, would be ripe for the taking as the homeworld crumbled into eco-catastrophe. Now something else had happened that nobody could even begin to find an explanation for, and a race that might otherwise have become extinct within days was still thriving, though none the wiser.

Perhaps another way could be found? Perhaps.

'You understand that keeping such matters quiet would imply a certain complicity,' continued DeLinz, ignoring Eddie's question.

Eddie smiled tightly. 'I've been the victim of that kind of complicity before,' he said. 'So you can understand why I wouldn't feel inclined to consider becoming a co-conspirator myself.'

'Mr Gabarra, you're correct in referring to what has happened here as a conspiracy. Conspiracies fail when they become unearthed, and you've played no small part in that unearthing. But there is much more going on here than that.'

'I don't quite follow you.'

'We've witnessed something that we can't explain,' said DeLinz. 'That protective field that appeared around Kasper before the radiation struck, you can't seriously say that was a natural phenomenon.' DeLinz regarded Eddie with curious eyes. 'Or could you? Please, I'd be interested in your scientific opinion.'

Eddie remained quiet for a few seconds, then finally spoke. 'It wasn't natural, no. That it should just appear at . . . at the right time, right place, then begin to fade away again. The most obvious candidate for producing this level of interference with the radiation is the Citadel itself. Not even a hundredth of that place has been explored.'

'Almost certainly, yes. And now that this matter seems to have been cleared up, what next?'

'I don't understand.'

'Earth is dying, Mr Gabarra. I've seen some reports that you haven't. Well, perhaps not dying, but certainly close to becoming a terminal patient. The only alternative to billions of deaths, over the next several decades, is almost certainly some form of relocation.'

Eddie was silent for a moment. 'Miss DeLinz, I understand what you're saying. The Kaspians may already be aware of our existence anyway. It's reasonable to assume that the Primalists who abandoned this Station early in the duration of the Hiatus may also have had some kind of contact meanwhile with the aliens. The footage we've seen of shuttle craft in the Kaspian atmosphere, along with the Goblin wreckage down there, does strongly imply a level of human interference which may well now be irreversible. I know some will call for colonization of Kasper. But there are other possibilities, too.' Such slim possibilities, of course, but real ones.

'Such as?'

'The bugs,' he said. 'They exited through the singularity, but they did not emerge anywhere along the known network. That means there are nodes in the Angel Station chain which we haven't yet found. They too may have habitable worlds. And then there are the probes we sent to the galactic core.'

'I wasn't aware you possessed clearance for that kind of information,' said DeLinz sharply.

'Please rest assured that I do.'

'The faster-than-light technology that made the Core missions possible only allows for the transportation of the tiniest probes across the galaxy,' said DeLinz. 'Hardly sufficient for the transportation of human beings in any numbers.'

'You forgot the important word, *yet*. We can't do it *yet*, but I think we will.'

'But not in time.'

'Maybe. Maybe not. Remember what the Core missions discovered: several stellar-sized artefacts close to the galactic hub.'

'There's no proof they're artificial in origin.'

'I'd be prepared to bet my professional career on it. I suspect they were emitting signals, talking to each other.' Starships of some kind, he assumed, not that he was prepared to suggest that to anyone else just yet. In other words, something very, very advanced, possibly originating from the galactic core. Maybe something that could trigger thousands of stars to detonate within a few years of each other. They would never have known, if some expedition into the Citadel itself hadn't revealed the secret of ftl technology.

But what it all meant, Eddie Gabarra couldn't begin to guess.

Kim

A dozen people had died on either side of the struggle. It had been over in minutes, a truce yelled out between ancient boulders. Elias had taken the opportunity to head into the depths of the Citadel, following after Trencher. Now Trencher was gone, and she could see he still couldn't understand the reason why.

When they realized Vaughn really was gone, the Primalists on both sides had begun to argue loudly amongst themselves. Elias and Kim had shepherded the two aliens away towards the shuttle he had captured earlier. She wondered what would happen to the Primalists now, but for the moment she found it hard to care. Fortunately, none of the Primalists thought to reclaim their stolen shuttle.

Kim still had her smartsheet with her. She took it out, and used it to communicate crudely with the aliens, as they proceeded.

'What are you saying to them?' asked Elias.

'I'm asking them where they would like to go now,' she said.

'Oh.' That made sense. They couldn't abandon them out here in the icy wilderness. They boarded the shuttle, only four of them now. Elias sat down behind the console, and stared at it as if he'd never seen anything like it before.

'I don't think this thing could get itself into orbit,'

said Elias. 'It's too old. I wouldn't want to chance it. Any other ideas?'

'I've already sent out a distress message through the smartsheet.'

'You know, we're going to have a lot to explain to anyone who comes and rescues us. To them and also to the Station Authority.'

'Yeah, well. I just spoke with the Kaspians. I'm not sure if I've got the location right, but we've got enough fuel to take them where they want to go.'

'Which is?'

'Some place south, near the ocean bordering the bottom edge of this continent.'

'And then?'

'Then we've got some business to take care of, Elias.'

Roke

They flew south, and after a few hours, the shuttle dropped down and landed on a barren, icy plain. As far as they could tell, they had no witnesses to their descent. Kim exchanged a last few words with the aliens, via the smartsheet, and then the two creatures stepped away across the plain and watched as the shuttle took off again.

For a long time Ursu and Roke both stood staring into the sky.

'How far is it now?' asked Roke, at last.

Ursu looked around him. 'That way.' He pointed. 'I think we should be there by sunset.' He looked at Roke curiously. 'I admit to surprise that you intend to join me here.'

'I abandoned an imperial expedition in order to satisfy my own curiosity, so I suspect the empire is better off without me. And anyway, I would prefer a quiet life – for a little while, at least.'

'There may be imperial soldiers in the city.'

'Who will have no idea who I am unless I tell them – or you do. *You* have more to worry about, Ursu.'

'Then we'll just have to see what happens.'

Perhaps when they arrived in Nubala, thought Roke, he would tell Ursu about the object he had taken. He had come across another of these glowing sheets the Shai used. The larger Shai had put it down shortly after they boarded the flying craft, and Roke had slipped it into the folds of his robe, hoping that they were too busy with other matters to notice.

Remembering how the symbols and shapes of their alien language had flowed across its surface, Roke wondered if they might find a way of understanding what exactly it said.

They plodded on, the walls of Nubala now visible upon the horizon, arriving just in time to hear the news from further south. The Emperor Xan had been deposed, and was dead.

Kim

Finding their way back to the Kaspians' camp was harder than expected. The forest that extended just beyond the northern ice sheets was vast but, in the end, Elias traced a route that followed the bend of a river until he spotted the trail of destruction the Goblin had gouged from the forest.

They flew over the area several times until fairly sure the encampment was abandoned. After they landed, they found the cage they had once been kept in, but there was absolutely no sign of Vincent's body. Elias took up a rifle for protection, and wandered around for a while until he was sure there were no Kaspians hiding nearby. After a little while it started to get dark. Leaning back against one of the shuttle's landing struts, they sat and stared up at the stars.

Kim then studied her smartsheet, glowing under the darkening sky. So far she had managed to elicit a response to their SOS; it came from one of the military escorts. *We're in a lot of trouble*, she thought. *It's going to take a lot of explaining.* Explanations? She smiled at the thought. Who would ever believe them?

Kim was not inclined to ritual, but found herself understanding why some people needed it. After a while she got up and searched out pieces of wood, constructing something that resembled a cross. Elias then found a small lasertool to burn Vincent's name on it. Finally, he helped her gather some stones to prop the cross up in the centre of the clearing. Kim wondered about saying something solemn, but nothing came to mind.

'You know,' said Elias, after a while, 'we really should be feeling better about ourselves. I think we just saved a planet.' He turned and peered at her in the darkness. 'Don't get much of an opportunity to say that, do you?'

'Yeah, I guess when you put it like that.' She smiled. 'What will you do when you get back there?'

'Get back? You know, I never really believed I would be getting back.'

'I'm not sure what you mean.'

'I mean I never really looked beyond this point.' He frowned deeply. 'And now that I think about it . . . I'm not sure I could go back. There's never really been anywhere I felt safe, where I could be left alone in the way I wanted to be. I'm . . . not sure there's anywhere for me to get back to.'

'Elias, you could go home.' He'd talked earlier about his life in London. 'The Primalists only wanted Trencher, not you.'

Elias shook his head. 'No, just think about it. Look at what happened to them; Trencher, Sam, even Vaughn. They all underwent similar gene therapy to mine. It made them more than human, and less at the same time. I can see that now: it was nothing but a burden.' He sighed. 'I don't have it as bad as them, of course. You know what Trencher said to me on our way to the Citadel? That I didn't really see into the future: I only saw reflections of what they saw.'

'But you underwent the same treatment, right?'

'No, remember – Trencher and the rest were modified from before birth. They were born that way. I wasn't. That's the difference.'

'So can you still foresee things?'

'No, I can't, and it's a relief. I don't have one damn idea what's going to happen next.'

'We can make guesses though, boards of enquiry, scandal . . . whatever the hell they're going to do with all those Primalists up in the mountains.'

'I was thinking about other things,' he said. 'Somebody once said something to me, about how bad things were getting on Earth. I've experienced first-hand what the Slow Blight can do to a man.' He stared at her. 'How long will anyone carry on giving a shit about the Kaspians if a lot of people back home start dying?'

Kim glanced at the darkened forest around her, and the thought of this landscape being filled with other humans seemed strangely depressing.

'I've got a suggestion for you,' said Elias. 'When you're up there again – telling them about what happened down here – you should claim I kidnapped you, forced you here against your will.'

She stared at him. 'Elias, you *did* kidnap me, and force me here against my will.'

'But you'd have come anyway, surely, if you'd known *why* I was doing what I was doing?'

Anger flared in her for a moment, but subsided almost immediately. She decided to say nothing, but was afraid Elias might be right. 'Why don't *you* tell them, then.'

'Because you should be coming out of this smelling of roses. Crazy guy kidnaps you to surface of alien planet. Fights with other crazy guys. World saved. They'll love it. You'll be a hero. Heroine, I mean.'

She laughed, despite herself. 'Yeah? So what happens to you?'

'I'll go somewhere where I won't be bugged.'

'Where?'

Elias shook his head, stared upwards.

Kim realized that a message was flashing on her smartsheet. She touched it, and watched the words dance across its surface in response. 'They're on their way,' she said.

Elias rose slowly to his feet. 'Who is?'

She shook her head. 'I don't know. One of the escort ships, I think. It's just some kind of acknowledgement of our signal.'

'How long do we have?'

'Not sure.' She tapped again at the 'sheet. 'Not long, anyway. Maybe twenty hours?'

Elias smiled gently. 'That's good. Good for *you*.'

'Good for both of us, Elias.' She watched him,

noticed his hand shaking, the thin beads of sweat rapidly forming on his brow.

When Kim woke, as the cool light of dawn revealed itself beyond the shuttle's viewport, she knew instantly he was gone. She had already known he would be gone, without really admitting it to herself. It was a strange experience to wake alone, in the dark, on a world so far from home.

She stepped out of the shuttle and, for the first time in a very long time, Kim felt very, very alone. *I've regained my taste for human company*, she realized, then thought, *I still have the last of the Books.* Susan would still be in there somewhere, like a ghost always hovering at the back of her mind.

A thin dew clung to the ground, and Elias was, indeed, very gone. He hadn't left a note this time. Perhaps he'd head for the sea, or perhaps for the mountains. Somehow she didn't think he would head for the Citadel again. Or perhaps he would; she couldn't begin to guess at the paths his thoughts might follow.

There were things she wished she could have talked to him about: about Sam, and about Trencher, where they might have gone. Or were they still there in the Citadel somewhere – somewhere inaccessible and unreachable? That wasn't a pleasant thought.

Then she had an idea.

She dug out the last few Books of Susan's memories,

as usual letting one dissolve on her tongue. Memories of their time together filled her mind once more, happier times, good times.

When the experience had passed, and the sun had risen in the afternoon sky, Kim went back to the cage they'd been held captive in and broke off some more pieces of wood. She took them to the spot where they had left a marker for Vincent, and imprinted Susan's name with the same laser-tool. Then she dug a shallow hole with a wide-bladed knife, and buried the last of the Susan Books there.

Kim returned to the safety of the shuttle. Some time later, she looked up through the viewscreen, to see a trail of fire across the sky; a glint of sunlight on metal, far above.